W. A. Harbinson was born in Belfast in 1941. He has published over a dozen novels, plus biographies of Charles Bronson, George C. Scott, Eva Peron and Elvis Presley, the latter being a number one bestseller in the United States, with over a million copies sold.

His novels *Genesis* and *Revelation* were bestsellers on both sides of the Atlantic and won considerable critical acclaim. The *Los Angeles Times* said of *Genesis*: 'It's superbly written, crammed with food for thought; it explores powerful and unusual emotions. It's a hit, and it should be.' In Britain, *Publishing News* described *Revelation* as: 'An extraordinary combination of love story, occult, horror and science fiction based on the second coming of Christ. An electrifying read that deserves the widest exposure.'

W. A. Harbinson's books have been translated into Dutch, Italian, Spanish and French. His most recent novel, *Otherworld*, was described by *The Bookseller* as 'a haunting portrayal of mysticism and the powers of darkness within the depths of the Amazonian rain forest.'

W. A. Harbinson has also contributed to numerous magazines and journals, has worked in an editorial capacity for various magazines, and has written for radio and television.

Also by W. A. Harbinson

GENESIS
REVELATION
OTHERWORLD

and published by Corgi Books

THE LIGHT OF EDEN

W. A. Harbinson

CORGI BOOKS

THE LIGHT OF EDEN

A CORGI BOOK   0 552 12650 0

First publication in Great Britain

PRINTING HISTORY

Corgi edition published 1987

This book is set in 10/11 pt Palatino

Corgi Books are published by Transworld Publishers Ltd.,
61-63 Uxbridge Road, Ealing, London W5 5SA, in Australia
by Transworld Publishers (Australia) Pty. Ltd., 15-23 Helles
Avenue, Moorebank, NSW 2170, and in New Zealand by
Transworld Publishers (N.Z.) Ltd., Cnr. Moselle and
Waipareira Avenues, Henderson, Auckland.

Printed and bound in Great Britain by
Cox & Wyman Ltd, Reading

For Lesley

THE LIGHT OF EDEN

PROLOGUE

The magnetic forces of water and air tugged Miles Ashcombe out of his restless sleep. Opening his eyes, he stared into the darkness, still held in the web of his dream, the fear briefly freezing him. He took a deep breath and sat upright, sensing a presence in the room, then swung his legs off the bed and walked to the window.

He looked out. The sun was rising slowly over the dark Mendip Hills, surrounding the black cone of Glastonbury Tor with a thin rim of crimson light. The light expanded as the sun climbed higher, erasing the stars above the clouds, turning the dawn darkness into a pale, shifting yellow that lent definition to the still, sleeping landscape and let a solitary tower emerge from the night to dominate the legendary hill.

The sun was a crescent-shaped, silver-limned fire forming an arch over the conical Tor. It continued rising, growing bigger and brighter, and eventually took the shape of a perfectly round, phosphorescent globe, partially eclipsed by the parapeted tower on the silhouetted hill's summit, over five hundred feet above sea level.

Now a heavenly halo around the majestic Tor, the sun also shone through the arch-shaped doorways of the tower and looked, from where Miles Ashcombe was standing, like a single, very brilliant eye, focused directly upon him.

Later, when the sun had been defeated by advancing mist, Miles Ashcombe drove from his home just west of Glastonbury, parked his car on the narrow, stone-walled road by Chalice Well, and walked up the steep slopes of the Tor until he stood on the summit, by the base of the hollow tower which was all that remained of the fourteenth-century church of St Michael.

Standing on that windswept summit, shivering with cold and fear, he thought of St Michael, the Archangel, that flaming, winged creature who floated between heaven and hell. He felt the tug of air and water, a magic portend deep within, then gazed all around him, at the remarkably smooth, sloping green fields, and thought of what this place represented: the Land of the Dead; a centre for Great Goddess fertility rites and celebrations; a Druid initiation centre; a magic mountain; the Arthurian hill-fort or Grail castle of Avalon; a ley-line crossroads and magnetic power-point over which flying-saucers were often seen.

He looked around him and shivered, whipped by wind, chilled by fear. He felt the forces of air and water, tugging at him, draining his mind, then rubbed his weary eyes and stared southwest, across the sublimely curving, emerald-green Bushy Coombe, to where the red-roofed modern houses of the ancient town seemed to float in the drifting mist.

Glastonbury had once been an island — an ancient Celt burial ground, the Isle of Glass — and now, with the mist drifting around numerous patches of green, it eerily resembled that primal, watery marshland out of which it had originally been formed.

Ashcombe was frightened. The landscape seemed unreal. He stared across Bushy Coombe, at the town thrusting up through the mist, and saw a cube-shaped patch of darkness materialising magically over the slender spire of St John's church.

He blinked, looked again, wondering what he was staring at, and saw the darkness growing spectrally in the morning's grey light: an incorporeal mass that had materialised out of nothing — like a ghost or mirage — and now seemed to float in thin air, immense, slightly transparent and pulsating oddly.

It was about half a mile wide, its height slightly more than that, inching southward as it descended vertically and very slowly, its nearest side forming a shifting wall that stretched across most of the town-centre.

Though unable to believe his own eyes, Miles Ashcombe now found himself staring at an enormous, perpendicular rectangle of darkness which seemed to cover the whole town-centre, was slowly descending upon it and, just as slowly, advancing south across the town, towards the hill upon which he was standing.

First stunned, then terrifed, Ashcombe watched that faintly transparent, mysterious mass as it expanded in all directions, growing taller and wider, its nearest side now hovering just over the lower slopes of Chalice Hill, before the darkness fell over the small town like the funnel of a great, cosmic chimney.

The town started to disappear.

Ashcombe choked back a sob. The sound of his pounding heart filled his head. He tried desperately to cling to his sanity, but what he saw was too much for him. That awesome dark mass kept advancing. It eventually swallowed the whole town. Ashcombe raised his hands to his face, saw the darkness on the hill below, then, convinced that he was going mad, he stepped back onto gravel.

Still staring at the advancing dark mass, wondering what had happened to the town, he backed through the arched doorway of the fourteenth-century tower — and only then did the fear force his eyes shut.

It was colder inside the tower. The ground started to shake beneath him. He heard noise — a rising symphony of unfamiliar, distant sounds — then, hearing the ancient stones reverberating and shaking violently, he opened his eyes and looked directly above him.

His body went numb first, but then his mind also froze. An icy coldness clamped around him and he lost more of himself when he saw an incorporeal darkness sliding across the tower's open roof to block out the sky.

Whimpering like a child, he pressed his face with his hands, shivering as the icy-cold stung his skin, feeling the ground shaking beneath his feet as strange noises surrounded him.

He lowered his head and closed his eyes, terror rooting him to the spot. The ground shook beneath his feet, his ears were stinging from the cold, and he heard the distant noises all around him and found himself trying to sort them out ... A bass rumbling ... Strange growlings ... A sharp squawk and beating wings ... The rushing of wind, falling rain, volcanic explosions and splitting earth.

He opened his eyes again, glancing wildly around him. He saw the ancient walls shaking and spitting dust — then he ran from the tower.

Once outside, on the lofty summit of the ancient Tor, he found himself at the edge of a great wall of darkness that had obviously passed over the town-centre, over the slopes of Chalice Hill, and was now inching south like a dense mist dissolving into dawn light.

That mist swirled around him, an icy, freezing shroud, as he stared down at Glastonbury and saw, where the town should have been, a broad swathe of steaming marshlands, water gleaming between green grass, prehistoric beasts moving along well-trampled, muddy banks; while beyond them, where the lush Mendip Hills should have been, a volcanic mountain belched purple fire and black smoke over a glittering mosaic of waterways, lagoons and tree-filled, steaming swamps.

He heard beating wings. His dazed eyes turned towards the sky. A prehistoric pteranodon flew overhead, its enormous beak pointing down in his direction, its wings of skin beating awkwardly.

Miles Ashcombe started screaming. He sensed that someone was coming towards him. He kept screaming in the hope that that someone would disappear with the rest of it.

His own screaming finished him.

PART ONE: THE PAST

CHAPTER ONE

' — disappeared,' Frances said, turning her head to stare at Laurence, who was driving them along the desert road, his red hair whipped by the wind that was also sweeping the dust in dense clouds across the path of the shuddering jeep. 'Most of Glastonbury, apparently. It just disappeared overnight — and no-one knows how.'

Laurence nodded, his lean face caked in dust, hair flattened against his forehead as he gripped the steering-wheel more firmly. 'Unbelievable,' he replied, speaking loudly against the wind. 'Completely out of this world. The scientists can't find a rational explanation for it, and apparently most ordinary folk are having trouble in accepting that it's actually happened. Lots of traumas already.'

Frances herself could not accept it and still felt very shaken. She had been in her apartment in Ashar, in Basra, relaxing on her patio and gazing out over the Shatt al Arab river, when the news, spoken in Arabic, had come over the radio. Staring beyond the palm-fringed bank of the broad, muddy river, her gaze lazily following the colourful spectacle of large-sailed trading boats, primitive canoes, circular rafts, paddle-steamers, motor launches and ocean-going steamers, she had thought at first that she had misinterpreted the broadcast, her Arabic not being all that good at the best of times. However, when she had changed to an English-language channel and heard the same news delivered in a tone of muted hysteria, she had felt herself slipping into dazed disbelief as the bizarre, frightening story unfolded.

The ancient town of Glastonbury and its unfortunate inhabitants had disappeared inexplicably from the face of the earth, leaving only lush marshlands where the town-centre had formerly stood, as well as a few hysterical witnesses from the immediate vicinity, all of whom had insisted that the town had been 'swallowed' by an immense pillar of darkness. And then there, on television, was the actual site of the miraculous event: a perfectly linear square-mile of lush green, watery marshland, surrounded by a military cordon of soldiers, baffled scientists, hysterical witnesses and gathering journalists, the television-cameras scanning over the whole area as if hoping to show the invisible.

No, Frances could not accept it — and most of the world was sharing her problem — but a small town back home had disappeared, leaving no trace behind.

Frances kept staring at Laurence, hardly knowing she was doing so. Beyond him, the desert of dry, seasonal marsh was like the landscape of a dream, the dust billowing and swirling above a featureless, flat terrain that ran out in all directions until it dissolved into the murky sky. To the uninitiated it would have been an awesomely desolate sight, but Frances was used to it, was actually getting to need it, and now, having let its vast desolation console her, she gazed through the windscreen again.

More dust-swept desolation. An achromatic terrain. Frances felt drawn to that windswept, howling emptiness, having dreamed of it often. The jeep passed a palm grove, then bounced over a pothole, causing the medicine chests, one on top of the other, to squeak and rattle in protest. Frances twisted around in her seat to push the chests closer together, and by the time she had turned back to the front the strong wind was weakening.

'Dammit,' Laurence said, shaking his head disbelievingly. 'I always wanted to visit Glastonbury. We don't have places like that in America — and now it's all gone.'

Frances shivered. She tried to visualise what had happened, but failed dismally to do so: she could only recall what she had seen on the small television screen: that placid, empty marshland surrounded by monitoring equipment and dazed scientists. And, remembering that, she could not shake from her head the thought of the enormous amount of grief, confusion and terror that would be shared by those whose loved ones had been stolen away as if by God's hand.

'I can't think clearly about it,' she said. 'I don't even want to try. So let's not talk about it anymore. Let's talk about work.'

'Are we getting close?'

'Yes, we'll soon be there.'

'Hallelujah for work,' Laurence said. 'At least it keeps us distracted.'

'A stiff gin and tonic,' Frances replied. 'That, sir, is what *I* need for distraction.'

'As a Christian let me state that I'm glad we're not carrying booze with us.'

'You don't have to sound so pleased,' Frances said.

Laurence grinned. 'I'll try not to.'

The landscape was still desolate, the dust drifting over the flatlands, but gradually, as the dust subsided, as the moaning wind fell into silence, the late-afternoon light returned, started burning through the haze, and revealed what at first seemed like a mirage in the desert: the glint of distant water, swaying bulrushes and fig trees, then reed houses springing out of the flatlands as Laurence drove straight towards them.

It was not a mirage, but it did seem slightly incongruous since suddenly, there, where the desert should

17

have been, was a broad swathe of marshlands, water gleaming between green banks, the tall bulrushes swaying against a ripening, crimson sky while the reed houses of the marsh Arabs shifted rapidly into black silhouette.

Frances brushed strands of dark hair from her mouth as Laurence slowed down, drove past some reed houses that were nestling under dusty fig-palms, and braked to a halt where the first of the bridges led across the irrigation ditches to the centre of the somnolent village. Laurence wiped dust from his face, glanced around him as the first Arab children approached, then threw Frances a teasing grin.

'This is it?' he asked.

'Yes,' Frances replied as they both climbed down from the jeep, 'this is it. You're about halfway between biblical Babylon and Ur — the Tigris river to the east, the Euphrates to the west — and this is the home of the Ma'dan — the marsh Arabs. Between the two great rivers are the marshes; beyond them, the desert.'

'Mesopotamia,' Laurence murmured, gazing dreamily about him. 'The Cradle of Civilisation ... Lord, I can't believe I'm here.'

Frances was amused by Laurence's reverential tone. 'Don't get too romantic about it,' she said. 'It's not the place you imagine. It's no more magical than Glastonbury was — and Glastonbury, my mystical friend, was just another small market-town.'

'It *was*,' Laurence emphasised. 'Before it disappeared without cause. That strikes *me* as magical.'

Wishing she hadn't mentioned the missing town, Frances looked down as the Arab children surrounded her, their eyes large and shy, the strings of beads dangling from their restless fingers being clicked rhythmically. A few of them were naked, holding spears or poisoned fish-bait, but most of them were wearing the customary headcloth, the *keffia*, draped over their head and shoulders, as well as the *dish-disha*, a long,

18

unadorned shirt reaching from the throat to the feet, usually plain, sometimes striped in modest colours.

She greeted the children in her very basic Arabic, smiling at those she recognised from previous visits to the village, then introduced Laurence as her 'new friend', though he was, in reality, only her new assistant.

Laurence, having spent most of his first six weeks in Iraq, locked up in the mission-house in Baghdad and now visiting the marsh Arabs for the first time, was instantly intoxicated when he took in the surrounding reed houses and, beyond them, the dimly glittering mosaic of watery marsh and lagoons which were fed by the two great rivers that became one near Basra and, as the Shatt al Arab, flowed on into the Persian Gulf.

He managed to tear his gaze from the scenery around him, glanced down at the milling children, then grinned again at Frances and followed her onto the bridge which crossed a water-filled ditch and led them into the heart of the village and, more specifically, to the *mudhif*, or guest-house, of the sheikh.

The *mudhif*, shaped rather like an immense Swiss-roll and much larger than any of the houses surrounding it, had been constructed out of a series of arches which had been woven, like the smaller village houses, from the giant reeds that grew in the marshes. Frances and Laurence, approaching the flat end that was turned towards Mecca, were greeted by one of the sheikh's servants and, after kicking off their shoes, led through the low, arched entrance into the *mudhif's* dimly-lit interior.

With its thirteen high arches, elaborate roof and flickering, dim lighting, the *mudhif* resembled a spartan, gloomy cathedral. It contained no furniture, but the servants had spread woven rugs on the floor of reed matting, and Sheikh Hamaid was already sitting there, legs crossed in the customary fashion, beside the coffee hearth with its exotic row of brass and copper pots. The light from the flames of an open fire in the hearth blended with that of the hurricane lamps which, swaying dangerously on the walls of the *mudhif* and giving off an acrid smoke, illuminated the inquisitive eyes of the many villagers who had crowded inside to observe the ritualistic socialising of their sheikh and his guests.

Frances greeted the sheikh by shaking his hand and then placing her own hand over her heart. 'Peace be with you,' she said in Arabic, before stepping back to let Laurence do the same. 'On you be peace,' the sheikh replied, also in Arabic, waving one hand to indicate that they should sit in front of him. Frances sat on the woven rugs, curling her legs under her and tugging the hem of her grey dress down over her knees, while Laurence, close beside her, sat cross-legged as all men were supposed to. The reed fire, crackling beyond him, filled the air with spiralling smoke, casting flickering shadows over his lean, pleasant face.

Sheikh Hamaid was not the handsome Bouduin warrior so beloved to the Western imagination, but an unshaven, hollow-cheeked man with skin so sunscorched and wrinkled that his true age was impossible to determine. With black hair sprouting from his nostrils, meeting like the fine wires of an old shoe-brush over the bridge of his Semitic nose, and sprouting thickly over the brown eyes that were shadowed by the *keffia* covering his head and shoulders, he looked like a sly old trader, or one of the marshland's cut-throat bandits, rather than a linear descendant of Mohammed, which he and a great many other marsh Arabs claimed to be. This first impression of primitive slyness was, however, soon belied by the lively intelligence of his steady gaze, and by the quiet arrogance and sly mockery of his full, sensual-lipped smile and good-natured mockery.

'It is most pleasant to see you again, Miss Devereux,' he said, speaking in excellent, if slightly formal, English. 'My people always appreciate your kind attentions — and I, of course, enjoy the pleasure of your company.'

His eyes moved questioningly towards Laurence, so Frances, anticipating him, said, 'This is my new medical assistant, Laurence Gilbride, presently a student at the Friends to Christ mission in Baghdad. Naturally, like most of the students in that mission, Laurence is studying medicine, as well as theology.'

The sheikh nodded, examining Laurence in a candid manner; then, noting his embarrassment, turned back towards Frances.

'Ah, yes,' he said. 'That *is* a good thing. Since we believe in Mohammed, where you Christians do not, it is better that you concentrate on our physical ailments and let us be the shepherds of our own souls.' He smiled with sly mockery, placing his hands beneath his unshaven chin. 'Of course you, Miss Devereux, are not religious at all, so it is odd that you should have religious assistants.'

'Not odd,' Frances replied. 'The hospital in Baghdad is desperately short of trained staff — so, in return for their assistance in running the wards, we give free training to the students of the mission.'

'A fair trade, Miss Devereux. We Arabs understand such arrangements. As for yourself, instead of living in the comforts of England, you come to this bleak place to help the Ma'dan — so you must, in your secret heart, be a religious person . . . or, at least, a truly spiritual woman.'

Frances smiled at that, amused to be thought of as a spiritual woman, but also pleased to be distracted from the fears that the disappearance of Glastonbury had raised.

'I'm not a spiritual woman,' she said. 'Quite the opposite, in fact. Now Laurence, here, *he's* a spiritual person — and deep down disapproves of me.'

The sheikh raised one eyebrow and stared quizzically at Laurence. 'This is true?' he asked.

'No,' Laurence replied, shaking his head, his grin open. 'I *do* have some concern for Miss Devereux's soul, but I think highly of her.'

21

The sheikh thoughtfully studied Laurence, eventually nodded and smiled, then turned towards the servants and clapped his hands lightly, thus indicating that the food should be served.

One of the servants emerged quickly and silently from the smoky, lamplit gloom near the cushion-lined wall of the *mudhif* to pass around the small bowl in which they could rinse their fingers. Even as they were doing this, the other servants were busily setting bowls of mutton, chicken and gravy — all placed around a mound of rice — on the floor between the sheikh and his guests, while an extremely old man, sitting cross-legged not far away, struck up a tune on his 78-stringed *al-qanoun*, the musical instrument most loved by the Arabs after the lute.

As was customary with the Ma'dan, the food was eaten quickly if awkwardly, the rice being soaked in the gravy and then scooped up with the right hand and forced by the thumb out of the palm and into the mouth. It was a messy way to eat and was clearly causing Laurence some problems, since he kept spilling handfuls of rice down his shirt-front and onto his crossed legs, much to the silent mirth of the perceptive sheikh.

Laurence, physically awkward at the best of times, was becoming more so under the amused scrutiny of the sheikh and his chattering villagers, but was saved from humiliation by his ability to laugh at himself. Nonetheless, he was obviously relieved when the meal ended and the plates were removed, the village children swooping in to grab the uneaten food, the servants expertly clearing away the bones and rice littering the mats.

'The Arabs believe in quantity rather than quality,' the sheikh explained to him, 'and what to the Western observer might be an unpleasant mess, is to the Arab but a sign of satisfaction.'

Frances, who prior to this field trip had only known Laurence through her monthly visits to the mission in

Baghdad, and who had found him to be attractively good-humoured, now took a mischievous pleasure from his discomfort and, as she again rinsed her fingers in the bowl proffered by a bowing servant, could not resist smiling wickedly at him. Laurence grinned back and brushed the red hair from his lean face, then uncomfortably shifted his crossed legs and gave his attention to the music being played on the ancient instrument. The sheikh, after glancing round the crowded tent, gave his attention to Frances.

'The food was to your satisfaction?'

'Yes, thank you. It was fine.'

'You will share coffee with me?'

'Of course.'

'Then we can have entertainment.'

While they had been eating, a servant, having prepared the coffee, was pouring it from one pot into another where they stood, like brightly ornamented birds, around the strip of uncovered earth.

The sheikh sniffed, as if testing the aroma of the coffee fumes, then clapped his hands to call for the entertainment to commence. The first performance was by an amateur singing group: four young men who provided high-pitched, nasal, dramatically quavering laments of the most alien and inexplicable poignancy. Shortly after this performance had started the servant rose from the smouldering coffee hearth and approached the matted area to offer Frances and Laurence each a tiny cup into which he poured steaming coffee. The coffee was hot, aromatic and exceptionally strong, and when Frances, too distracted and moved by the singing, was handing her cup to the servant after her third drink, she shook it to indicate that she wanted no more.

'They sing of the pleasures of the flesh,' the sheikh explained, 'and of how all those pleasures come to dust when payment is due.'

'Must the pleasures always be paid for?'

'If not materially, then spiritually.'

23

'That sounds very depressing,' Frances said.

'It is natural and proper.'

Frances gazed at the sheikh and saw his smile through swirling smoke. He was having his little joke at her expense, but also sexually challenging her.

The smoke stung her eyes; the increasing heat was making her sweat; the noise, ricocheting in the crowded *mudhif*, was making her dizzy. She started to imagine that she was melting and dripping down through her own core, but was jolted back to reality by the sudden ending of the last, aching song.

Before the abrupt silence could take command, some professional dancers stepped forward and began to dance in the flickering light from the hurricane lamps. All young men, but with their hair long and loose, they first mimed a few stories of misfortune and triumphs, but all too quickly moved on to some graphically explicit sexual pantomime. There could be no doubting what was being enacted by these sinuously swaying and shuddering boys, and Frances, though she had seen it all before, was helplessly aroused by it.

The boys writhed in the swirling smoke, lithe bodies glistening with sweat, hips swaying and groins thrusting rhythmically. Frances couldn't help herself: she wanted to reach out and touch them, to let her fingers slide over their knotted muscles and then have them envelop her.

She glanced across at the religious Laurence, saw him shifting uncomfortably, smiled with amusement and then looked to the front to catch the searching gaze of Sheikh Hamaid. His dark, deep-set eyes, glittering perceptively in his ageless face, displayed the sly amusement and frank desire of a man who understood women.

'The dancing is to your liking, Miss Devereux?'

'Its strangeness is interesting.'

The sheikh smiled at that, his gaze very steady upon her, then eventually, after nodding in a judicious manner, returned his gaze to the dancers.

The entertainment went on a long time, the villagers shouting constant enouragement, and eventually the tent became very hot and filled up with the smoke from the cigarettes, pipes and hurricane lamps. At once exhausted and sexually aroused, feeling the sweat soaking her clothing, Frances was glad when it finally ended and the villagers, all chattering excitedly, filed out of the tent.

When the villagers had departed, leaving silence behind them, the sheikh called for tea, which was served by the servants in minute glasses half-filled with sugar. While Frances was sipping at her tea, the sheikh gave instructions to the remaining servants, who quickly tidied up the *mudhif* and then discreetly disappeared, leaving Frances, Laurence and the sheikh in a silence broken only by the soft snapping of the still burning fire, and by the wind that was starting to moan across the marshes beyond the walls of the *mudhif*. The sheikh, apparently cool in his roped headcloth and robes, sighed and stared thoughtfully at Frances.

'Now you must be tired,' he said.

'I am.'

'Then I must take my leave.'

However, instead of leaving, he merely glanced at the silent Laurence, offering him a neutral smile, then again stared very directly at Frances.

'Please let me say, Miss Devereux, as I am sure I have said before, that I greatly admire your courage in continuing to visit my people throughout these dangerous times.'

'It was never dangerous for me,' Frances replied. 'And the war is finally over.'

'Yes, Miss Devereux, the war is over at last — Iraq and Iran are now at peace — nevertheless, you continued to visit us while the war raged in these marshlands, as well as in Basra where you live. I think that was courageous.'

Even as he spoke, the sheikh was staring at Frances

with a calm and candid sexual interest, his gaze flickering from her eyes to her body in open inspection. Frances was not offended — in fact, she found his attentions pleasing — but she kept her gaze steady and gravely attentive, as if unaware of his silent invitation.

'It was a very bad war,' she said, 'and I'm glad that it's over. I wasn't frightened when the shells were exploding, but I didn't like what I saw.'

'Death bothers you?'

'Yes.'

'To the Arabs it is natural. The desert has no mercy on the weak, so it is they who fall first.'

'That may well be true. Nonetheless, I am delighted that the destruction and killing have ended.'

'And do you think that this peace, which so delights you, will last forever?'

'Nothing lasts forever,' Frances replied, 'but I hope it lasts for a long time.'

Laurence, obviously keen to involve himself in the conversation, leaned forward and coughed into his clenched fist.

'It should at least last for a reasonable period,' he said. 'The mass of Iranians have had enough of the old ways, so it's unlikely that another war with Iraq is on their current agenda.'

The sheikh raised both his hands in a histrionic gesture. 'But the dead are still rotting in the desert and marshes,' he said, 'and that is something many Iraqis cannot forget . . . So, it might start again.' He lowered his hands again, letting them rest on his thighs, then offered a loud sigh. 'The horrors of war are repugnant to the Western mind,' he said, 'but to us they are as natural as the wind — and like the wind, will not cease. War is not a mystery, nor an aberration or sickness — though there *are* certain mysteries which even this humble Arab cannot explain.'

Frances remembered what had happened the day before in Glastonbury, but the very thought of that

26

awesome event sent a chill down her spine.

'Such as?' she asked.

The sheikh shrugged his shoulders in a gesture of bewilderment, then uncrossed his legs and stood up.

'Come,' he said, addressing them both. 'Stand up. Let me show you.'

Frances and Laurence did as they were bid, then followed the surprisingly small, ungainly sheikh along the gloomy *mudhif*, walking under the thirteen high woven arches until they arrived at the very far end.

There, lying flat on his back on blankets spread out on the reed matting, was an apparently sleeping, lightly bearded white man dressed in blue denims and jacket, a soiled rucksack propped up not far from his head.

Frances studied him, wondering how he could sleep so stiffly, then turned back to the sheikh.

The sheikh shrugged again, almost forlornly. 'It is not normal sleep,' he explained. 'He has been unconscious for a long time. A fisherman found him this morning, lying on the riverbank near the mouth of the Shatt al Arab. Seeing that he was unharmed, the fisherman tried in vain to revive him — then, not knowing what else to do, brought him back here. He is healthy — yet no-one here can waken him, which seems very strange. I am hoping that you, with your medical experience, can do what we cannot.'

Frances and Laurence automatically stared at one another, then Frances knelt down to examine the man on the floor. The sheikh took a step backwards, letting his shadow fall away from the unconscious man — and at that moment, when Frances saw the man's face properly, she felt something lurching within her, as if in surprised — and fearful — recognition.

Instantly confused, trying to ignore her racing heart, and wondering why she should imagine that she knew this perfect stranger, Frances blinked and studied him more intently.

Looking down at his lamplit face, which was

unshaven, middle-aged, slightly brutal and possibly corrupt, she shivered and hastily averted her gaze, shocked to realise that she simultaneously felt repelled by him and attracted to him, for reasons which lay somewhere just out of her reach.

She shivered again, suddenly aware of the moaning wind, her head filled with a vision of the marshlands outside, the lagoons black and glittering beneath the stars in that cold, frightening darkness. Then, filled with inexplicable repugnance and desire, she bent low to press her ear to the stranger's chest and hear his healthy heart beating — a distant drum calling to her.

CHAPTER TWO

Cheryl had never been noted for her punctuality, and Michael, who had arrived only five minutes early, was well into his second glass of white wine before he saw her standing in the doorway, silhouetted in the summery London light outside. Her head moved left and right as she scanned the packed, noisy brasserie, then she saw him, waved and moved towards him, wending her way skilfully between the many tables which were crowded with the beautiful young things, male and female, who had already managed to make Michael feel much older than his forty-three years.

Moving away from the sunlight and advancing through the smoky haze, Cheryl eventually reached his table and stood in front of him, that inner radiance which she threw out with the calm assurance of her twenty years instantly obliterating his lingering aggravation at being forced to sit alone in this rather fashionable, art-deco brasserie, being stared at, often far too frankly, by expensively dressed, attractive ladies who were, as he recognised with jaundiced humour, roughly the same age as his daughter.

'Hi!' Cheryl exclaimed, raising her right hand in the air. 'Sorry I'm late again.'

'I just arrived a few minutes ago,' Michael lied, delighted to see her. 'And I've really enjoyed being surrounded by these lovely young creatures.'

'You should have come to the dance-studio,' Cheryl said. 'They're even prettier there.'

A model agency's dream of slyly casual elegance, she was wearing a dark-blue cotton Monsoon shirt with embroidered front and matching flowery braces, the latter holding up her cotton suedette jodhpurs which, tucked into canvas boots with buckled sides, emphasised the legs supporting her slim body. A dark alpaca wool shawl had been dangling with calculated carelessness from her shoulders, and now, as she pulled the bamboo chair back and sat opposite Michael, she let the shawl slip from her and fall, as if placed there by an invisible waiter, across the back of the chair.

'My handsome father!' she said. 'What a treat! And he's all mine for lunch!'

'The pleasure is all mine,' Michael replied. 'And well worth the wait.'

'You *were* early.' That was a sly reprimand. 'A drink will buy you forgiveness.'

She placed her small tan-suede shoulder-bag on the table by her left hand, leaned forward to kiss him lightly on the cheek, then cupping her perfectly proportioned, suntanned face in her hands, stared very directly at him, her ravishingly blue, rather too open eyes, emphasised by the slightly boyish fringe of blonde hair that fell down from the slanting brim of her men's wide felt hat.

'Just call the waiter. *I'll* order it. You wouldn't know where to start.'

Michael was not offended by his charming daughter's brash impertinence. Like so many of the bars and restaurants in London, this brasserie specialised in a line of cocktails so complicated in their ingredients that a university degree would soon be needed to master the drinks list. Getting the mini-skirted and peaked-capped waitress to their table with surprising speed, he insisted

30

on sticking to white wine, whereas Cheryl, after perusing the list at considerable length, ordered a very exotic cocktail.

The waitress, who had been growing visibly impatient with Cheryl's procrastinations, departed gladly back through the crowded tables, her tight mini-skirt and very high heels making her long legs look delectable.

'Stop thinking about it,' Cheryl said. 'A man like you should know better. As a clinical psychologist, you know perfectly well what happens during the male-menopause. And, apart from being too young for you, she's also too dumb.'

'How do you know that? Is she a friend?'

'No. I just know the type.'

'And I suppose you know your father's type as well. The male-menopause type.'

'Oh, mein Papa, that was just a joke!'

She lowered her head slightly to let her eyes widen, her broad smile puffing out her golden cheeks in an irresistible manner. Michael returned her smile, amused and warmed by her, but was uncomfortably reminded of how much like her mother she looked when, after the waitress had brought their drinks, he studied her thoughtfully.

'Well,' he said, 'you *are* looking beautiful.'

'I'm glad,' she replied. 'That's why I suffer so much in that so-called dance studio. It's not the dancing that makes me lose pounds — it's the aerobics — so I'm glad you approve.'

'You're more suntanned every time I see you.'

'It's all the travelling. I've been doing a lot of it recently, as you know. And if you're interested, I've just returned from the south of France.'

'Cannes?'

'No. Nice. We're shooting a low-budget feature film in the old city, and the purchaser had to check on soaring costs, so he dragged me along. We were there for five hectic days — and every one was a scorcher.'

Michael sighed enviously at the thought of his daughter's life-style. Although still only twenty, Cheryl had already travelled extensively as the personal assistant to the top executive of one of the few thriving film-producing companies left in London. When not at a film festival in Cannes, Los Angeles, Berlin or Manila, she was visiting locations in such tax-advantageous countries as southern Spain, the Philippines, Israel and the Far East. His envy of her constant travelling, and his gratitude that she had such a good job in these days of high unemployment, was tempered by his occasional unease at the effects of her way of life on her still forming and highly impressionable personality, most of which doubts had arisen during the infrequent film previews or publicity parties to which she had invited him. Extreme extroversion, casual promiscuity and a ruthless desire to succeed at any cost appeared to be the prevalent traits of the majority of those whom Michael had met at such gatherings, and it sometimes made him apprehensive to think that Cheryl — who was in many ways still remarkably immature — might fall under their spell.

'You don't supplement that tan with a sun-ray lamp, do you?' he asked her.

Cheryl actually blushed. 'Now, Daddy, don't — '

'You do, don't you?'

'Not often, but sometimes. It prevents me from getting too burnt when I have to suddenly fly off to some sunny spot.'

'Nonsense,' Michael said, quietly despairing of her childish vanity. 'You only do it because you can't bear the thought of stepping out in front of your fancy friends with normal white skin.'

'Well, what's the matter with that?' Cheryl responded, smiling at him, but with a hint of defiance brightening her blue eyes.

'You know damned well what's the matter with it. If I've told you once, I've told you a thousand times — that sun-ray lamp will eventually ruin your skin.'

'Oh, tosh! Let's order.'

With pouting lips and a theatrical toss of her head she picked up the large menu and buried her nose in it. Michael wearily shook his own head and then likewise picked up a menu, letting his gaze run down a list of dishes which were mostly of the American fast-food variety, but embellished with currently popular Tex-Mex trimmings, such as enchaladas and chilli.

'You *eat* this stuff?' he asked.

'When I'm in a casual mood.'

'Now I know why you're attending aerobics classes. You're working off what you eat.'

Cheryl giggled at that and Michael called the waitress. Cheryl was still undecided, so Michael ordered his own meal — an unappealing combination of hamburger, French-fries, chilli-dressing and green beans — and sat back to endure the usual silent tension of Cheryl's procrastinations.

Every table in the brasserie was now taken and the exotically costumed, blonde, teenage waitress was obviously under some pressure to attend to them, but she managed to roll her eyes good-humouredly at Michael and give him a sardonic grin while Cheryl, as was her custom, kept muttering and changing her mind. Michael, normally patient, was just about to lose that patience, when Cheryl suddenly gave her order, watched the grateful waitress hurry away, then folded her hands under her chin and leaned slightly towards him, her radiant smile erasing his temper.

'Don't think I didn't notice you and that waitress,' she said. 'I'd be offended, except I'm so proud that my father's still so attractive.'

'I don't know what you're talking about,' Michael replied, amused by her cheek.

'You were eyeing-up one another.'

'Nonsense. She was rolling her eyes because you were taking so long to decide what to order. Her eyes suggested no more than the frustration that comes from

33

dealing with customers such as yourself. Not, I fear, a case of sexual yearning.'

'You found her attractive, didn't you?'

'I find a lot of the young ladies in this place attractive. That doesn't mean much.'

'You're still a womaniser, Daddy.'

'I retain a fondness for the ladies — true. However, I *do* tend to stick to my own age-group, so don't play any games, girl.'

'When are you going to stop playing the bachelor and settle down like a decent man?'

'I *am* a decent man. I'm just not settled. And what's wrong with that?'

'I think Mother still misses you.'

'It's been *eight years*, Cheryl.'

'Time means nothing to a woman in love. You should bear that in mind.'

Michael killed that subject by glancing around the busy brasserie. Arc lights flashed off silver railings and ornate, art-deco mirrors, illuminating in different colours the many bizarre hairstyles and the equally strange clothing of the privileged youth of the land, most of whom were eating instant food while drinking cocktails or champagne. He had never had that at their age, and could scarcely credit their having it; and he wondered, as he studied them, how they could all look so unconcerned, bearing in mind the extraordinary event of that morning.

Even now, thinking about it, he felt the dark cloak of the unknown falling over him. Given the inexplicable, terrifying disappearance of Glastonbury, it was difficult to accept that he could actually sit here with his daughter, surrounded by undisturbed laughter and joyous pop music.

'Did you get a paper this morning?' he asked Cheryl.

'No,' she replied. 'I always watch the news on telly.'

'So you know about Glastonbury?'

'Oh, God, yes,' she said, her glowing smile

disappearing. 'I actually saw it on the morning news. I still can't believe it's actually happened. I don't think anyone can.'

'Frightening,' Michael said.

'Yes, frightening. Let's not talk about it.'

'A whole town disappears,' Michael said, ignoring her plea. 'So do most of its inhabitants. Where a great Tor once dominated the landscape there is now only marshland, still steaming and flat. It just doesn't seem possible.'

Cheryl shivered. 'I keep thinking about it — and it makes me feel unreal. I think everyone I've talked to feels the same way. They all feel that they're dreaming.'

'It will change a lot of people's way of thinking. It may change the whole world.'

'Don't talk about it. I don't want to think about it. Let's talk about something else.'

Noting how disturbed she was, Michael decided to drop the subject, but could not resist looking around him again at the packed, noisy brasserie. He thought of the scenes on television — of the weeping and hysteria — and could scarcely credit that here, in the middle of Covent Garden, London, life continued as if nothing had happened. Blinking, suddenly feeling unreal, he turned back to Cheryl.

'And how is your mother?' he asked her. 'No problems, I hope.'

'Oh, she's fine,' Cheryl replied, clearly relieved at the change of subject. 'She just gets a bit lonely now and then.'

'We *all* get that way now and then. It's part of the human condition.'

'You don't, Daddy. You *like* living alone. You're a natural bachelor.'

'Yes, I am. But your mother always refused to believe that. She mistakes my need for independence as a lack of paternal instincts. In other words, she thinks I don't care enough about you.'

35

'I know you care.'

'Well, that's good. Because I care very deeply.'

It was an unusually emotional confession that left them both a little embarrassed, so the arrival of the waitress with their lunch was a welcome distraction. Soon regaining her ebullience, Cheryl kept up a lively stream of conversation during the meal, mostly about her experiences in the very unstable but still colourful British film industry; and Michael, enjoying himself, taking pleasure from her youthful optimism, nonetheless found himself listening with only half of his attention, the rest being taken up with the increasing disbelief that this beautiful young woman could really be his daughter.

He had married Cheryl's mother, Janet, at the age of twenty-four, two years before Cheryl's birth and just after he had gained his M.B. and was starting as house physician in psychiatry at the Maudsley Hospital in London. He and Janet, who was then also in psychiatry, had been deeply attracted to one another, and the marriage during its earliest years was, if not particularly passionate, emotionally satisfying. However, with increasing maturity and a self-knowledge gleaned from his further work in clinical psychology, Michael had gradually come to accept the truth of his own nature. Not a particularly passionate man, he nonetheless enjoyed sex; not a particularly emotional man, he still had the need to experience many different women, and, beyond that, to live a life unrestrained by domestic trivia. It was a combination of these factors that had led to his divorce from Janet — but only in recent months had he come to realise that if he had been able to go through with the divorce with minimum damage to himself, he had certainly caused some damage not only to his former wife, but to Cheryl, an only child, who had been a sensitive twelve-year-old at the time.

So, as he studied his lovely daughter, he wondered if the pain he had caused her eight years ago still lurked in the back of her mind. Cheryl was attractive, well-educated and adored, but a part of her refused to grow up, a trait which tended to make her highly impressionable and too dependent upon others. Michael not only wondered if his divorce had caused that insecurity, but also dreaded the thought that sooner or later someone, most likely from the world of films, would sense it and ruthlessly exploit it.

It was possibly that concern which prompted him, while drinking his Irish coffee, to casually ask her about her love-life.

Her reply began with a careless shrug of her shoulders. 'Oh,' she said, 'it comes and goes.'

'No-one special at the moment?'

'They *all* seem so special during the initial heady encounters. Unfortunately — or fortunately — that feeling never lasts for too long.'

'I think fortunately,' Michael said. 'I'd rather you experience a lot more before settling down. One of the most damaging aspects of marrying young is that one tends to still have too many desires and ambitions unfulfilled — desires and ambitions which marriage simply cannot permit.'

'Such as?'

'Oh, travel — not the kind you're presently doing as part of your work, but the kind which one chooses for oneself and does independently. That, and perhaps a more ambitious career — one requiring free time and a minimum of other commitments.'

'I *have* a career, Daddy.'

'You have a *job*, Cheryl. I would hardly call a secretary's job a career. More a stop-gap.'

'I'm not a common *secretary*. I'm a very responsible P.A. to a movie producer. And a very talented, attractive one at that. So I'm quite happy, thanks.'

'Sounds like you're doting on this fellow.'

'I'm not doting on him. I just feel very lucky to be working with him.'

'Handsome?'

'Correct.'

'About your age?'

'Not correct. He's in his late-thirties and is happily married with two kids. He's just my *boss*, Daddy.'

Michael smiled at that. 'I still think you should stay free as long as possible — to give yourself time to think out what you really want to do. And, of course, to learn more about men and what kind you could seriously live with.'

'That's a very logical attitude to life, Daddy.'

'I'm a very logical man.'

'Maybe. And maybe you're simply justifying your reasons for leaving Mother. *You're* a practising psychologist, but we can't all apply that kind of objectivity to our personal lives.'

Michael finished his coffee and sat back in his chair, surprised at Cheryl's display of self-awareness.

'Well, well,' he said eventually. 'For a very romantic, highly impressionable young lady you can be quite hard-headed.'

'I get that from you.' She flashed him a dazzling smile, her blue eyes bright with mischief, and he realised once more, with a mixture of pride and trepidation, just how attractive she would surely be to most men.

'You still share that flat in Bayswater with those three other girls?'

'Yes,' Cheryl replied. 'And go home to Mother every weekend, which I think keeps her happy. So, what about *your* love-life? What's happening there?'

'I have to get back to the hospital,' Michael replied, 'so let's pay-up and leave.'

'Well, *that's* a neat cop-out!'

Cheryl chuckled triumphantly while Michael waved to the waitress, indicating that he wanted to go. When the bill eventually arrived, he paid with cash and tipped generously, thus receiving a warm smile from the waitress before she departed. Cheryl watched the girl weaving her way between the tables, then gave Michael a knowing glance before letting him take her by the elbow and lead her out of the brasserie, which now, with its loud music and smoke, was making him feel claustrophobic.

'Well,' he said, when they had both stepped into the bright light of Henrietta Street, 'that's a relief.'

'You didn't like my choice of restaurant?'

'The company at my table was wonderful,' he replied, 'but I felt a little out of place with that music and all those pretty young things. I was starting to feel very *old*.'

'I can't stand pretty young things, male or female,' Cheryl said. 'I prefer more mature gentlemen like yourself. Tall, broad and handsome. Distinguished academic career. Now Principal Clinical Psychologist of the psychiatric wing of a leading hospital in upper middle-class Hampstead. A real catch to any bitch with foul intentions — but all mine for lunch.'

'Dear daughter, you make me feel so young — as Frank Sinatra once sang.'

'That *does* age you, Daddy.'

Nodding his agreement, Michael took her by the elbow and led her along the street into the Central Piazza which, on this warm, sunny day, was filled with camera-laden tourists, people eating and drinking at the outside tables of the numerous restaurants and cafes, impatiently hurrying office workers, and various colourfully attired and made-up street-entertainers.

In the square in front of the Tuscan columns of St Paul's Church, a crowd was gathering around two men dressed up as clowns. One of the men was holding a very large balloon which had been painted as the globe of the earth, playing with it rather as Charles Chaplin had done in his film *The Great Dictator*.

Michael and Cheryl stopped to watch as the clown, juggling the balloon, comically tried to avoid the second clown who was balletically attempting to prick the balloon with a giant hat-pin. The attack and retreat of the two clowns was performed as a pantomime, by turns comic and threatening; but as the performance drew to its climax, with the balletic movements becoming more frantic and the onlookers by turns laughing, gasping, booing or shouting encouragement, the mood of the play edged away from comedy altogether and closer to something distinctly macabre, until eventually, with a demonic shriek of triumph, the clown brandishing the giant hat-pin managed to prick the balloon, thus causing the globe of the earth to explode.

The onlookers broke into prolonged applause, and, as the first clown stood with his head hanging in shame and the remains of the balloon dangling forlornly from his fingers, his partner started passing around his hat. Michael gave him some loose change, then shivered and walked on, leading Cheryl across the crowded, noisy Piazza, past the packed stalls of the market in the middle.

'What's the matter?' Cheryl asked him. 'You suddenly look *terribly* thoughtful.'

'It was the clowns' pantomime,' Michael replied. 'They were mocking the millennium. I think they got the idea from Glastonbury — the way it inexplicably disappeared this morning. A lot of people are already claiming that that awesome event marks the beginning of the end of the world — and the two clowns were poking fun at that theory.'

'Well,' Cheryl said, 'it *is* a frightening business — almost unbelievable, in fact — and no doubt that when what happened really sinks in, we'll *all* be frightened by the thought of what it might mean.'

'Does it frighten you?'

'I'm still trying to grasp it. I mean, it's almost like a movie in one's head — very vivid, yet unreal. Anyway, let's not talk about it. Let's not spoil that nice lunch. Are you now going to meet some lovely lady and carry her off somewhere?'

'No lovely lady today — apart from the one that I'm with. I'm taking the tube straight back to the hospital. What about you?'

'Straight back to Wardour Street by public footpath. Soothed by the wine.'

They passed the people dining at the tables outside the Hard Rock Cafe, walked up the crowded pavement of James Street, and stood facing one another outside the entrance to Covent Garden underground station in Long Acre, beside the racks of newspapers, the front pages of which were dominated by the disappearance of Glastonbury.

Michael glanced only briefly at the newspapers, then distracted himself by studying his daughter's beautiful, suntanned face, slim body, and very attractive, slightly androgynous clothing — all of which only served to remind him again that Cheryl was no longer a child and that he, who had held her on his knee not long ago, was now the middle-aged father of a very desirable young woman. Disconcerted by this, and touched by a fleeting paternal anxiety, he leaned down and kissed her on the cheek and then straightened up again.

'Take care,' he said. 'And don't forget to call me when you feel like another free lunch.'

'Don't worry. I won't.'

She stood on tip-toe to return his kiss, then turned away and plunged into the swarming crowd, her wide hat bobbing like a boat before disappearing behind a sea of heads.

Michael stood there for some time, filled with love and concern, then eventually went into the station to catch the train back to work.

CHAPTER THREE

'Did you have a good sleep?' Laurence asked, setting down his glass of sweet tea and picking up a piece of thin, golden coloured bread. He was sitting cross-legged at the other side of the coffee hearth, directly facing Frances, his face hazed by the smoke from the small fire upon which the coffee was heating.

'No,' Frances replied. 'I hardly slept a wink. I kept thinking of Glastonbury and that man lying beside us, and finally I just gave up and went out for a walk. Naturally, because of all their bloody dogs, I didn't get very far.'

'Yes, I've already noticed that they've all got vicious dogs.'

'*Lots* of them,' Frances emphasised. 'All large and unfriendly and *noisy*, barking all day and night.'

She shook her head with a weary gesture. First awakened by that relentless barking, then kept awake by haunting thoughts of the missing Glastonbury and the unconscious man lying close by, she had risen in the cold, grey dawn, crept quietly from the *mudhif* still wearing the clothes she had lain down in, and crossed a couple of the narrow, scum-covered ditches that threaded the village until she passed through some palm groves and emerged at the bank of the Euphrates river. There had been no boats on the river, making it

42

seem oddly ominous, and beyond it, on the flat and barren horizon, had been a featureless dark strip which she knew to be the densely reeded perimeter of the permanent marshes. All in all, a desolate sight, devoid of colour and warmth.

'You sound angry,' Laurence said. 'I get the impression that you don't like it here — and yet you've chosen to work here of your own accord.'

'I'm not angry,' Frances replied, sipping her coffee and wincing. 'I'm just irritable because I'm tired. I don't like their vicious dogs at the best of times, and when I'm tired, I could kill them.'

'We're all God's creatures, Frances.'

'You're entitled to that belief.'

Laurence smiled. 'You're a very tough woman. I wouldn't like to cross swords with you.'

'Oh, I'm not really *that* tough,' Frances said, returning his smile. '*My* bark's worse than my bite.'

The sheikh's servant was kneeling at the tall coffee pot in the smouldering hearth, and Frances stared past him, through the lazily coiling smoke, at the man lying at the far end of the *mudhif*. He was still unconscious, breathing deeply and evenly, lying flat on his back with that slightly unnatural stiffness, a strip of darkness falling across his body, while the hurricane lamp, strung from a post just above him, painted his face with wavering lines of yellow and black.

The very sight of him frightened Frances — or at least confused and disturbed her — since she was forced to recollect what she had felt as she lay beside him during the long, restless night.

In truth, it was not the dogs that had kept her awake, but the sound of that stranger's breathing: a rhythmic rising and falling of air that had eventually taken hold of her and convinced her that her heart, which had been racing, was in fact beating mysteriously in time with his.

She had seen his face throughout that night — visualising it behind her closed eyes — and had felt her body tingling with desire and inexplicable revulsion.

'It's not natural,' she said thoughtfully, still staring along the gloomy *mudhif*. 'I can't find a thing wrong with that man — and yet he won't wake up.'

Laurence shrugged and raised his hands in bewilderment. 'Some sort of coma,' he said. 'We just don't know what caused it.'

'Some sort of coma, yes. But no kind that *I* know about. He wasn't *knocked* unconscious — there's no sign of bruising — and his heart-beat, pulse and skin-tone are perfectly normal, just like those of a sleeping man. So, whatever kind of coma it is, it's a mystery to me.'

'Shivery,' Laurence said.

'Yes,' Frances replied. 'Just like the disappearance of Glastonbury . . . And *that* kept me awake as well.'

She glanced once more along the gloomy *mudhif*, saw the shadows flickering over the stranger where he lay on his back on the reed matting, simultaneously experienced a rush of desire and fear, then turned back to Laurence.

'No matter,' she said. 'It's a new day today and we've got our work to do. Let's attend to the Arabs and then, when we're finished, we can take that unconscious man back to Basra and put him into the hospital for observation. Let *them* deal with the mystery.'

Standing up together, they went outside to find the grey morning giving way to brilliant sunlight, letting the village stand out in untidy clarity. Frances instructed two of the villagers to bring the medical chests from the jeep parked at the other side of the palm-log bridges, and while a great many of the Arabs started gathering around expectantly, she saw Laurence surveying the village, his gaze taking in the scum-covered water drifting around the stilts of the reed houses that were poised precariously over the mudbanked ditches.

A light wind was blowing, picking up dust, sand and small fragments of reed, then sweeping them together in a cloud that spiralled lazily around the gathering Arabs. Beyond the village, the horizon was flat and featureless, but here, by the river, the tall bulrushes parted noisily as the fishermen pushed them aside and moved in their long, thin canoes out onto the broad, calm lagoons. Smoke poured out of the reed houses, dogs barked, chickens squawked, and the smell of coffee and baked bread filled the warming air, briefly defeating the unpleasant stench of the criss-crossing ditches.

'It's not like I imagined it,' Laurence said. 'It's not nearly as exotic as I thought it would be . . . In fact it's all fairly colourless.'

'That's what travelling does for you,' Frances replied. 'It strips the most exotic places of their glamour and forces you to realise that what on a postcard is local colour, is in reality just poverty. And most of the places we think of as exotic are in fact simply *poor*.'

'You don't have any illusions about it, do you?'

'No,' Frances replied, watching a group of young males struggling across one of the palm-log bridges with her two medicine chests rocking between them.

'Then why are you practising medicine here instead of back in the comforts of England?'

'Because I like my independence. Because here, in Iraq, I can live my own life without worrying about what people will think of me.'

'And why would people worry about that?'

'Oh,' Frances replied, shrugging, hardly aware of what she was saying, 'I like total freedom — to do what I like with whom I want — and here they just assume that all white women behave that way naturally. Back home, in London, my behaviour can be offensive; but here, in Basra or Baghdad, I can quietly do what I want. I'm an exotic flower to the Moslems — to be discussed but not touched — and since most of the white men are just passing through, I have few complications.'

A very large, long table was carried out and set down

in front of the *mudhif*, the medicine chests were placed on the table and opened, then the expectant villagers — most of whom, when they were not seriously ill, treated the clinic as a marketplace where they could bargain and plead for the tablets and medicines they so loved — were lined up in an orderly fashion to be examined and treated.

The marsh Arabs were riddled with many acutely infectious diseases, and as Frances examined them, and diagnosed the various cases of dysentery, yaws, ringworm, hookworm and bilharzia, she thoughtlessly barked her instructions at Laurence who, starting to sweat in the brightening sunlight and growing heat, swabbed weals, infectious cuts and cataracted eyes, lanced suppurating boils and rashes, took blood and urine samples, administered various injections, stitched a wide variety of revolting wounds, and handed out a few hundred of the pills that the Arabs loved as a child loves its candy.

Sweating more with each passing minute, his eyes squinting against the brightening glare, and obviously trying to adjust to the sight of the often appalling wounds and disfigurements of the Arabs, Laurence eventually distracted himself by asking Frances how long she had been visiting the villages of the marshlands.

'Two years,' Frances replied. 'I spend three days a week visiting the various villages, work another two days a week in the hospital in Basra, and spend my weekends either in Basra or Baghdad.'

'Then you must know Sheikh Hamaid fairly well,' Laurence said, holding up his hypodermic to check it.

Frances glanced at him, then smiled to herself. 'Yes,' she said, 'I know him fairly well. Why do you ask?'

'Oh,' Laurence replied, sounding casual, almost abstracted, 'I just thought he was a bit of a character . . . and was obviously making some kind of pass at you.'

'Don't be so coy,' Frances replied. 'He *was* making a pass. And he does so every time I visit this village.'

'You don't seem to mind,' Laurence said. 'In fact, you seemed to enjoy it.'

'That's right — I enjoyed it.'

Still holding the wrist of the Arab whose bitten hand she had been examining, Frances stared at Laurence, keeping her eyes upon him as he expertly slid the needle of his hypodermic into an upraised brown rump.

'And why shouldn't I enjoy it?' she asked rhetorically. 'I've always been attracted to strong-willed men. I don't go much for coyness.'

Laurence slapped the naked, brown rump and allowed his patient to straighten up, waving one hand to indicate that the man could leave.

'Coyness,' he said mischievously, 'seems more applicable to women than to men.'

'Not to *this* woman.'

'I *have* noticed that,' Laurence said with a chuckle. 'Am I allowed to ask you why you never married?'

'I'm still unmarried because I don't want children, I don't want to be a housewife, I don't want to be dependent on the whims of any man — and, most crucially, because I like sex, but don't want to have to pay for it with domestic slavery. Would you like to know what *kind* of sex I like? Or can I keep that a secret?'

Laurence blushed and smiled, taking pleasure from his Christian shock, then avoided Frances' mirthful mockery by simply giving his undivided attention to his next expectant patient, an old woman with a boil as big as an egg, disfiguring her withered face. The old woman handed Laurence the treatment instructions that had been scribbled down by Frances, and as he read them, his face turned slightly sideways, he said, 'Well, that's a fairly straight reply to an impertinent question.'

Frances, enjoying their banter, kept talking while attending to her next patient, one of the many villagers suffering from dysentery after drinking the excrementfilled water that lapped against the walls of his reed house.

'Let's change the subject, Laurence. Let's talk about you instead. How's *your* love-life?'

'I think you know perfectly well, Frances, that I — '

'You don't have a love-life — I know. It's not approved outside of marriage. But that must be very difficult, Laurence, for someone of your age.'

'All right, Frances,' Laurence said as he spread some ointment on lint and prepared to clean the boil of the old woman. 'I think this conversation's gone far enough. Let's change the subject again.'

'No,' Frances replied. 'I'm enjoying this. Tell me how you stay celibate. Celibacy, like coyness, is something that only women are meant to practise — so how do you manage it?'

'Perhaps I don't want it as much as you do,' Laurence said, applying the lint to the enormous boil and making the nervous woman groan audibly. 'We're not all that desperate, you know.'

'You're not, eh?' Frances smiled maliciously at him, then lowered her head to the desk while she scribbled a prescription for her dysentery-sufferer. 'So, let's indeed change the subject. What did you think of the Arab dancing last night?'

'Interesting,' Laurence murmered.

'It was highly erotic,' Frances said.

'Yes, I suppose it was.'

'In fact,' Frances insisted, exhilarated by Laurence's discomfort, 'it was about as sexually explicit as you can get without actually doing it.'

Now truly embarrassed, the celibate Laurence threw his piece of used lint into the rubbish bag beside the table, brought a smile to the face of the suffering Arab woman by giving her a handful of tablets, and then stared directly at Frances for the first time.

'Okay, Frances,' he said, placing his hands on his hips, 'it was explicit and I found it embarrassing.

48

Does that thought amuse you?'

'You weren't *just* embarrassed,' Frances said. 'Admit it: you found it exciting — and *that's* what made you uncomfortable.'

The dysentery-sufferer left Frances and, with his prescription in his shaking hand, joined the end of the queue facing Laurence. Snatching Frances' written instructions off his next patient, Laurence studied them with more intensity than they warranted, then, after taking a deep breath, spoke again while rummaging through one of the medicine chests to find the tablets he needed.

'You're a very attractive lady,' he said, 'but you're also a ruthless one. To protect my mortal pride, I'm refusing to discuss this matter any more.'

'That might be wise, Laurence.'

Smiling, she glanced at him, having enjoyed winding him up, amused to see him blush as he handed out more pills and prepared to swab an ugly boar-bite. He caught her glance and grinned at her, accepting defeat with grace, then returned his attention to the ugly wound, while Frances, having dispensed with her last patient, called to a servant to prepare a pot of tea.

At that moment, Sheikh Hamaid, who had obviously been watching her from the doorway of his very large reed house, and had waited until she was finished with her patients (though Laurence was still attending to the diminishing queue of those waiting to be treated), walked across the clearing towards her, his dark robes and headcloth fluttering lightly in the breeze, sunlight glinting off the studs and buckles of his webbed belts and straps. When he reached Frances, he bent down to pat the heads of the smaller, mostly naked children, after which he straightened up, glanced at the working Laurence, then finally offered his slow, full-lipped, sensual smile.

'So,' he said, raising his hands in a benediction,

'again you have cured the ills of my suffering people. You are our angel of mercy.'

'You're very generous with your compliments, Sheikh Hamaid, but I'm just doing my job and you know it, which means that you're teasing me.'

'Women like to be teased,' the sheikh replied. 'It is part of their nature.'

Frances smiled at that, but didn't offer a reply, knowing just how far to go with this man who could normally get what he wanted. She glanced past him, across the village, saw the buffaloes in the river, a line of Arabs standing upright in their canoes, all with forked spears in their hands, their eyes fixed on the fish swimming below them. Beyond the Arabs, the lagoons formed a glittering tapestry of light and shadow that was bordered by the thin dark line of the reeds which marked the visible edge of the permanent marshes. The sky above was bright and very blue, but filling up with white clouds.

'And how is the man in the *mudhif*?' the sheikh asked her.

'Still the same,' Frances replied, the simple mention of the man making her feel that she had been slapped. 'He didn't move all night. He's still in his coma, but otherwise seems perfectly normal. It's a mystery to me.'

'You will take him back with you to Basra this morning?'

'Yes.'

'I am relieved to hear that.'

'Why?'

The sheikh shrugged and waved a languid right hand to indicate the villagers milling about them. 'My people are superstitious,' he said, 'and think this man is bad luck.'

'Because he is a mystery?'

'Yes ... and as such he could possibly be an evil omen.'

'As you said, that is pure superstition.'

50

'Perhaps,' the sheikh said. 'Perhaps not. There are still unanswered questions ... How did that man come to be lying unconscious on the riverbank with not a mark on him — and with no footprints at all in the mud around him? And why, if he is physically perfectly normal, can he not be awakened ...? No, there are certain riddles here — and my people whisper of magic.'

'Magic can sometimes be good.'

'It is more often frightening.'

Feeling more uneasy each minute, Frances glanced across at Laurence and noted that he had dispensed with the last patient and was starting to clear up the cluttered table by putting bottles and instruments back into the medicine chests in preparation for their departure from the village.

'A good day's work?' she asked him.

'Yes,' Laurence replied. 'Fascinating. And I'm amazed at how many patients we got through in that short time — probably because so few of them ask questions.'

'That's exactly right,' Frances said.

They smiled at one another, then Frances turned back to the sheikh who was staring steadily at her.

'Don't worry,' she said. 'We'll take him away for you. He'll be in a hospital in Basra by this afternoon, and then you'll have no further cause for concern.'

The sheikh nodded and smiled, his gaze steady and flirtatious. 'I think that will be best for all concerned,' he said. 'And, of course, my personal *tarada* will be at your disposal.'

'My thanks.'

'My *pleasure*.'

'You sound as if you would like to get rid of me, Sheikh Hamaid.'

The sheikh immediately put his hands to his own lips, indicating that Frances was speaking a kind of blasphemy.

'No, no!' he exclaimed. 'That is definitely not true! It always gladdens my heart to see you coming here — not only because you tend to my people, but also because of the personal pleasure your company gives me. However, what is also true is that I would, on a personal level, prefer the pleasure of your company in Basra, in less public circumstances.'

'Whatever do you mean by that, Sheikh Hamaid?'

'Whatever you *want* it to mean.'

Frances could never resist such sexual boldness and this instance proved to be no exception. Immediately suffused with warmth, her head teeming with fleeting images of clandestine trysts with the wealthy sheikh, she was nonetheless aware of the basic foolishness of her imaginings even as she experienced them. Feeling helpless at her own weakness, but also exhilarated, she almost broke her own rule about not getting involved with extremely autocratic Arab chieftains by opening her mouth to start giving the sheikh encouragement — then stopped herself, remembering what it could lead to, and let the silence return her to commonsense.

That brief silence was suddenly slashed by the sound of vicious snarling. Frances twitched and glanced past the sheikh's head to see two very large, badly scarred, wolf-like dogs savagely fighting one another, teeth bared, paws swinging, tattered tails lashing up the dust as they jumped, rolled and yelped. Some villagers giggled and pointed, others ran for a closer look; but Frances shivered, again feeling unreasonably fearful, then turned her gaze away, not wanting to see more — now feeling, rather oddly, that she was not only avoiding the bloody savagery of the fighting dogs, but also searching, as if impelled by irresistible impulse, for a magical sign of her own inexorable fate.

Obviously recovered from his long and inexplicable sleep, the unknown man, still wearing the denim jacket, trousers and leather boots he had worn since being discovered, was standing in front of the *mudhif*, gazing around him in growing surprise.

He raised his left hand, scratched his head, rubbed his forehead, then stared across the busy clearing — at the squatting women and naked children, at the canoes and buffaloes in the river, at the glittering lagoons and swaying bulrushes along the marshes — then at Frances, Sheikh Hamaid and Laurence ... and then once more at Frances.

Her cheeks were burning, she felt lightheaded and weak; then she started when the man moved towards her before stopping again. He thoughtfully studied her, as if trying to place her face, and eventually, as if recovering his senses, let his lips curve into a thin, slightly mocking, oddly frightening smile.

Bewildered by her rising panic, heart racing, cheeks flushed, Frances glanced blindly at a puzzled Laurence, at the surprised, staring sheikh, seeing the village and river and broad, glittering lagoons with an incandescence that made them singularly unreal, if overwhelmingly *present*. Then, controlling herself, feeling the ground beneath her feet, yet again filled with desire and a contradictory revulsion, she returned her gaze to the man standing in the clearing and saw the steel in his smile.

He waved his left hand in greeting.

CHAPTER FOUR

'What the hell ...?' the stranger said, spreading his hands in bewilderment, his confused gaze taking in the Arab village and the watery marshes beyond. 'Am I dreaming? Is this some kind of trick? Just where the hell *am* I?'

'Not far from where we found you,' the sheikh replied. 'Just a few miles upriver.'

Still obviously confused, but surprisingly unshaken, the stranger stared directly at Sheikh Hamaid with no great sign of warmth.

'*Upriver?*' he said. '*What* river? There *was* no river! I was in the middle of the goddamned English country-side. And now these *Arabs* ... for Christ's sake!'

He glanced around him again, trying to take in what he was seeing, then lowered his hands to his sides and shook his head in perplexity, before staring with unsettling boldness at Frances.

'So,' he said, managing a crooked grin, 'what the hell's going *down* here?'

Now, observing him up close and in the sunlit clarity of the morning, Frances was both repelled and erotically aroused by the arrogance and hint of cruelty in his face. It was a thin, hawklike face, matching the man's tall, lanky body, his hollow, unshaven cheeks framing a patrician nose and thin lips which, when they curved into a crooked smile, displayed a sly sneer instead of humour. He was in his late thirties and his brown hair was tinged with grey, but his eyes had the darkness of pitch and seemed just as opaque.

'Am I dreaming — or what?' he asked aggressively.

'You were found lying unconscious by the river,' Frances explained. 'Don't you remember being there?'

'*What* river?' the man repeated in growing impatience. 'And what's with this goddamned Arab village? I mean, where the hell *am* I?'

'You were found on the bank of the Shatt al Arab river,' Frances said in rising confusion. 'You're in southern Iraq.'

The man's impenetrable brown eyes stared steadily at Frances for some time, then, as his brow furrowed, moved briefly left and right, taking in Sheikh Hamaid, Laurence and the milling Arabs, then the glittering expanse of the nearest lagoon and the thin, dark line of the distant marshes.

'I'm going crazy,' he said, sounding absolutely sane. 'The last thing I remember is falling asleep on a bench in Glastonbury, in England. I *can't* be in . . . *Iraq*?'

He offered a tentative grin and Frances took a deep breath, feeling her shock turn into fear at what all this might mean.

Glastonbury, in England — the town that vanished overnight . . . the town whose disappearance had haunted her dreams with remarkable intensity . . . She looked at the man in front of her, trying to keep her senses together, aware of how unnatural his calmness was, given what had occurred.

'I'm afraid you *are* in Iraq,' Laurence said. 'Do you know *who* you are?'

'Yeah . . . yeah, I do.' The man studied Laurence at length, as if measuring his possible worth, then grinned in a quietly contemptuous manner and turned his gaze on Sheikh Hamaid.

'Jack Schul,' he said. 'From Atlantic City in the States.

55

I'm not married, I live in a crappy apartment located conveniently near the race track in Pleasantville, and I work the amusement piers of the Boardwalk, scamming the tourists.'

He grinned tightly at Sheikh Hamaid, whose painfully polite attentiveness could not hide the distaste he was obviously feeling in the presence of this crude intruder, then turned his head and stared directly at Frances, his eyes moving up and down her body in immodest appraisal.

'No,' he said, 'no doubts about who I am. I remember everything that happened until I fell asleep in England — and woke up in *this* country. Jesus, I still can't believe it! Are you gonna tell me what happened? I mean, how long have I been sleeping, for Chrissakes? And who brought me here?'

'I think you better sit down,' Frances said. 'Let's all have some tea.'

'Tea? I could do with a fucking beer.'

'We only have tea,' Frances said.

Laurence and Sheikh Hamaid were both obviously offended by Schul's obscenity, but neither said anything, the sheikh merely nodding at Frances and then leading them all into the *mudhif* where, after they had removed their shoes (much to Schul's cynical amusement) they sat cross-legged in a circle near the hearth and were served tea in tiny cups by the waiting servants.

Schul reached out for his first cup with his left hand, but was prevented from taking it by Frances, who quietly told him that he must use his right. Schul did not apologise, but merely grinned cynically and explained that he was left-handed, after which he had his first sip of tea and visibly winced. Then, after everyone had been introduced to him, and as the ritualistic tea-sipping continued, he told them how he had ended up in Glastonbury.

'I didn't know nothin' about Glastonbury when I

went there,' he explained. 'I had no special interest in it. It's just that I like to kick around a lot and I had this old friend who used to drive a cab in Atlantic City and then married this English broad and went back to live with her in Glastonbury, where she had come from. Anyways, he tol' me to come see him if I ever got to England, so when I scraped up a little money, and got bored with the Boardwalk, I decided to hitchhike around England and also pay him a visit, if only for the free bed and breakfast. So, I spent a day and night with him in Glastonbury, hung one on, forgot what I was doing, made a play for his old woman and got thrown out. This, you understand, was in the middle of the night, so I decided to sleep on a bench and then try for a lift when the traffic had started to flow. Just before dawn, I found a bench on that great fucking hill with the old church on top of it, was still drunk enough to fall asleep pretty fast, had really weird dreams about prehistoric days ... and then woke up here, thinking that I was still dreamin' — 'cause the marshes here look just like the marshes that I saw in my dreams.'

Remembering the television films of the lush, watery marshlands where the town of Glastonbury had formerly stood, Frances felt a cold chill going through her.

'And that's all you remember?' she asked him.

'Yeah,' he replied. 'I fell asleep on that hill in Glastonbury, had some pretty weird dreams, then woke up in this Arab hut in Iraq. I mean, who *brought* me here?'

He stared quizzically at each of them in turn, then eventually let his gaze rest on Frances. She felt the hardness in him — the calculation and aggression — and was lost in the conflict between her revulsion and helpless desire.

'We can't answer that question,' Laurence said. 'It's a mystery to us. However, what we *do* know is that the whole town of Glastonbury disappeared without trace a few hours before the Arabs found you on that riverbank near Al Qurna, at the confluence of the Euphrates and Tigris rivers.'

Now Schul turned his head to stare at Laurence, his expression frankly amazed. 'The whole town ... *disappeared?*'

'That's right,' Laurence said. 'It vanished, and no-one knows how ... or where it has gone.'

'It wasn't *destroyed*? It just *vanished*?'

'Yes. It obviously vanished when you were lying on that hill — and now, here you are.'

There was a brief, uncomfortable silence, during which Schul, his dark eyes alert and hard, gazed around the large, smoke-filled *mudhif*, stared at the village outside, thoughtfully surveyed the sunlit marshes beyond the lagoons and then concentrated his attention on Sheikh Hamaid who, at that very moment, was gazing at Frances with open admiration. Schul grinned knowingly at seeing that, then turned the same grin upon Frances, his eyes brightening suggestively.

'Are you hungry?' Frances asked, observing Schul's expression and aware of what it meant.

'Yeah,' Schul replied, 'I'm hungry. And I'm thirsty as hell.'

'Have some more tea.'

'I was thinking of something stronger than that.'

'You can have something stronger when we get back to Basra and you've been medically examined.'

'Basra?'

'It's the second-biggest city in Iraq, situated on the bank of the Shatt al Arab river, down south, not too far from the Persian Gulf. It's about an hour from here by car, but we won't get there till nightfall, since Laurence and I have to attend to some more villages near Al Qurna and, also, we'll be making the rest of the journey by boat. If you're hungry, stay here and have some bread while Laurence and I put our things in the boat. We'll be leaving in fifteen minutes or half an hour. Okay?'

'And what happens when I've been examined in Basra?'

'Do you still have your passport?'

'Yeah. Everything's still intact in my rucksack.'

'Then we'll get the American Embassy to fly you from Basra to Baghdad, and from there on back to New York.'

'I could sell this fucking story to the papers.'

'That's right: you could do that.'

Offended by Schul's arrogance, greed and crass indifference to the miraculous nature of his appearance here in Iraq, but also uncomfortably aware that she was helplessly drawn to his particular kind, Frances tried to keep her face blank and voice neutral; then, as Schul grinned at her, his gaze roaming with insulting suggestiveness over her body, she felt a pressing urge to stand up and rush out of the tent.

She managed to control that urge, but she did stand up, thanking the sheikh for his hospitality and then leading Laurence out of the *mudhif* while Jack Schul, still sitting cross-legged on the reed mats near the smoking coffee hearth, grinned crookedly as the sheikh's servants brought him slices of golden-coloured bread. 'Christ!' Frances heard him exclaim, 'I just can't believe all this!' Then, feeling released, but with her sweating flesh excited, she let the morning sunlight burst over her and dazzle her eyes.

It was late in the afternoon when they completed their work in the last village near Al Qurna and reboarded the large war canoe of Sheikh Hamaid, to be rowed along the river to Basra. The *tarada* was nearly forty feet long and no more than four feet at its widest beam, thus forcing Frances, Laurence and Jack Schul to sit on separate plank-seats. Laurence was seated near the stern, between Frances and the two Arab oarsmen; Frances was in front of him, her back turned towards him, sitting face to face with Jack Schul, who had more or less insisted on that position. Schul's knees were almost touching Frances' knees, and his head was framed by the high, slender prow that curved up towards the sky like a gigantic inverted bird's beak.

From Frances' position, in the middle of the long canoe, she was forced to stare either directly at Schul (which she knew had been his intention) or beyond the high prow, and a third Arab oarsman who stood beside it, at the banks of the narrow, reed-lined tributary through which they were moving.

The oarsman standing beside the high prow was, while the oarsmen at the stern did the actual rowing, expertly controlling the canoe's course with a long pole reaching down to the bed of the river; and Frances studied him as much as possible, not only out of genuine interest, but also to avoid the increasing insinuation and challenge in Schul's conversation.

Already torn between her attraction to sexually aggressive men and her self-loathing for that apparently uncontrollable weakness, she was soon feeling drained by the constant effort of trying to remain distant while Schul, throughout the long day, kept up a relentless monologue composed of bad jokes, obscenities, boasts about his skill as an Atlantic City Boardwalk card-sharp, and an exhausting amount of sexual innuendo aimed directly at her.

To make matters worse, it quickly became apparent that there could be no bridging of the distance between the religious, sexually naive Laurence and his widely experienced and amoral American counterpart; and indeed, as the hours passed, and as Laurence became increasingly exhausted from treating the Arabs in the various villages they stopped at, his patience with Schul visibly deteriorated and gave way to anger at the crude manner in which he was trying to capture Frances' attention.

Even as the sun sank lower over the marshes and the canoe brushed past some beds of tall bulrushes, and while Laurence sat in sullen silence behind her, Frances could not prevent Schul's knee from touching hers, nor avoid talking to him.

' — always found it easy,' he was saying. 'My scam was to cheat those tourists out of everything in their billfolds and then, when I felt like relaxin', pick up some broad on the Boardwalk, often the wife of one of my goddamned suckers. And a woman's always hottest when she's cheatin', which is one of life's harsh facts.'

'I wouldn't know,' Frances said.

'No?'

'I'm not married.'

'But not without the odd man in your life, right?'

'That's none of your business.'

Schul simply grinned at that — a grin more like a sneer — then glanced over Frances' shoulder at Laurence, as if measuring his silence.

'He's got the hots for you,' he said.

'Please keep your voice down.'

'That's why he doesn't like me talking to you,' Schul continued, unperturbed. 'That kid, your religious virgin, is secretly carrying a torch for his boss. He's jerking off in his mind, there.'

Frances tried to put Schul down with her silent contempt; then, failing, glanced past him to see the darkening azure sky moving over the tall prow. The standing oarsman was silhouetted, his body leaning across the pole, giant palm-leaves brushing against his head as the canoe grazed the nearest bank. Here the water was muddy, the giant grass like bamboo; there were dark clouds of mosquitoes around the reeds that thrust up from the water.

'I don't understand you,' she said, hardly aware of her own voice. 'You fell asleep in England, the whole town disappeared, then you woke up in southern Iraq — and you don't seem to be bothered. That experience would frighten most people; at the very least it would bother them.'

'Why should I be bothered?' Schul replied. 'I can't do

nuthin' about it. It's weird — I'm willin' to admit that —
but what's done has been done.'

'And that's all you think about it?'

'What else *is* there to think? Something weird made
that town and everyone in it disappear, and somehow I
ended up here. So, fuck it. I'm still alive and unharmed.
I don't give a shit about the others: I'm alive and feel
great.'

'The mystery doesn't intrigue you?'

'Sure it does. I'd like to know what happened as much
as you — but that's as far as it goes. Maybe the town will
reappear and maybe it won't; but either way there's
nothing I can do — and I'm not about to lose sleep over
that fact.'

The reaction was incomprehensible to Frances, and
she lowered her eyes to look at Schul, almost seeing
herself reflected in his dark eyes and their impenetrable
depths. Schul was a brute, unfeeling, self-serving, but
to her shame, it was his callous aggression that drew her
helplessly towards him.

She shivered, feeling confused, getting lost in conflicting feelings, and distracted herself by studying the
riverside village that they were just passing by. Smoke
rose from the reed houses; dogs barked and snapped
above the tall grass; the women and children silently
watched the canoe passing while the buffaloes,
enormous and hairy, drank the muddy water below
them, their shadows stretching further across the river
as the sun kept on sinking. Frances felt Schul's eyes
crawling up her legs as if they belonged to him.

'You're a real attractive woman,' he said, grinning
lecherously. 'I can't understand why you're not
married. You musta been pretty popular.'

'Popularity,' Frances replied, 'has got nothing to do
with it. I just never fancied living with any man.'

'Why? Your dad used to beat your mom when you
were a kid?'

'No,' Frances replied levelly, ignoring his sarcasm.

'My dad *died* when I was a kid, but I remember him as being a lovely man. As for my mother, she and I are very close — and in fact I still live with her when I'm at home.'

'What about your love-life?' Schul asked bluntly.

'What about it?' Frances replied.

'Do you have one?'

'Yes. Intermittently. With any man I fancy.'

'And you don't hold yourself cheap for that?'

'I hold *the men* cheap.'

Schul snorted at that, slapping his hands on his knees, then glanced over her shoulder, obviously studying the silent Laurence, then crooked his lips in a sneering grin.

'You're some sweetheart,' he said.

The canoe was now taking them past the smoke of burning reed beds, more small villages planted untidily above the muddy water, the dripping, hump-backed buffaloes silhouetted in crimson as the sun started sinking behind the flat horizon and spread its light across the distant marshes. Eventually, when the sun had sank completely and been replaced by an enormous moon and brilliant stars, they were assailed by the crying of geese, the croaking of frogs, the rise and fall of ghostly voices that came from the torchlit darkness above the rustling reeds of the wind-tossed riverbank. Here a brief burst of laughter, there children calling to children, now a boy singing beautifully, his voice first quavering out of nowhere, then his face materialising in flickering firelight in a dark village clearing.

Frances stared at him, entranced, letting his lonely voice stroke her heart; then his face disappeared, was lost behind a line of fig-palms, as the canoe moved along a gradually broadening stretch of river and came to a glittering lake which appeared to be about three-quarters of a mile wide.

'There is no sign of wind,' said the Arab standing

upright. 'I think it will be safe to cross the lake.'

The lakes had always frightened Frances and this one was no exception. As a child she had frequently dreamed of getting lost in a place like this and drifting forever through eternal night; thus, as she stared past Schul's head at that immense body of water, black, striped with moonlight, the fear took hold and refused to release her.

'It's all right,' she heard her own voice saying, 'but let's get across quickly.'

The oarsman at the prow nodded, dipped his long pole into the water, and pushed the canoe out into the lake. Frances glanced back over her shoulder to see Laurence's thin face, his gaze obviously fixed resentfully on Schul. She turned back to the front, but could not avoid Schul's knees when they deliberately pressed against her own.

Again, she distracted herself by studying her surroundings, saw a flock of ducks, disturbed by the canoe, winging into the starry sky. The silence was complete and pervasive, almost palpably present.

'Weird,' Schul muttered, glancing around him. 'Something odd about this place ...'

His voice trailed off into the silence and he continued staring around him, his brow furrowed in concentration, his eyes moving left and right in searching motions, taking in the whole lake. Frances did likewise, wondering what he was trying to find, and saw nothing but the dark, limpid water and a broad stretch of starry sky.

'What do you mean?' she asked him. 'What are you looking for?'

'I'm not sure,' he replied, still scanning the surrounding night, 'but I seem to be losing my sense of direction.' He pointed with one finger. 'See that bank we're heading for? It doesn't seem to have moved at all. I mean, we've been moving towards it for ten minutes, yet it doesn't seem to be any closer ... And the stars ... I don't recognise the stars. I looked up at the stars and I recognised them all; then I looked at you and looked up again — and the stars had changed. I *know* the stars, lady. I *know* them ... but not those stars up there.'

Frances, who knew nothing about the stars, saw nothing unusual. She stared hard at Schul, *felt* the silence, shivered slightly, then looked all around her, at that broad expanse of black water, then at the darker strip of land towards which they were heading. The canoe kept moving forward, but the land drew no closer; then, when the Arab standing upright muttered something, Frances saw him wiping sweat from his brow as his eyes widened fearfully.

'He's right,' she heard Laurence say behind her. 'Those aren't the stars that are normally in this sky. There's something strange going on ...'

Like Schul, Laurence let his voice trail off into the silence while he tried to take in what was happening. The oarsmen behind him had stopped rowing and were muttering to one another, their heads bobbing in a conspiratorial manner, their voices sounding hysterical. The Arab standing at the prow had raised his long pole out of the water and was staring about him, his eyes growing larger as he realised that the land was no closer than it had been five minutes ago.

'Oh, my God, have mercy upon us!' he whispered. 'Oh, my God, lead the way!'

At that moment the wind rose, whipping lightly across the water, making its placid surface ripple in low waves that shook the canoe. The standing Arab yelped in panic and let go of his pole; he watched it sliding down into the lake and then, groaning audibly, sat down behind Schul and covered his face with his hands.

The wind blew more strongly, whipping up higher waves, then the canoe was carried sideways into a darkness that filled Frances with dread.

She gripped the sides of the boat, noticing Schul's increasing amazement, then blinked and examined the darkness into which they were moving.

'What the hell ...?' she heard Schul say.

The three Arab oarsmen were now groaning and muttering prayers while the wind, growing unnaturally fierce, pushed the canoe well off course, away from the distant strip of land to which they had been heading and deeper into the great darkness that seemed to be even more unnatural than the wind.

Staring into the darkness made Frances feel disorientated, her stomach lurching as she tried to work out why that might be so. The wind howled and whipped the waves up, making the boat rise and fall, and Frances, holding her seat with one hand, rubbed her eyes with the other. She kept staring into the darkness, trying to work out what it was, and then felt that she was being sucked into it, as if into the vortex of a whirlpool that was turned on its side.

'That's what's wrong!' Schul suddenly exclaimed. *'There are no stars out there!'*

The sound of Schul's voice, screaming against the wind, made Frances study the night more fully and, to her horror, see that Schul was right — that the darkness into which they were being forced contained no moon or stars.

Even more disorientated, feeling as if she were actually falling, she gripped the side of the now violently rocking canoe and tried to make sense of what she was seeing.

There were stars to the west, and to the north and south; but to the east there was only a great wall of unnatural darkness with roughly vertical edges which, limned with silvery light and pulsating rhythmically, had eclipsed the stars encompassed by her field of vision.

Stunned, Frances still managed to tear her gaze away. Glancing up in an attempt to gauge how high that darkness was, she saw the stars shining all around it where it merged with the sky. It was shaped like a great pillar, almost certainly rectangular, about half a mile wide on each side, its peak lost in the clouds. It was darker than the night, yet oddly transparent, displaying what appeared to be a faint line of forest beyond its light-flecked, rhythmically pulsating base.

Frances struggled to define what it was that she was seeing, gripping the boat, breathing deeply, trying to calm her racing heart; but she struggled in vain, her senses confused and deceitful, then collapsed into the well of a terror that made her feel naked.

'What — ?' Schul started to ask.

'God have mercy!' an Arab cried.

'We're not being *pushed* off course!' Laurence screamed. '*That thing's sucking us in!*'

The wind howled around the boat, being sucked into that strange mass, and the canoe was drawn forward on the water as it swirled and splashed over them. Frances was drenched and almost choked; she heard the water drumming against the boat's hull and then she looked up again. Schul was reaching out to grab her. She felt his demanding fingers. The Arab at the prow stood up, babbling wildly and waving his hands; he swayed dangerously as the boat surged high on the swirling waves and then, his arms flapping like wings, threw himself overboard.

Frances saw him disappearing, a foaming wave washing over him; then another wave, much bigger, a roaring surfer's peak, curled high above the boat, briefly forming a tunnel around it, blotting out the moon and stars and that distant stretch of land, then smashed down with the force of a giant hammer as Schul fell upon her.

She was battered and deafened, then numbed by the cold. She saw a swathe of stars tilting, a spinning cloud, a shifting moon, then was sucked down into the watery depths again and swept through streaming darkness.

Not pushed: *sucked*. She would remember that all her life. She was sucked in and surrounded by the darkness, then hurled into oblivion.

CHAPTER FIVE

Rendered pleasantly drowsy by another wine-bar lunch, and reminded of the hour he had spent a week ago with his daughter, Michael was jerked out of his reverie by the buzzing of the telephone on his desk.

Glancing out of his fourth-floor window at the rolling slopes of Hampstead Heath, he picked up the telephone and listened more alertly while his secretary informed him that a Mr Lionel Sampson, from the Ministry of Defence, had arrived for his three-thirty appointment. Michael told the girl to show the visitor in, then he sat back in his chair and again felt the confusion he had experienced when Mr Sampson had phoned that morning, saying that he had to see him urgently, that it was government business, and that Michael was to tell no-one that he was coming.

Not knowing Mr Sampson, nor anyone else in government circles, Michael clasped his hands under his chair and raised his eyes expectantly to the opening door.

The man whom Michael's secretary ushered into the office was short, well-fed, rosy-cheeked and slightly bald, his waist-coat buttoned tightly over a protruding belly, his pinstriped suit immaculate. Once the introductions had been completed, Michael's secretary left the office, closing the door quietly behind her, and

Michael indicated that Mr Sampson should take a seat at the opposite side of his desk. This he did, setting the black-leather pilot case he had been carrying on the floor beside him, then crossing his legs and offering a cheerful smile.

'It's very good of you to see me at such short notice,' he said. 'I assure you, my department appreciates it.'

'And what department would that be?' Michael asked.

'Sorry. I'm the Chief Projects Officer for the Department of Atmospheric and Meteorological Phenomena.'

'At the Ministry of Defence?'

'Correct.'

'Atmospherics and meteorological phenomena?' Michael said. 'I'm intrigued. What on earth have you come to see *me* for?'

Sampson grinned, as if amused by Michael's bewilderment. 'Well,' he said, 'it's obviously a bit unusual — but we do have our reasons.'

'Which are?'

'Well, according to our information, you, Dr Phillips, are heading the most advanced experimental clinic in the country regarding psychological disorders or traumas induced by extreme shock.'

'In layman's terms, that's correct.'

'In your field I *am* a layman, Dr Phillips.'

'Of course. I didn't mean to be facetious.'

Sampson smiled again, crossed his legs the other way, then patted the bald patch on his head as if searching for hair. 'The function of my department,' he said, 'is to monitor, analyse and assess ambiguous or inexplicable atmospheric or meteorological phenomenon, including comets, meteors, plasmoid and corona discharges, ball-lightning, temperature inversions, all manner of unidentified flying objects, and unusual electromagnetic and other atmospheric disturbances — such as those which may relate to the remarkable disappearance of Glastonbury. So, that's why I'm here.' He leaned forward and gazed more intently at Michael, his basically cheerful face solemn. 'Presumably,' he said, 'you *know* what happened at Glastonbury?'

Michael instantly recalled the two clowns in Covent Garden, the darkening expression on Cheryl's face when he had mentioned that very same subject.

'Of course,' he said. 'But whatever occurred, it would seem to be a scientific matter — hardly a psychological one.'

'Not necessarily,' Sampson replied. 'This is, after all, an unprecedented event — and one with the most terrible consequences and implications. *People* are involved, Dr Phillips — not only those who disappeared with most of the town, but those in the surrounding area, many of whom have been very seriously disturbed by what has happened, whether or not they had relatives involved. There is also the fact that at least *one* of those who *should* have disappeared was found — alive if rather crazed — near the critical radius.'

'The what?'

'The critical radius. It's ...' Mr Sampson stopped talking, nodded and smiled ruefully. 'I'm sorry,' he said. 'I'm running ahead too fast. Please, listen to this.'

So saying, he picked up his black-leather pilot case, placed it on his knee, opened it and produced a miniature cassette-recorder. He set this down on the desk, pushed it halfway to Michael, pressed the play-button and sat back in his chair when the tape started turning.

At first there was only the sound of the winding tape, then the hissing of static, then eventually the very audible groanings of an obviously tormented human being.

Michael leaned forward to listen more intently as the groaning became louder and increasingly fearful in tone, then eventually turned into a babble of hysterical words. Initially incoherent, but gradually making a kind

71

of sense, the words soon formed a litany which expressed some kind of vivid imagining — or nightmarish experience — in which there were repeated fearful references to an icy coldness, steaming swamps where Glastonbury should have been, then prehistoric birds, dinosaurs, other unrecognisable animals, then the threatening advance of what the speaker obviously thought were ape-men. His demented voice went on a long time, repeating the same bizarre words, eventually managing to paint a picture of a prehistoric world which seemed more real in his mind than the real one.

The more he talked, the quicker he talked, until he was simply babbling, rendered senseless as he repeated that an icy-coldness had enveloped him, that the landscape was *changing*, and that an ape-man was advancing threateningly upon him. At that point his shrieked words trailed off into tormented moaning, which in turn faded away into static and a click as the tape stopped.

Sampson leaned forward and switched off the machine, then stared steadily at Michael.

In the silence that followed that tormented, haunting voice, Michael found himself thinking of the films of Glastonbury on television, of the cameras scanning over the terrible stillness and silence of the marshes where Glastonbury had stood. He also thought of the traumatic terror that the voice on the cassette-tape had revealed, and wondered just what that man had experienced . . . or, more likely, imagined.

He was pondering this when Mr Sampson broke the silence, speaking clearly and calmly.

'Now you know why I've come here,' he said.' We need someone to treat that man.'

'Who is he?' Michael asked.

'Miles Ashcombe. A well-known writer and resident of Glastonbury. The Army found him when they moved in to cordon off the area. He was lying unconscious by the edge of the marshes, just about where Glastonbury Tor had formerly stood — on the perimeter, as it were, of what we already refer to as the "vanishing zone", and what might well be the dark mass's critical radius.'

'Ah,' Michael said, 'that phrase again!'

'We'll get back to it in a moment,' Sampson replied. 'The point is that Ashcombe was discovered at what was almost certainly the outer edge of the area that disappeared — he might even have been slightly inside it — and maybe, because of that, he escaped. I repeat: he was unconscious when the Army found him. But then, as soon as he awakened, he started screaming and babbling, most of which was exactly the same as we have on that tape.'

'He's still hysterical?'

'Yes. But if you can bring him back to a reasonable level of normality, he might tell us much more about what happened to him inside that dark mass.'

'What do *you* think happened to him?'

Sampson shrugged. 'We've no idea. We only know that he's possibly still screaming about what drove him crazy.'

At first Michael wasn't sure that he had heard right; then, when he accepted that he had indeed done so, he leaned forward again.

'Are you trying to tell me that you think he might have *seen* what he's babbling about?'

Sampson very deliberately returned Michael's steady gaze. 'I know it sounds crazy,' he said, 'but he *has* been through an extraordinary, theoretically impossible experience, and all he can talk about, delirious or not, is what he describes on that tape.'

'He's traumatised,' Michael said. 'He has to have something to cling to — something with which he can identify and claim as reality.'

'A *prehistoric* world?' Sampson said with blunt scepticism. 'Surely that would be the most *remote* thing he could possibly cling to. What about the world he vanished from? The world that he *knew?*'

'You think that what he experienced was *real?*'

Sampson shrugged. 'Who knows?' he said. 'All *we* know is that what happened at Glastonbury has happened elsewhere. Not in this country — I can't say where — but it's happened before.'

Now Michael, for all his pragmatism, experienced a shock of disbelief out of which arose, like smoke from burning tinder, the grey breath of fear. For the first time, he was being compelled to face the impossible, and it threatened everything he believed in.

'You mean that man disappeared with Glastonbury, but then reappeared again?'

'Yes,' Mr Sampson said. 'And we want to know if what he experienced was real or imagined.'

'Imagined, surely,' Michael said, startled that Sampson should seriously suggest otherwise.

'We can't be too sure of that,' Sampson replied. 'We can't be too sure at all. Do you mind if I smoke?'

'No,' Michael said. 'I smoke myself. Here, have one of mine.'

He removed a packet of cigarettes from a drawer in his desk, gave one to Sampson, took one himself, then let Sampson give him a light and inhaled with great pleasure.

Sampson blew a smoke ring in the air, then squinted through it. 'Tell me,' he said. 'Have you *any* idea what *actually* happened at Glastonbury?'

'Only that it disappeared in an impossible manner. That's *all* I know.'

'Right, Dr Phillips, it disappeared. No explosion, no earthquake, no flood — it just disappeared.'

Sampson stood up, went to the window and stared out at the smooth slopes of Hampstead Heath. He stood there for some time, lost in thought, then turned back to Michael.

'Do you know what a black hole is?' he asked.

'I've a very rough idea,' Michael replied, 'but I didn't think — '

'That's right,' Sampson quickly intervened, antici-

74

pating Michael's train of thought. 'It *wasn't* a black hole. If it had been, we wouldn't be here right now — the *whole world* would have disappeared. However, we *are* receiving reports that it was a great dark mass that more or less *swallowed* Glastonbury.'

Michael said nothing, patiently waiting to hear more, automatically behaving as he did with most of his patients. Mr Sampson, scratching one ruddy cheek, offered another bemused smile.

'Let me explain,' he said. 'The whole area of Glastonbury has been cordoned off by the Army and is presently being surveyed by my department with a variety of scientific instruments.' He patted the bald spot on his head and sat in his chair again. 'Already we've ascertained that, one, it contains an unusually high density of electromagnetic radiation and, two, it has an exceptionally strong, though gradually weakening, gravitational pull. In other words, if we're not dealing with a legitimate black hole, we certainly seem to be dealing with something that greatly *resembles* such a phenomenon.'

'And whatever it was, that man you recorded, Miles Ashcombe, was also swallowed by the dark mass, but then, instead of disappearing for good like the rest of them, mysteriously materialised back on earth.'

'Correct. We don't know what that dark mass is, and it certainly defies all known knowledge, so let's use the black hole as a convenient analogy.'

Sampson inhaled on his cigarette, blew some more smoke-rings, watched them growing larger and disappearing, then turned back to Michael.

'Theoretically speaking, a black hole represents the ultimately compressed state of matter. Because of its immeasurable gravitational field, the black hole permanently traps light and all other forms of electromagnetic radiation — including infra, ultraviolet and radio Xrays — inside it. Because light cannot escape, the objects are termed 'black holes', but this term refers to a physical condition rather than a true colour, since in theory black holes have *no* colour.'

'Which suggests the dark mass that covered Glaston-bury,' Michael said.

'Right,' Sampson replied. 'Most of the witnesses who viewed the dark mass from a distance were in agreement that although it *seemed* dark, it also appeared to be incorporeal and *colourless* in some way they could not quite define. So, in that sense, it's a *kind* of black hole.'

'So, how did it make Glastonbury disappear?'

'Well, accepting our black hole hypothesis, it is possible that the dark mass — our so-called black hole — *sucked* Glastonbury in past its critical radius, either to crush it out of existence or to spew it out somewhere else — as a black hole might do.'

'The critical radius,' Michael said. 'That's the phrase you used before . . .'

'Ah, yes,' Sampson replied, nodding and smiling almost apologetically. 'The *critical radius* — more widely known as the *event horizon* — marks the point beyond which there is no escape from the black hole.'

'Which rather destroys your analogy,' Michael said. 'Since, if there is no escape from the black hole, your Miles Ashcombe should not have escaped from the dark mass.'

'Clever,' Sampson said, 'but not quite right. Our investigations have already raised the possibility that the dark mass which swallowed Glastonbury, and other places I cannot name, might possess a similar critical radius — but one that waxes and wanes in strength, refusing for the most part to release what it sucks in, but *occasionally*, perhaps when its strength lessens, allowing some object, or person, to escape — as in the case of Miles Ashcombe.'

'Fine,' Michael said. 'I'm with you so far. I'm accepting your black hole analogy for the dark mass. So, what do you think happened *inside* it? Since, as you said, what gets sucked into a black hole is probably crushed out of existence.'

'That's true of a *stationary* black hole,' Sampson replied without pause. 'However, it is a widely held scientific belief that since stars spin, black holes must spin also. Ergo, if this is true, an object heading into a spinning black hole could follow a course which does *not* take it to the obliterating centre of the black hole — the singularity of its core — which in turn leads to the theory that if the aforesaid object does *not* get crushed out of existence, yet cannot re-emerge to its own universe, then it must end up somewhere else — which could be a distant region of our universe or, just as likely, given the remarkable distortions of time that must exist within the black hole, in some *other* time, after a journey through instantaneous interstellar travel.'

Michael took a deep breath and stared steadily at Mr Sampson. Had it not been for the fact that he was from the Ministry of Defence, Michael would have thought of this bizarre conversation as some kind of insane joke.

'Some kind of *time*-machine?' he asked disbelievingly.

Sampson shrugged. 'I know it sounds ridiculous, but it's possible that the dark mass, in a manner *similar* to that of a black hole, distorts time and space inside its critical radius. Or — perhaps less remarkable and therefore more conceivable — actually *traps* time in some way and holds it forever. Certainly, theoretically speaking, a black hole would do that.'

'You mean that Miles Ashcombe, when he was rendered invisible, actually *witnessed* the past?'

Sampson glanced at his dwindling cigarette, shrugged and stubbed it out in an ashtray, then crossed his legs again.

'If we accept the possibility that black holes do exist, we must then accept that they can distort and ultimately *freeze* time. The notion of time travel also contains the hidden supposition that there are thousands of parallel universes, each a mere fraction of a second ahead or behind this one, each with its own past and future — and, if this is so, and if those parallel worlds exist within the black hole, then some similar phenomenon might exist beyond the critical radius of the dark mass that spirited Glastonbury away.'

'Are you trying to tell me that Ashcombe may not only have *witnessed* the past, but actually *lived* it?'

'What can I say, Dr Phillips? We only know that that dark mass was an extraordinary phenomenon — one that defies all our scientific knowledge — and that Miles Ashcombe, in his delirium, but also under hypnosis, has forced us to consider every possibility.'

Michael glanced out the window, then realised what he was doing: he was trying to focus his attention on something real . . . the tangible world.

'I'm confused,' he confessed. 'Even accepting your rather mind-boggling hypothesis, surely, if Ashcombe was sucked into, or spirited away to, some other time and place, he must have ceased existing in *this* time. And even if he had been somehow lost in history, to return he would have to travel *forward* in time, which is just inconceivable.'

Sampson sighed, gazed down at his own crossed legs, picked a piece of lint off his trousers and let it fall to the carpet. 'I have sleepless nights thinking about it,' he said, 'but *all* things are possible.'

'Two-way *time* travel?' Michael said sceptically, hardly able to credit that he, a sane man, was actually tolerating this conversation.

Sampson sighed again and raised his gaze from his striped trousers. 'Beyond the black hole,' he said, 'time and space are distorted. Theoretically speaking, for someone travelling through a black hole time would gradually slow down and eventually cease altogether — though our hypothetical person, completely unaware of it, would continue to live his normal life in some kind of bizarre, eternal present. Given this, Miles Ashcombe *could* have briefly regressed through his other selves and then, in some equally remarkable manner, returned to his present self.'

'And all the others? The ones who didn't come back?'

Sampson shrugged and uncrossed his legs. 'The point of no return. Who knows *where* they are?'

Now it was Michael's turn to stand up and go to the window, to stare down at the green hills of Hampstead Heath and reassure himself that he actually existed and was not simply dreaming. If what he had just heard had come from the lips of anyone else, he would surely have thought them mad, but when he turned away from the window, and looked down at the still seated Mr Sampson, he knew that he was dealing with a very experienced, level-headed civil-servant.

Sighing, he sat down again, folding his hands on his desk.

'This is all too unbelievable,' he said. 'It's simply too much to grasp.'

Mr Sampson smiled and spread his hands in a rueful gesture. 'It's too much for *us* to grasp,' he said, 'but we're having to deal with it.'

'I don't think *I* can deal with it,' Michael said. 'My head's reeling already.'

'You're a psychologist,' Mr Sampson said. 'That *should* be a help.'

Michael smiled at that, drummed a pencil on the desk, became aware of what he was doing, dropped the pencil and looked up.

'I take it,' he said, 'that you want me to attend to this Miles Ashcombe and, if possible, ascertain just where imagination ends and reality begins.'

'That's it. Precisely.'

'He'll be brought to the hospital?'

'Yes — without papers. We believe you have private wards for special people and we want him in one of

79

those. A room well-barred and guarded. No name on the door. We'll deliver him with false identification, then it's all up to you. So, will you do it?'

Michael wanted another cigarette, but thought better of it. He stared around his office, at the material world, shook his head as if to clear it of cobwebs and then sighed disbelievingly.

'It's the case of the century,' he said. 'It's one I simply can't miss.'

Sampson removed the cassette-tape from the recorder, left the tape on the desk, slipped the recorder back into his pilot case. Then he stood up and pointed at the tape, his smile brightening his ruddy cheeks.

'You can keep the tape,' he said. 'I'm sure you'll play it often. I'll phone later to make arrangements for the delivery of your patient. The best of luck, Dr Phillips.'

He turned away and walked out, closing the door quietly behind him, leaving Michael sitting there in the chilling silence of the afternoon's deepening gloom.

CHAPTER SIX

Frances blinked against a bright haze, licked her lips, rubbed her eyes, moved her head experimentally from left to right, then took a deep breath. How long had she been unconscious? Had she broken any bones? Perhaps she had actually died in that darkness and was now *imagining* her body. She took another deep breath, touched herself, *felt* herself, then raised herself onto her right hip, her hand pressed to the damp grass. She was wet and steaming slightly as the heat dried her clothes. She shook her head, squinted through the haze and saw Laurence watching her.

'You've been unconscious all night,' Laurence said. 'You were knocked about a fair bit.'

Frances sat upright, feeling feverish and dizzy, shivered and studied Laurence again. His hair was untidy, he badly needed a shave, his eyes seemed slightly dazed and bloodshot. He was covered in dirt, and his clothing, also wet, was dishevelled.

'God,' she said, 'you look a mess.'

'So do you,' he replied.

'Then I must look exactly as I feel.'

'You're not alone,' Laurence said.

The great lake was behind him, its surface vitreous in the morning light, but when Frances tried to ascertain the exact position of the sun, she was almost blinded by the constant, brilliant haze.

'I've been unconscious all night?' she asked, hardly recognising her own voice.

'Yes,' Laurence replied. He was holding a gnarled stick in his right hand, scoring rings in a small patch of mud surrounded by shiny stones. 'You were hammered repeatedly into the bank before Schul and I managed to drag you out of the water. Naturally, by the time we got you out, you'd been knocked unconscious.'

Frances ran her hand experimentally over head and limbs. 'No serious damage,' she said eventually, 'so it must have been shock.'

'Yes, maybe so.'

'And the others?'

Laurence shrugged. 'The canoe was smashed to pieces against the bank of the lake, Schul and I managed between us to drag you ashore, and the Arab oarsmen seem to have vanished with the remains of the boat.'

Squinting into the brilliant haze, Frances saw that she was in a clearing by the lake, in what seemed like a natural garden of orange and lemon trees, fig-palms, and a lush profusion of buttercups, box thorn, saltbrush, tall rushes and uncommonly rich, untended green grass. She felt very strange when she studied it, but she didn't know why.

'The Arabs must have drowned,' Laurence said. 'There's no sign of them anywhere.'

'And Schul?'

Laurence languidly waved his hand to indicate the forest behind Frances. 'He's somewhere in there,' he said. 'He's been wandering about all night, trying to get some help, but so far he hasn't found a soul.'

'That's not particularly unusual: he's not likely to find anyone between here and Al Qurna — and he probably doesn't know where that is.'

'Let's hope that's been his only problem.' Laurence raised his short, gnarled stick and plunged it into the patch of muddy earth, scoring coils and circles abstractedly, but with suppressed nervous violence. 'Do you remember anything else about last night?' he asked.

'Just that darkness ...'

'That's right.' Laurence threw the stick onto the ground, rubbed his dirt-smeared hands on his trousers, then wiped his lips with the back of one hand. 'That great wall of darkness,' he said. 'There wasn't anything natural about it: that thing was real strange. It had a definite shape. It was rectangular and very high. It blotted out the stars, but it seemed slightly transparent and had flecks of light darting about inside it. I don't know what it was, but it was frightening. It wasn't natural at all.'

Frances remembered and knew just what Laurence meant: she closed her eyes and saw that great mass towering above as its pulsating darkness drew the canoe in on the turbulent water.

'Yes,' she said, wiping sweat from her forehead. 'And that thing sucked us into it.'

Laurence stood up and walked to the water's edge, his body framed by the glittering surface of the lake, his feet close to a mass of bulrushes that swayed by the muddy bank.

'Yes,' he said, 'but into *what*? The only thing that Schul and I can remember is that the stars disappeared. There was darkness — a terrible darkness — and flecks of light were darting around us. It was cold — *freezing* cold — then it grew warmer as the darkness faded away. The stars returned, but they weren't the stars we knew: they were the same stars that suddenly appeared just before last night's storm. It was a different sky, Frances — a *different* sky — but we don't know *what* sky.'

Frances hardly knew herself. She had never felt so strange. Staring across the forest clearing, trying not to breathe too quickly, she saw Laurence as a black silhouette framed by rippling, silvery light.

The lake, she thought. *It's only the lake. I must not start imagining things* . . .

'Please, Laurence,' she said. 'Do me a favour. Don't talk with your back to me.'

Laurence sighed audibly, walked towards her and stopped a few feet away.

'While I watched you,' he said, 'Schul went looking for help — but each time he went into that forest, he lost his sense of direction.'

'Schul doesn't know the area, Laurence. What's strange about that?'

'Do *you* know where we are, Frances?'

'Yes. We're just a couple of miles north of Al Qurna. We could walk there in no time.'

'That's what *I* thought,' Laurence said. 'But Schul couldn't find Al Qurna — or anywhere else.'

Already disorientated, Frances now felt more confused, her thoughts writhing in the thickets of that darkness which had swallowed her senses.

'He can't find Al Qurna. He can't find a living soul. He went looking three times during the night — and he's looking right now.'

'I repeat,' Frances said, aware of the strain in her own voice, 'Schul doesn't know the area. He's probably just — '

'No, Frances, it's something other than that. Schul's a Vietnam veteran, well-trained and possessing a compass, and could normally find his way anywhere. I told him where Al Qurna was, but no matter how far along the bank he walked, he ended up right back here. He can't figure it out — and neither can I. It's as if we're on some kind of island . . . except it *isn't* an island.'

Frances was exhausted, drained by the fierce humidity; when she stood up, rising awkwardly, she realised just how badly she had been bruised when thrown out of the boat.

She placed her hands above her head, stretched herself, loosening up, then looked around the clearing again, surprised by its beauty. The grass was remarkably lush, the green splashed with yellow buttercups, the trees rich with oranges, lemons and figs, the foliage resplendent with wildflowers.

Schul's rucksack was on the ground, lying under one of the trees, opened, its flap hanging down.

'Does he have any food in that rucksack?' she asked.

'I don't think so,' Laurence said.

'He's a veteran from Vietnam,' Frances said. 'Perhaps he can find us some.'

She walked past Laurence and stopped at the muddy bank, looking out over the limpid water, into that strange, dazzling haze.

Why strange? She wasn't sure. She rubbed her eyes and kept staring. The rippling, silvery water gradually merged with the shimmering white sky, revealing no land at the far side, no dark line of bulrushes.

She shivered and turned away, hearing birdsong from the trees, but aware that the singing was encased in a great dome of silence. Laurence was still standing there, his gaze intense and a little frightened, then she heard snapping twigs, shifting foliage, and looked to her right.

It was Schul. He was emerging from the forest and coming towards her, stripped to the waist, denims rolled up to his knees, carrying a makeshift fishing-pole across one well-muscled shoulder, with three or four fish in the small net dangling from his left hand. His naked torso was suntanned, badly scarred, hard with muscle; and even his walk, Frances noted immediately, was clearly aggressive.

He stopped just in front of her, took a deep breath, wiped sweat from his brow.

'So,' he said, 'you're awake at last.'

'Yes,' Frances replied.

'Oh, man, that was some sleep you had ... First me and then you.'

'I don't think there's a connection.'

'Maybe, maybe not. There's odd things going on here.' He held his small net up high, displaying the freshwater fish. 'You like 'em?' he asked. 'I caught 'em in a pool back there. There's no shortage of food in this place — and we might need a lot of it.'

'You kept that net in your rucksack?'

'That's right, lady,' Schul replied. '*And* a compass, matches, an all-purpose knife and lots more. I'm a sensible traveller.'

He sneered at Laurence, then threw the fish at his feet. 'Do you know how to light a fire, kid? If so, we can eat.'

Laurence looked down at the fish, the blush on his cheeks displaying anger. 'No,' he said. 'I can't light an open fire. I was never in the Boy Scouts.'

Schul laughed at that, slapping one hand on his hip. 'Shit,' he said. 'The Boy Scouts! *That's* a good one. I didn't pick it up *there*, kid.'

'We *know* you've been to Vietnam,' Laurence said with quiet sarcasm.

'Fuckin' right, kid. And learned a lot.' As if dismissing a minion, Schul waved his left hand. 'To hell with it,' he said. 'I'll light the fire myself — *and* I'll cook the damned fish.'

He turned away from Laurence to fix his attention on Frances; she noticed the sweat trickling down brown skin and making his hard muscles shine.

'We've been shipwrecked,' he said, his lips curling into that crooked grin. 'We're gonna have to fend for ourselves, and I'm experienced that way.'

'It shouldn't be too long,' Frances said, speaking more hopefully than she felt. 'If I'm not back at Basra by tonight the hospital will contact the sheikh — and if he tells them we left his village yesterday, they'll send a helicopter to search for us.'

'Oh, yeah?'

'Yes.'

Schul grinned sarcastically, shook his head from side

to side, then nodded contemptuously at Laurence and said, 'Do you know the situation we're in? Do you know what's going on?'

'He told me that we seem to be lost,' Frances said, 'but I'm sure there's a rational explanation.'

'And what's your rational explanation for what we saw last night?'

'I don't have one.'

'Right, you don't have one. And do you have a rational explanation for why I can't find that town your friend here sent me to?'

'Obviously — '

'Shit,' Schul said brutally. 'I could find my way anywhere just by tracking the stars, but those stars we saw last night don't conform to any stars that we know. As for the town, Al Qurna, that's supposed to be south of here ... well, let me tell you, there's *nothing* south of here — nothing at all. As a matter of fact, lady, if you follow the water's edge you just end up right back here — which at first made me think this was an island. But then, when I cut straight across this island, I ended up right back here *again*. Here there's no north or south. There's no east or west. Believe me, you walk in any direction and you'll end up right here.'

'That's impossible,' Frances said.

'*Impossible*?' Schul replied, then, rubbing a hand across his bronzed, hairy chest, nodded again, this time indicating the sky. 'Look up there,' he said, 'and tell me what you see ... Or what you *don't* see.'

Frances shaded her eyes with one hand and looked up, squinting painfully. 'I ... Just the light. It's very bright.'

'Yeah,' Schul said, 'it's *too* bright. And where's the sun? Tell me *that*, doctor-lady! *There's no sun in that sky!*'

The light flashed in front of Frances, making Schul seem unreal, but she blinked until her vision returned and brought with it the mystery: the lake merging with the sky, the sky sunless, air hazy, Laurence framed by a rippling, silvery light behind Schul who, in his in-explicable arrogance and lack of fear, had himself given shape to this dream by springing out of nowhere.

Frances wiped sweat from her brow, feeling hot, yet shivering. She rubbed her eyes and tried to make real this unnatural garden. No north nor south, no east nor west, just a peculiar, brilliant haze that made everything seem even more unreal.

'Christ,' Schul said. 'Let's get to work. Let's think it out while we eat.'

But before they ate, Schul decided to prepare for a long stay by the lake and took pleasure in showing them how to survive in the wilds. From what had seemed like a fairly normal rucksack, he unpacked a two-man Wenzel Flamezel Mountain tent, 5lb Coleman down sleeping bag, Trangia Storm methylated stove com-prising an aluminium cook set with two large frying pans, frypan and pot lifter, lightweight Flaghouse canteen including cooking and eating utensils for two, first-aid kit, torch, some brillo pads, toilet paper, spare clothing and a pack of waterproof matches.

'I've also got some emergency rations,' he said, grinning maliciously. 'Glucose tablets, chocolate, dried fruit and other shit — but that'll stay in the rucksack until we're desperate — or, to be more precise, until *I'm* desperate. You people, you don't come prepared, you deserve what you get.'

Frances felt as sheepish as Laurence looked while Schul, frequently casting them mocking glances, gathered some brush and made a fire which he lit with his fire-starter tablets and a large, waterproof match. He sliced the head and tail off the fish with a 5-inch sheath knife, expertly removed its bones, fried it in a pan heated on the stove and served it with relish.

'I've got some salt in the rucksack,' he said, 'but we might need it later.'

Frances ate her meal in silence, using a fork and nervous fingers, slightly nauseated by the dry, unsalted fish but grateful to have it. She was aware of Schul watching her, his lips curled in a licentious grin, and although she felt removed from herself, her warming flesh captured her. *What's happening*? she wondered. *Where are we? Is this real?* She dissolved into a realm of confusion, feeling time slipping past her.

'Here,' Schul said huskily. 'Have some Scotch. I always carry this hip-flask.'

Frances accepted the offer, letting the drink anaesthetise her, turning away from Laurence's reproachful stare and offering Schul a small smile. The Scotch burned quickly through her, illuminating her dazed mind, pushing time even further away and making the dream more acceptable.

'It's getting colder,' she finally murmured.

'Yeah,' Schul said. 'That's right. It's afternoon already — Jesus Christ! — and the sun's goin' down.'

'There *is* no sun,' Laurence said.

'Christ, man, I forgot that! Still, it's gettin' colder and darker . . . *Too* cold . . . And too quickly.'

Frances noticed that the hazy brilliance had turned grey, though was still oddly unreal. She stared across the wide lake, trying to see the marshes beyond, but saw only a slowly shifting mist where glittering water met darkening sky.

'Cold,' she murmured. 'It's turning much, much too cold.'

'Yeah,' Schul replied, sounding almost hoarse, 'and it's gonna get worse.'

'It shouldn't,' Frances said. 'It never gets that cold here. I don't know why it should be that way now — nor, for that matter, why it should be turning so dark this early.'

'What the hell *is* the time?' Schul asked. He studied his wrist-watch, furrowed his brow in surprise, shook the watch close to his ear and then registered more surprise.

'It's stopped,' he said. 'It's never done that before.

It stopped thirty-five minutes ago.'

Frances and Laurence both checked their own wristwatches and discovered that they, too, had stopped.

'The same,' Laurence said. 'They stopped at the same time. That's approximately when it started getting dark.'

'But that was only two-thirty in the *afternoon*,' Schul replied, 'so it shouldn't be dark *or* cold right now.'

Laurence coughed into his fist, his gaze wandering back to Frances. 'That struck me last night,' he said, speaking directly to her. 'One minute we were out there in the warmth of the lake, the next we were inside that dark mass where the cold nearly froze us. You were unconscious through it all, but believe me, you were shivering all night.'

Frances yawned, no longer frightened, feeling drunk, and saw that the greyness was deepening into a strange, swimming darkness. She raised her head but saw no stars, examined the sky but saw no sun, placed her right hand, fingers outspread, on the grass and felt the cold earth.

'Christ,' Schul said, 'I'm drunk.'

'So am I,' Frances replied.

'I've never got drunk so fast before. I think I'll have to lie down.'

'You're not drunk,' Laurence said. 'Neither of you is drunk. I didn't have anything to drink and yet I feel the same way.'

'It's this darkness,' Frances said, rubbing her forehead. 'It's making *all* of us tired.'

There was no sun in the sky, but it kept growing darker as Schul jumped to his feet and then, swaying a little, started putting up his two-man tent. Frances watched him, amused, more so because of Laurence, impelled perversely by his visible anger to move closer to Schul.

There was something weird here. Schul knew it and would protect her. Like a lot of men — or at least like

90

most of those she had known — he was driven by a brutish, selfish ego that would not let him rest. What he wanted, he must have — she understood that, having known it — and, if the impulse often made her feel revulsion, it just as often made her surrender to her need for oblivion.

He's a brute, she thought. *Look at him: flexing his muscles and smirking.*

And yet, even realising that, she felt her flesh flowing towards him.

'Okay,' Schul said, 'the tent's ready . . . And I've got room for one more.'

His grin had two sides, inviting Frances, mocking Lawrence. He put his hands up in the air, palms turned towards the sky.

'It's *my* tent,' he said. 'So that means I can use it. That leaves space for one of you — and ladies come first.'

He kept the wolfish grin on his face, looking at each of them in turn, his hands still held out in the air as if preparing to grab something. It was growing darker every second, though the darkness seemed strange: it appeared to be materialising like smoke from the air all around them. Schul obviously didn't care; he possessed an unnatural lack of fear; he lived on the surface of his skin and knew nothing beneath it. So, he kept grinning, fixing his hard gaze on Laurence, who had sat down on the grass beneath a tree, resting his hands on his raised knees. He was staring very steadily at Schul, keeping himself in control, but his anger brightened his eyes to a degree that made them pierce through the gathering gloom.

'You and I can sleep out here,' he said. 'Frances can sleep in the tent.'

'It's *my* tent,' Schul repeated.

'That's hardly the issue,' Laurence replied.

'It doesn't matter,' Frances interrupted. 'I'd rather sleep outside.'

Schul threw her his wolfish grin. 'What's the matter?

You don't like me? You're gonna freeze your arse out here, lady, so why not share the tent?'

'And what about Laurence?'

'Where he sleeps is his problem.'

'To hell with you,' Frances said contemptuously. 'I'll sleep out here with Laurence.'

Schul stopped grinning, then took a deep breath, the lake and marshes beyond him dissolving rapidly into the strange dusk. Frances returned his hard stare, trying to keep her face blank, not daring to show him what she felt, knowing how he would use it.

Then Schul shook his head, very slowly, in mock despair. 'Okay,' he said, 'stay out here. You'll come crawling in soon enough.'

He shivered and spat, muttered an oath about the cold, grinned in a contemptuous manner at Laurence and crawled into his tent. Frances smiled nervously at Laurence, received a grateful smile in return, then glanced at the darkening forest around her and out to the lake.

Something was wrong: it was too early to be dark. And the darkness itself had a quality that she couldn't pinpoint. She studied the lake and felt peculiar. It didn't seem to be dark out there. The darkness was gathering here, wrapping its chilly wings around her, but out there, beyond the darkness, was what seemed to be normal daylight.

In fact, studying the lake and marshes, Frances had the distinct impression that she was looking through a sheet of tinted glass. The darkness was *here*, gathering around her, but it wasn't out there.

She glanced at Schul's tent, remembering his well-muscled, sweating torso, then stood up and walked across to the lemon tree and sat down beside Laurence.

'God,' she said, 'it's cold.'

'Yes,' Laurence replied. 'You better swallow your pride and share Schul's tent.'

'No, thanks,' Frances said.

It was now as dark as night, but Laurence's face was illuminated by numerous darting lights, which, first in their hundreds, then in their thousands, were pulsating as they drifted to and fro. The lights multiplied constantly, streaking the gloom with their shifting brilliance, resembling shoals of luminous, silvery minnows in the depths of a river.

Frances felt drugged and sleepy, but she stretched out her hand, spreading her fingers to catch one of the sparkling lights and see what it was. The lights passed through her hand, through her arm, then through her head, so she closed her eyes and let herself drift through a spiralling galaxy.

'What's *happening?*' Laurence whispered. 'Is this *real?*'

He stared at Frances with wide eyes, his face a quiltwork of light and shadow, then automatically placed his arms around her and drew her close to him. When he did so, Frances heard a mechanical whirring sound in her ear, and looked down to see the hands on Laurence's wrist-watch spinning into a blur.

Startled, she jerked her head back and pulled his wrist away; she examined the spinning hands on his watch and then looked at her own. When she saw that it was doing the same, she felt the breath of insanity.

'Hold me, Laurence!' she whispered. 'Just *hold* me! I have to know this is *real!*'

They took warmth from one another, soothing their fear in togetherness, and then Frances squinted through that darkness filled with drifting, sparkling lights to see a series of completely different landscapes taking shape magically.

The scenery moved. It changed. It was never the same for long. First volcanoes and fire, then boiling water and sprouting greenery, then bizarre creatures flapping their wings overhead while large plants bloomed and died. Seasons came and went, dissolving into one another, and the landscape changed from molten rock to desert, from that to lush foliage and wildflowers. It was real, but obscured, as if viewed through tinted glass; and the thousands, perhaps millions, of tiny, sparkling lights darted to and fro, and drifted up and down, cascading in mysterious, dreamlike grandeur before her dazed eyes.

Frances felt drugged and sleepy. Her body was very heavy. She felt that she was turning into stone and sinking into the ground. The earth was pulling her down. Gravity had clearly grown much stronger. She glanced at Laurence and saw that he was sleeping, and that made her smile. She breathed deeply and looked above her, but the sky was unfamiliar. She lowered her head and closed her weary eyes and fell asleep almost instantly.

She dreamed about humming lights. She dreamed that someone was coming towards her. She stayed silent in the hope that that someone would disappear with the rest of it.

CHAPTER SEVEN

She awakened to a ghostly chorus of frogs, geese, singing birds and swarming mosquitoes. Opening her eyes, she squinted into morning sunlight and saw Schul at the centre of the clearing, lighting a fire. Stiff with cold, she moved painfully, sitting up and stretching herself, then stared across the glassy, placid lake at the marshes beyond. Everything seemed normal, making her wonder if she had been dreaming. Then Laurence, sitting beside her, also yawned and faced the new day.

'Is it normal?'

'Yes,' Frances said.

'Thank God for that.'

Laurence sat up, rubbing his eyes, shaking his head, distastefully took note of the working Schul then glanced up at the sky.

'Look,' he said, pointing with his finger. 'We've even got the sun back.'

It was true. The familiar sun had returned and the morning light seemed natural, blazing down upon the water and earth to burn the coldness away. Schul struck a match and set fire to his pile of twigs; when the flames burst into life, he threw Frances and Laurence a crooked grin.

'You look frozen,' he said.

'We *are* frozen,' Frances replied.

'You had your chance, lady,' Schul said. 'It was real cozy inside that tent, and you could have been with me.'

Frances didn't bother replying, but she and Laurence stood up together, then walked over to the fire as Schul heaped larger sticks on the burning twigs. They both knelt down by the fire, opened their frozen hands to the flames, and shuddered as the warmth filtered into them.

'I think we should try to get out of here,' Schul said, 'while everything's normal. You want coffee?'

'Yes.'

Schul had filled a metal pot with water from the river; now he dropped a couple of purifying tablets into the water, then put the pot onto the fire to boil. While he rinsed out his two tin cups, then put coffee and sugar into them, Frances took comfort from the fire and thought of her strange night.

She remembered the streaming darkness, the thousands of darting lights, the scenery that changed as the hands on her watch spun in a blur. She had grown very weighty, as if turning to stone; then, while the scenery kept changing, she had fallen asleep.

What had she dreamed about? She now struggled to remember. The dreams had been so vivid at the time, but now she couldn't recall them. She remembered humming lights, perhaps someone coming towards her, her silent prayer that that 'someone' would disappear with everything else.

'I hope you two appreciate what I'm doing for you,' Schul said. 'First I catch and fry the fish, now I'm giving you my coffee. You don't seem too grateful for my efforts.'

'Why be grateful?' Frances replied. 'You're getting satisfaction out of it. It gives you a sense of power to have us so completely dependent upon you. It makes you feel you're in charge.'

'I *am* in charge, lady. That's automatic in this case.

I'm in charge because I'm the one most capable of getting us out of here. I've been to Vietnam. I know how to live off the land. That means I get to make the decisions and you do as I say.'

'God,' Frances replied, 'you're obnoxious. You really *do* need to be in charge and lay down your orders.'

'You know that 'cause you understand the type. Deep-down I'm the kind you like, lady. I know what you want.'

'I just want your coffee.'

The conversation had embarrassed Laurence, but Schul just grinned maliciously. 'Anyway,' he said, 'it looks like everything here is back to normal, so we might be able to find our way to that town. That weird darkness has been and gone, but it might come back again, and I want us to get out of here while the going is good.'

'Did you sleep all night?' Frances asked him.

'Yeah. Like a bird.'

'Then you didn't see what happened after you left us?'

'No, not a thing.'

Frances summarised what she and Laurence had witnessed, but Schul, though he wrinkled his brow, still seemed unafraid.

'Weird,' he murmured. 'Real weird ... And I slept through it all.'

He examined the pot on the fire, saw that the water was boiling, made the coffee and handed each of them a cup. While they sipped, he made himself another in the hollow lid of the pot. He drank some, then glanced across the lake, raising his eyes to the sun.

'Well,' he said, 'we've still got the sun and everything else seems normal, so we better try to get out of here as soon as possible. Maybe what happened last night was just an odd occurence, but just in case it wasn't — in case it comes back — we better forget breakfast and try to get as far away from here as possible before anything happens.'

'Let's try to get to Al Qurna,' Frances said.

'Sure,' Schul said. '*Anywhere.*'

While Schul doused the fire and Laurence simply looked on grimly, Frances washed the tin cups in the lake, then gave them to Schul. He expertly dismantled his tent and packed it in the rucksack, then glanced at the sun, checked his compass and led them out of the clearing.

Since it would naturally lead to the continuation of the river, they stuck to the muddy bank of the lagoon, Schul walking out ahead, Frances just behind him, and with Laurence as the last link in the chain. The sun was high in the sky, making the lagoon look like glass, and the heat had an unrelenting ferocity that drained them of strength. Mosquitoes buzzed all around them, attracted to their running sweat, swarming up from the trampled grass and bulrushes, darkening the bright light.

Frances wiped sweat from her forehead, licked it from her upper lip, felt it trickling from under her armpits, down her neck to her breasts. Exhaustion claimed her quickly, making her sag, draining her mind, and she sank into the well of her senses, hardly aware of her own thoughts.

Schul had removed his shirt again and had it flapping from his rucksack; Frances followed that whipping flag like a donkey after a carrot, then tried to gather together her scattered thoughts by lowering her gaze. Schul had also removed his trousers and was now wearing only shorts; Frances saw his deeply tanned, hairy legs moving under the rucksack.

She kept staring at those legs, mesmerised by their hard muscles, her gaze following a line of glistening sweat that wound through his dark hairs. She licked her lips and shook her head, trying to get back her senses, feeling strangely out of control, her flesh melting away.

'A couple of miles?' Schul asked, looking back over his shoulder. 'Al Qurna's only a couple of miles from here? Is that what you said?'

'That's right,' Frances replied. 'It's not far. Another few minutes should do it.'

Yet even as she spoke, she sensed that something was wrong, her gaze taking in the sweep of the great lagoon but not recognising it. They should have passed the lagoon by now — it should have narrowed down to become the river — but instead the opposite side was as far away as ever, the marshes dissolving in a haze that grew brighter each minute.

'Oh, God,' Frances murmured.

She realised what was happening, jerked her eyes up to confirm it, and saw, where the sun should have been, only a sweeping white haze.

'Oh, God!' she repeated, this time loudly. 'The sun's disappeared again!'

Schul stopped walking and glanced at the sky, shading his eyes with his hands and shaking his head.

'Oh, shit,' he whispered.

'That means it's starting again,' Laurence said. 'That's what happened yesterday.'

Schul glanced at his wrist-watch. 'It's stopped again,' he said. Frances and Laurence both checked their own wrist-watches and found the same thing. 'Fuck it,' Schul said, 'let's keep going anyway. We're probably out of the range of that thing and might get to Al Qurna. Let's move it. *Right now!*'

Remaining close together, they continued along the muddy bank, almost blinded by the dazzling white haze that covered sky and lagoon. Frances glanced across the water, trying to see the far side, saw only that same blinding haze and then turned to her left. She was passing orange and lemon trees, the fruit packed close together, but their colouring had been washed out completely and the trees were mere shadows. She wiped tears from her stinging eyes, then focused on the ground; the bulrushes were swaying by the bank as a breeze rippled through them.

'Oh, God,' she said, far too loudly, 'that wind is returning!'

The heavy rucksack bounced in front of her; then, as a shifting shadow, his features erased by the swimming haze, Schul was turning towards her to grab her hand and pull her close to him. She felt his arm against her own, his skin sweat-slicked and electric, then he dragged her along the muddy bank, trying to make her go faster. She thought about Laurence behind her, wondered if they would lose him, forgot him when she noticed that the fierce haze was starting to darken.

'Shit!' Schul hissed. 'Too late!'

As he tugged even more urgently at Frances' hand, the wind rose dramatically, sweeping violently across them, almost forcing them into the trees which were bending and rustling. Frances stifled a sob, squinting into the changing light, aware that they should have reached Al Qurna by now and hoping to see it.

What she saw destroyed that hope, plunging her spirit into despair: the great darkness was returning, materialising magically from nothing, blocking out the sun's light and warmth as it deepened inexorably.

'Where is it?' Schul shouted. '*Where's Al Qurna?*'

'I don't know!' Frances cried.

The darkness had taken command, turning the day into night, and it forced them to stop and take shelter beneath the shivering trees. They huddled together for some time, but then the wind suddenly ceased—and too bewildered for words they all looked across the lake to see what appeared to be normal daylight beyond the unnatural darkness.

Frances couldn't believe her eyes and felt increasingly unreal as she took in that daylight at the other side of the darkness, then focused on the bank where it curved away from her and disappeared into light-flecked gloom.

She shivered with cold, wrapped her arms around her raised knees, blinked and squinted into the sparkling gloom to see the lights multiplying. They were tiny, pulsating lights, first in their hundreds, then their thousands, bursting out of the distant darkness and suddenly swirling about her, then moving to and fro, up and down, in loops and circles, forming cartwheels and winding streams of silver which dazzled the eyes.

'Oh, dear God,' she heard Laurence whisper. 'What *are* they? *Where* are we?'

Schul muttered something, then stretched out his left hand, fingers spread like a net to catch the darting lights.

'Damn!' he muttered. 'They just pass right through me. I must be losing my mind!'

Frances raised her own hands, watched the lights passing through them, examined her body and legs, saw the same thing.

The darkness kept growing brighter, throwing the lake into clear perspective, but the marshes at the other side of the water started melting, then growing. First the dark line of reeds, then low dunes and windswept sand . . . then the dunes dissolved and turned into hills that were sunscorched and barren.

Frances heard beating wings and turned her gaze towards the sky. There was no sun up there, but the sky was very bright, and a prehistoric pteranodon flew overhead, its wings of skin beating awkwardly. It grew hazy as it approached her, disappeared in a flash of light, emerged as a great golden eagle that passed silently overhead. Then the darkness faded completely and the trees changed some more, the greenery too lush, the bark toasted a deep mahogany, the figs, oranges and lemons in dense clusters, the branches shedding white pollen.

101

'It's hot again,' Schul said, staring at Frances. 'And the sun's disappeared again.'

'No north or south,' Laurence murmured. 'No east or west ...'

The light-flecked darkness was no more, but a sunless sky arched over them, bathing the landscape in a heat-haze of unusual intensity. The land beyond the lake was different, a series of sun-scorched, ragged hills, while around them the trees seemed familiar, though subtly altered.

'It all looks like stage-scenery,' Laurence said. 'Or scenery painted by God ...'

Schul snorted without mirth. 'Don't give me God,' he said. 'We're all going nuts in this heat — and that's all there is to it.'

Frances studied the two men, trying to take comfort from them, hoping that the reality of their presence would keep her senses together. They looked strange in that bizarre light, their skin as white as marble, their eyes gleaming with a brilliance that made them seem glassy and mad.

'Let's keep walking,' Schul said. 'Let's try it one more time. Let's move while the going is good and see where we end up.'

'It's hopeless,' Laurence replied. 'You tried before and got nowhere. You always ended up in that same clearing, so we'd be wasting our time.'

'And what do we gain by staying here? Not a god-damned thing, kid. We don't know what time it is or where we are or what's happening, and staying here won't help a goddamned bit. I say we keep moving. I say give it another shot. What the hell? We've got nothing to lose, so let's get off our asses.'

Laurence reached down to help Frances to her feet and, as he did so, she saw that his face was pale with anger, his lips forming a grim line. She tried to smile at him, but singularly failed to do so, so she covered her embarrassment by turning away and falling in behind Schul.

Schul twisted back towards her, revealing his unshaven chin, his grin sardonic and his eyes bright with a humour that sprang out of arrogance. Frances was glad when he straightened up, his head cut off by the rucksack, but she felt an obscure, nagging desire as she marched close behind him.

They marched a long time, through that blinding, sunless haze, forced to rely on pure chance since the compass was useless. Their wrist-watches raced wildly, stopped, raced again, while the flowers blossomed only to die and be instantly renewed. Time shifted back and forth, changed the scenery, changed it back, encircled them and scattered their thoughts into a common delirium. Schul started to laugh hysterically, then stopped and stared at them; he leered invitingly at Frances, then glared at Laurence and marched forward again. The sky remained sunless. Snowy-white clouds moved across it. Frances noticed that the light, though intense, produced no shadows at all.

No sun: no shadows. The light had no fixed direction. She heard her own sigh as she turned her head lethargically to see Laurence stumbling close behind her, clearly dazed and exhausted. She wanted to sympathise, but felt drained of all emotion, so instead she wiped the sweat from her stinging eyes and concentrated on walking.

They walked a long time, but did not find Al Qurna. They kept following the muddy bank until they returned to the original clearing; then, at Schul's insistence, they cut straight across the 'island' and, after another arduous walk, arrived at what seemed to be the very same clearing. The dark mass did not return; nor did the normal sun. They followed the shoreline again, gave up and went inland, but always arrived back at the same place and eventually accepted defeat.

'Okay,' Schul said magnanimously to Laurence, 'you were right. We're trapped here.'

'We'll stay here?' Laurence replied.

'We don't seem to have a choice. But don't give me that goddamned smirk, kid. You ain't that fucking smart.'

Schul's gaze was very direct and now more patently aggressive. He stared Laurence down, snorted triumphantly when he moved away; then he turned his attention on Frances, his grin sexually challenging.

'Let's hope that that helicopter actually comes,' he said. 'Otherwise we're gonna be trapped here forever.'

'It'll come,' Frances replied, wearily sitting down on the grass, leaning her back against the trunk of a fig-palm, taking deep, even breaths. 'However, since we can't seem to find Al Qurna anymore, how's the helicopter going to find *us*?'

'Oh, Christ, that's right.'

Obviously frustrated, Schul angrily kicked some grass, then stared thoughtfully out over the placid lake. His shirt was tied around his neck, leaving him bare to the waist; Frances saw the sweat trickling down his chest, over his hard, sun-tanned belly.

'It's getting darker,' Laurence said. 'I don't know how, but it's getting darker. Not that dark mass, but more like a normal darkness — though I still can't see a sun in the sky.'

'Evening,' Frances replied. 'This place has its own kind of evening. My watch has started working again — at more or less normal speed.'

'*And* mine,' Schul said. 'Time seems to stop and start here, runs too fast, runs too slow, and sometimes it even seems to be normal. What the hell's going on?' He took a deep breath, then shrugged as if defeated. 'Well,' he said, 'no matter what it is, we're gonna have to stay here a while. I better catch us something to eat before the light disappears; after that, we might as well try to sleep — or at least say our prayers.'

With that parting shot at Laurence, he walked away from them, stooping briefly to slip under the nearest trees and vanish behind them. When he had gone, Laurence sighed and sat beside Frances, not touching her, but very close to her, his breathing uneven. They were silent for some time, neither knowing what to say, but eventually, and with a certain reluctance, Laurence sighed and spoke softly.

'I can't help it,' he said. 'I just can't stand that Schul. I remind myself that he's a fellow-American and that I'm a practising Christian, but I can't help but think uncharitable thoughts each time I look at him.'

'Don't look at him,' Frances replied.

'I can't help it,' Laurence said. 'He's hardly stopped talking since we met him, he's full of sarcasm and innuendo, and I feel that my face is being slapped every time he opens his mouth.'

'He's a bit aggressive, I know.'

'He's more than that,' Laurence insisted. 'There's something perfectly evil about him — and also something unnatural.'

'*Unnatural?*'

'Yes, unnatural,' Laurence insisted. 'How did he get from England to here? And why is he not even disturbed? He seems normal, but he's missing something — natural nervousness, fear, a sense of wonder at what has already happened to him and is happening to us right now — and that missing part of him convinces me that he's somehow abnormal.'

Frances studied Laurence thoughtfully, seeing only his shadowed profile, then she let her gaze roam across the darkening lake and back to the clearing.

The clearing was crescent-shaped, its straight edge the muddy bank; the bank had originally run from east to west, though that was now problematical. Frances and Laurence were under a tree, both facing east, and down there, at the far end of the clearing, was a natural arch of more fig-palms.

Laurence sighed loudly and shook his head from side to side. 'What with Schul and all these strange events,

I think I'm losing my senses. Either that, or we're actually in purgatory — and will remain here forever.'

'No,' Frances said. 'Not purgatory ... Maybe somewhere more magical.'

She leaned forward a little, studying the clearing more intently, feeling a distinct surge of excitement at what she was thinking. The light was still fading, turning the air a pale crimson, giving everything a strange dream-like quality, as if viewed through fine gauze. Unseen birds were singing in the trees; leaves rustled, twigs snapped. Frances sensed the great silence over all, coming down with the darkness.

'Presuming we no longer know *exactly* where we are,' she said, 'we *do* know that when the storm blew up we were nearing Al Qurna.'

'That's right,' Laurence replied. 'No question about it. Al Qurna should be somewhere in this area, but it's mysteriously disappeared.'

'And what's in Al Qurna?'

'I don't know. Surprise me.'

'The possible site of the Garden of Eden.'

She looked expectantly at Laurence, her excitement tinged with fear, and saw his eyes glittering in the shadow that was falling down over him.

'You know the story,' she said, hardly aware of her own voice, only conscious of the light in Laurence's eyes where they shone in the gathering gloom. 'According to *Genesis*, Eden is east of Israel, in an area out of which flowed a river that then divided into four others. Those rivers were the Gihon, which may have been the Nile; the Pishon, which was most likely in the Persian Gulf, just south of here; and, of course, the Tigris and the Euphrates. The latter two rivers meet near Al Qurna, where they form the Shatt al Arab River, which actually flows down into the Persian Gulf. So, the most widely accepted location of the Garden of Eden is Mesopotamia — or, to be more precise, Al Qurna.'

'But Al Qurna has disappeared,' Laurence said.

'To *where?*' Frances asked him.

Laurence did not reply immediately, but Frances knew what he was thinking: that the place they had been seeking might be right here — all around them. Unseen.

'Oh, Lord,' Laurence whispered eventually. 'I just can't believe this.'

Feeling remote from herself, her skin tingling with an odd heat, Frances squinted through the growing darkness at the natural arch of trees that stood on the eastern corner of the clearing. She stared at it a long time, almost hypnotised by it, then let her gaze fall on the very large fig-palm that stood alone in the centre of the clearing.

Looking at that particular tree, at its fat, clustered figs, she thought of the walled-in tree in Al Qurna — and of the sign placed beside it... *In this holy spot, where Tigris meets Euphrates, this holy tree of our Father Adam grew, symbolising the Garden of Eden on Earth* ... Frances closed her eyes, saw that site in her mind's eye, wondered where it was right now ... or where she and the others had been transported by this bizarre, timeless zone.

'This *could* be it,' she said. 'We don't know. Nothing else makes sense anyway.'

'Now it's *you* who's reading too much into things,' Laurence replied. 'You better watch yourself, Frances.'

She opened her eyes to see him smiling, without malice, almost gently, and was touched enough to reach out towards him. She didn't know what she had intended — perhaps just to shake him gently — but at that moment the sound of snapping twigs announced Schul's return.

He emerged from the trees, holding up a dead rabbit, the darkness hiding the blood that had doubtless drenched his hands, but not able to dim the triumph in the eyes that were staring down at them.

'Let's eat,' he said.

After the meal, when the darkness had descended, Frances stretched out near Laurence and watched Schul creeping into his tent. She ignored his inviting wave, closed her eyes, tried to sleep, but tossed and turned under her sheet, feeling cold and tormented.

Laurence was right: there was something odd about Schul. She thought of him making the camp fire, remembered how he had prepared the rabbit, recalled the relish with which he had skinned it before roasting it for them. *He's an animal*, she thought, still tossing and turning, trying to sleep. *There's something primitive and rapacious about him; he thinks little, feels less* ... Yet even thinking thus, she felt desire for him, overwhelming her shame and latent guilt, making her wanton.

She was cold, but felt on fire. The thin sheet was suffocating her. She glanced through the darkness at Schul's tent, but saw no movement inside. *He knows*, she thought despairingly. *He has the instincts of the beast. He knows that sooner or later I'll come and let him do what he wants with me* ... And so thinking, she almost groaned, biting her lower lip to stifle it, distracted herself by studying the sky and saw a vast, starless darkness.

Frightened, she closed her eyes again, hoping for escape, but was immediately tormented by her body and its sweaty, demanding flesh. She thought of Laurence lying near her, worried about her, caring for her, then understood that she was not attracted by his decency, but by Schul's crude, aggressive lust.

She kept tossing and turning, her skin slippery with sweat, then lay flat on her back and imagined Schul pressing on top of her. He would show little tenderness. He would crush her and subdue her. She groaned softly, then licked her parched lips and let sleep ease her shame . . .

The experience was very vivid. It might even have been a dream. The ground started shaking beneath her and made her open her eyes. The landscape had changed. The great lake was a cratered plain. An alien word, *edinu*, was whispered and she knew what it meant. There it was where the lake had been: a great plain like a dust-bowl. A savage light was beaming out of the sunless sky and turning the stony earth white.

The ground was still shaking when she sat up and grunted. Not many trees here — just a few between scorched rocks — but she recognised the one bearing strange fruit. Her fear had filled her belly with hunger, but she didn't dare stand up: she just stared at the tree with inchoate longing and thoughtlessly scratched herself. The others were grunting loudly. She understood and shared their feelings. She started making as much noise as she could, though she sensed it was useless.

Within the light more light was growing. The ground shook and made strange sounds, one of which gradually rose above the others to make her head tighten. She soon lost all her senses, first grunting, then shrieking, finally covering her eyes with her hands and whimpering helplessly.

The brightening light scorched through her fingers, showing the bones beneath the skin; she stared through her hands into the brightness and watched *them* coming towards her.

She was frozen when they gathered around her to carry her off.

Edinu: plain. The only world that she knew or wanted. They picked her up and carried her from the plain as terror shattered her senses . . .

Frances awakened, groaning loudly and sobbing. Laurence was placing his hand on her burning forehead and whispering to comfort her. She stared wildly around her, saw the trees in white haze, and beyond them, the broad expanse of the lake where the cratered plain had once been.

It was morning and the darkness had departed to leave her back in this mirage.

Gasping, clutching the grass, trying to control her fear, she lay back on the ground and breathed deeply.

'I'm all right,' she said.

CHAPTER EIGHT

The voice of Capital Radio informed Michael, as he sat in his car in a traffic-jam in Finchley Road, that the Finchley Road should be avoided if at all possible. Cursing, Michael switched to Radio 3 to hear Haydn's Sonata in A flat. Sighing with relief, he let the music flow around him, inched forward with the other traffic, and thought pleasurably of the long night he had just spent with Rebecca.

An occasional lover for the past five years, Rebecca was a tall, raven-haired, Jewish career-woman who, in the double-bed in her elegant period-house in Golder's Green, had told Michael that his attention was wandering at the very worst time. Now, remembering that, and well aware of what had caused it, Michael smiled and slipped into the nearside lane to turn up Frognal Lane.

Driving more freely up the winding tree-lined road, past the houses now inhabited by Third World ambassadors and the wealthier English, he felt increasing excitement at the thought of seeing Miles Ashcombe for the first time.

He had in fact received a telephone call from the hospital the previous evening, just before leaving his own flat in Belsize Park to visit Rebecca, telling him that his patient had been delivered to the hospital; and there could be no doubt that it was his thoughts about

Ashcombe that had made him rather distracted when in his lady's bed. He had long ago developed to perfection his ability to separate his work from his private life, and it was a tribute to the magnitude of this new case, and to his fascination with the vanished Glastonbury, that he had been unable to keep it out of his mind even when in Rebecca's warm embrace.

It took a considerable amount of time and patience to manoeuvre the car through the relatively brief length of Hampstead Village, but as he did it he found himself smiling again at the thought of his distracted love-making the previous night. Rebecca's laconic criticism would doubtless have amused his daughter, Cheryl, who was fond of teasing him about his bachelor's life. In truth, if he liked women and suffered no shortage of them, his bachelor's life was, for the most part, devoted to work; and it was, as he often joked, dealing with the insane that kept him sane.

As the Sonata washed over him, he studied the dense traffic crawling down Rosslyn Hill and wondered that the world could continue as normal after the awesome disappearance of Glastonbury. Not a day passed without some mystified reappraisal of the event on television, radio or in the newspapers, yet most people were simply going about their business as if nothing had happened. The ability of the human psyche to narrow itself down to its own concerns irrespective of what was going on around it had never ceased to fascinate Michael; but now, even as he smiled ruefully, his rising excitement over the impending meeting with his new patient drove those very thoughts out of his own head.

Eventually, he turned into Pond Street, then right into the hospital grounds; and when at last he parked his car and entered the large, modern building, the weariness caused by the traffic-jam was already falling away from him.

His mood of keen anticipation was rudely broken when, having taken the lift up to the fourth floor, he entered his office and found his former wife, Janet, waiting for him in his secretary's reception area.

Standing up to greet him, Janet was almost as tall as Michael, a fact emphasised by her slimness, her high-heeled shoes, and the subdued elegance of her tight-fitting dress and knee-length, classic woollen overcoat. She gave him a fleeting smile and nervously stroked her short blonde hair—which reminded him again, as it always did, of how like Cheryl she was.

'Surprise, surprise,' Michael said.

'I'm sorry, Michael. I should have phoned . . .'

'It's all right,' Michael said, glancing down at his secretary, Mrs Beaumont, and noting her shrugging shoulders and rolling eyes. 'Come into my office.'

He held the door open to let her walk in, felt her brushing past him, glanced backwards to see Mrs Beaumont's sardonic smile, then stepped in himself and closed the door. Janet sighed as if nervous, her spine visibly straightening, and he walked around her, indicating that she should sit down. She responded by merely shaking her head in a negative manner.

'I'd rather stand,' she said, her accent pure Cambridge, her voice still a little smoky and distinctly sensual. 'I'm sorry. I should have called,' she repeated. 'So, how are you?'

'You don't have to call,' Michael replied, secretly wishing she had. 'And I'm fine.'

'You disapprove. I can tell.'

'Nonsense,' Michael lied, wondering what the problem was. 'I'm delighted to see you — and delighted that you're looking so well.'

'Liar.'

'Absolutely not.'

Janet nodded and smiled, nervously bit her lower lip, then started pacing to and fro in front of the desk. Watching her, Michael realised that his automatic compliment was well deserved; but he also wondered what new problem his former wife was about to pass on to him.

Although they had been separated for eight years, and actually divorced for five, Janet, who like him had never remarried, tended to treat him as if their own marriage was still intact, depending upon him to sort out her problems, both material and emotional. In the sense that this situation had ensured that Cheryl did not become involved in any tug-of-war between her parents, Michael thought the effort worthwhile; but there were times, such as today, when he could not resist feeling resentment at what he felt was an unwarranted intrusion upon his work. Indeed, his former wife's preoccupation with material matters and ephemeral concerns was inclined to stretch his patience to the limit; so now, watching her pace up and down in front of his desk, he sighed and prepared himself for the latest of her generally trivial concerns.

'Stop pacing the floor,' he said levelly, 'and just tell me your problem.'

'Problem?' she replied, standing still and staring at him. '*My* problem?'

'Well, I assumed — '

'Not just *my* problem,' she said. '*Your* problem as well.'

'Oh? Something wrong with the house ...?'

It was one of the ironies of their separation that Janet should have retained their spacious, five-bedroomed house in Esher, which Michael, who could now only afford to keep a modest flat in Belsize Park, was still called upon to keep in good repair. It was not a legal obligation, but, rather, one based on Janet's assumption that Michael, until someone else came along, was still the head of the family.

'No,' she said firmly, 'it's not the house. I wouldn't come here uninvited just for *that*.'

She would and she had, but Michael would not say so. Instead, eager to be free to see Miles Ashcombe, he simply said, 'So, what *is* it?'

'It's your daughter,' Janet said. 'Your *beloved* daughter. She's involved with some man.'

'That's hardly surprising,' Michael said, though he suffered a sinking feeling, some instinct preparing him for bad news. 'She's twenty years old, which is certainly old enough for such involvements.'

'It's not old enough for this,' Janet replied. 'She's involved with a *married* man.'

She threw him an accusing glance which did not soothe the shock that jolted through him with unexpected severity. There was a moment of disbelief, a sharp rise and fall of grief, but he managed to hold Janet's gaze and keep his voice steady.

'With a *married* man?' he asked, rather stupidly.

'Yes, Michael, that's what I said.'

'Are you *sure*?'

Janet rolled her eyes and stared up at the ceiling. 'Oh, God,' she said. 'Am I *sure*? Why do you think I've *come* here?' It was a purely rhetorical question uttered clearly as a reprimand; she then shuddered and sat in the chair at the other side of the desk. 'Yes,' she said. 'I'm absolutely sure. She's having an affair with her boss.'

Feeling a pain which was surprisingly sharp, Michael was forced to accept that for once his wife's concern was not trivial. He glanced down at his desk, closed his eyes, took a deep breath, massaged his eyelids with his fingers and remembered his lunch with his daughter *... I'm a very responsible P.A. to a movie producer. And a very talented, attractive one at that. So I'm quite happy, thanks ...* Her praiseworthy words and skittish support for that nameless man now came back to Michael with painful clarity. He had sensed something then, but had chosen to ignore it, and so, as he opened his eyes to take in his former wife, he felt the inexorable rise of a primitive hatred for the man who was possessing his daughter.

Which was not, as he instantly realised, an intelligent response.

'When we had lunch,' he said wonderingly, 'she joked about how attractive he was. But I didn't really imagine that ...'

'No. Why should you? You don't live with her.'

'Now, Janet, I don't think — '

'If she had a proper father — '

'I hardly think that's the issue. People her age fall in love. That's all there is to it.'

'That's *all* there is to it?' Janet's voice quavered with outrage. 'Is that what's known as psychological objectivity? Your own daughter can have an affair with a married man — and that's *all* there is to it?'

'That's not what I meant, and you know it,' Michael replied, trying to keep the despair out of his voice. 'But for God's sake, let's discuss this as calmly as possible. For a start, are you *sure* it's an active affair and not just an infatuation that hasn't yet — ?'

'It's an affair,' Janet intervened. 'I *know* it's an affair. They've just spent a weekend together in a hotel outside Bath — and it's not the first time that they've done so.'

'How do you know?'

'I overheard Cheryl talking to that bastard on the telephone.'

'You were listening to her *phone* calls?'

'Of course not, Michael. I was going to make a phone call myself from my bedroom — and I picked up the phone and heard them speaking. Naturally, in normal circumstances, I would have hung up instantly; but something in the tone of their voices — something rather conspiratorial — made me listen in ... They were discussing their last weekend together, the other times they had spent a weekend in the same hotel, and the fact that they'll be together again when they return to Nice for more location work on that bastard's film.'

'He may not be the bastard you think he is.'

'He's married and has two adolescent children. I would call that being a bastard.'

Janet crossed one leg over the other, took a deep

breath, glanced at the window that overlooked Hampstead Heath. She was still a very beautiful lady, though less attractive when angry, and when she turned back towards him, green eyes flashing, she was very angry indeed.

'So,' she said, 'what are you going to do about it?'

He hardly knew what to think, let alone what to say. For the first time in a long time he was almost lost for words, knowing nothing but the chaos of emotions which he had thought were long since buried. He had always been proud of his logic and self-control, but now he could only think of his daughter with a fierce sense of loss. His confusion and pain were palpable, shaking him leaf and bough, shaming him with the knowledge that he was actually struggling to keep himself calm. Love made logic redundant and children out of men; and as he shifted uneasily, aware of his racing heart, he was wounded by the realisation that he shared that same weakness.

'I'm not at all sure that there's anything I *can* do about it. I can talk to her, of course, but I doubt that it will be very effective. If she's already *involved* in this affair — '

'She is!'

' — any disapproval on *our* part will only drive her even closer to him.'

'You mean we do . . . *nothing*?'

Michael shrugged, still hiding his rage and pain, feeling utterly helpless. 'You know what she's like,' he said. 'She can be very contrary. As I said, if you want I'll talk to her — but that might be the very worst thing to do.'

'You can talk to *him*,' Janet said. 'You can put an end to it. You can tell him to fire her from her job and not see her again.'

'And if he refuses?'

'Threaten to tell his wife.'

'I don't think so, Janet.'

She uncrossed her long legs, glared at him, then stood up again.

117

'She's our only child,' she said, 'and she's having an affair with a *married* man. I won't have her used and then cast aside — which, beyond any shadow of doubt, is what's going to happen.'

'Perhaps he's in love with *her*.'

'Oh, Christ!' Janet snapped. 'You don't believe that anymore than I do. It's just sex, pure and simple.'

She blushed and pursed her lips, expressing disdain and shame at once, perhaps remembering that her own life with Michael had been sexually incomplete. Most of Janet's sensuality resided in her voice and had never happily expressed itself in bed. For a long time Michael had thought the failure was his own, but the intervening years had shown the opposite. Before and after his marriage he had enjoyed sex very much, whereas Janet, in a kind of quiet desperation, had led the life of a nun.

'Anyway,' she continued, unaware of his line of thought, 'that's what *I* believe, so either you talk to our daughter or you talk to her boss. If you don't, *I* will — and if I don't receive a positive response, I'll talk to his wife.'

'That would be cruel.'

'No worse than what he's doing.'

'Let's try to keep his family out of this.'

'That's up to you, dear.'

Michael sighed. 'All right, Janet, I'll talk to Cheryl first. Please don't do anything rash until then. I'll keep you informed.'

Janet stared gravely at him, then nodded and turned away; she walked to the window and looked out, as most visitors did.

'Fine,' she said eventually. 'But when? I can't let this continue.'

'I'll ring her tonight,' Michael said.

'Good,' Janet said. 'Excellent.'

She turned back to face him, offering a grateful smile; and aware once more of how attractive she still was,

118

Michael felt a familiar spasm of guilt because their marriage had failed.

'I have to get to work now, Janet.'

'This isn't a *favour*, Michael.'

'I know. It's just that — '

'She is *our* daughter, after all. And if you weren't so casual about your *own* love-life, she might not have — '

'Please, Janet, that's unfair, and we've been through all this before.'

'And your work comes first. I should have *known* that. I'm leaving right now.'

The sarcasm was familiar and had its roots in insecurity; for that reason he did not respond to it, but simply stared at her. She shrugged, as if apologising, then said, 'Well, not the best of circumstances, but it *was* nice to see you.'

'And you,' he said gently.

He stood up and walked around the desk to give her a kiss on the cheek. It was a rather prim kiss, almost brotherly in fact, and she responded by sniffing and stepping back to turn away from him. She opened the door, then stopped to stare at him; eventually, with a tremulous smile, she shook her head sadly.

'God protect us from our children,' she said softly.

'They're our only future,' Michael replied.

Janet nodded and stepped out, closing the door behind her, and Michael simply stood there for a moment, giving her time to depart. In that silence he was exposed to his own very human frailty, stung by the realisation that his professional objectivity was useless when it came to personal matters. He remembered his lunch with Cheryl — the concern he had felt for her — then experienced a keen sense of betrayal and smouldering rage. What he had feared had come to pass — his daughter was doubtless being exploited — and unlike a psychologist, but very much like a normal father, he could not help but feel a growing hatred for the man who was using her.

'Damn!' he whispered. 'Why *now*?'

Still badly shaken, he entered Mrs Beaumont's office, first noting with relief that Janet had actually gone, then seeing the sardonic glint in his secretary's eyes. Raising his hands in mock despair, thus disguising the despair he felt, he walked past her desk, opened the other door and stepped into the corridor. He hurried along it, feeling confused, his stirred emotions in conflict, his excitement at the thought of seeing his patient, Miles Ashcombe, now blending with his feelings of betrayal, anger and shame.

Why shame? he wondered, as he passed through some swinging doors, and sensed, even as the question was raised, what the answer might be. *You don't live with her*, Janet had said. *If she had a proper father* ... The implication that he had been derelict in his duty had not been made for the first time. No, indeed not. Janet had often implied the same thing, her voice vibrant with the thrill of accusation and a certain self-righteousness. Janet's vanity was soothed by suffering, by the martyrdom of her position, yet Michael knew, even understanding this much, that her accusations were valid. He *was* guilty of selfishness, of placing himself before his family; and thus, as he approached the barred room containing his new patient, he realised that what Cheryl had done was — indirectly and probably unwittingly — pay him back for his betrayal of long ago.

He arrived at a locked door, was admitted by a male nurse, walked along another, shorter corridor to the rooms that were always barred. Saddened by the news of Cheryl, perhaps more by its implications, he was abruptly plunged into a much deeper gloom when he realised that just like his fellow-motorists that morning, he, too, was placing his own, relatively petty concerns above the monumental Glastonbury event.

Further shaken by this awareness, he stopped halfway down the corridor, at a lime-green painted door which had, instead of a normal glass window, a moveable panel of wood. He took a deep breath, forced his family from his thoughts, then unlocked the panel, slid it open and looked into the room.

The new patient, Miles Ashcombe, was stretched out on the bed, staring up at the ceiling and murmuring a constant stream of demented words. He did, however, jerk upright almost as soon as Michael looked in, and stared directly at the peep-hole with widening, crazed eyes.

Michael was used to madness and its bright, glacial vacancy, but in this case the eyes staring upwards mesmerised him, drawing him into a world that lay beyond all known perimeters and for which he had no prior frame of reference.

For the first time in his professional career, Michael actually *felt* terror.

CHAPTER NINE

Frances continued dreaming while they all lost track of time. The great pillar of darkness would appear without warning, fade away, then return to torment them. During its absence the world would seem perfectly normal, but when it had covered them again, forming a shroud of quiescent beauty, the geography of the stars would be different from what they knew, and the world outside their strange prison incorporeal and unreal.

The mysterious phenomenon came and went, obeying some law of its own, materialising like smoke from the air and disappearing back into it. It continued playing bizarre tricks — distorting time, changing the scenery — and when it disappeared the world returned to normal ... or what *seemed* to be normal.

It was the gravity that was different. They all noticed it in the end. Each time they were surrounded by the shifting, light-flecked darkness, they felt heavier, more sluggish and very sleepy, which afflictions became more pronounced with each passing day.

Yet what was a day now? They could no longer tell. They were measuring their days by the arrival and departure of the phenomenon, but knew in their hearts that this bore little relation to normal time. They slept in the flickering gloom, awakened to the dazzling haze, saw their wrist-watches racing crazily, slowing down, gradually stopping, and soon lost all concept of duration and former reality, until eventually the unnatural became natural, the magical, mundane.

'Where's Al Qurna?' Frances asked. 'Where are we at the moment? What time is it? What day or *month* is it? We can't answer such questions anymore — and might be trapped here forever.'

That possibility was very real and made them share the breath of fear. Time kept changing before their eyes, though not as rapidly as before, and when the plants bloomed and died to be reborn as different species, when the great lake became a cratered plain filled with dust, when a golden eagle suddenly turned into a flapping pteranodon, the rate of change seemed to be slower, the new landscape more lasting.

Time kept slowing down until it came to a halt, finally leaving them in an oasis which appeared to have sprung miraculously from a former landscape of desolate lakes and mist-covered swamps. They caught fish in the nearest lake, plucked the fruit from the trees, and as the landscape had changed, so they also changed, losing their civilised habits and becoming more primitive.

No-one discussed this change, but Frances felt it in herself: her thoughts thickened like mud forced through a pipe while her body grew heavier. She felt awkward, uneasy, divorced from her former vigour, and she stumbled with the new weight of her dead flesh through the dream of an ancient past.

That past eventually became the present and seemed to be here for good: various eons had come and gone to leave only this strange garden whose beauty had a magical, haunting quality that permeated the senses.

The garden was crescent-shaped and ran roughly from east to west; it was hemmed in by a forest whose every path led straight back here, and it lay by the side of the broad, placid lake which, in her dreams, Frances had seen as a great dust-filled plain encircled by mountains.

'We're in the past,' she said to Laurence. 'Perhaps the original Garden of Eden. But in my dreams I go back even further — to the real dawn of mankind. In those dreams there are always others present, but I can't see them clearly.'

Her dreams were so vivid they might have been hallucinations — or real events viewed through the haze of a disarrayed mind. She was always in the same place — right here in Eden — but in her dreams the landscape changed as time moved back to an even more distant age.

The great lake would be drained, turning into a dust-filled plain; and beyond, where once the marshes had been, volcanic mountains appeared. There was a fierce, sunless sky — or light so bright that it hazed the sun — and the relentless heat deadened her mind as well as her body.

Yet in that heat, more heat; in that light, a greater light. The light expanded like an opening eye, became a whirlpool in the sky, increasing rapidly in size as it descended and spread out above her. The swirling wind whipped the dust up; the heat scorched her skin. In her dream she always fell on hands and knees to hide her face in the dirt.

God was descending to punish or reward her. God, in His benevolence or wrath, would bring joy or pain. And then the air was filled with strange noise — the music of the spheres — and she tore her hair and gnashed aching teeth as voiceless singing surrounded her.

God roared and pulsated above her, making the very air vibrate, while His angels, rendered featureless in the silvery haze, looked silently at her. Then a brighter light, more heat, the sudden bite of pain, then she usually slipped into a protective daze until they departed ...

The dreams were frightening to recall. Were they dreams or hallucinations? Were they even, in fact, actual events which she wished to deny?

Haunted by such questions, Frances passed them on to Laurence. He simply stared oddly at her, then moved off across the clearing — while Schul, who had been watching them both, offered a mocking grin.

'He thinks you're going crazy,' he said. 'He's just too embarrassed to say so. He's got the hots for you, but he gets frightened when you say those things to him. He thinks you're losing your mind.'

Schul's presence made things worse, causing more fear and dissension. His oddly inhuman lack of concern, his unnatural ability to ignore this miracle, made him seem positively demoniac — perhaps the dream's sole creator. Also, he was threatening, growing more aggressive daily, assuming the mantle of leadership over them and demanding submission.

It was Schul who caught the food, skinned and gutted the fish and animals, showed them how to light the fire, cook the food and generally survive in the forest. Given this, they were dependent upon him, and he knew it and abused it, humiliating them with relentless, cruel mockery and increasing contempt.

'You need me,' he said. 'You *both* need me. And that makes me the king here.'

Surprisingly, given their circumstances, Schul's base concerns remained unchanged; and while Frances suffered her dreams and Laurence retreated into silence, Schul behaved as if their world was perfectly normal and this was merely a camping trip. Untouched by fear or wonder, still wrapped in his former ego, he responded to the situation by merely giving in to his baser appetites. Becoming king of his small domain, he started lusting for further conquests and, in his growing hunger for Frances, invited her into his tent.

'Anytime you want,' he said to her, 'you just crawl right in . . . And you'll want soon enough.'

He had set up the tent near the arch of fig-palms and was turning it into a symbol of his authority. Seemingly undisturbed by being trapped in an alien world, he was intent on utilising it to his personal advantage, and thus, in the shimmering, sunless light of this strange place, he more frequently flaunted the tent to remind them of their dependence upon him.

'You're freezing out there every night,' he said to Frances. 'Come into my tent and share my sleeping-bag. That way we'll *both* keep warm.'

He owned everything else and now he wanted her. Frances knew it and was tempted, even despising herself for her weakness, feeling revolted by Schul's crude animalism but wanting what he could give her: the illusion of security, the warmth of the tent each night, a release from personal responsibility during this frightening experience.

All that, and something else — something that Schul knew all about — the temporary obliteration of the self in ephemeral passion. Yes, she saw herself exposed (she wanted to lie down like a whore) and as the days came and went, as the Garden of Eden became more permanent, her sensuality flared out of the growing fear that she might be trapped here forever.

'You want it,' Schul said, reducing all emotions to basics. 'You're purring like a bitch-cat in heat, which is why you can't sleep at nights.'

She couldn't sleep because of fear — and the fear increased her sexual desire — because the dreams or hallucinations were becoming more real each night. Now, when she lay on the ground in the darkness, Laurence on one side of her, Schul's tent on the other, she was convinced that she was not really sleeping when the world changed about her . . .

The eye of God descended as a whirlpool of pure light, freezing her mind and burning her body as His angels surrounded her. Their voiceless singing split the silence, filled her head and dimmed her thoughts, until she slipped into a daze, experienced more strange dreams, and awakened at dawn to see the trees in the Garden of Eden, Laurence still tossing and turning in restless sleep, no visible movement from Schul's tent.

She started yearning for that tent, desperately wanting its protection, then accepted, with the sorrow of the lost, that Schul would soon have her.

Schul knew it as well, and constantly used it on Laurence, humiliating him by sneering at his unrequited passion for Frances. That passion, which was naked, was rapidly growing stronger; and as each day passed and their mutual fear became contagious, Laurence took refuge in the love he could no longer hide. Schul observed him with amusement, took pleasure from mocking him, rarely missed an opportunity to remind him that his love served no purpose.

'You want her,' he said, 'and you think that's what matters; but what matters is nerve and conviction — and you don't possess those. You think your love will win her — that your respect is enough — but the only thing she wants is sexual heat with someone who knows how to raise it. She may find your innocence touching, kid, but she needs more than that.'

'Shut your filthy mouth!' Laurence replied.

He was frightened of Schul and had little defence against him, but his resentment over what was being said was driving him close to the edge. His hatred, now more obvious, was more frequently stated, and Frances sensed that Schul would soon have the confrontation he so obviously longed for.

Schul wanted to crush Laurence, to break his pride and spirit, and combined with his own lust for Frances that need came to obsess him. He was goading Laurence more often, using Frances as his weapon, and she, even knowing how Laurence felt, knew whom she would go to.

She genuinely despised Schul, yet was forced to face the fact that in the end she would be drawn to his strength. Lord knows, she had always needed it (and had often suffered for it) and now, with her fear growing, stirred by thoughts of her unknown future, she wanted even more to submit to another's will, to lose herself in that particular kind of bondage, swept away by her melting flesh.

'You wouldn't do that, would you?' Laurence eventually asked her, his changing voice reduced to a whisper. 'Not while I'm here?'

'Oh, dear God!' Frances groaned.

Because she knew that she would, that Schul was aware of it, and that nothing would prevent it but the sudden reappearance of the normal world. That was what she was praying for, every day, every hour, but this strange, lovely garden, with its impossible, sunless sky, seemed to have become a permanent feature in an unchanging, alien world.

Apparently they were trapped here, beyond time and space, in a world which bent back upon itself to render former laws meaningless. And as that realisation grew, boring through her disbelief, Frances knew that she would only find escape by erasing herself.

Neither dreams nor hallucinations: she was convinced that they were real, that God's angels, when they came in the night, were as real as this garden. The garden itself was ancient history — it existed in times long gone — but the great swirling light which whipped up the dust was doing so in an even earlier time — at the very dawn of mankind. Only she experienced it (Laurence and Schul both slept through it), but she knew with the certainty of the doomed that the visitations were real.

Real and becoming more so — in body as well as spirit. She now lived in dread of the breaking silence of the night, and quivered when that single, staring eye became a bright light expanding. She had lived then and now — in the past and in the present — but when God breathed upon her, scorching her with His breath, she was cooled by the touch of His angels as they silently studied her.

She surrendered to God as she would soon give in to Schul, neither knowing nor caring what would happen, only wanting protection. She and Laurence thought Schul a demon, an inexplicable, mysterious visitor, whose bizarre arrival in their midst had convinced them that he could not be normal. Indeed, they thought him supernatural — and decidedly evil. And being evil, he was banal, ignoring miracles, concerned with trivia, his conversation revealing his ignorance of all outside himself.

He wanted total obedience — their physical and moral subjugation ... and one particular evening, when they were huddled around the camp-fire, as Schul fried some fish and Frances wearily watched him, he pressed again for the victory which he knew would eventually come to him.

'Not him,' he said of Laurence. 'Not this dumb kid, here. You may respect this kid because he's decent, but you know what you *need*. And what you *need*, lady, is the animal that ruts in your hottest dreams.'

Frances ignored the remark, even knowing it to be accurate, but Laurence, as he usually did when he could not bear such talk, hurriedly walked away from the warm fire to kneel by the lake. Frances glanced at him, saw the slump to his shoulders, then found herself focusing on Schul with her heart beating too fast. He was grinning, his eyes bright with mockery, as he forked the fish in the frying-pan.

'You wanna eat?' he asked her.

'I've lost my appetite,' she replied.

'I don't think so,' Schul said. 'I think that's something you'll always have. You're a woman who wants everything or nothing. I specialise in the type.'

He forked out some fish while Frances glanced across at Laurence and saw him still kneeling by the water with his back turned towards her. He was staring out across the lake, into that darkening, sunless haze, silhouetted where lake and sky were

129

divided by a thin line of marsh reeds.

The descending night was normal — it was not the magical dark mass — but it was falling in this long-ago time to bring dread and confusion. The scenery had stopped changing and was now their sole environment, dominated by this lush, enchanted garden which should not have existed. The evening light was fading, its white haze turning grey, and across it flew brightly-coloured, prehistoric birds whose shadows, gliding along the earth, fell on other strange animals. Time had moved back and forth, constantly crossing its own path, but eventually it had slid to a halt at this particular moment.

Here, all ages met and all places became the one, forming a world beyond imagining and trapping them in it. Yet the fruit and fish were edible, the water clear and pure: they could live here forever if they had to . . . though they tried not to think of that.

Tried not to, but did — as Laurence was doing right now, his gaze focused on the marshes beyond the lake which could not be crossed. He was looking for an exit that no longer existed, praying for a sign that would show the way . . . the way out of this purgatory.

Frances returned her gaze to Schul, staring into his hard, bright eyes. 'Am I crazy?' she asked him. 'Is that it? Am I just going mad?'

Schul handed her a plate of fish. 'Here,' he said. 'Eat. I only like strong, healthy women, so I want you well-fed.'

Frances accepted the plate, but crossed the clearing to give it to Laurence, kneeling beside him by the lake as the greying haze dimmed. Laurence stared at the proffered meal, raised his gaze to her face, took the plate from her with a nod which expressed more than thanks. Then, though he was starving, he picked half-heartedly at the food, but suddenly burst forth with the words that had been locked up inside him.

'What's happening here?' he said. 'Are we dreaming

or awake? Where are we and how long have we been here and *why* are we here? I ask these questions every day and they're driving me crazy — yet what's driving me even crazier is the thought of you surrendering to Schul. He's not human, Frances. He doesn't feel the way we do. No-one human could react as he does to what's happening here. Don't do it, Frances. Promise me that. Not with Schul. Not while *I'm* here.'

Frances was touched, but she simply nodded agreement, then stroked his cheek with shivering fingers and hurried back to the camp-fire. Schul was still there, pouring water on the dying embers; he gave her a crooked grin, then, with a nod, indicated the tent near the fig-palms.

Frances simply stared at him, fascinated by his cold, bright gaze, wondering who he was and where he had come from, then feeling dread when she thought of the possible answers. Schul spoke with a forked tongue and derived his pleasure from inflicting pain, yet Frances knew, even sinking into shame, that she would go to him soon.

'Tonight,' Schul said. 'I feel it in my bones. I'm burning up just to think of it.'

That echo of her own thoughts drove her away from Schul. She stretched out on the rubber-sheet he had lent her and pretended to sleep. *I am burning*, she thought. *My skin is on fire* . . . She opened her eyes again, looked at the sky, saw the stars in the new night. She didn't recognise those stars, but otherwise the sky seemed normal, making her think of her home in London, the view from her bedroom window, the stars cascading down on Hampstead Heath and the trees draped in mist. Then her burning turned to pain, to the bitterness of her loss, and she closed her eyes again to visualise that lost home, hoping to find in that singular image something to cling to. She almost heard her mother's music — a soothing violin or piano — and then the crushing reality of her situation swept her towards sleep . . .

131

It was not a dream this time. The ground was definitely shaking beneath her. She let out a soft, frightened moan, then looked up at the sky. That single eye was descending, growing larger as it dropped lower, becoming a whirlpool of light with brilliant stars in its vortex.

She had to look away, dazzled, burning as if with fever, then she blinked and saw scorched rocks and parched earth where the forest had been. The great lake had disappeared and was now a dust-filled plain. Laurence was running towards her out of an expanding light-haze, his eyes large in the thin wedge of his face, displaying his panic.

No, it was not a dream. Laurence was obviously seeing it, too. Frances looked the other way, at the arch of fig-palms, and saw Schul's tent as a triangular silhouette in the brightening light. The flaps of the tent were beating as the wind swept across it. There was noise — a voiceless singing rising out of bass humming — but she heard Schul cursing loudly inside the tent, which was now shaking visibly.

She was blinded by the light, but felt Laurence close beside her. He grabbed her by the wrist, but she sobbed and jerked away, then jumped up and ran through the streaming haze, past the voiceless singing and distorted, silhouetted, human-shaped figures which were emerging like ghosts from the ether.

Heat. Dazzling radiance. The awareness of beating hearts. The singing was like the music of the spheres, ethereal and magical.

Frances sobbed and fell, moved forward on hands and knees, heard Laurence calling out some kind of plea and then crawled into Schul's tent. 'What the hell ...?' Schul began, his bright eyes staring wildly, his hands reaching out to pull her in and hold her close to him. She felt his racing heart, his body's sweat, flesh and bone, then she buried herself in his embrace as the ground shook again.

'Sonofabitch!' Schul exclaimed, holding her tighter, pulling her down. 'What the hell *is* that out there? What the fuck's going on?'

Frances did not reply but simply sobbed and held him tighter, her fingers sliding under his shirt and digging into his chest. He was muscle and bone, solid, her one contact with the real world, and when the ground stopped its shaking, when the light disappeared, when the fierce heat was replaced by the cold, she still would not let him go.

Her clothes fell easily from her, littering the ground around her body, then Schul pulled her legs apart with brutal urgency and rolled quickly upon her. He entered her immediately, not concerned that she wasn't ready, and she cried out as he pierced her dry tightness and thrust up inside her.

Someone sobbed outside the tent, and she bit her lip, remembering Laurence. The shame whipped her, but could not make her stop as Schul pressed down upon her. *God forgive me. Obliterate me.* She thought of Laurence outside the tent. She knew that he could not avoid seeing what was going on in here.

Strangely, she saw it, too: herself and Schul locked together, two silhouettes, one on top of the other in carnal embrace. *God forgive me for what I'm doing. Obliterate me, for I am shameless.* She heard Laurence sobbing outside, then a sudden, anguished cursing, then footsteps hurrying away towards the lake, leaving silence behind. *Fill me up with your flesh.* Schul was sucking her swollen nipples. She writhed beneath him as his belly rose and fell to slap down on her own. *Don't stop. Destroy me. Let me punish myself with guilt.* She saw Laurence kneeling by the lake, adding his tears to the water.

After this, he would hate her. No forgiveness would be forthcoming. His love would understandably turn to poison and make matters worse. *God, forgive me*, she started thinking, but feeling her body, failed to finish, losing her senses as she melted inside her flesh and plunged into sensation.

Schul was pulling her thighs higher and wider, his fingers kneading her aching skin. Whipped by shame, she obliged; defeated by lust, she surrendered. She arched her spine to give him more, gripped him fiercely, pulled him closer; let him gasp and grunt hungrily in her face as they both became animals.

Obliteration. *Yes! Take me, satan, for I have sinned. Pick me up and cast me down from the heavenly hosts and let me burn in hell's fires.* Weep no more for me. No more.

Frances and Schul writhed in love's convulsions while Laurence wept by the great lake.

CHAPTER TEN

Miles Ashcombe opened his eyes, licked his lips nervously, shuddered and sat upright on the bed, glancing around him.

'Me no fear,' he said, using a primitive form of English. 'Me have courage. Go outside.'

Obviously thinking he was going outside, he swung his legs off the bed, tested the floor with his toes, then very carefully stood up — or as near to standing as he could manage in his present condition.

'Dark now,' he said. 'But light coming. Soon sight will clear.'

Michael observed him through the peephole, again marvelling at what he was seeing, trying to fathom how Ashcombe could have regressed so completely to this primitive state. Ashcombe was not standing properly — he was badly stooped, hands hanging loose. He moved away from the bed, swinging his arms like an ape, his feet barely lifting off the floor, nostrils twitching and sniffing.

Michael was looking at an ape-man. There could be no doubt about it. Miles Ashcombe — reportedly an educated, professional writer, only in his mid-thirties but prematurely grey-haired and aged — had turned into a Neanderthal man in all but physical appearance.

Now, as Michael observed him, he reached the wall

opposite the bed, scratched curiously at it, as if trying to ascertain what it was, then in sudden fury hammered upon it with a white-knuckled, clenched fist. He snarled something and turned away, sniffed the air, glanced at the peep-hole, shambled forward and stared directly at Michael with bright-eyed malevolence.

Looking into those eyes, which were devoid of human feeling, Michael once more experienced fear of the most primitive kind. He tried to hold Ashcombe's gaze — to conquer his fear that way — but those eyes seemed to glow with the chilling light of a strange moon, and Michael turned away, ashamed of himself, his heart racing uncomfortably.

Frank Mullard, the male nurse, had been standing beside him and, holding the door keys in one hand, offered a teasing smile.

'It's okay,' he said, 'you can enter. He's not violent at all.'

'I can tell you don't like me,' Michael replied. 'That's why you're encouraging me to go in there and get my brains smashed out. Seriously, though, how has he been since yesterday?'

Frank's grin widened, then he shrugged his broad shoulders. 'Peaceful,' he said. 'He really *is* okay. He sometimes hammers the wall with his fist, as you've just seen, but he only does that when he's alone. If you go in there, he'll sniff at you and explore you tentatively with his fingers. He'll even try to make conversation, though he still finds that difficult. I think he's puzzled — he's not too sure of who or *what* we are — and he certainly seems to need space to roam in, which is why the walls bother him.'

'He doesn't scare you?' Michael asked.

'I avoid his eyes,' Frank replied. 'But I know what you mean when you say they bother you — they remind me of my very worst nightmares.'

Michael knew what Frank meant and nodded his agreement, thinking of the bad dreams he had suffered since first meeting Ashcombe. The man had more than regressed — he was *inhabiting* the mind and soul of a primitive — and looking into his eyes, with their curiously hard, inhuman brilliance, gave one a feeling of falling into vertiginous depths.

This new Ashcombe was a creature of primal awareness and brute impulse. He had in fact become a part of that same primitive world which either he had witnessed or actually *experienced* when inside the dark mass. Thinking of that, Michael shivered again, starting to doubt his own senses.

He turned back towards the barred door and looked at the peep-hole. Ashcombe was staring straight at him with alien intensity.

'Hello,' Michael said lamely. 'I'm your doctor, Mr Phillips.'

There was no spoken response, merely a quickening of Ashcombe's breathing, a visible widening of those oddly luminous, animal eyes. Michael felt the fear again and quickly walked up to the door, slid the wooden panel back across the peep-hole, then looked at the male nurse.

'Have you heard even *one* sentence in proper English?' he asked.

'No,' Frank replied. 'I'm pretty certain that he's actually *talking* more, but it's still fairly basic. So, are you going in, Doctor?'

'No,' Michael replied. 'Not yet. Talking to him just confuses me. I'm going back to my office to read my notes and then collapse into madness.'

'Sounds like fun,' Frank replied.

Michael returned to his office and noticed, when he walked in, that the sun was sinking over the hills of the heath below. Since his office was already darkening, he switched on his desk-lamp, then leaned over to study his notes.

Scrawled on a piece of paper tucked under his notes was the single question '*Cheryl*?' Seeing it, Michael remembered that for the past week or so he had been trying in vain to contact his daughter. He reached out for the telephone, thought of Ashcombe's fierce gaze, was stabbed by a shaft of familiar fear and decided to try Cheryl later.

Lighting a cigarette, which he had sworn not to do today, he inhaled, blew the smoke out, then squinted down through it at his unusually hesitant, confused notes about his patient, Miles Ashcombe.

Patient is 35 years old. Born and raised in Glastonbury, and still resident there until its disappearance. Never married. Well educated. No prior history of mental disorder. Successful author of speculative books on the more mystical aspects of Glastonbury — the Celts and Druids; Medieval, Christian and Arthurian associations; flying saucers, et al.

Any bearing on present condition?

Even under drugs or hypnosis is convinced he is inhabiting what would seem to be a primitive or prehistoric world. Displays great terror, but speaks normal English. However, when unaffected by drugs or freed from hypnosis, reverts to a very basic form of English, as if only able to express the most simple thoughts — again, perhaps primitive, or even prehistoric.

Possible link between this and subject's literary work? i.e., life-long obsession with ancient past and mythology manifesting itself as an alternate reality induced by trauma caused by experience inside the dark mass.

A form of schizophrenia? Obviously not in the sense of being a 'split personality' but, rather, a withdrawal from reality.

Disassociation? Certainly from the present. Possibly replacing the present with the myths of the past ...

No. More than that. His new 'personality' is too complete and exact for that. He is not 'behaving' but actually 'living' as this strikingly primitive personality. Has in fact been 'taken over' and actually 'sees' that other world, whatever it might be.

The world inside the dark mass? Existing outside the known time-scale? Is it actually possible, as Sampson suggested, that Ashcombe 'experienced' rather than 'witnessed' the past and still thinks he is part of it?

Unacceptable. Not comprehensible. Too removed from known psychological or psychoanalytical theories . . . Yet no positive response to drugs or hypnosis. No sign yet of a reversion to normality.

Present condition: Patient moves and talks like some kind of primitive creature. Possesses certain sensory perceptions lacking in 'civilised' human beings — acute hearing and keen sense of smell — and often displays a kind of mental telepathy — just like certain animals . . . or, according to numerous theories, like our primitive ancestors.

What happened inside the dark mass?

Will Ashcombe recover?

Will he tell . . . ?

Having finished reading the notes, Michael continued to stare down at them, not seeing them, but reading them repeatedly in his weary, confused mind. The light outside was growing darker, the day giving way to evening, and he felt that darkness closing in on his thoughts as if threatening to blot them out. He had worked for ten days on this case (it seemed more like ten months) and now was no nearer to curing his patient than he had been at the start.

He tried to put himself into Ashcombe's shoes, to imagine being inside the dark mass, but to do so was to invite a clammy fear and greater incomprehension. He tried to think of it as a black hole, a void beyond space and time, but that only led into a series of concepts which threatened his reasoning. There was no way to treat Ashcombe — since his condition defied psychology. His affliction, if indeed it was such, was beyond rational analysis.

Michael sighed, feeling impotent, surrendering to an old man's tiredness, his handwritten words blurring before his eyes and forming a mist in his brain. He thought of Ashcombe and the dark mass, remembered his own bad dreams, and was just about to slip into a reverie when the telephone rang.

He picked it up automatically, expecting to hear his secretary, but instead heard the voice of his daughter, Cheryl, sounding unusually nervous.

'Daddy?'

'Cheryl!'

The very sound of her voice was enough to bring the past week rushing back — reminding him of his former wife and what she had told him; of the phone calls he had made in vain every day to Cheryl's flat; and of the calls he had *received* every day from her mother, demanding to know if he had spoken to her. Now, with Cheryl actually on the other end of the line, Michael felt his familial responsibilities impinging upon him again.

'Where are you?' he asked. 'Back in your flat?'

'Yes.'

'I've been trying to get you all week. Your flat-mate didn't seem to know when you were due back, so I rang every day.'

'I was in France.'

'I know that. Your friend did at least know that much. She just didn't know when you were coming back — and you didn't leave a phone number.'

'I forgot.'

'No, you didn't,' Michael said. 'She said you *never* leave your number when you go away these days. Now why would that be?'

'Oh,' Cheryl replied, sounding suspicious. 'I don't know ... I just don't think, I suppose ... So,' she continued, as if collecting her thoughts, 'what was so urgent?'

'I have to talk to you. I think we should meet.'

'Oh, Lord,' she said, trying for a note of levity, 'that sounds so *serious*.'

'It *is* serious.' he replied.

'Is it Mother? Is something wrong?'

'There's nothing wrong with your Mother,' he assured her quickly, 'but she *did* raise the subject.'

There was a hesitant silence at the other end of the line, and Michael, closing his eyes, had a clear picture of Cheryl, biting her lower lip and nervously stroking her blonde hair, sensing that something unpleasant was forthcoming. He thought he heard her breathing, but wasn't sure; then she managed to speak again.

'You mean it's me,' she said.

'Yes,' he replied, 'it's you. Your mother came here to see me.'

This time he *did* hear her breathing, or at least giving an audible sigh, but said nothing, giving her time to think, not wanting to panic her.

'I can't meet you for a few days,' she said, 'so you might as well tell me.'

'You know what it is?'

'I didn't say that. Why don't you tell me?'

At that moment Michael felt the despair of a father who knows he has lost his daughter. There was a sharpening edge to her voice that he could not fail to recognise: she intuitively knew what he was about to say, and was already resisting him.

Feeling like an assassin, Michael took a deep breath. 'All right,' he said, 'I'll get straight to the point. Your mother says you're having an affair with the man you work for — a married man with two children.'

There was no cry of outrage, no faltering denial; only a brief silence and the question: 'How did she know?'

'Christ!' Michael exclaimed.

'Pardon?'

'So it's true!'

'Yes,' Cheryl replied, sounding calm. 'So, how *did* she know?'

'She didn't put a detective on to you, if that's what you mean. She simply happened to use the upstairs phone at the very worst time.'

'Oh,' Cheryl said. 'I see.'

'Yes,' Michael said. 'And now that it's out, I think we should meet and discuss it fully.'

'I don't *want* to discuss it, Daddy.'

'I'm not concerned with what you want. I'm considerably more concerned about your future and what this could do to it.'

'For heaven's sake, Daddy — '

'Don't tell me I'm being silly. I want you and I to have a talk before this goes any further.'

'I don't want to meet you. I don't want to talk about it. You're only going to give me a lot of clichés about how wrong it is. Well, right or wrong I'm involved — and I won't be talked out of it.'

'Let's meet.'

'No.'

'Dammit, Cheryl, don't be so silly! I'm your father and I have a right to talk, so don't give me this nonsense!'

Having just warned her not to use the word 'silly', he felt silly at using it himself. God, he sometimes hated emotions — for the lack of commonsense they engendered — but when it came to his beloved daughter's welfare, his objectivity failed him.

'I won't meet you,' Cheryl said, after what seemed like a long time. 'I'll talk to you on this phone anytime — but I'm not going to meet you.'

'A married man. Christ, why a *married* man?'

'There *are* no 'whys', Daddy. These things just happen — which is something you certainly know.'

'What does that mean? Is it a reference to my *own* love-life? If so, it's decidedly out of place in this particular context. You're not my age — you're still only twenty — and you're involved with a married man.'

'So?'

'Stop sounding petulant. Now tell me: just how *serious* is this affair?'

'It's serious.'

'On his part? Or just on yours?'

'He's serious.'

'Has he said that?'

'He doesn't have to. I know it.'

'Is he willing to leave his wife and children?'

'Why should he? I haven't asked him to. Oh, for God's sake, this — '

'How serious is it with *you*, then? Tell me that.'

'I love him.'

'Oh, Christ!'

'I don't expect you to understand.'

'I understand that he's married and has two children not much younger than you.'

'That isn't fair, Daddy!'

'Where's this affair going to end? How long can you continue to love this man who returns home each night?'

'It's not important at this stage.'

'How do you feel when he goes home? Do you wonder what he's like with his wife and children? Do you dream of his leaving them!'

'Oh, Daddy! You *bastard!*'

The line went dead abruptly and he knew she had slammed the phone down.

Shocked, he simply stared at his own phone as if examining a bomb. He only did it for a moment, but it seemed a lot longer, then feeling angry and hurt he dialled her number again.

'Yes,' she said, very quickly and nervously.

'Cheryl, it's me again.'

'I don't want to — '

'Cheryl, listen to me for a moment. Neither your mother nor I would normally interfere in such a personal matter, but in this case it's clearly very necessary. Your personal life is your own, and in the end you'll have to run it, but you can't expect your mother or I to keep our mouths shut when it comes to something we know is very wrong. No good can come of this, Cheryl. This isn't just another boyfriend. The very fact that you're having an affair with a *married* man is proof that you're serious. I know you, Cheryl. You're still relatively immature. You're very easily impressed and far too dependent on others — and falling for an older man with children is, sad to say, your misguided way of dealing with your own weaknesses. Being older, he gives you a sense of security; being married he absolves you from any decisions regarding your future. But it won't work, Cheryl, because your own love will trap you; sooner or later, you'll want him as a permanent fixture in your life — and when you do, you'll probably find that he doesn't want *you* — and that's when the real pain will start. Don't let yourself become his mistress, Cheryl. If you do, you'll be finished.'

She was silent for some time and again he imagined seeing her: doubtless leaning against the wall, biting her lower lip, blushing, perhaps stroking the blonde hair out of her eyes in her insecure manner. Thus imagining her, he loved her, with a pure, anguished heart, and felt the rising tide of his contempt for the man who was using her.

'All right,' she finally said, her voice quavering with nervousness. 'You've had your uninterrupted say, and now I'm going to hang up.'

'Let's meet.'

'No.'

'Dammit, Cheryl, just for a *talk*!'

'I don't want to talk about it, Daddy. I want to live my own life.'

'I'm not stopping you doing that. I'm just trying to protect you.'

'I don't want your protection. I don't need it. I'll deal with this in my own way.'

'The only way to do that is to leave your job *and* your boss.'

'I won't do that, and that's all there is to it. I'm hanging up now.'

'Cheryl, *meet* with me!'

'No.'

'Then I'll come to see you.'

'No!'

'Damn you, I'll come without an invitation! I won't be put off this way!'

'Don't do that, Daddy! If you do, I'll never speak to you again! Do you understand? *I mean that!*'

'Then when am I next going to see you?'

'When I call. Goodnight, Daddy.'

The line suddenly went dead and he knew she had hung up again. He put his own phone back on its cradle and stared out the window. The sky was dark and cloudy; the streetlamps below were lit. He studied the people in Pond Street, watched cars and buses pass, then raised his gaze to look at the darkened hills and the moon high above them.

He shivered, feeling helpless, thinking of Ashcombe and Cheryl, two problems that now dominated his life and cast their shadows across him. One problem was very human, brutally painful yet commonplace; but the other came from outside normal experience and suggested the magical.

Michael felt exhausted, drained by fear and confusion, but his thoughts kept bouncing back and forth between Cheryl and Ashcombe. The father in him was hurt, the psychologist rendered impotent, and he grieved that the vanity of man could transcend even miracles.

Miracles? Yes, the Glastonbury event could be so classified. And he, a normal father with very human concerns, had to deal with his personal problems whilst wrestling at the same time with the seemingly insoluble riddle of an extraordinary happening.

Still shaking from the vehemence of his beloved daughter's rejection, Michael sighed, rubbed his eyes, stood up and walked from his office. He went straight to the psychiatric wing, to the door with the sliding panel, slid the panel open and looked in.

Ashcombe was sitting upright on the bed, returning his stare.

He stared at Michael for a long time, hardly blinking at all. He was sitting up very straight, his shoulders no longer slumped; and his eyes, even from where Michael stood, were still visibly bright.

Michael said nothing. He was waiting for Ashcombe's speech. He waited for a long time, but Ashcombe said nothing, so eventually, unlocking the door with his own key, Michael entered the cell.

'Good evening,' he said.

Ashcombe stared at him with diamond-bright, insane eyes, then offered a slow, macabre smile and climbed to his feet. He took a deep breath, glanced left and right, sniffed a little, then gave that frightening smile again and slowly advanced.

Michael shivered instantly, surrendering to fear, even though he sensed that Ashcombe would not harm him and only wanted to talk. Nonetheless, the fear gripped him, squeezing the breath from his lungs, and he felt his senses slipping away to render him helpless.

He looked into Ashcombe's eyes and saw the unknown in their depths. He stood there, quite numb, his fear giving way to passivity, and only noticed that two hands not his own were being raised in the air. Those hands waved very gently, fingers opening and closing, as if trying to grasp something invisible and crush the life out of it. Then they fell onto his shoulders. He felt the strength of restless fingers. He was shaken and just as quickly released and saw Ashcombe's macabre smile.

'I know you,' Ashcombe said. 'You have been there as well. Soon, in the near future, you will go back to where you have come from. Me tired. Me sleep long night.'

Ashcombe turned back to the bed, his shoulders slumping again. He fell into a pool of inky shadow and seemed to sleep instantly.

Michael stood there like a man on a gallows — awaiting his doom.

CHAPTER ELEVEN

God did not return to Eden, but other things remained, most notably the daily sunless haze and Schul's merciless dominance. Having possessed Frances, he had stripped Laurence of his will-power and now used him for labour or sport, with a Pharoah's contempt. Frances saw it and was ashamed, knowing what had broken Laurence, but she now shared Schul's tent on a regular basis and had little to say.

At last they had all accepted that they might be here forever. The dark mass no longer surrounded them, the scenery no longer changed, but since all of them had jointly experienced the last manifestation, they now believed implicitly that they were indeed caught in a nightmare.

Even Schul was frightened, although he refused to show it. The deeper his fear grew, the more autocratic he became. As his secret desperation increased, his attacks on Laurence grew worse.

'She's mine,' he said of Frances. 'This bitch now belongs to me. She and I share the tent, and you sleep outside, and if I ever catch you looking at her sideways I'll cut your throat with this knife. We're probably here for life, see? We'll probably stay here till we die. So don't think I'm gonna worry about what I do, 'cause laws don't mean shit here.'

Laurence did not reply — he rarely did anymore — but he quivered with the rage of the helpless and lowered his gaze. He now lived as a ghost, with the slave's natural invisibility, complying with every demand, shouldering every injustice, but quietly boiling in the vats of his resentment and nurturing his hatred.

Frances knew that when she saw him, but tried to forget it, avoiding his soulful gaze whenever possible and retreating into herself. Just as much a slave as Laurence, she not only shared Schul's bed, but suffered the many humiliations heaped upon her, both mental and physical.

'Do it this way,' Schul said.

'Oh, Christ,' Frances replied. '*Please!*'

'Shut up, you bitch, and do as I say. You'll soon learn to like it.'

Frances sought release in dreams, in those visions of descending light, feeling terror, but also yearning for salvation from the hell she was in. When she thought about it, she felt crazy, convinced that there was no hope, and she sensed that she was about to explode out of her steadily mounting dread. She had almost lost her old self, and had actually watched it vanishing, awakening each morning to find less of herself to take hold of. The Garden of Eden was her new home, unchanging, inescapable, and the lake that stretched out to the horizon only led straight back here.

The vegetation was lush and luminous; the water crystal-clear. The whole place was impossibly beautiful — and decidedly unreal. Surrounding her, it drained her, turning her into someone else: a more primal version of the woman she had once been: a creature physically sluggish and mentally dull, hardly knowing her own name. Yet that creature knew fear — a fear of everything outside herself — fear of water and sky, of the demon-darkness, of Schul's swift retribution.

'Take your clothes off,' he said. 'Let's do it now. I want it right here.'

'Oh, God, no!' she protested. 'Not here. Not in the open. Not with Laurence sitting over there. Even you, Schul . . . not *that!*'

'Take them off or I'll rip them off, you bitch. I want it here and right now.'

The first time, when she tried refusing, he slapped her face and ripped her clothes off; the next time she didn't bother trying and scarcely knew what was happening. Nonetheless, she heard Laurence weeping and saw him fleeing into the forest. He was gone a long time — doubtless trying to escape — but returned in despair a few hours later, prepared for his punishment.

Schul had made a whip from marsh reeds and he punished Laurence with it. Laurence bit his lip and whimpered, but made no other sound; and when Schul let him go he nursed his wounds in the lake's healing water.

Thereafter it became normal practice — Schul enjoyed the open air — and he and Frances fornicated in the clearing while Laurence tried not to look at them. Frances felt like an animal, dull-witted and egoless; but sometimes, with Schul heaving on top of her, she would hear the sky's silent screaming — a lament that actually came from within herself to justify her humanity.

Very much a lost humanity, remembered only in fleeting moments, a question-mark flicking at her thoughts as lightly as feathers. Such moments were very bad, giving rise to dark emotions, making her feel that she was looking into an abyss of bottomless darkness. To drop into it would be fatal — she would drown in her own memories — and those memories would drive her into the madness of an utterly vain hope.

'We're on our own now,' Schul said. 'We're the only three here. I'm lord of the whole goddamned universe, and you two are my people. Laurence is my servant, and my descendants will come from you. The world begins and ends in this place — and my word is law.'

This was too much for Laurence and actually made

him display some spirit. 'That's blasphemy!' he hissed with eyes blazing. 'I won't let you say such things!'

This time Schul used his fists, beating Laurence very badly, then kicking him when he finally fell to the ground, gasping with pain. It was a highly professional beating, causing no visible damage, and Frances sensed that Laurence had not really tried to resist.

This was common to her *and* Laurence: they had both lost pride and willpower. The bizarre experience through which they were living had rendered them powerless. It had simply overwhelmed them, destroying confidence and self-esteem, making them retreat into themselves and live for each moment.

Even Schul had changed — though in quite the opposite way. He had responded to his new world by taking command of it, escaping from his fear and bewilderment by giving vent to his cruelty.

So it was that they existed like savages in paradise, with Frances and Laurence living only to be ruled, Schul to be ruler.

God did not return, but Frances often looked for Him — on the one hand terrified that He might actually reappear, on the other yearning desperately for salvation from the hell of her new life.

God was the sunless sky and the light-reflecting lake; he was also the stars that shone at night and the wind in the marsh reeds. God was neither here nor there, but was simply hope and promise, He who could cast out the night to let the dawn break. Schul now thought that *he* was God — and in one sense he was — but to Frances, in the dimness of her reasoning, earth and sky were her masters. He was of the earth and water, and His voice was the wind, but when He came back, which she knew must happen eventually, He would come from the sky.

'Eat!' Schul commanded, tearing white flesh from fish-bones, throwing the lesser morsels to Laurence as if feeding a dog. 'Eat!' he snarled at Frances, his voice oddly distorted and hollow. 'You hardly eat a thing anymore and look like a skeleton. So, eat! I like my women fatter. I want something worth holding.'

Frances did as she was told, then lay down to be used, was then allowed to wash herself in the lake while Laurence muttered nearby. Laurence now looked like an ape (perhaps she did, as well), but his eyes held the fire of a zealot who was finding his cause. He still believed in God — his original God from remembered times — and he heard Schul's every word as a blasphemy deserving of punishment.

A flicker of will was returning to Laurence. It was the glow of spiritual faith. He was being shaken out of his paralysis by the strength of his outrage. Also, there was a primal sexual hunger. Laurence, one of the only two men on earth, wanted the earth's only woman.

'Why him?' he said. 'Me!'

Frances stared at him, bewildered. He had not spoken to her for many moons and now his voice sounded different.

'Me?' she asked. 'You?'

'Me better,' Laurence said.

Frances didn't think it sounded like speech at all, but that's what she heard him say.

'Bad,' she replied. 'Trouble. No speak. Go now you.' And she turned, when he looked blankly at her, and crawled back into Schul's tent.

So time moved or stood still in this place where time was not, while the landscape, which was not of their own time, remained constant and startling. Frances felt the earth's heartbeat, heard its whispering voice night-times, sensed the living creatures forestwise with her nose, worshipped silently earth and sky. She lived by dream and instinct, her senses flowing to the light and colour, knowing terror and exultation without reason and surrendering helplessly.

She was not herself at all, and yet part of her

151

remained. She now lived with the instincts of a primitive, but still recognised human things.

Mostly Laurence and Schul: she knew their names and who they were, knew that Schul had not always owned her and that Laurence now wanted her. Schul and Laurence fought a lot. Or at least, Schul beat Laurence. Schul now liked to draw blood from Laurence when he lay in the dirt.

'I kill him,' Laurence said, his voice throttled by his leaning shoulders. 'Silent I make him. And still. And then God can return.'

Frances whimpered and tried to hide, but Schul found her soon enough, roughly rolling her onto her back and pushing her legs apart. She thought of silence as he moved inside her, tried to visualise him as nothing; but his presence permeated her whole being and made her cling to him. She was then rolled onto her belly and he took her that way also. She felt the earth's heartbeat through her breasts and was touched with the spirit. She saw time passing through her. The fecund garden turned to barren rocks. The glittering lake became a great plain over which dust-clouds drifted.

Edinu, meaning 'plain'. Its whispered name gave it life. She was taken from the rear in the dust while her own kind surrounded her. Neither caring nor looking at her, huddled by firewarmth, shoulders stooped, grunting words that had once made sense to her as he panted behind her. She felt something flooding her insides, making her heavy body shake, then she squealed and crawled away, released from his hungry hands, and gratefully huddled whimpering in the rock-hole, filled with food-thoughts and slavering.

She raised her gaze to the sky, which was a dazzling white haze. She was blinded by the light, rubbed her eyes and saw Schul when she opened them.

'Good,' Schul growled. 'Feel better. Soon night-time we hide.'

They always hid at night-time, lying together in the

tent, now terrified that God and His angels might come back to route them. Even Schul, who ruled the earth, feared the dark ones from the sky, and ashamed, he would take it out on Laurence, beating him viciously. Laurence sometimes fought back, but always bled and lost his pride; on other occasions he did not fight at all, but merely stood there and took it.

His bright blood frightened Frances, as did his burning eyes. He stared at her with hunger and rage, then tore the bark from the trees.

'Me weak,' he whispered. 'He strong. Me need strength in hand.'

Dimly aware of what was happening, Frances lived in growing fear, her gaze focused frequently on the sky from which God might descend. The eye of God did not appear, nor did His light or angels, but she prayed that He might intervene before it was too late.

Laurence shuffled to and fro, his shoulders stooped, his gait awkward, and Frances noticed the hunger making his nostrils flare when he came too close to her. Schul saw that, also, and usually snarled his resentment; then, if Laurence failed to retreat immediately, he savagely beat him. Laurence often licked his bloody wounds, whimpering under the fig-palms; and the bright light, when his eyes moved out of the shadows, illuminated his growing rage.

'Kill!' he hissed. 'Need stronger hand. Disappear him. Forever!'

Schul knew what was happening and started beating Laurence more brutally; then, because he knew that Laurence wanted her, turned his fists on Frances as well. She received the blows silently, but in sullen, rising resentment, aware that Laurence was trembling with anger, his fists opening and closing. Later, she smiled at him, scarcely knowing what that implied, and he responded by stroking her arm with his enlarged, hairy hand.

'You, me,' he whispered. 'Soon to be. When his

153

silence is always. Kill him with stronger hand.'

He found his strong hand soon enough, in the shape of a thick, gnarled branch, picking it up when his rage flared out of control and he had to give vent to it.

It happened during the great change, when fear tore them all apart, when Schul realised that the change was taking them back to the present — to where he could not have dominion and would be just like other men.

Schul saw his own end in that.

The sunless sky had darkened and night lay upon the lake when Frances, placing her ears to the ground, heard the earth's quickening heartbeat. Startled, she jerked upright, saw Schul's coarse-haired body beside her, heard God's voice whispering on the wind and started to crawl from the tent.

Awakened, Schul grabbed at her, his free hand on his stiffened member, but she kicked him, hardly knowing what she was doing, and hurried into the cold night.

Schul's frustrated snarl pursued her, but was swept away on the wind, and still on hands and knees, Frances looked up and was stunned by the stars.

Stars streaming and cascading, forming waterfalls and pools, curving into immense loops and coils which blended into a brilliant haze.

Frances whimpered and clutched the grass, felt the earth's quickening heartbeat, saw Laurence, eyes skyward, reaching out to pull her close to him. The surrounding land was changing, as was the lake and sky, with alien flowers blooming and dying to be reborn, the distant marshes altering subtly to become more familiar, and the stars, in their multiplicity and brilliance, forming patterns that soon became recognisable as those of the former world.

The ground shook as its heart raced, the darkness glowed and pulsated strangely, then a snarling Schul crawled speedily from his tent and stared around him in wonder.

Lost. All lost. He was losing everything he had gained. As his slightly bestial, snarling face became more human, he glanced up at the changing sky.

He recognised the stars of earth. His shocked expression revealed that much. He saw that time was moving again and returning them to the normal world, but that was something he no longer wanted, nor could possibly deal with.

Schul sat back on his haunches, raised his face to the sky, then howled in the anguish of his loss. He was baying at the moon, letting it know he had seen it, outraged that it should suddenly have returned to that glittering, normal sky. He tore the grass from the soil, shoved it into his shivering lips, spat it out again, then looked at Frances and howled even louder.

His changing form was striped by moonlight. Frances saw his human skin. She felt the sluggishness leaving her own body, and touched her raw, newborn flesh. Laurence sobbed and leaned forward, pressing his forehead to the ground, quivering as he thanked God for this deliverance from the bondage of frozen time.

Schul snarled and vented his rage, swinging his left fist in an arc, the blow slapping Frances' face sideways and making her cry out. Then Schul was upon her, tearing away her flimsy rags, trying to force her unwilling legs apart in order to take her one last time. Frances struggled and screamed in protest, now aware of her true identity, and Laurence, lifting his forehead from the ground, stared at them with startled eyes.

'No!' he cried. '*Not again!*'

It was then, as a snarling Schul turned away from Frances, that Laurence took hold of the thick, gnarled branch that had been lying on the ground beside him, and, with his body arched, silhouetted against the moonlit lake, raised the weapon high above his head. Schul was already halfway through the air, his greedy hands outstretched, when Laurence, with a quavering, high-pitched, almost feminine wailing, brought the branch down on his skull, making Schul careen sideways and roll over on the grass with blood already splashing from his first wound.

It was the first but not the last, since as Schul attempted to rise again, Laurence repeatedly struck him over the head and face with a fury which, accompanied by his peculiar, demented wailing, merely emphasised the extent of his long-buried resentment and anguish.

Frances screamed at Laurence to stop, hardly believing what she was seeing, but Laurence kept striking Schul with that terrible, helpless rage, sobbing even as he was doing it, aware of his guilt. Schul's hands dropped to his sides, revealing a head like a pomegranate, then as Frances finally managed to pull Laurence away, Schul fell onto his side, tried in vain to get up again, shuddered in a long, drawn-out spasm, fell back and was still.

Spent by his own violence, Laurence dropped the bloody branch, sat back on his haunches, and stared at Schul's prostrate body with wide, disbelieving eyes. Frances also stared at Schul, her senses returning to her; she was aware of what that terrible stillness meant, but reluctant to dwell on it.

She studied Schul's bloody head, then the stars glittering above, then looked out and saw that the lake was the one she had known in former days.

The familiar disorientated her, ironically making her feel more unreal, but she managed at last to explore Schul with professional fingers. *I'm a nurse*, she thought wonderingly. *I'm back to being what I was before.* Her experienced fingers examined Schul's bloody skull, then fell on his naked chest. Schul's heart was still. He was silent. And that silence was permanent.

'He's dead,' she said, speaking in her normal voice.

'Are you sure?'

'Yes. You've killed him.'

Laurence had also returned to normal, but seemed completely dazed, and he covered his face with his

156

hands and sobbed for what he had done. Frances, in a similar turmoil, her relief destroyed by shock, went to him, put her arms around him and held him close to her. He wept like a real person — returned to consciousness and conscience, to the very human awareness of his guilt regarding the murder — then, in that same awareness, he glanced wildly around him, studied the lagoon for some time, before returning his attention to Frances, breathing into her face.

'We've got to get rid of him!' he said. 'And we've got to do it immediately!'

'The lake,' Frances replied, surprised by her own words. 'Let's take the raft and drop him into the lake and then get out while we can.'

'Yes!' Laurence exclaimed gratefully. 'Let's do that! *God forgive us, let's do it!*'

Frances would not forget the next few hours for as long as she lived. Together, she and Laurence dragged the bloody remains of Schul across the grass to the water's edge, where the crude raft was swaying gently against the bulrushes, its wooden planks bathed in moonlight. Schul was very heavy and his head was a ghastly mess, so Laurence gagged and retched while Frances sobbed and they dragged the corpse after them. Although the night was cold, they were soon drenched in sweat, and as they manhandled Schul onto the bobbing raft, they were both gasping painfully.

Frances felt her old self returning and exposing her to guilt, but as she rested on hands and knees on the rolling, creaking raft, trying to get back her breath as she leaned over Schul's body, she gazed out across the lake and almost wept for joy when she recognised the outline of the far shore, which would lead to Al Qurna.

The world had returned to normal, but she still dwelt in fear, aware that the dark mass could return at any moment and plunge her back into the same nightmare. Taking a deep breath, she looked down at Schul's eyes

— two dead orbs reflecting the moonlight with wide-open, blind clarity.

Frances jerked upright and turned away quickly. She sat back on her haunches, refusing to believe what was happening, while Laurence, occasionally sobbing, once throwing up on the bank, hacked off lengths of bulrush and tied them around heavy stones, then tied the same stones to the lifeless Schul, some to his wrists and ankles, others around his waist and neck. When Laurence had finished, Schul looked monstrous, a Neanderthal man preserved in stone, and Frances shivered and took another deep breath, trying to swallow her horror.

Moonlight striped the water and lent the ripples a silvery quality as Laurence rowed the raft out into the lake. He seemed calmer now, but his eyes were dazed and disbelieving; and occasionally he wiped tears from his cheeks and glanced down at the dead Schul.

Frances also studied Schul, shivering each time she did so, wondering obsessively who he had been, trying to accept that Laurence had murdered him, and haunted by the knowledge that she was about to become a partner in the crime. She could not believe that this was she — Frances Devereux, of London, England; once a mature, 35-year old woman and respectable doctor.

Shaken even more, she studied the far shore of the lake, her gaze following the line of marsh reeds where they curved back to rejoin the Shatt al Arab river and the rest of the land she knew so well. The sight of the marshes overwhelmed her, filling her with longing; but when she glanced up at the sky and saw familiar stars, she found herself waiting fearfully for them to change and plunge her back into hell.

'God,' she murmured, 'just let me get out of here. I just want to go home.'

'Here!' Laurence snapped. '*Here!*'

He was obviously lost for words, his moonlit face

white and strained, his eyes glazed with shock and disbelief. He stared about him like a startled deer, first at Schul, then at the lake; and Frances, following his gaze, saw the water rippling in silvery lines around the sides of the raft. The water was very black, but reflected the large white moon. The moon seemed to be very deep in the water and drawing everything to it.

Laurence pushed Schul's body overboard, so quickly that Frances missed it. She just heard the splash and looked down to see the body rolling over with the weight of the stones and sinking under its own waves. The waves bubbled and gurgled, then turned into a small whirlpool, resembled water being sucked down a plug-hole, then became still again.

Frances shuddered and closed her eyes, imagining Schul's body, wrapped in bulrushes, weighted with stones, sinking silently into the cold, eternal darkness of his watery grave. When she opened her eyes again, she saw Laurence, bathed in sweat, his face anguished.

'Are you all right?' she asked him.

'I feel feverish,' he replied. '*Oh, dear God!*'

He covered his face with his hands and wept. Eventually, when he managed to control himself, he took the oar in his shaking hands and rowed the raft on towards the far bank. Once there, he followed the shoreline, heading south towards Al Qurna, finally leaving the lake behind and heading along the placid river, between rustling rows of fig-palms.

The darkness gave way to light, the dawn to bright morning, while Frances, feeling haunted by what had happened, tried to conquer her trembling. The sky was a white sheet, but no longer sunless, and she had to shade her eyes to see the clouds drifting over the tree-tops. The raft passed waterside villages, hump-backed buffaloes and other canoes; and gradually, as such familiar scenes closed in about her, she felt herself returning to sanity and a certain control.

Then she heard a descending roaring, glanced up and

was dazzled, collapsed into a well of fresh terror as the noise grew louder above her. She screamed 'No!' and was whipped by wind. The raft rocked and water splashed her. Gusts of hot air were suddenly whipping around her, then settling down again.

Frances sobbed in despair and fear, imagining God descending upon her. When she thought of what she might have to endure again, she came close to hysteria.

Then she felt hands on her shoulders. Someone was shaking her and shouting. Feeling hysterical, she opened her eyes and saw Laurence in front of her, holding her and shouting to calm her down. She licked her lips and held onto his shoulders, letting him know she was all right.

The roaring above was diminishing as God ascended on high again. Frances glanced up, shading her eyes, and saw the brilliant light shrinking, first flaring out of that roaring mass in silvery striations, then disappearing back into a duller core beneath large, beating wings.

Not wings: rotor-blades. The sunlight was actually flaring out around an ascending dome; and the dome, made of metal and glass, was reflecting the sunlight.

Someone was leaning out of that dome. Frances saw a white hand waving. She gasped in relief, then fell back into Laurence's arms, laughing hysterically in the realisation that it was actually a helicopter above her.

The rescue team had arrived.

PART TWO: THE PRESENT

CHAPTER TWELVE

Home. Frances Devereux, a mature, 35-year old woman and respectable doctor wearing a buttoned-up grey trenchcoat, slacks and high-heeled leather boots and looking a little older than her years, stood on the summit of Hampstead Heath and stared abstractedly out over the green hills of the Vale of Health at the spires and concrete towers of distant London. *Home*, she thought. *Thank God. Now it all seems so unreal.* She shuddered as a gust of wind slapped her, then started walking.

The winding, well-trodden path led her away from the sounds of traffic and down into the soothing silence of the Vale of Health. She was further soothed by the birdsong, but not entirely so, since to a passing stranger she would have seemed nervous — blinking too much, her gazing roaming restlessly, her right hand constantly brushing at her hair where it fell on her forehead. *God,* she thought, *I've aged. I'm not the woman I used to be.* She hesitated on the lower slopes, studied the sky that Constable had painted, then made her way into the tiny street named Byron Villas, stopping in front of the home of D. H. Lawrence.

The famous writer had lived here in 1915 with Frieda von Richhofen, the woman who had eloped with him three years earlier. It was, according to Lawrence, the year the old world ended; and Frances, thinking about that in an attempt to forget her own recent experience, was only reminded that her personal 'old world' had ended in Mesopotamia. *I cannot forget*, she thought. *The world conspires to remind me of it*. And she trembled again, this time untouched by the wind, then walked away from the dead writer's home to circle the pond.

She could not forget it, although she tried during these walks, breathing deeply of the damp English air and enjoying the grass underfoot. Yet everything reminded her of it — a glint of sunlight, a bird-call, the very grass she enjoyed underfoot — and now, as she circled the pond, looking down at the English bulrushes, she was reminded of the bulrushes of the marshes in southern Iraq.

They said we were missing for twenty-four hours, but it must have been longer than that. We spent months there. We aged. We changed . . . Yet they said it was only twenty-four hours.

She continued walking around the pond, distracting herself by trying to visualise this place as it had originally been — not a vale of health, but a very unhealthy swamp that had to be drained before being turned into a second reservoir to the town's water supply. *An unhealthy swamp*, she thought, then remembered the marshes of Eden, the dark line of reeds around the lake where time had played bizarre games.

How long had she been back? A month? Two months? It hardly made any difference to her, since she dreamed of it constantly.

Home, she thought as she cut across East Heath, heading towards the twin pools of Heath Pond. *There is no such place as home anymore . . . and there never will be*. She felt broken in mind and spirit, robbed of her sense of reality, and knew that she would now be aware of time for as long as she lived.

Time — and mortality. The prismatic face of the eternal present. She had gone back in time and returned again, so now had to learn to live as two people. *What time was it that I inhabited? What kind of creature was I then? What dream did I have of God's eye coming down from the heavens?* She felt cold just to remember it, numbed by its awesome nature, realising that the present, this very moment, was less real than the dream.

She soon passed the two ponds where people were fishing beneath the cyprus trees, a scene so unchanging that Constable had painted virtually the same one in the early 1820s.

Unchanging? she thought. *A mere century and a half ago. And the Tudors actually made the ponds with water that came from the River Fleet; and before that, the river was a sea, and before that ...*

Dear God. Before that, more changes. And other changes before them. Time moving back to eons yet unknown, to the very birth of the dawnlight ...

Frances passed the ponds, trying to stop her nervous blinking, then hurried through the ugly car-park beyond until she arrived at East Heath Road. Still not used to the city traffic, she glanced left and right, kept doing so for a long time, eventually managed to find a gap between roaring vehicles and darted across.

She passed the garden of the Freemasons Arms, then the mock-Tudor main building, contemplated going in for a drink, but decided against it. *Too much drinking lately*, she thought. *And it only makes things worse.* Thus determined but feeling deprived, and therefore wanting a drink even more, she walked along the elegant Downshire Hill until she came to her own gate. She put her hand on the latch, started opening it, hesitated. *Home*, she thought. *Think of it that way. It's all you have left now.* Then she pulled the latch down, opened the gate and walked up the garden-path.

Home was an elegant Regency villa with elaborately wrought-iron balcony railings around the windows, finely gabled sloping roofs, and gardens profuse with shrubbery, trees and flowers. Inside, the house had an

165

air of genteel decay, with large, high-ceilinged rooms, a lot of very valuable antique furniture, and white-painted walls covered by paintings and books, most of which were the works of the notably famous Hampstead residents, past and present.

Standing in the hallway, glancing up the charming stairwell, Frances felt like the little girl she had been long ago. There was the sound of music — as there seemed to have been every day of her life — and she instantly recognised Handel's *Largo*, played superbly on a good piano. She listened for a moment, then walked along the hall, into the music-room where her mother was playing.

Her mother was small and slim, with a weather-beaten, bird-like beauty, her face flushed and webbed with lines, grey hair piled on her head and pinned together with ebony combs of a colouring that perfectly matched her Victorian dress. She was perched on a piano-stool and appeared to be an extension of it, her cigarette smouldering in the ash-tray on top of the Steinway.

She was playing the *Largo* with great tenderness, leaning forward in a dreamy manner, but she sensed immediately that someone had entered the room, which made her turn towards Frances. Her eyes, unusually large, were as blue as a summer's sky, focusing intently on Frances, but with no great surprise.

'Ah,' she said, 'my daughter is back. I thought it might be a rapist.' She stopped playing and returned Frances' smile as she placed her hands on her lap. 'So,' she said, 'you had another walk.'

'Yes,' Frances said.

Her mother sighed histrionically. 'I don't know how you stand all that bird-shit and those men in their gaberdines.'

'You don't have to try to shock me, Mother. I'm too old for that, now.'

'No-one's ever too old to be shocked — and it *can* be

166

therapeutic.' Mrs Devereux, who at sixty-one years old was still filled with aggressive energy, raised herself from the piano-stool and walked across the room to the drinks cabinet.

'Did you drop into the Freemasons Arms for a drink?' she asked.

'No,' Frances replied.

'Then I'll reward you with a little dry sherry.'

'You're too generous,' Frances said.

Her mother smiled fleetingly, put on a pair of spectacles, then peered owlishly at the well-stocked drinks cabinet. 'A little *amontillados*,' she said, picking up one of the bottles. 'That should be safe enough.' She filled up two glasses and gave one to Frances. 'I'm only generous,' she said, sampling her drink, 'because I had to have one myself — so you needn't feel guilty.'

'I don't feel guilty.. It's just that you've recently been nagging me about my drinking.'

'Naturally, dear, I *nag*. I *nag* because you start drinking at noon and don't stop until bedtime. *Nagging* is what mothers are *for*, dear.'

Frances smiled, though she didn't feel good-humoured. 'I've only been doing that since I returned from Iraq. I never did it before.'

'The point, my child, is that you're *doing* it — and I simply won't stand for it.'

Frances had a sip of sherry, then after removing her trench-coat, sat in a chair and lit a cigarette.

'My,' she said, blowing smoke out, 'I *do* love this house.'

'Naturally,' her mother replied. 'Your father had exquisite taste in all things. The name Devereux, after all, is the family name of the viscounts Hereford and, though we may not be immediately related, we *are* surely connected, so it's understandable that we should be a family of distinction.'

'You're such a snob, Mother.'

'Perhaps. Perhaps not. But I *do* wish that your father

hadn't died so early and left you without a man to look up to.'

'Mother!'

'All right! I won't start!'

Mrs Devereux walked away from Frances and sat on the sofa opposite, her back turned to the French windows which, overlooking the rear garden, framed wisteria and wildflowers. Frances thought of her childhood, fatherless, filled with love, then saw her mother, radiantly beautiful and spoiled, a long time ago. Time moved back and forth, both in memory and speculation, and now, studying her mother, Frances was filled with love and despair. Her mother was beauty ravaged, spirit turned into eccentricity, a lovely creature reaching the end of her life and trying to keep her head high.

'About the drink,' Frances said. 'I still have bad dreams and I need the drink to relax me ... to help me forget them.'

'Too much drink will only make the dreams worse,' her mother replied. 'And what you need to make you forget is a decent man — not your usual low types.'

'I don't think we should be discussing my taste in men, Mother.'

'Why on earth not? I should think that *any* mother would show an interest in her daugher's love-life, particularly if it seemed a trifle *bizarre*, as yours surely does.'

'Any bizarre traits I must have picked up from you.'

'I do not have a love-life, and haven't had one for years, so you certainly picked up nothing from me in *that* particular field. You're such an intelligent woman in every other respect — but your men! Dear, oh dear! There's a touch of the masochist in you — of that I am certain.'

Frances sipped her sherry, wishing it was something stronger, disturbed by her mother's deduction, but forced to accept it. She remembered Ravello in southern Italy, dizzying gorges and corkscrew roads, its Roman steps and arches leading through riotous wildflowers into cool, shaded courtyards of vine and mosaic tiles. She had been bored in Ravello, then she fell in love, surrendering her virtue at seventeen to a man twice her own age. They had made love in the sweltering afternoons in his apartment off the main square, with the bells of the church tolling away the hours. That man had taught her everything, enslaving her en route, before breaking her and leaving her addicted to shameless desires.

Intelligent? Possibly she was ... but not when it came to sex.

'I refuse to let you bring up Ravello, Mother, which is what you are clearly planning to do. So, just don't try it.'

'I just want you to accept — '

'I don't have to accept anything. Least of all something that happened eighteen years ago. What I have to accept, Mother, is what happened in Iraq a few *weeks* ago.'

'You still find it hard to believe that it actually happened?'

'First I do, then I don't. It just doesn't seem possible.'

'Well, dear, as you know, I am certainly *one* person who believes that *all* things are possible.'

'Yes, Mother,' Frances said, suddenly weary.

'Please don't adopt that patronising tone with me. I am simply saying that the story you told me, fantastic or not, could have certain perfectly reasonable explanations.'

'There's no way to explain what happened, Mother. No way at all.'

Standing at the cabinet, she stared out the window, raising her gaze above the clinging vines and flowers to the grey sky above. She remembered that other sky, the sunless haze above Eden, then the helicopter descending like God's eye to take her away.

'You've been back six weeks,' her mother reminded her, 'and in all that time you haven't told the real story

169

to anyone but me. I'm sure that if you simply *talked* to someone, you would find sleep much easier, dear.'

Frances did not reply. She had told her mother the story — not all of it, but most — and now, as she remembered the rest of it, the horror returned ... Schul — and their fornication. Schul's murder — by Laurence's hand. Schul's body sinking into the lake, weighed down with heavy stones ... Frances closed her eyes, let the dread and revulsion whip her, then sighed and poured another sherry, taking a large drink.

'That's enough,' her mother's voice said from behind her. 'That's a very strong drop, dear.'

Luckily, after the rescue, when she and Laurence had given their false, plausible story, there had only been a few questions asked, most of them perfunctory. And indeed, who would have doubted their version of events? According to their rescuers, they had only been lost for twenty-four hours, and pieces of the wreckage had confirmed their story about the canoe being wrecked in a storm. Regarding the fact that their Arab oarsmen and the American passenger had disappeared — well, given the wide area over which the boat's debris had been found, it could reasonably be assumed that they had indeed (as Frances and Laurence had implied) been swept downriver and drowned.

Subsequently, there being nothing in their story to arouse undue suspicion, Frances and Laurence had been routinely examined in a hospital in Basra, then flown back to their respective homes in England and America, leaving the American Embassy the task of ascertaining Schul's proper identity and informing his nearest relatives, if such existed, of his untimely death.

It had all been a very bad dream, but at least it was over.

'God,' Frances said, 'I'm weary. I feel that I haven't really been awake since I returned from that place.'

'The experience certainly aged you,' her mother said with customary candour. 'But then I always *did* believe

170

that a little maturity goes a long way. Youthfulness is such a terrible burden when one has to live with it.'

'Do I look *that* bad?' Frances asked.

'Not *that* bad, dear, just more *lived-in*. And after all, you're thirty-five years of age, which speaks for itself.'

Frances smiled, feeling bleak, aware of time moving constantly, but no longer sure if it moved forward or in both directions. Returning from the drinks cabinet, she sat facing her mother, studying her weathered bird-like face for a moment, then gazing around the room, which held so many memories.

Her father had once worked here, composing film music, and although he had died when she was too young to remember him, she liked to imagine him sitting here with her, as a child, on his lap. It was not a very mature thing to do, but it gave her some comfort.

She kept looking around her, still entranced by the room, trying to visualise her father squinting at his sheet-music while his wife played the piano for him in that long-ago time. Her childhood had been filled with music — and the emotional resonance it provided — and these days, when her mother played, she often chose her husband's compositions, filling Frances with un-utterable longing for the man she could never have.

'Memories,' Frances murmured, hardly hearing her own voice. 'Everything reminds me of something. Everything haunts me . . .'

'*What* was that, dear?' her mother asked sharply, cocking her head to hear more clearly.

Frances blinked and stared at her, as if seeing a ghost, then had another sip of sherry. 'Nothing,' she said, sighing. 'I simply can't believe what happened to me — nor can I forget it.'

'You *won't* forget it,' her mother replied. 'You'll just have to learn to live with it. There's no other way.'

'Do *you* believe that what I told you was true?'

Mrs Devereux shrugged. 'Well,' she said, 'strange things are happening every day, so I'm inclined to accept that something peculiar happened to you. And after all, the whole town of Glastonbury *did* disappear shortly before your own extraordinary adventure. And that American who turned up so mysteriously *did* say he had fallen asleep near the Tor — so there *might* be a connection between those two events. However, I still don't see why you won't talk to someone about it as I've been suggesting. I mean, that nice Dr Phillips in the Royal Free Hospital, who is working in conjunction with those officially investigating the Glastonbury event, would, I'm sure, be very interested to talk to you.'

'He's a shrink.'

'You may need him.'

'I won't talk about it, Mother. I just can't — and that's all there is to it.'

Her mother's brow wrinkled, as if she was wondering just what Frances had left out of her story. Frances knew what she hadn't told her — and could hardly bear to think about it: that she had been an unwilling partner to murder and the body's disposal. She didn't want to talk about that, nor about her relationship with Schul, since even now, when it came into her mind, she was filled with revulsion.

Like an animal . . . She had behaved like a primitive beast . . . and she could never confess to that.

'Frances,' her mother said, leaning forward in her chair, head tilted slightly. 'You know of course that we Devereuxs are a very *psychic* family.'

'Don't start, Mother.'

'Well, it's true, isn't it? And I'm not just talking about myself. I also think that you might have such powers but simply don't know it.'

'That's nonsense, Mother.'

'Are *my* powers nonsense?'

'That's different.'

'Not really.'

Frances' mother was a practising spiritualist medium

172

who held seances right here at home every week and had been trying for years to contact her dead husband. She had not succeeded in that, but she *had* succeeded in bringing to the house each week a collection of extremely odd characters and in producing, during the seances, some very odd effects.

At her mother's insistence, but with very great reluctance, Frances had sat in on a few of those seances and been very surprised by what she had witnessed. The round table had rocked and actually risen in the air. Pencils and papers had also floated in the air while her mother spoke an indecipherable, alien language. There was clearly no trickery involved — Frances trusted her mother implicitly — and so, if bewildered, she had also been nervous about what had occurred.

'Do you *remember* what happened at those seances?' her mother asked, lighting a cigarette.

'Yes, Mother, I do.'

'They were impressive, were they not?'

'Yes, Mother, they were.'

Her mother nodded contentedly and leaned a bit closer. 'Well,' she said, 'I'm going to tell you something that I never told you before. We never obtained such impressive results when you were *absent* from the seances. The things you saw — those very powerful manifestations — were produced by *your* presence.'

Mrs Devereux nodded vigorously, exhaling cigarette smoke, her eyes glittering behind the round spectacles when they focused on Frances.

'I don't get what you're driving at,' Frances said, wanting to stand up and leave.

'I think you're highly psychic,' her mother said. 'And if that's true, it makes you powerful. It would mean that you can see things most mortals cannot see, make visible what is normally invisible, travel outside your own body and contact the spirit-world.'

'Please, Mother, *stop* this!'

'No, dear, I won't! You just have to face up to the

173

possibilities. And the point, my dear, is that you possess unusual psychic powers which could be the cause of, or a contributing factor to, what happened to you and those with you. There *are*, after all, other worlds — *spirit* worlds, for want of a better term — where time and space have no meaning in any sense that *we* understand. What is death, dear? We simply don't know. And where does human energy go when the soul leaves the body? Again, we don't know, but logic demands that it must go *somewhere*. And it *is* widely believed — and certainly believed by *me* — that that energy must remain in circulation, possibly in a kind of parallel world where it can still serve some purpose.'

'I'm sorry, Mother,' Frances intervened, 'but this conversation is going to give me a headache, and I think we should —'

'Nonsense,' her mother replied. 'You're just trying to wriggle out of this. What I'm saying is that psychic phenomena, other phenomena such as flying-saucers and inexplicable disappearances, and even so-called hallucinations, could simply be manifestations of parallel worlds. Ghosts, my dear, don't have to rattle chains — they might be perfectly normal.'

'Why don't you take up knitting or something, Mother? I'm sure it's much healthier.'

'Sticks and stones, dear. I am immune to your sarcasm. But I must insist on reiterating that a lot of strange things have been happening recently — indeed, to an unprecedented degree. Glastonbury Tor *did* disappear and has never returned; that American, Schul, *did* insist that he had fallen asleep in Glastonbury before awakening in Iraq; and there *are* an increasing number of stories in the papers about people and objects disappearing. In fact, only yesterday there was an awful story on television about a woman, in Surrey, whose child walked into the middle of their garden, abruptly disappeared, and though apparently invisible kept calling repeatedly for her mother until, after an hour or so, the poor child's voice faded away completely — and that child has not been seen since. So, my dear, I'm sure you must get my drift by now. What happened to you is not an isolated incident. The only difference is that you returned to tell me about it.'

Agitated, Frances stood up and walked past the piano to the window. The sun was going down, and the fading light, turning the garden grey, also darkened her mind.

I'm going crazy, she thought. *I cannot believe what I am hearing. Perhaps I'm not hearing it at all; maybe I'm simply imagining it.*

Home? Was this it? Had she actually expected to find a cure here? In this house with its music, memories of loss and spiritualist seances? She was angry at herself, then directed it at her mother, but when she turned around to look at the old lady, she felt love's cleansing emotion.

Her mother was squinting up through her spectacles, her face wreathed in cigarette smoke, her lips pursed rather primly.

'I don't want to think about this,' Frances said, 'so I'm going to bed.'

'A jury cannot ignore what it has just heard,' her mother replied, 'even though it may be stricken from the record.' She nodded, smiled with triumph, then sat straight in her chair, tensing like a bird about to snatch up a field-mouse. 'Sooner or later you'll remember what I've just said . . . and it might start to make sense.'

It did not make sense that night when Frances tossed and turned in bed, her thoughts colliding like cars at a junction, bringing chaos and pain. She was back in civilisation, but did not feel that way, her clothing and demeanour concealing emotions that were close to the primal. She dreaded sleep because of the dreams, seemed to dream when still awake, closed her eyes to the shadows on the walls and instantly saw what she still feared.

It was the bright, sunless sky over the garden of Eden, the great lake and marshes turning into a vast dust-bowl, while another light, greater than the sunless day, burned a hole right above her. It was that — a familiar memory — but it was also something else: she had always sensed the presences around her, but now she could see them.

They were there and then gone, materialising and disappearing, faceless, distorted shadows in the burning haze that made eyes and flesh weep. Were they human shapes or not? Had they faces or were they masked? In that light, and given her blinding fear, it was impossible to tell.

Frances cried out in that dream, but heard her own voice in the darkness, forcing her to open her eyes and stare fearfully around her. She was alone in the room, her gaze focused on the window, which framed the grey-smudged darkness of the northern sky between the fine white-lace curtains.

Her gaze roamed, still fearful, taking in the rest of the room, letting familiar items materialise out of the gloom and lend reassurance. She had slept in this same room as a child, and inside was that same child.

Now she viewed the past and present as a single, haunting entity. Her memories, brightly lit and vivid, simply would not release her. She saw herself on her father's knee, felt his breath, heard his voice, then felt a searing pain and fell through darkness to arrive at a graveyard. Her father's grave was a mound of earth (they had obviously buried him years ago), but she wept and threw herself on the dirt and tried to bring him to life again.

She opened her eyes to the sunlight, feeling older but no happier. The bells of the town church were ringing out above the hills of Ravello. *I love you*, the Italian murmured. *My beautiful English rose*. Naked, at seventeen, she lay beneath him and was gradually crushed by him. Frances groaned at the memory of it.

176

First love, then humiliation. 'My beautiful English slut,' he had whispered in his melodious Italian. She had wept, but accepted it, wanting someone older and wiser, then one form of dependence became another and left her enslaved.

She saw herself on her hands and knees, felt him stretched out on her spine; she strained against the thongs of silk in a helpless anguish that soon turned to ecstasy. 'You were born for this,' he said. 'To submit. To be a slave.' And she knew that to be true when she found herself in Eden, submitting to Schul's domination and rapacious demands.

Frances tossed and turned all night, as she had done for so long now, caught in the conflicting web of guilt and lust, trying to reconcile opposites. She fell in and out of sleep, finding exhaustion rather than rest, and once having found it lay stupefied all morning, letting the hands on her wrist-watch turn towards noon, but still unable to rise.

She suffered dark premonitions, sensed disaster in the air . . . then her mother entered the room and stood beside the bed, peering down through her spectacles, her flushed, bird-like head tilting a little as she coughed into a clenched fist.

'You better get up,' she said. 'You have a visitor . . . It's that American, Laurence.'

CHAPTER THIRTEEN

Frances took Laurence to Jack Straw's Castle for lunch, feeling as she did so that she was walking beside a ghost. The journey to that famous pub was accompanied by a conversation whose long, awkward silences were only broken by words of the utmost banality. During this time they desperately avoided one another's eyes, but once seated in the upstairs restaurant, overlooking the sea of trees on the hills of West Heath, Frances, forced to stare directly at Laurence, was shocked to see just how pale and aged he looked.

He obviously knew what her startled glance signified, for he shrugged, grinned painfully, and said, 'Lots of sleepless nights in Virginia. Lots of very bad dreams.'

In a moderate way, the acknowledgement that Laurence had shared Frances' traumas, albeit from a great distance, was enough to ease the embarrassment and shame between them. Since Laurence was an American on his first visit to England, Frances relaxed him more by telling him a little about the old hotel, most notably that Jack Straw had nothing to do with it, but that Charles Dickens, Washington Irving, Karl Marx and Max Beerbohm had frequently visited it — then, still in the spirit of entertaining a foreigner, she ordered Roast Beef and Yorkshire Pudding for both of them.

While they were waiting for the food to come, and settling their ragged nerves with a bottle of red wine, Frances, hardly knowing where to begin, said, 'Well, it's a shock.'

'*Touché*,' Laurence replied. 'I can hardly believe I'm here, but I just had to come.'

'Why?'

Laurence shrugged. 'Lots of sleepless nights,' he repeated. 'Too many, in fact. Wondering if it had really happened. Going crazy because I couldn't discuss it with anyone — except you, of course. In the end, I think I *was* a little crazy, so I just had to see you.'

'To hear me confirm that it actually happened?'

'Yes.'

'It happened. Now what?'

Laurence shrugged again. 'I don't know,' he said. 'I have to find a way to forget it. And I think that to do that I'll have to find some kind of rational explanation.'

'I can't give you one, Laurence — '

'I know that.'

' — and I don't think you came all this way just for that. I know no more about what happened than you, so why have you come here?'

Laurence rubbed his eyelids with his forefinger and thumb; when he looked up, his eyes were slightly bloodshot, doubtless from weariness.

'I just had to talk,' he said. 'And who else can I talk to? Only someone who shared the experience with me could believe that it happened.'

'I'm sorry, Laurence, but *I* don't want to talk about it. In fact, I can't even bear to think about it — for understandable reasons.'

Laurence blushed when she said that, then he gazed out of the window, trying to find escape in the Heath which rose and fell under low clouds.

'You've nothing to be ashamed of,' he said. 'You weren't yourself and neither was I. *None* of us was.'

The unconscious reference to the dead Schul made

them both uncomfortable, but Laurence, no longer an amiable innocent, was able to force his gaze back upon her.

'I've more to be ashamed of than you,' he said. 'And you know what I'm talking about.'

Frances thought of Schul's body sinking into the lake, and was relieved when the waitress arrived with their food. While Laurence was tentatively tackling his typical English pub lunch, Frances filled up both glasses with more red wine, appreciative of its anaesthetising qualities during discomfiting experiences. The bottle, she noted with alarm, was almost empty already.

'You used not to drink,' she said to Laurence.

'I started when I got back from Iraq,' he said. 'At least it's safer than drugs.'

'The sleepless nights?'

'Yes.'

'So we're both having trouble sleeping,' she said. 'In our separate beds, of course.'

Laurence blushed again and busied himself with his eating, while Frances, amused even in her general depression, sipped some more wine.

'It wasn't us,' Laurence said eventually, putting down his knife and fork. 'I don't know who Schul was — man or monster, or just a victim — but I *do* know that it wasn't the normal you or I who took part in those terrible events.'

'It was us, Laurence. Let's face it: it was us. We may not have been rational at the time, but certainly it was us.'

'No, I'm not sure of that. I think we were *inhabited* — that when time changed and we found ourselves in that other world, we were actually taken over in some way and weren't remotely ourselves.'

'If that's so, then you needn't feel guilty.'

'Yet I feel it. It haunts me.'

He shuddered, then glanced down at his plate, studying the unfinished food in a distracted manner.

'I feel guilty because I was aware of who I was and what was happening — but I *still* feel that I was somehow inhabited — that the three of us were. We were in another time, another place, but we were being . . . *controlled*.'

They were silent after that, unhappily struggling through the meal; then, when the waitress came to remove their plates, Frances ordered another bottle of wine. When it was delivered, she filled up both their glasses, then settled back in her chair, feeling a little bit better.

'I killed a man,' Laurence said, 'and I'm not sure why I did it. And even now, I wonder who Schul was or how he came to be there.'

He was staring intently at her, trying to gauge her reaction, but she simply had a sip of her wine and remained very cool.

'You said that when you got back to the States you were going to check with the authorities to find out what they'd discovered about Schul. Did you ever do that?'

'Yes,' Laurence replied. 'And that's why I'm even more baffled. ''Schul'' was his name alright. Jack Schul. He was a perfectly normal American citizen, born and bred in Atlantic City, and with a long list of petty misdemeanours to his credit. Mainly Boardwalk confidence tricks and muggings — nothing too serious — but he'd been in and out of corrective institutions and jails most of his life. Nothing special about his parents, either: his father a garage mechanic, his mother a cleaning-lady, both dead in a freeway pile-up when Schul was still just a kid. And, yes, the immigration department had a record of Schul leaving New York for a trip to Europe — exactly when Schul said he had done so — and it was also confirmed that he had an American friend who was married to an English woman and lived with her in Glastonbury. Finally, I discovered that our misleading report of Schul's drowning in Iraq is the only record they have of him since his initial arrival in Great

Britain. So, it would seem that when Glastonbury disappeared, Schul did indeed vanish with it.'

'When Glastonbury disappeared, so did most of its inhabitants. However, none of those people was ever seen again, whereas Schul turned up in Iraq.'

'Right,' Laurence said.

His cheeks were flushed, either with alcohol or excitement, and he had another sip of his wine, then nodded abstractedly.

'This was not an isolated incident — ' he began.

'My mother said that,' Frances intervened.

'Well, your mother was right. Since the disappearance of Glastonbury, there's been a worldwide series of reports of disappearances — mainly of individuals and vehicles — many of which were related to UFO reports. Naturally it was widely assumed that such reports were largely hysterical reactions to the Glastonbury disappearance, but it soon became clear that many of the reports *were* in fact genuine mysteries, most of them remarkably similar. All the reports came from seemingly sane people who claimed to have watched friends or relatives disappearing abruptly before their eyes. And, naturally, what was most horrible was that most of the victims were reported to have called out repeatedly for help from the very area into which they had disappeared, their voices often crying out for hours before fading away completely.'

Through the window, Frances saw the clouds moving over the green hills of the Heath, casting their shadows on the winding, red-rust paths that wound through the densely clustered trees. The clouds were starting to cover the sun and turn the afternoon grey.

'Anyway,' Laurence continued, 'according to various newspaper reports, examination of some of the more notable sites has shown them to be displaying an unusually high degree of magnetic fluctuation — which, as you may recall, is exactly what we noticed when the dark mass first started dropping around us.'

182

'Magnetism?' Frances said, feeling drunk and a little confused.

'Gravity,' Laurence explained. 'Gravity — or magnetism. When that dark mass dropped over us, we all felt a lot heavier, as if the earth's gravity had increased and was pulling us down; then, during those periods when the dark mass had disappeared, the pull of gravity, or earth's magnetism, returned to normal.'

'I still don't get what you're driving at,' Frances said, pouring herself another glass of wine.

'Examination of the Glastonbury area,' Laurence continued, 'has so far revealed that it's undergoing very dramatic magnetic fluctuations. Also, the few witnesses who luckily managed to remain outside the so-called 'vanishing zone' confirmed that what appeared to be an enormous dark mass — just like the one we saw near Al Qurna — dropped over the area that disappeared. Finally, a great many of the other 'vanishing zones' have shown the same kind of unusual geo-magnetic disturbances. So Glastonbury, Al Qurna and those other, smaller areas all seem to be part of the same phenomenon.'

'*What* phenomenon?' Frances asked.

'I don't know,' Laurence replied. 'Obviously they represent some kind of spatial-time zone which can suck people and objects into it, and from which no escape is likely.'

'*We* escaped,' Frances said, wanting to stand up and run away. '*We* finally got out.'

'Right,' Laurence said. 'And that only makes it more baffling. But I think it may be tied to the fluctuating nature of the geo-magnetism.'

'Laurence, can we please talk about something else?'

'No,' he replied, sipping some wine and looking excited, which only made Frances feel more fearful and disorientated. 'That dark mass kept dropping over us and disappearing again, as if affected by the fluctuating magnetic field. However, each time it returned, it stayed for longer than the time before, which suggests that it was gradually gaining strength and durability with each of its visits. So it's possible that at Glastonbury and those smaller areas, the 'vanishing' zones were strong enough to suck in the present, then, when the masses moved elsewhere, carry off the present with them. While that *may* have happened, it's also possible that in our case the dark mass was only gradually gaining strength — which is why it was still coming and going — so we may have made our escape just before it became permanent and trapped us for good.'

'And where did all those *other* poor bastards get transported to?' Frances asked sarcastically.

'I don't know,' Laurence replied, ignoring her sarcasm, 'but it's possible that in one sense they could be exactly where they were before, but in some kind of invisible, parallel world outside known time and space.'

Frances thought of what her mother had said about this same subject, and that made her feel even more uneasy ... *Ghosts don't have to rattle chains*, her mother had said. *They might be perfectly normal* ... Recalling those words, and also thinking of her own secret condition, Frances could not prevent her hand shaking when she picked up her glass.

'Are you all right?' Laurence asked.

'Yes,' Frances replied, sipping her drink. 'So what about Schul?'

Laurence sighed. 'God knows. I've thought about it often enough, but the more I think of it, the more it baffles me. Apparently he fell asleep on a bench on the lower slopes of the Tor, just outside the range of the "vanishing zone". Maybe that's why he didn't disappear for good. Maybe he was just trapped in the fringe of the "vanishing zone" and was transported somehow to Al Qurna. I'm convinced that the two dark masses were linked together some way — that they were gateways through time and space — and that Schul, being sucked in through one gate, was spat out the other.' He shrugged. 'It's a mystery.'

The afternoon had turned grey and the pastoral heath seemed ominous; the shadows of the trees stained the paths that coiled into the darkness.

Frances heard her own sigh, emanating from her fear, and her left hand, which was resting in the middle of the table, started nervously tapping a silver spoon against its silver-rimmed sugar-bowl.

'So,' she said eventually, hardly knowing what she meant. 'You've come all the way from the States just to discuss this?'

She felt his thin fingers tightening over her hand, forcing her to stop her nervous tapping and turn back towards him.

'No,' he said. 'It's not the *only* reason I'm here. I'm also here because I can't forget what happened between us in that awful place.'

'Between *us*?' Frances replied. 'It was between me and *Schul*. And God knows, given the circumstances, anything that happened between *us* has no meaning now — other than as some kind of nightmare which we have to try to forget.'

'No, Frances, I don't think we should do that. And I don't want to forget what I did because Schul was abusing you. There's a meaning to all this. I think it may have been preordained. According to all the evidence we were near the original Garden of Eden — and I'm convinced that in some way we were re-living the birth of mankind.'

'Oh, dear God,' Frances murmured.

'It's *possible*, Frances! I'm certain of it! That thing took us back in time, to when we were still clearly human — to Eden. Then it took us back even farther — to the dawn of mankind.'

Frances stared wildly around the restaurant, noting how crowded were the tables, trying to lose herself in that generalised human chatter but dismally failing to do so. Laurence was squeezing her hand more tightly, tugging at it to draw her attention ... and it was then that she remembered her condition and thought of a way to protect herself.

'Don't you see?' Laurence said. 'It might have been preordained. I wanted you, Frances — in that hell I learned to love you — and I killed Schul, the serpent in our Eden, because of that love. I loved you then, Frances, as I love you now ... and I think it was preordained.'

Frances jerked her hand from his, feeling as if she had been stung, then sat up very straight in her chair while she studied his face. His hazel eyes were almost weeping, brimming over with emotion; his lower lip was visibly trembling as he breathed far too loudly. *Religious mania*, she thought. *Maybe he had that tendency* ... But she thought of what had happened in Iraq and her fear washed that hope away. Her mother's words rang in her head — *Ghosts don't have to rattle chains* — then she thought of the condition she was in and almost gagged in her panic.

She soon managed to control herself and sat up straight in her chair, after which, stretching her hands out on the table, she spoke in a level tone.

'I think you need a good sleep,' she said. 'You must be suffering from jet-lag.'

And forced a smile when she said it.

She was not smiling that evening when, after Laurence had gone to bed, she had a brandy and coffee with her mother in the elegant drawing-room. Her mother immediately launched into a discussion about Laurence, eventually arriving at the conclusion that he seemed a decent sort, if rather nervous.

'He might be good for you, dear,' she said. 'At least he's not gross and bullying. And we should not let the fact that he's an American detract from his main virtue, namely, a distinct sense of decency which should make him worth having.'

'I'm not interested in him, Mother.'

'Why not? He's besotted with you. And I *do* think that a younger man — and one who worships you — could give you stability.'

'I'm stable enough, thanks.'

'No, you're not.'

'Then I have good reason not to be.'

After the wine in the restaurant and a third, even stronger bottle over the evening meal with her mother, Frances was hoping that the large brandy would help her to sleep. Unfortunately, even as she sat there talking to her mother, she realised that she had drunk herself beyond sleep and would probably be in for another restless night.

'Don't torment me, Mother,' she said. 'I feel bad enough already. And Laurence turning up here doesn't help — it just makes me feel even more haunted. I keep re-living what happened, over and over again, to the point where I'm losing track of the real world, or maybe going insane.'

'Nonsense,' her mother said. 'Not while *I'm* here. So, what did he say to you over lunch that made it all worse?'

'Parallel worlds,' Frances replied. 'Almost the same thing you said. Except that he seems to think it was pre-ordained for some as yet unknown purpose.'

Her mother stared oddly at her, as if disturbed by her own thoughts.

'Well, my dear,' she said eventually, 'he may be correct. Who knows in such matters? As for turning the event over and over in your mind, I need only remind you that many so-called ghosts are noted for endlessly repeating the same action, and that most of we mediums have always insisted that the world is full of bewildered spirits who, unaware that they are dead, wander around helplessly. Accepting, then, that death does not really exist — as I do — we are left with the question of just *where* such creatures are wandering about. Parallel worlds? Thought-matter imprinted upon time and space? A world where past and future do not exist, but only the eternal, ever-recurring present? It's worth thinking about.'

'Are you saying we were re-living our lives in an eternally recurring present? That we were witnessing the ghosts of *ourselves*? That *Schul* was a ghost?'

'It's possible, dear. *All* things are.'

Frances wasn't amused at all. In fact, she felt panic. The walls of the room seemed to be closing in on her, threatening to crush her.

Her mother sniffed, obviously thinking, then glanced across the room, her eyes magnified by her spectacles and clearly still intelligent, taking in the furniture, paintings and antiques with an expression that suggested she was recalling her whole life by so doing.

All human lives were artifacts, constructed from bits and pieces, marked at their passing by possessions and a lifetime of paperwork. This room was time immemorial — past and future in the present — and Frances felt, as her own childhood came alive before her eyes, that what had happened in the Garden of Eden may not have been so miraculous.

She shivered, badly shaken, thinking of Laurence in the room upstairs . . . and, in so doing, was inevitably reminded of her own secret, frightening condition.

Her fear turned to a terror that actually made her hands shake, but she managed to put the glass to her lips and finish the last of her brandy. It burned down inside her, then made her mind glow; she felt wide-awake to the point of incandescence, seeing everything brilliantly.

Yet what she saw with such clarity was an unremitting nightmare, a mystery whose nature, if revealed, could be beyond her poor reasoning. She could not face that alone, nor endure it in noble silence, and as she thought of Laurence sleeping, and of what she must do, she turned to the only person she could trust, then gave voice to her terror.

'Don't tell me that Schul was a ghost,' she said. 'I'm carrying his child.'

CHAPTER FOURTEEN

Frances tossed and turned in bed, feeling as if her skin was burning, torn between some last vestige of puritanism and her desperation and lust. The room was dark but moonlit, pale light beaming in through the window, and she saw her pale, ghostly reflection in the mirror across the room.

She sighed and cursed softly, gripped the sheets, stroked herself, remembered being an adolescent in this same room, tossing and turning the same way.

She decided to do it, but abruptly changed her mind. She changed her mind again and decided to do it, then muttered a soft oath. She thought of her mother in the adjoining room, and of Laurence along the hall, then torn between shame and need, accepted that need would prevail.

Eventually it did and she slid out of the bed, put on her nightgown, tied the belt loosely around her waist and stood there for a moment. She let her eyes adjust to the darkness, listened for movement outside, heard nothing, so quietly opened the door and looked into the hall.

All the lights were out. There was no sound from her mother's room. Her mother was asleep and could not easily be wakened, and Frances, knowing that, stepped into the landing and quietly closed the door behind her.

She then walked along the carpeted landing on her bare feet and, without knocking, opened the door of the guest-room and walked in, then closed the door behind her and stood there with her spine pressed against it, studying Laurence.

He had been lying flat on his back, his gaze on the ceiling, but startled by her unexpected entrance, he pushed himself upright and whispered her name in the form of a question-mark.

'Frances?' he whispered.

'It's all right,' Frances said. 'Don't say anything. Just lie back on the bed.'

'What — ?' he replied, confused.

'You heard me,' Frances said, speaking firmly. 'Just lie back and be quiet.'

Laurence made no move, but merely stared disbelievingly at her, so she walked up to the bed and stood there, looking down at him. He seemed a lot less naïve than he had been when they first met, but his upward gaze still held the light of a mild sexual panic.

Taking a deep breath and slowly untying her nightgown's belt, Frances remembered how the Italian had stood over her in a similar manner — smiling at her, first with tender regard, then with arrogant mockery. She did not smile at Laurence, but simply held him with her gaze. Then she let the belt fall, opened her nightgown and watched his eyes widening.

'Frances, we — '

'Don't say a word. Just lie back on the bed.'

He did as he was bid, sliding down under the sheets, letting the moonlight fall back over his face and naked, white shoulders. Frances let her robe drop off, knowing just what she was doing, and felt the cool air on her warm skin, making it tingle. Then she jerked the sheet away and slipped in beside Laurence, turning sideways, her breasts pressing against his arm, stomach touching his hip.

'Your mother — ' he began hoarsely.

'She's well asleep,' Frances said. 'And she couldn't be wakened by a bomb, so there's no need to worry.'

He offered no reply, but she heard his heavy breathing, felt the heat of his arm against her breasts, his hard, heavy hip. He was wearing pyjama bottoms, which discovery mildly amused her, and when she placed her outspread fingers on his chest, his heart started racing.

'Are you a virgin?' she asked him.

'Frances, *please*, you know I can't — '

'All right,' she murmured, breathing into his ear. 'You don't have to answer.'

She pressed herself closer to him, breasts flattening against his arm, felt a tremor rippling through him, his thigh's heat at her stomach. He closed his eyes — like a virgin — then his body quivered lightly. His shoulder's heat was enough to harden her nipples as she breathed in his ear. He kept his eyes closed while she bit his ear-lobe. She slid her tongue into his ear, licked and sucked, and he gave a light gasp.

Her fingers were still spread out on his chest above his quickening heartbeat.

'Oh, Frances,' he sighed.

She did not kiss him. Instead, she ran her tongue over his cheek and closed lips, slid it down his unshaven chin, opened her lips to suck the side of his sweating neck. He sighed, breathing quicker. She ran her fingers across his chest. She remembered the Italian running his fingers over her belly as she did the same thing to Laurence. The Italian had been an expert, removing her clothing as if by magic; she thought of that as her fingers crept down Laurence and slid through his pubic hair.

'Oh!' he groaned as he hardened, unable to resist his growing flesh; then she removed her clinging lips from his neck, sucked his chest, then a nipple.

'*Please*, Frances,' he whispered.

Yet he made no move towards her, but just lay there,

192

quivering lightly, momentarily paralysed by his own innocence, lost in his helpless needs.

She slid her fingers down lower, touched the root of his rising penis, sucked his chest as she turned her hand around to undo his buttons. She felt his fingers around her wrist, trying to tug her hand away, but she merely bit his nipple and felt his fingers slide off her, his hand falling back onto the mattress with the sound of a light slap. His body arched as she unbuttoned him and pulled his clothing apart; she smiled and pressed the palm of her hand into his groin, her thumb and forefinger forming a ring that slipped smoothly over him.

'Take them off!' she commanded. '*Take them off!*'

He did as he was bid, automatically, like a child, instinctively managing to wriggle out of his clothing without slipping out of her grasp or moving away from her body.

She was still lying on her side, breasts and belly pressed against him, but she curled up, knees sliding across him, to press her lips to his stomach. He quivered like a bow-string, breathing in spasms, gasping loudly, while she slid her tongue into his navel and felt his groin heaving.

The Italian had done that to her and she melted at the memory of it: he had turned his wet tongue inside her until she was sobbing. Now Laurence was actually groaning, rolling his groin against her mouth, and she squeezed the bone-hard muscle searching for her as she lapped up his sweat.

The bells seemed to be ringing over the rooftops of Ravello as she pulled the sheet off Laurence's body and curled over his white skin.

'Oh, Frances! *Oh, God!*'

He had finally nerved himself to touch her, but only to stop her foraging, fingers sliding through her hair to grip her head and try to pull her back up. Frances knew what he wanted — the absolution of a normal kiss — but

193

she also knew that would return him to an inhibiting awareness of his lack of sexual experience.

So, she ignored him and simply moved a little lower, forcing him to release her head and instead place his hands on her bent back. His erection was hot and smooth, slipping easily through her fingers; she let the tip of his penis graze her lips as she breathed warmly over him. He gasped and groaned some senseless words. She thought of how the Italian had taught her. He had thrust in and out in languid motions that made every nerve sing. His hands on her hips. Making her undulate and roll. He had waited until he had coaxed her into a state where will and pride had no meaning. Her skin melting divinely. Rivulets of flesh and sweat. He had waited until her lips had lost control and then pressed his thumb over them. She remembered as she breathed on Laurence, her lips opening, tongue extending: the Italian had insistently pressed her lips with his thumb until she had sucked it into her mouth like a child with a nipple. So hungry to have it. Sucking greedily, seeking life. She had hardly noticed the difference between his thumb and the larger probe of his penis. Her lips had parted to let him in, without awareness, drinking thirstily; and after that, again, then again and again, until, with awareness, came greed and yet another addiction.

So it was now with Laurence. His erection had no pride. Frances opened her lips and sucked him in as his groans sounded distantly.

'Oh, Christ!' he blasphemed.

His groans sounded like distant bells, filling her head in that stifling apartment, people chattering in the street just below where the white walls met Roman stones. It was summertime in Ravello, the afternoon bright and hot, and she watched her sweat dripping off her breasts and falling onto his belly. '*Si*,' he murmured. 'My little whore. You learn so well, so quickly.' And touched her with his hardness, divided her thighs and lips, showed

194

her how to lean across him as she now did with Laurence, moving her lips up and down the smooth, pulsing length of him.

Laurence groaned and whispered something. He took hold of her head again. This time he didn't try to pull her away, but instead coaxed her lower. She held him in her hand, lightly pressing on his scrotum. When he quivered she slid her lips off him and slowly sat upright.

He was writhing on his back, his hands clawing at empty air. He opened his eyes to stare blindly upwards through oblique lines of moonlight. 'What — ?' he said, his voice hoarse, hands falling back by his sides, rolling his groin to raise himself higher as she slid one leg over him.

An innocent ... no more. She would enslave him through his flesh. She raised herself on her knees above his body, her legs spread out across him. *Slut*, she thought. *Opportunist*. And was also receiving satisfaction. She felt her sweat trickling down between her breasts as his eyes fixed upon them. Dazed eyes, almost mad. Eyes drinking in her body. She leaned forward while rolling her hips to locate and then hold him. He touched lightly, divided her, slid smoothly in, entering as she leaned lower, still swinging her hips, to let his hungry mouth suck her breast and release more old memories ...

Night. The silvery moonlight. The Italian had taught her well. She thought of her mother sleeping in the next room as Laurence pushed up more frantically. Filling her. Melting her. Making her lose her senses. She moved her other breast to his mouth to let that be sucked as well. He was thrusting up, quivering, and she slid her hands beneath him, taking hold of his constricting buttocks and pulling him higher.

'God!' he sobbed. 'Oh, that's wonderful!'

She sat upright again, still rolling her hips, turning left and then right, staring down and taking pleasure from

195

his face, which was a wide-eyed, slack-jawed mask of ecstasy. He was running his hands around her body, exciting himself by watching, then she felt herself rising off him, sinking back and flowing warmly around him.

The Italian had taught her to lose herself and she was starting to do that now; her head filled with fleeting visions and echoing sounds: of motes of dust at play in striations of sunlight while churchbells tolled mournfully from the square above the steep, pirouetting roads. Italy: *Ravello*. A mother and daughter on vacation. She had seen her own virgin blood on the white sheet and blushed like a child. A beginning. No more than that. First love, then humiliation: she had ended on hands and knees on the floor, being told what to do.

How could she have resisted? No more than Laurence could right now. He was crying out, convulsing, spilling himself inside her, as a clock chimed downstairs in the dark hall, announcing the midnight hour.

'Oh, God!' he cried. *'God!'*

Frances sank back upon him, plunging into her own feelings, letting his convulsions subside before rising off him. She twisted onto her back, felt him trembling inside her, again placed her hand on his chest to feel his heart racing wildly.

She kept her hand there for some time, listening patiently to his gasping, aware that she had wanted him desperately as her only protection. She was pregnant with Schul's child and could not face that alone. She didn't know who Schul had been, nor what his child might become, and the possibilities lay upon her thoughts like acid on bare skin. Terror shook her leaf and bough, reminding her of what she was doing here: she had to enslave Laurence through his love and make him stay with her.

She started again for that very purpose, massaging him, making him harden, spreading her legs as he groaned and rolled on top of her, his eyes blind with rapture.

'God, I love you!' he whispered, poised above her, bewildered, his body shaking with the tension of desire, beads of sweat on his skin.

She raised her hips to take him in, curling her legs around him, pulled him down and tasted his tongue for the very first time. He sobbed, his tears glistening. She stroked his spine and sweaty flanks. She heard the bells of Ravello, saw the light outside the window, felt the Italian pressing upon her before burning up into her. He had taught her many things and now she passed them on to Laurence, carrying him up to where love became so strong that it rendered him senseless.

'Oh, God!' he sobbed. '*Please!*'

He moved rapidly in and out, penetrating her deeply, his instincts taking over his inhibitions and giving him confidence. He moved faster, still faster, breathing harshly and groaning loudly, until she felt him coming, the spasms starting deep inside him, rippling up through his straining body before exploding out of him, making him go into a series of convulsions, then quiver and sob.

He writhed helplessly on top of her, twisting this way and that, then raised his body and pressed down with his groin, gripping her so hard she hurt. The spasms whipped repeatedly through him, making him seem like a man in torment, but eventually, with a loud gasp, he fell back down upon her, collapsing within himself, then pressed his left cheek to her breasts, to just lie there, trying to get his breath back.

Frances slid her hands over him, stroked his tangled hair, studying the moonlit ceiling above her and remembering Italy.

Shortly after, Laurence wept, kissed her breasts, sucked her fingers. He dried his eyes, then lay beside her in the darkness, staring up at the moonlight. Neither spoke for a long time. Frances let the silence linger. She knew that sooner or later the silence would force him to speak to her.

Eventually, he did, taking a deep breath, sounding nervous. He told her that he loved her, that he would never stop doing so, that he worshipped the very air she breathed and would do anything for her.

When he had told her that she smiled, slightly, enigmatically, then rolled over with the elegance of a cat, onto her stomach. She stretched out her right hand, groping blindly behind her, searching for him and, quickly finding him, guiding him into her.

'Do it this way,' she said.

CHAPTER FIFTEEN

It was soon clear that Laurence didn't know what he had let himself in for. He didn't so much move formally into the house with Frances as simply, at her request, make no visible attempt to leave. At first he had been reluctant, being embarrassed about her mother, but Frances insisted that it was absolutely necessary, and her conviction, plus the fact that Laurence now felt feverish just looking at her, guaranteed his acquiescence in the matter.

'You've got to stay,' she said. 'I can't bear to face it alone. I think that what you told me is true — that this was all preordained. You and I were meant to meet — we were destined to share what's coming — and whatever it is, good or bad, we have to face it together. So stay here. You *know* you want to stay. You know you want *me*.'

She didn't tell him she was pregnant, least of all by Jack Schul, and admonished her mother not to tell him either, lest he hurry back home. He might still have the will to do that — it was highly unlikely, but possible — and she wanted to be sure that when her pregnancy became obvious, he would then be so addicted to her, he would find it impossible to leave.

'You should tell him you're pregnant,' her mother chastised her. 'What you're doing is immoral. You're keeping him here under false pretences, which will only make things worse later, but I'm sure that if you tell him the truth, he will treat the matter most sensibly.'

'I *can't* tell him, Mother. He'd just take fright and run. He still can hardly bear the mention of Jack Schul's name, so discovering that I'm carrying Schul's child will, particularly at this point, scare him into doing God knows what.'

'Perhaps you're right, dear. In this matter you may know best. And it may indeed have been preordained, so the child must be protected.'

The thought of the child terrified Frances and overwhelmed her shame, helping her to justify the deception involved in her whore's game. She sincerely believed that Laurence was part of this, that he was somehow meant to be here, but she also knew that what she was doing with him was more than she had to. She certainly did not love him, but genuinely felt bound to him, perhaps because of what they had been through together in that place which still haunted her. There was that and her own lust, her desperate need for obliteration; and because since her return she had not been able to approach any other men, Laurence, if not her usual type, was at least someone to cling to.

And cling to him she did, letting her body find expression, drowning her fear in that overriding sensuality which, though always a weakness, had recently become even more pronounced, fanning the flames of lust night and day. So she made love in Laurence's bedroom like a whore in a brothel, and Laurence, though unable to resist her, was appalled and ashamed.

'What does your mother think?' he asked her. 'She must know what's going on.'

'She thinks we're a young couple in love,' Frances lied, 'and she's a very modern mother in that way.'

Laurence was sceptical but tried not to show it, already caught in the web of his desire and puritanical

200

guilt. He wanted Frances — yes, he could hardly wait to touch and be touched — but his lust was like a rose caught in the thorns of disbelief and inhibition. He had often thought of love, wanting the heat of its tender flame, but nothing had prepared him for the shock he had felt that first night at the discovery that Frances, the woman he loved, knew tricks which he had never imagined decent women would practise.

'Do it this way,' she said.

'Frances, no!'

'I like it — so do it.'

Frances knew what she was doing to him, but extracted pleasure from it, remembering that apartment in Ravello where her childhood had ended. She passed on what she had been taught, letting pleasure lead to addiction, often thinking of Laurence looking on in revulsion as she did the same things with Schul.

She thought constantly of Eden, of that lush garden beyond time, of that even earlier time in which a bitch-beast had rutted in the dust, squealing either in pleasure or in rage. Had the other beast been Schul or some bizarre apparition? She was haunted night and day by that question, and knew that Laurence was, also. So, she used that, making him do what Schul had done, letting his ecstasy overrule his moral qualms, turning him into her slave.

'You like it,' she said to him.

'*Please*, Frances! Dear God!'

'If you find it that disgusting, just stop.'

'You *know* I can't! God forgive me!'

She used his religious beliefs against him, destroying his faith as she freed his lust, turning him into an addict who lives for his fix. She showed him what she had been taught, blandly ignoring his disgust, then observed his disbelief at what he was doing, even as he surrendered.

He was shocked, humiliated, tormented by his growing needs — and ashamed of himself at night, he would be more so by day when he had to sit in the drawing-room with Frances and her mother, sipping tea and making idle chit-chat. He could barely look in a mirror, much less at Mrs Devereux, but the old lady lacked similar inhibitions when she fixed her gaze on him.

'You had a good sleep, Laurence, dear?'

'Yes, Mrs Devereux, fine.'

'Most Americans don't know how to relax, dear, but you're obviously more sensible.'

Laurence thought that Mrs Devereux knew nothing about Eden, and so, given instructions by Frances, he avoided raising the subject. However, Frances talked about it — frequently and fearfully — usually when they were in Laurence's bedroom in a tangle of soaked sheets. She often did it when they were naked, tangled up just like the sheets, their sweat glistening in the fractured, moonlit darkness, their words cleaving the silence. She talked even as Laurence groaned, quivering helplessly at her silken touch, coming into the velvet glove of her fingers while she nibbled his ear.

'I knew what I was doing,' she said, 'but didn't always know who I was. When we went back in time, right back to the dawn of man, I *felt* things, rather than thinking them, though I did have awareness. Sometimes I remembered names. I was aware that you were watching. Even when we did it on all-fours, like animals, I was only dimly aware of my shame, and might not really have felt it — I might just have remembered it.'

When she talked about it, she excited him almost to the point of mania, rendering vivid in his mind what he had witnessed in outrage and revulsion. Yet even loathing it, he wanted it; despising himself, he had to have it; and often shivering at the thought of his weakness, he still had to give in to it.

Frances knew by his beating heart, gauged his needs from his widening eyes, made him keep them open and focused upon her while she spread her legs and lowered herself patiently on his hard, slick erection. She writhed in abandonment above him, rising and falling with blatant relish, tugging his hands to her breasts, to her buttocks, sliding herself through his sweating palms. She did all that and more — much more — and made him keep his eyes open.

'You have to *look*,' she said. 'Seeing is almost as good as touching. You think you love me, but you really lust after me because of what you have seen: Schul and I in that awful place, both naked, on the ground, me either on my knees while I used my mouth on him, or on hands and knees with him behind me, displaying his strength. That excited you — yes, you explored yourself because of that — and doing that, you had to remember what you had seen and re-live it in darkness. I saw you. We *both* saw you. Trying to satisfy yourself. And Schul, when watching *you*, would become excited and have to take me again.'

Laurence cringed at such stories, but became more aggressive, almost fighting through his puritanical, Christian guilt to dominate her more fully. She wanted that, needed it, could not be satisfied without it, and plunged him into new depths of despair because he could not make her climax.

She writhed wildly in her frustration, gripped the sodden sheets, groaned and cursed, clawed his spine as she pulled him down and rolled upon him to slide her body along him. In that soaked bed in the dark room, in that house in the silent night, Frances took him and made him a part of her until they both became one, moulded to the pores of each other's flesh by the heat of their passion.

Yet Laurence, though exhausted and dripping with sweat, could only express his despair.

'This isn't love,' he said. 'It's lust and self-satisfaction. It's not even healthy sex — it's depravity — and it cheapens us both. Why do you act like this? Why do you make us do these things? I despise myself for doing what we do, yet once I start I can't stop. You like that, don't you? It turns you on more than the sex. Maybe it *was* the real you in that place, performing for Schul. Oh, my God, I feel sick.'

'There's more,' Frances replied, her voice mellow. 'We haven't really begun yet. Now pass me the oil.'

Most assuredly, Laurence didn't know what he had let himself in for. And as the days came and went, as his lust swamped his disgust, he began to feel even more bewildered by what had happened in Iraq, was happening right here in London, and would surely come to some kind of conclusion in the frightening future. Frances talked constantly about it, when Laurence was calm or in a fever, and soon, when he wasn't being tormented by that subject, he was being haunted by the conviction that this house itself might be unreal, filled as it was with ghostly knockings and bizarre manifestations.

'That's just Mother,' Frances explained.

Laurence had already been compelled to adjust to the stream of elderly people, many of them very strange indeed, who poured twice each week into Mrs Devereux's drawing-room where, before the doors were shut in his face, he would see them partake of tea and biscuits.

When Frances explained to him that the people were gathered there to have a spiritualist seance, Laurence at first put it down to typical English eccentricity; however, during one of those evenings — when he was flat on his back in the darkened bedroom, with Frances' lips sliding diabolically over and along him; when he had just clutched at the bedsheets and opened his eyes to beg 'No more!'; when in fact he was on the verge of another delicious, guilt-ridden climax — he was jerked out of his reverie by a distant, steady knocking that seemed to emanate from the floor directly below him and reverberate, as if magically amplified, through his dazed, spinning thoughts.

'Oh, God,' he groaned, 'what's *that?*'

'That's just Mother,' said Frances.

On that and subsequent nights he was forced to continue making love to Frances (or, more precisely, being made love to) while the floor resounded with knocking, tables tapped, crockery rattled, or macabre shrieks and groans arose from the elegant drawing-room situated directly under his bedroom.

Already lost in a bewildering, hallucinatory world of flesh, sweat, moonlit darkness and burning breath; of tears, entreaties; prayers and whispered obscenities; of mortal shame and profane desires that often carried him close to delirium — already trapped in that incandescent dream of sexual madness, Laurence could scarcely take in the reality of this latest enchantment.

Indeed, with his every pleasure tainted by the persistent thought that Mrs Devereux might overhear his ecstatic cries and gasps, Laurence was thrown deeper into the vats of his fear and confusion by the knowledge that a collection of English lunatics was attempting to speak to the dead in the room below him, even as he was engaged in sexual adventure of the most unspeakable kind.

Unspeakable at least to him, or to the puritan he had been, since he wanted to love and be loved in return, but instead found himself with a woman whose appetites outraged his moral nature even as, in attempting to satisfy her, he was shuddering helplessly.

'What's *that?*' he whispered.

'That's just Mother,' Frances said. 'She's a medium and claims the spirits speak through her, which is what you're hearing right now. They groan and shriek a lot. I really don't know why. I haven't joined in on a seance for years. Now pass me the oil.'

He passed over the oil and let her soaking hands massage him, felt himself melting into her fingers and becoming part of her. He often stared in amazement at her, disbelieving her lewdness, hardly able to credit that she was actually Frances Devereux, unable to reconcile that cool, middle-class English doctor with this aggressively wanton woman who, naked and un-ashamed, displayed the most unsavoury appetites imaginable, making demands that he tried to resist even as they aroused him.

'You drive me wild,' he said. 'You reduce me to moral turpitude. You get me to do things that I can't believe I'm actually doing — and yet it isn't enough for you. You never seem to get satisfaction, and you hate me for that.'

'Tie me up,' she replied.

'Oh, my God! No, I won't!'

'There's no harm in it. You just have to render me helpless.'

'It's not right! *I won't do it!*'

At such times he could take no more and would break down into tears, these often leading to waves of religious guilt and the need to confess. A good Catholic, a mission-worker, he would fall to his knees on the floor and there, stark naked, tears flowing, pray with deep fervour.

Yet even that was no solution, and certainly no protection from Frances, since she would often, even then, in the very middle of his praying, move directly in front of him, her groin close to his face, silk panties small enough to accentuate her mons Veneris; then, as he was praying, slip her fingers between his lips, immediately stopping his talk, transforming his confession into a greedy devouring and making his shame crumble before his lust. So, there, in that fraught darkness, signifying a fresh surrender, he would try to take his fill, drinking drunkenly of her essence, his senses flying away as he heard her seductive whispering, felt her fingers in his hair, smelt the oil on her writhing, gleaming skin when his nose lightly grazed it. Then she would drop down past his face, spreading herself out below him, making him bury his face in her, smelling and tasting her, his lust blending with guilt and inevitable remorse.

The latter would make him tremble when, the next morning, he would have to sit in the drawing-room, nibbling biscuits and sipping tea, listening to Frances' mother, the very peculiar Mrs Devereux, offer the hope that her spiritualist activities in the drawing-room directly below him had not disturbed the sleep he surely needed.

'No, Mrs Devereux, not at all.'

'I'm *so* glad,' Mrs Devereux said, biting delicately into a biscuit, then tilting her head to peer at him through her spectacles. 'Thing is, my dear boy, that the seances *are* important in that they do, if nothing else, bring great comfort to the poor wretches who come here. They have all, you see, at one time or another, lost someone quite close to them.'

'I hear groaning and shrieking,' Laurence said. 'I wonder what it is.'

'The dead speaking,' Mrs Devereux replied. 'Alas, communication is imperfect. There seems to be a great lack of comprehension between the dead and the living. Thus, they make the table tap — once for yes, twice for no — and when angry, or possibly just frustrated, they throw things about. The groaning? The shrieks? I must apologise, since that is me. Not *really* me, of course, but one of my spirit-guides speaking through me — either in some unknown babble or in the sounds that you heard. Do you have an interest in such matters, Mr Gilbride? Then perhaps you should join us.'

Frances had told Laurence that her mother knew little about their experience in Iraq, but sometimes, when Mrs Devereux spoke to him, Laurence was convinced that she was reading his mind. She was of course a spiritualist medium, and had hinted that Frances might by psychic as well, but Laurence only knew that he felt strangely uncomfortable when she gave him her sweet smile.

He meant to ask Frances about it, and tried to keep his mind on it, but when she came to his room that night, and crept seductively into his bed, her oiled body too quickly found his hardness and splintered his every thought. He was blinded by the pale moon, hypnotised by the fluttering curtains; and bent across Frances, seeing the white line of her spine, feeling her small breasts in his hands and her rump against his belly, he was shriven in the heat of his revulsion and swept back through time.

He saw the fig-leafed gates of Eden melting into the dazzling haze, the green trees turning into stone that was bleached by the sunless sky. She was in the middle of the clearing, hands and knees in the dirt; he knew her name but could not quite remember it as she grunted and heaved. He was filled with lust for her, wanting to do what the other did, and when he looked at the other thrusting behind her, he wanted to kill him.

Then it all dissolved before him, the sky brightening and descending, a fierce light spreading out to obliterate the features of those standing around him. God it was who came down, then His angels took command, making everyone feel terror or awe as they went into hiding.

In the rock-hole he still saw her, being taken again, grunting. He whimpered as the other, standing behind her, displayed his great pleasure. Then the cave was flooded with light and silhouetted creatures entered, advancing on those trembling just out of reach. Different creatures, tall and upright, not speaking, but making strange music as oblivion came . . .

' — love you, Frances! I love you!'

Returning to her arched spine and the rolling of her buttocks, he would hear himself whispering those words with an almost anguished intensity. Yet she never replied, but merely drove him to a greater frenzy, moving with the suppleness of a cat, her heat making his blood boil. He worked at her, in despair, vainly performing as she had taught him, but always found himself exploding ecstatically into a great isolation — aware that once more she had not come and would display her frustration.

'Christ!'

'*Please*, Frances!'

'Jesus Christ! Oh, my God!'

'*Please*, Frances!'

'Just tie me up and that will do it. *Damn you, I need that!*'

He refused such demands, his body shuddering with revulsion, his mind still unable to grasp that his love had brought him to this. Was it love? He wasn't sure. He didn't want to face the question. He only knew that he was no longer capable of telling the difference between love and this relentless, enslaving lust and the shame it engendered. Her demands disgusted him, but his compliance shocked him more, and when she begged him to tie her to the bed, he made that the limit — since he sensed that his compliance would cause him to be totally damned.

'Why do you want that?' he asked her. '*Why?* It's not natural! It's *sick!*'

She laughed harshly at that, throwing her head back on the pillow, her swollen breasts thrusting up towards him, her thighs trapping his sweaty hand.

'Natural?' she said mockingly. 'You don't know what that word means! What's natural is what comes easily to us — as this does to me. Tie me to the bed, damn you! You've had your pleasure, now give me mine. I can only get satisfaction when I'm helpless, so for Christ's sake unbend.'

'Don't blaspheme!' he said.

And yet he thought it *all* a blasphemy, a denial of his faith, and continued, even as he was sinning, to pray for forgiveness. And with those prayers, another, an entreaty for revelation, for the truth of what was happening and *had* happened to be revealed to him.

209

He was still haunted by Eden, by constant visions of that nightmare, and often, even as he made love to Frances, thought of Schul and her doing it. She had said that she did the same, so he tried to hide behind that, convincing himself that her perverse, shocking needs were a form of escape.

She cupped his testicles in her hand, slid him through well-oiled fingers, licked him and very gently bit him until he was whimpering — yet her skill, which was diabolical, had its roots in despair, her exquisite refinement of touch seemed to spring from her torment.

He often begged her to tell him who had taught her such things, thus reducing her to such baseness, but invariably she replied with a soft, mocking laugh, before making him quiver once more in passion's uplifting agony.

'God forgive me!' he gasped.

With his guilt growing daily in direct proportion to his desire, Laurence still had to suffer the memory of what had happened in Eden. Indeed there were times when, making love to Frances, he would have of that awful place a recollection so vivid that it would take on an hallucinatory quality. He knew that Frances suffered the same, and that her lust was mixed with fear, but this knowledge did not help to ease the pain that was growing inside him.

In fact, as he gained experience with her, learning the manifold ways of sex, wallowing in his lust and viewing his desires as depravity, his guilt and shame grew, sweeping away his romantic notions, eventually leaving him in a mire of hatred for her because of what she had made of him.

'You've destroyed me,' he accused her. 'Stripped me of love and pride. You've shown me the gutter, rubbed my nose in the mud, and ensured that I'd become addicted to it, no matter how it disgusts me. Even knowing what I was — a practising Christian — you did all that to me.'

'Stop being so hypocritical,' she replied. 'I gave you what you were yearning for.'

'I'm going home,' he said. 'I'm returning to the States. I can't live with this any longer, so I'm going to leave.'

'Leave?' she replied dreamily, on her knees, between his legs, her warm breath pouring over him as she spoke, to make him erect. 'I don't think so. Not yet . . .'

He closed his eyes — she now let him close his eyes — and concentrated all his senses on his groin, his new soul, to experience sensations of unbearable intensity, his body quivering like a bow-string, his pores rippling like grains of sand, his fingers electrical on her scalp, seeming to sparkle down her spine, his heart racing as he grew and kept expanding to the point of explosion. And there she stopped him, controlled him, using the contracting rings of her fingers, holding him back while she stroked him to a sensual pitch beyond which lay delirium.

Even then, he learned to hate her, because of the power she had over him, and would view her as some kind of dark witch who could exalt or debase him. Just that: her expert fingers; his mouth filled with her swollen breast; her white skin gleaming under a sheen of oil against which he could rub himself. Moonlit darkness, writhing limbs, oil, sweat and heat, nimble fingers playing delicate refrains, mouths and tongues joining greedily.

All that and more: Mrs Devereux; the house itself; the twice-weekly seances; the dead communicating in strange tongues or with sounds that made his flesh crawl. He plunged into despair and rage, hating himself as well as Frances — and then grew more paranoid each time he had to descend the stairs to have tea with the eccentric Mrs Devereux in that elegant drawing-room.

'Frances isn't happy,' Mrs Devereux said. 'Alas, poor

child, she never was. And unfortunately I do not think your presence here has made an improvement. I must confess, I had hoped for more — but please don't misunderstand me. If I say this, it is not to blame you, but simply to point out the facts. She has *always* been unhappy. I blame that on the loss of her father. I also blame it on that unfortunate affair in Italy, about which, the less said the better.'

'Italy?' Laurence murmered. 'An affair . . .?'

'No,' Mrs Devereux continued, smoking a cigarette, puffing smoke, 'that was her affair and I refuse to resurrect it. I would just like to discuss, my dear Laurence, your relationship with her. You both shared a terrible experience — we need not dwell on the details — and this has naturally drawn you closer together than you might have been otherwise. It is therefore good that you should be here — I think the positive aspects are obvious — but I *have* noticed disturbing changes in Frances that cannot be ignored. I think she is having a breakdown, Laurence. She cannot forget what has happened to her. And for that reason, no matter your own feelings, I think you should stay on.'

'Is Frances psychic?' Laurence asked.

'I beg your pardon?'

'Is she psychic?'

'Her psychic powers are greater than mine, but she refuses to face that fact. She *feels* things, Laurence — things beyond our normal perceptions — and I think that's her problem. So, will you stay on?'

'Yes,' Laurence said.

So, he agreed to stay — because he thought Frances might be psychic, because he felt that if she *were* indeed psychic, that might explain what had happened. He understood what was happening here — it was why he had turned to God — he had always felt the breath of the spirit-world breathing over his shoulder. Thus it was possible, as Mrs Devereux seemed to think, that his adventure with Frances and Schul had been preordained.

'*Why?*' he asked Frances.

'God,' she said, 'I don't know. I only know that I want to forget about it, but I can't seem to do that.'

'Are you all right?'

'All right?'

'You don't feel ill or — ?'

'Deranged?'

'I just meant — '

'Just tie me to the bed, Laurence. I can't come any other way.'

In that instance she said it mockingly, but he knew that she also meant it, and he felt his resolve to stay fading away in the light of what she was asking. He stared at her, frightened, wondering who he was looking at, still bewildered by what he felt was her depravity and almost too shocked to speak.

She was sitting in front of him, wearing only her nightgown, having just padded in on bare feet to avoid waking her mother. Her brown hair was bathed in moonlight, dark eyes glinting steadily, and she sat on the edge of the bed with her very long legs crossed, the lower half of the gown falling off her thighs in a provocative manner.

Laurence despised his hapless lust but remained a victim of it, his breath quickening immediately when he gazed at her pale, unlined skin. He was lost to her and knew it, wanting her more than life itself, but as his hand fell on her knee, clearly out of his control, he tried with the last of his willpower to resist what was coming.

'Tell me about Italy,' he said. 'I want to know all about it.'

She didn't actually move, but he sensed a change in her, then saw an almost imperceptible stiffening of her lithe, treacherous body. His hand slid up and over, finding a space between her crossed legs, and he felt himself hardening as he watched her, wondering how he could do this.

She just stared steadily at him, offering an enigmatic smile, then raised one leg a little, letting his fingers slip into her, and slyly pressed her tender inner-thigh back down on his knuckles.

'Italy?' she whispered, while his hand burned and he hardened more. 'Why do you want to know about Italy? Has my mother been talking?'

Laurence moved his hand up farther, hardly knowing what he was doing, only aware that the radiant heat from her was flooding his loins. He squeezed and stroked her automatically, his hand trapped between her thighs, and was captured by the fathomless depths of her ambiguous, brown gaze. His body shuddered against his will — he tried to stop it, but failed — then he found his fingers touching that softness where one thigh joined the other.

'She just mentioned Italy,' he murmured throatily. 'Some trouble you had there ... Now I want to know everything.'

Frances opened herself to him, making his heart leap dramatically, and he touched that melting warmth with a thrill that threatened to drown him in pleasure. She sensed that, and smiled, stretching her body like a snake, then managed with a slight roll of her hips to take his fingers right into her.

'Pornography,' she whispered. 'That was Italy ... And that's what you want.'

He heard his own choked sobbing, a strange, childish sound, as she smiled, sat up straight, placed her hand on her neck, then slowly, theatrically, with a stripper's practised skill, tugged the dressing-gown off her gleaming shoulders and smooth arms, until it was lying behind her on the bed, leaving her top half exposed.

He saw the marble of her bare skin, the rise and fall of her bosom, then his gaze was captivated by her nipples as they visibly stiffened. *Italy*, he thought obliquely. *I want to know what happened there*. He was

214

contemplating that when her legs moved and his fingers slid farther into her. He sucked his breath in simultaneously, heart racing as he stared at her, then sobbed again, scarcely knowing he was doing it, and, with his free hand resting lightly between her breasts, gradually pushed her back onto the bed.

'God, I want you!' he groaned.

'If you tie me to the bed,' she replied, murmuring, 'I'll tell you all about Italy.'

Laurence felt himself breaking, unable to resist his own greed, and he untied the knot at her waist and jerked the gown from her hips. He stared at her, breathing harshly, leaning over her like an ape, only aware of her supine, naked body and his aching erection. His consciousness drained down to there, flooding into his loins, responding in a flare of awareness to the touch of her hand. Her fingertips stroked his penis, one nail scraping along it, and he heard his own breathing like a storm blowing through a deep gorge. Her body lay beneath him, oil-slicked limbs curved in surrender, pale skin smooth on shoulders, soft breasts and a sublime mound of belly.

He shook with shame and longing. Her free hand held his erection. Her fingers slid like well-greased rings along him when he tried to resist her. At that moment he was doomed. His tears came when he saw her smile. He thought of her in that awful place, then of Schul penetrating her, and was starting to fall upon her burning body when her other hand stopped him.

'No!' she said. 'Not yet!'

She was supporting him with her free hand, pressing him back with surprising strength. Her other hand was sliding along his penis to press it gently against her. His body quivered like a bow-string and he failed to stop his tears. He stared down at her, stricken, comprehending her through his loins, then noticed something dangling from the hand that was holding him off her.

He cried out in despair. Her other hand slid him inside

215

her. He saw the cords of silk in her free hand, but by then it was too late.

'All right!' he gasped, blinded by tears. 'All right, damn you, *yes*!'

He tied her to the bed and did her bidding until the dawn broke. After that, they were enemies.

CHAPTER SIXTEEN

The woman who sat in front of Michael in his office in the psychiatric wing of the Royal Free Hospital, recounting her extraordinary experiences in southern Iraq and telling him about a murder which may well have taken place only in her imagination, did not give the appearance of someone suffering from any kind of mental disorder. A rather severe, dark beauty with her long hair hanging loose, she *did* look, in some manner which he could not quite define, slightly older than her stated age; but the simple elegance of her clothing and the unconscious dignity of her poise marked her indelibly as an educated, middle-class woman of considerable refinement.

She answered his questions precisely, talking softly but clearly, her hands folded primly in her lap, resting on top of her handbag. Her lovely legs were crossed, her skirt's hemline above the knees, and although it was true that in general she did not fidget, he noticed that her left leg, crossed over the right, frequently made an almost imperceptible swinging motion which suggested erotic arousal.

When most of the details of her strange adventure had been recounted into his tape-recorder, Michael gazed down at his extra notes and sighed disconcertedly. Buying time while he thought, he offered Miss

Devereux a cigarette; when she accepted, he lit the cigarette for her, then lit his own and inhaled.

'Do you smoke a lot?' he asked her.

'Very rarely,' she replied. 'I always carry a packet in my handbag, but I don't often smoke them.'

'A bad example to your patients, I suppose.'

'Maybe that's it,' she said.

She smiled at him for the first time, a remote smile, quietly radiant, and he realised how very attractive she was for someone her age.

'Before we go any further,' he said, 'can I just confirm this one vital point: What you're telling me is that God is speaking to you and that you may well be carrying His child. Is that correct?'

'Yes.'

'Do you have any conception of who, or what, this God is?'

'No. Just that He is.'

Michael nodded and inhaled on his cigarette, realising that he had a special case here and becoming more interested. 'Fine,' he said conversationally, exhaling the smoke and watching it disappear. 'We'll probably return to that later. Right now, however, I would like to ask you a series of questions, many of which may seem unduly personal and of no relevance to your case, but which are, I can assure you, of great importance. Should any of these questions offend you, please don't hesitate to say so, but try to answer as many of them as possible. Okay?'

'Yes, Doctor.'

'You're a doctor yourself, I believe.'

'Yes, a general practitioner, specialising in tropical medicine — but I haven't worked since I returned from Iraq.'

'How are you managing to support yourself?'

'I live with my mother, who has her own income.'

'Ah, yes, Mrs Devereux. I've talked to her. She told me she was a spiritualist medium and seemed to

218

take it quite seriously.'

'She takes it *very* seriously, Doctor.'

'She also said that psychic abilities ran in her family, and that you had inherited them to an exceptional degree. Is that true?'

'I didn't think so before because I wasn't really interested, but now I think my mother may be right. Normally, at her seances, she would only obtain routine results — communication through tapping furniture, the odd poltergeist effect, spirit-guides speaking through her — but each time I attended there was a dramatic improvement, including some extremely vivid images, or materialisations.'

'Of the dead?'

'Of people.' Miss Devereux shrugged, glancing at the framed diplomas which adorned the plain walls of the office.

'Do you think,' Michael asked, 'that your psychic abilities had anything to do with your experience in Iraq?'

'I don't know. I think constantly about it — constantly — but I simply don't know.'

'And your mother?'

'She believes that my psychic abilities are the channels through which I've been contacted.'

'And does *she* believe you're carrying God's child?'

'She says anything is possible. Of course my mother, as you've doubtless gathered, is a little eccentric.'

Michael had in fact been charmed by Mrs Devereux but not fooled by her. It seemed to him that if Mrs Devereux had, over the years, picked up more than a few eccentric habits and interests, she had nonetheless lost little of her sharp intelligence, intuition and perception — to the degree, indeed, where she simply could not be ignored.

'I take your mother's eccentricity with a pinch of salt,' he said. 'But tell me: Do you know *why* your mother sent you to this particular department?'

'Yes. She thinks I'm having a nervous breakdown.'

'Are you?'

'It's possible. I think about this thing night and day, and it's certainly affecting me.'

'That shows a healthy degree of self-awareness.'

'I'm no fool, Dr Phillips.'

Michael smiled at that, but lowered his head first, fixing his gaze on his notebook but not really seeing it. When he looked up again, she was staring steadily at him, her brown eyes very calm, the smoke from her cigarette spiralling in front of her pale face.

'Call me Michael,' he said.

'I'm sorry, but that's too familiar.'

'I don't mind that kind of familiarity.'

'I do, Dr Phillips.'

Michael studied her at length, surprised by her response, but also finding her severe beauty very attractive . . . indeed, oddly disturbing.

'And what about the man?' he asked. 'Laurence Gilbride. Is *he* having a breakdown?'

'Yes,' she replied. 'I think he's heading that way — and for more than one reason. I think — '

'We'll get back to that later. I need to know other things first.'

The very mention of Laurence Gilbride's name had made the woman start to gently swing her left leg again; and when Michael's attention had been drawn to that motion, his gaze automatically narrowing down to where the folds of her thin dress met in the cleft of her compressing thighs, she had instantly ceased the movement but smiled at him, as if reading his mind.

Michael, very much to his surprise, felt aroused and embarrassed.

'Your mother,' he explained, grateful for the distraction, 'didn't send you here *just* because she thought you were having a nervous breakdown. She also sent you because this particular department is engaged in research into psychological disturbances

220

relating to reported experiences with unusual phenomena. In that respect this department is also involved in investigating the psychological responses of those who have, in one way or another, been involved with the increasingly widespread incidences of human or material disappearances, notably Glastonbury and its inhabitants; encounters with so-called aliens; sightings of UFOs or mysterious masses of the kind that came down over Glastonbury — and, according to you, over that area in southern Iraq. Your mother, then, wanted you to come to me because your experience is not an isolated one, and because I specialise in just this kind of case.'

Miss Devereux leaned forward to stub out her cigarette. She stayed like that for some time, as if in a trance, but finally managed to shake herself from her reverie and sit straight again, crossing her legs in that elegantly sensual manner, leaving her knees and calves exposed to his increasingly disconcerted gaze.

'And you believe that such phenomena are now widespread?' she asked, speaking levelly.

'Yes — and increasingly so.' He folded his hands on the desk, strangely pleased by her interest. 'This department is currently filled with people who have either had nervous breakdowns, or gone totally insane because of — or can simply supply first-hand accounts of — bizarre and frightening events of the kind we cannot rationally explain. Now, while many of these cases undoubtedly are rooted in commonplace trauma, our main interest lies in those cases that are allied to a phenomenon which, though almost too incredible to credit, is becoming common worldwide: namely, the inexplicable, usually permanent, disappearance of people and objects after the materialisation of a linear dark mass of variable size ... As I said: the very same kind of mass that descended over Glastonbury and, according to you, over your so-called Garden of Eden in Iraq.'

221

'It was not *so-called*, Dr Phillips. It was definitely Eden.'

'Perhaps,' Michael replied, not ignoring her note of firmness. 'We can leave that aside for now. What matters is that you're convinced that you were transported to another space-time continuum, and your description of that experience tallies remarkably with those of most of our other patients.'

'Well,' Miss Devereux said tartly, 'it's heartening to know that at least I'm not *completely* alone in my lunacy.'

'No,' Michael replied with a gentle smile. 'Not completely.'

'May I have a drink?'

'Tea or coffee?'

'I mean alcohol.'

'No, I'm afraid not.'

She displayed a flash of anger, then glanced restlessly around his office, again studying the diplomas with what appeared to be professional interest, then letting her gaze roam out the window and up to the sky. She studied the sky for some time, then turned back towards him, watching him as he stubbed out his cigarette and leaned back in his chair.

'So,' she said, 'you've been investigating the dark masses. What have you found out?'

'Naturally my own concern is with the psychological and, in some cases, physiological effects on those patients who have either been actually engaged with, or witnessed, a dark mass.'

'What do you mean by ''actually engaged with''?'

'I mean those people who have actually found themselves *inside* a dark mass, but somehow managed to get out — people like you.'

She nodded solemnly. 'Go on,' she said.

'Let me repeat: my own concern is with the physical and mental health of the people involved — but my department *is* working hand-in-hand with a team of

222

specialists who have been attempting to ascertain, scientifically and with the aid of first-hand corroborative evidence, the exact nature of the dark masses — which, it now seems, are starting to gobble up whole portions of the earth. Much more of this has been happening than has generally been revealed by the media, but the situation is becoming more dramatic — *very* dramatic, in fact.'

'You mean an increasing number of dark masses are appearing?'

'That's right. A *lot* more.'

Miss Devereux uncrossed her legs, then crossed them the other way. Michael, to his consternation, found himself watching that movement with an intensity not experienced since his adolescence. When he managed to raise his gaze from the hands placed back in her lap, he saw that to her calm gaze she had added a slight, enigmatic smile.

'So,' she asked, *'what* are they?'

Relieved to be thus distracted, Michael clasped his hands under his chin and said: 'Do you know anything about the Earth's magnetism?'

'Hardly my best subject,' she replied, 'but I'm sure you'll forgive that.'

Michael smiled, actually pleased with her gentle sarcasm. 'All right,' he said. 'Let me give you some background. I'll be as brief as I can.'

'I'm very glad to hear *that*,' she replied, then sat back to listen.

'Two points about your own report,' Michael began. 'One: that when the dark mass was taking shape around you, the atmosphere turned very cold — '

'Correct.'

' — and, two: that once inside the dark mass, when the whole space-time continuum changed, you all felt a lot heavier, as if the magnetism of the Earth had increased.'

'Correct again.'

'Okay,' he said. 'The Earth's magnetic field is caused

by the electric currents set up in its core by the revolution of the planet about its own axis. However, the magnetic field isn't constant. Short-term variations in the magnetic field can be caused by disturbances of the electrical currents in the ionosphere — and those disturbances are in turn caused by the changeable properties of particular rock formations on the surface of the earth itself, notably the rock known as ''lodestone'', which loses its magnetic properties when heated, but gains *more* of those same properties when *cold*.'

He stopped for her response, but she simply smiled a little, then said, 'I am listening, Dr Phillips. I am all ears. Please *do* continue.'

He coughed into his fist, tried not to look at her long legs; that forced him to look at her face, which made him just as uneasy.

'It's already well established,' he continued, trying not to sound too pedantic, 'that under the action of an *external* magnetic force, *all* substances become magnetic to a greater or smaller degree. That's what seems to be happening all over the earth wherever one of those dark masses appears. It would seem that part of the composition of the dark mass is a dense core of electrons which are being affected by — or are utilising — the more extreme fluctuations of the earth's magnetism, such as those found in areas containing large deposits of the highly magnetic mineral magnetite — in other words, *lodestone*.'

Miss Devereux took a deep breath, then let it out again, thus causing her breasts to rise and fall under her thin cotton dress. Remarkably, although she still looked severe, her sexuality seemed radiant.

'And what areas might those be?' she enquired.

'Generally speaking, areas which are noted as convergence points for what in Britain would be called leylines; in China, *lungmei*, or the paths of the dragon; in Ireland, fairy paths; in Australia and North America, creation paths. What I'm talking about is geomancy:

224

the theory that the earth is criss-crossed with an enormous network of largely invisible straight lines — the most noted visible ones being those of the Nazca plains of Peru and the so-called, unnaturally straight "antelope" tracks of the Himalayas — and that such lines are known to possess unusually powerful currents of terrestrial magnetism of the kind that can cause atmospheric phenomena. For some unknown reason, all but the few visible magnetic paths converge at points noted for their large quartz or metal content — in other words, lodestone — or in areas to which lodestone has actually been transported and used for construction purposes, such as the numerous megalithic-stone rings of this country, or the pyramids or other great buildings around the world.'

He paused to gauge if Miss Devereux was actually following what he was saying. Clearly she was, since she merely stared steadily at him, then said, 'Go on.'

Michael sighed. 'Recent surveys have shown that in the past few months there has been an unprecedented drop in temperature — and subsequent increase in magnetic strength — in most of those areas, with some, such as Glastonbury, displaying a much greater fluctuation than others. Glastonbury, which quickly became the coldest and most magnetic of all, was the first to suffer the visitation of the mysterious dark mass; but some of the other, lesser-publicised areas that vanished displayed the same atmospheric conditions as Glastonbury, and so it's thought that if things continue as they are, we can anticipate the same fate for a large portion of the earth, including some of its most renowned sites, great cathedrals and buildings which are known to be built over highly magnetic, prehistoric mounds, and, of course, the world's most famous megalithic monuments, including Stonehenge and Silsbury.'

Miss Devereux was now studying him more intently, her handsome brow wrinkled in thought as she leaned forward slightly.

'And when the dark masses swallow up parts of the earth, they replace them with — ?'

'Marshland,' Michael intervened, 'Just like your Garden of Eden.'

She straightened up again, giving prominence to her breasts; and Michael, disconcerted by his own feelings, took another deep breath.

'And can I take it, Dr Phillips, that if we project this theory further, we have the prospect of a disappearing earth — and the emergence of a new one very much like the areas already affected. In short: a new world of primal marshlands.'

'So it seems,' Michael said.

Aware that he was thinking of Miss Devereux as an attractive woman as well as a patient, he shifted uneasily in his chair, vainly attempting to put his thoughts in order. He tried to distance himself from her, to think of her as a patient, but felt his senses slipping away into a sensual mist. She was sitting very straight, her brown eyes fixed upon him, revealing a peculiar, quiet mockery and sexual challenge. Was she mad? He thought not. Yet her condition was not normal: he sensed that her calm exterior was hiding terror and obsessional introspection.

God's child. She believed she was carrying God's child. That was something to think about.

She leaned towards him again, her elbow resting on one thigh, the movement pulling the dress back over one knee and emphasising her long legs. Michael, shocked to realise what he was thinking, kept his gaze on her face.

'I got out,' she said. 'Laurence and I both got out. How did we manage to escape when no-one else has?'

'You're wrong,' Michael said. 'Other people have escaped, also. Admittedly, most of those people were caught on the very edge of the dark mass — which probably explains your other American, that fellow

Schul — but certainly they've at least been sucked in and managed to get out again.'

'How?'

'I've already explained how the magnetism fluctuates and subsequently affects the electrons within the dark mass. So, when the mutual magnetic attraction between the dark mass and the earth is very strong, the dark mass — which we now call the "Gateway" to the other space-time continuum — temporarily materialises. However, it disappears again when the magnetic field weakens. Laurence and you were obviously sucked into the "Gateway" when the magnetic field was particularly strong; then, when the magnetic field started weakening — which, incidentally, is why your "visions" started fading away — the parallel world gradually disappeared and let you escape.'

'If that's so, why did Glastonbury and those other areas disappear for good?'

'Because the dark mass comes and goes, growing more powerful each time it returns, until eventually it gobbles up what it's covered and takes it away for good, leaving behind a part of the earth as it must have been many millions of years ago. You made your escape while your dark mass was still fluctuating, but sooner or later that area will disappear for good and the primal marshlands will be left in its place. In other words, your Garden of Eden will eventually be permanent.'

She shuddered visibly, glanced around the room, briefly massaged her forehead with her fingers, then stared at him again.

'So,' she said, 'what actually *started* all this?'

Michael shrugged and spread his hands out in front of him, palms turned upward in a sign of defeat.

'We don't know,' he said. 'However, our researches into the kind of people who have been involved with the manifestations have given us the notion, alas unconfirmed, that certain people — those who, whether or not they know it, possess exceptionally powerful psychic or paranormal abilities — may actually be releasing the magnetic attraction between the earth and the dark mass, possibly because they have a very high degree of mental disturbance of the kind that can actually affect certain elements — in this case, the electrons which cause magnetic fluctuations to react on the dark mass, thus causing its power to wax or wane.'

Miss Devereux responded with a disconcerting silence, before managing to shake herself out of her reverie.

'Then Schul, as well as Laurence, might have had psychic abilities?'

'Yes,' Michael replied, feeling drawn to the mystery surrounding her, 'that would seem very likely.'

'I don't think Laurence is aware that he has any such abilities. In fact, I think he's rather sceptical of such abilities in general.'

'But he is, according to your report, a deeply religious person.'

'He *was*,' she corrected him.

'Are you telling me that his experience in Iraq *destroyed* his faith, rather than strengthening it?'

'Why should it strengthen it?'

'It strengthened yours.'

'That's because my interpretation of what happened was very different from Laurence's — and for a very good reason.'

'Your pregnancy?'

'Yes.'

Michael thought of lighting another cigarette, but decided against it. Miss Devereux was staring at him, her face severe and oddly sensual, its beauty a combination of intelligence and controlled emotion — or possibly hysteria. There was something fierce and desperate about her, but she was keeping it bottled up, refusing to let it blow her apart as it was threatening to do.

228

Her left leg, crossed over the right, was still swinging slightly, forcing Michael to remove his gaze with the guilt of a schoolboy.

'Okay,' he said, trying to sound as casual as possible. 'Let's talk about this child you're going to have. According to this new report, Schul wasn't actually drowned *before* being sucked into the dark mass, but was killed by Laurence during your experience in the other space-time continuum.'

'Yes, that's correct.'

'And that explains why Laurence refused to come here with you?'

'That's one of the reasons.'

'And the other?'

'His present relationship with me.'

'Your sexual relationship?'

'Yes. He thinks that's all tied to the Garden of Eden and what happened there.'

'The murder?'

'*And* my relationship with Schul. He thought that I was possessed — that Schul was the devil's disciple — and that what subsequently occurred between him and me had turned him into a sinner. He was disgusted *and* frightened by our affair, so has turned those emotions directly against me.'

'You mean that now you personally frighten and disgust him?'

'Yes, Doctor. Precisely.'

'Which means that this child, whom you consider to be God's child, is to Laurence the child of the devil.'

'He's wrong,' she said instantly.

Her leg stopped swinging, her knuckles tightened in her lap, and her eyes, formerly calm, suddenly flared with a disturbing intensity. Michael, who prided himself on his objectivity, felt that tension sweep over him.

'You definitely had no sexual relations with Laurence in the Garden of Eden?'

'No,' she replied, relaxing again. 'Only with Schul.'

229

'And did Laurence develop the idea that you were possessed during that time?'

'No. Only after our sexual relationship here had terminated.'

'What finished the sexual relationship? Did it end when you told him about Schul's child?'

'No. It ended before that. It ended because of the nature of my sexual demands, which he thought were both excessive and unnatural.'

'How many times did you have sex each week?'

'Each week?' she asked him, 'or each night?'

Michael stared thoughtfully at her, slightly shocked, quietly amused, then said, 'I think you've answered my question.' She smiled at him, also amused, but with a challenge in her gaze, so he coughed into his fist, studied his notes and continued: 'It would help if you could tell me why he thought your sexual demands were unnatural.'

She shrugged at that, opened and shut her clasped hands, swinging her leg again as she recounted, in a clear, perfectly neutral tone of voice, exactly what she had taught the innocent Laurence each night in her guest-room.

Michael listened patiently, then with growing surprise, then found himself staring at her swinging leg and finally into her steady gaze. Her brown eyes were gleaming brightly, then they melted and turned to limpid pools which drew him in through their darkness to that quiet, moonlit bedroom.

No: not Frances Devereux. It could not be the same person. That severe beauty in the middle-class clothes would not be capable of such things. Yet he heard her and saw her, wanton, unashamed, and his disbelief was mixed with growing desire at what she was telling him.

He lit a cigarette, inhaled deeply, coughed the smoke out, rubbed his eyes and squinted through the smoke to see her slight, enigmatic smile. She had finally stopped talking and was now staring at him, aware of his helpless discomfort and obviously amused by it.

Michael, who was normally at ease with the opposite sex, endured a self-imposed silence that seemed to last forever, then coughed without reason into his right fist before speaking again.

'Why do you need all that?' he asked carefully. 'I wouldn't exactly call it unnatural, but it does seem . . . *extreme*.'

Miss Devereux smiled slightly, then shrugged. 'I just need it,' she said.

'There *must* have been a *reason*,' Michael insisted.

'It's all in the past,' Miss Devereux replied. 'It's simply what I got used to.'

'What you got *used* to?'

'Never mind.'

'And it brings you happiness?'

'Yes.'

'I don't think so.'

'Think what you will.' She did not say it angrily, but as a simple statement of fact, then leaned forward, over her crossed legs, to study him thoughtfully. 'Tell me, Doctor,' she said, 'are you married?'

'I'm divorced,' he replied, taken by surprise. 'It happened five years ago.'

'I'm sorry to hear that.'

She nodded and pursed her lips, obviously still deep in thought. 'Do you mind telling me your weight?' she asked eventually, surprising him even more.

'A hundred and seventy pounds,' he replied, trying to hide his bewilderment.

She nodded again, then sat back in her chair. 'You're very solid,' she said. 'That's good. I like a man of some substance.'

Again taken aback but trying not to show it, Michael inhaled on his cigarette and took his time blowing the smoke out. He tried to meet his patient's gaze, but could not do it for long, and soon found himself glancing down to take note of the fact that her left leg, still crossed over the right, had started swinging again.

Disconcerted, almost sighing, he returned his attention to her face, and was at least relieved to see that she was no longer smiling enigmatically, but was instead offering a mask of blank, middle-class composure. More confident, if drowsily sensual, he decided to press on.

'Has the intensity of your sexual needs increased since your remarkable experience?'

'Yes,' she said. 'Definitely.'

'Does this bother you?'

'Only in that it forces me to find men ... and I don't like being reduced to picking up strangers.'

'But it doesn't bother you otherwise?'

'No. Why should it? Sex is perfectly normal. In fact, its only abnormality is its ability to help us transcend ourselves. Sex is a doorway to another world, which is why it obsesses us.'

'Have you *always* seen sex that way? As a means of transcendence?'

'I've always needed sex very badly — *very* badly — but until my experience in the Garden of Eden, I had only thought of it as a form of release.'

'And since Eden?'

'I need it. I need it all the time. It takes me out of myself.'

'And why do you think this all started in Eden? Had it something to do with the new environment, or was it the manifestations?'

'They were *not* manifestations, Doctor. Those events were very real. God came down upon us — it was God: He could control us — and His angels, or children, encouraged Schul and I to do what was done. It was not like normal sex — it was transcendence through self-abasement — and its purpose was to raise us beyond ourselves and propagate a new species. Yes, Doctor, a new species: the seed of a new dawning. What I learned

in that place is that the body is more than mere flesh . . .
it's immortality's doorway.'

'So you feel no guilt about your relationship with
Schul in that other world?'

'I felt shame at the time — particularly because of
Laurence — but then I came to accept that it was God's
will: that He had wanted this pregnancy.'

'Schul, then, was His instrument?'

'Yes. And died by His hand.'

'Why God and not the devil?'

'The devil is in the mind, a creation of man's guilt. It
was the eye of God I saw — a great white light
descending — and then I felt His children all around me
and heard the song of their speech. Their language
sounds like singing, but it isn't singing — it's speech —
and I understood enough to learn from them that I was
one of the first.'

'Pardon? One of the first of *what*?'

'One of the mothers to mankind as we know it,'
Frances Devereux said. 'And now soon to be mother to
this child — God's child — which will be one of the first
children of that new world you've already described.'

She took a deep breath, stretching herself, smiling at
him, then spoke with an oddly quiet fervour which he
thought might be madness.

'Don't you see, Dr Phillips? When we were trapped in
that dark mass — what you term another space-time
continuum — we first found ourselves in what might
have been the Garden of Eden, but then we were taken
back to an *even earlier* age, at the very dawn of mankind.
We were like apes, Dr Phillips, with the most primitive
consciousness imaginable, but then that light came
down, and those beings surrounded us, and they somehow imprinted upon us what we *and* our offspring
would become. I was an *animal*, Doctor — existing at the
dawn of time — and then I gave birth to a child that was
very different from myself, and that child and his

offspring evolved into the first of the human race. Time shifts back and forth. All exists simultaneously. I found myself in a barren landscape, as some primitive controlled by gods, then I found myself in the Garden of Eden as at least a *recognisable* human-being. I was a mother to the human race — not alone, but one of many. Now I'm about to become a mother to the new race in the world that is dawning.'

Michael stared steadily at the woman in front of him, trying to stay calm and keep his thoughts ordered; to relate what he had just heard to the woman who had spoken, as well as to the extraordinary events of the past two or three months.

More dark masses were appearing all over the world, materialising, disappearing, returning again, then gobbling up whatever they had covered and depositing marshlands. Time was stealing back its creations, space was opening out to accept them, and springing out of the Nothing left behind was a clean, virgin Earth.

And now this woman sat in front of him, one of many spread worldwide, claiming to be pregnant with the first of a new generation.

Not *just* a new generation — according to her, a new species — and if that were true, what would the world be like when the last dark mass had come and gone?

Michael leaned forward, stubbed his cigarette out, then rested his elbows on the desk and his chin in his hands. He looked at the calm exterior of Frances Devereux and felt her stirring emotions.

'God's child!' he murmured.

CHAPTER SEVENTEEN

Michael told Frances that he wanted her to meet some-one, but first he relented and let her have her alcohol, escorting her to the staff canteen high above the city, where he bought her a large gin and tonic. Facing her across the table, his knees practically touching hers, he felt uncomfortably close to her, almost guilty of intimacy. He had purchased himself a can of beer and sipped at it with relief, aware that the woman's suppressed, chaotic emotions were somehow affecting him.

'Are you enjoying the gin?' he asked her.

'Wildly,' she replied.

'You drink a lot?'

'Yes, I drink a lot — at least since I returned from there.'

'Drink and sex.'

'Precisely.'

'What about your faith in God?'

'I believe that I'm carrying His child, but I don't know what He's like.'

'The thought of what He might be like frightens you?'

'It terrifies me. I'm scared because I don't know His nature — nor what my child will be.'

'What makes you so sure you're pregnant? Have you seen a gynaecologist?'

'I *don't want* to see a gynaecologist. I'm frightened of that as well.'

'Of what he might discover?'

'Yes, I suppose so.'

'I understand your concern, but you can't possibly say you're pregnant until — '

'I'm a woman *and* a doctor. I *know* the symptoms of pregnancy. I haven't had my period and can actually *feel* something inside me. Damn it, I *know*!'

She was obviously angry, so Michael grinned and shrugged, spreading his hands in a gesture of apology until she smiled her forgiveness.

Relaxing, she sipped her gin, obviously in need of it, then gazed around the crowded canteen with professional interest. 'White smocks and stethoscopes,' she murmured. 'It reminds me of old times.' She shook her head from side to side, smiling with weary self-mockery, then turned back towards him, studying him frankly. 'Michael,' she said. 'Michael Phillips. Why *not* be familiar?'

'Why not, indeed?' He grinned at her and raised his can as if offering a toast, then drank some beer with a thirst that revealed how tense he was. He started drumming with his fingers on the metal-topped table, but when he saw that this was annoying her, he stopped it immediately.

'Can I get back to your relationship with Laurence?' he asked her.

'You're the doctor,' she said.

'Why did you eventually tell him about the child?'

'Anger,' she replied. 'It was no more than that. When he refused to have more sex with me, when he found the courage to reject me, I simply flared up in a most unpleasant manner and told him the truth.'

'And?'

'It just made matters worse. My sexual demands had actually revolted him — convincing him that I was either perverted or possessed — then, when I told him about

236

the child, the news filled him with fear. Like me, he's not sure what kind of pregnancy this is, which is something that doesn't make him any happier.'

'And yet he still lives there with you and your mother.'

'Yes — because no matter what he thinks of me personally, he's convinced that all of this was pre-ordained and therefore has to be seen through to the end, no matter the outcome.'

'And your mother? How does *she* react to all this?'

Frances actually smiled, then shrugged in a laconic manner. 'My mother is convinced that Laurence and I are on the way to nervous breakdowns, which is why she encouraged me to come here. She wanted Laurence to do the same, but understandably he refuses to talk to you or anyone else.'

'Perhaps I could go to see *him*.'

'I have no objections.'

The canteen was very lively, filled with chatter and clattering plates, the air enriched with the pungent aromas of coffee, boiling vegetables and grilling meat. Michael felt Frances' knee grazing his under the table; whether an accident or not, it sent a slight electric tingle through him.

'What age are you, Michael?' she asked him, her gaze steady and candid.

'Forty-three,' he replied.

'You look it,' she said, 'but in the best possible way. Most men of your age are still schoolboys in disguise, but you look rather worldly and mature, which I find most attractive.'

'I'm delighted that you like older men.'

'I like *experienced* men, Michael.'

Aware that she was staring very directly at him, that her knee was still pressing insistently into his, and that he was helplessly sinking into a state of sensual drowsiness, Michael had another sip of his beer and tried to keep his mind clear. He could feel her throttled tension and tried to see her hidden demons, but he only received the formal smile of a well brought-up lady.

A *formal* smile? Not quite: that smile was also slyly challenging, as if, in defiance of her fear, she was determined to have autonomy over her fate, and if necessary, steal it.

Perhaps aware of the uneasy silence, she abruptly changed the subject, saying, 'Since you've met my mother more than once, are you aware of her ideas about the spirit-world?'

'More or less,' Michael replied. 'She seems to believe that we don't necessarily pass over to the spirit-world through death, but may in fact exist simultaneously in that world; that it's a mirror to our own world; and that past and future may *also* exist simultaneously in that parallel world.'

'Correct,' Frances said. 'And she also believes that just as we're trapped in our own time and can't see beyond it, so, too, are the beings in the parallel world — they exist in their own time-frame, repeating their lives endlessly, unaware of any other world or period ... Though sometimes, just occasionally, they get *lost* in another space-time frame and materialise as what we think are *ghosts*.'

'That might explain why you thought you'd been gone for months when you had, in fact, been gone for only twenty-four hours of Earth's time.'

'Yes,' she replied, 'that could solve *that* particular little riddle.'

'And do you believe in ghosts, Frances?'

'I'm not sure. I *almost* did last night. Because last night, perhaps trying to prove her point to me, Mother persuaded me to sit in on a seance, and during it I heard what I'm convinced were the same voices that I first heard in the Garden of Eden — voices speaking in a language that sounded oddly like singing — and also saw shadowy figures passing *through* the other women around the table. As that was happening, I became overwhelmed with the same feelings I had in Eden: primitive emotions and dull thoughts, dominated by inchoate fears. Then, just as those feelings became unbearable, I fainted. When I recovered, Mother told me that she, also, had heard the singing voices, that she had not recognised or understood them, but that she was convinced I had been in contact, *not* with the dead, but with creatures from a parallel world, which could have been in the past *or* the future . . . So, there could be something in what she says.'

Michael noticed that her eyes were glittering, no longer calm but fraught, so he reached out and patted her wrist as if comforting a child. When he did so, she placed her hand on his, her fingers pressing his skin.

'You feel nice,' she said. *'Warm.'*

Michael instantly withdrew his hand, feeling his heart racing suddenly.

'According to that theory,' he said, 'the people disappearing from this world are going to materialise elsewhere as ghosts.'

'That's it. That's her theory.'

'And do you think that you, Laurence and Schul were like spirits in your Garden of Eden?'

'Yes,' she replied, 'I think so. The experience was extraordinarily vivid, yet completely unreal.'

'And your child? How does that fit in?'

'Oh, dear God, my child.'

She shuddered and looked away, her gaze scanning the crowded canteen, taking in the doctors, nurses and administrators with eyes that were not really seeing them, but turning fearfully inward. Eventually, she returned her attention to him, letting her knee press against his, taking comfort from flesh and bone.

'I feel like running away,' she said. 'I just want to get out of here.'

'Not yet,' Michael replied. 'I want you to meet some-one first.'

'Who?'

239

'An in-patient.'

Before she could refuse, he stood up and took hold of her elbow to lead her away. Guiding her out of the noisy canteen, he marched her to the psychiatric block, entered it and stopped at a solid wooden door, painted lime-green, with a sliding panel instead of a window.

While Frances stood there, increasingly agitated but offering no verbal protest, Michael slid the small panel back and stared into the room. Satisfied at what he was seeing, he nodded, opened the door and walked her inside.

'Frances,' he said, 'this is Miles Ashcombe.'

Sitting quietly on the edge of his steel-framed, single bed, Ashcombe was wearing what appeared to be slightly oversized clothing — crumpled grey slacks, open-necked white shirt, blue-grey pullover — but a closer inspection revealed that he had in fact lost a lot of weight and, although completely white-haired, was actually only in his mid-thirties.

Frances seemed to be puzzled by him, her brow furrowing in thought; she glanced enquiringly at Michael, received no response, so shook her head and returned her gaze to the silent man. He met her gaze boldly, but did not attempt to rise, merely opening and shutting the fingers of the hands in his lap.

'I'm sorry,' Frances began hesitantly. 'I . . . '

'Miles is one of the victims of the Glastonbury disappearance,' Michael explained. 'He lived just west of Glastonbury, with a clear view of the Tor, and was professionally immersed in the area as a noted centre of magic. He is, in fact, a well-known writer who specialised in the history and myths of that area and was renowned for his unusual psychic gifts. He's now suffering extreme trauma, and for a few weeks after the event could only speak a kind of primitive English. Now he talks properly, but will only speak when spoken to — though we *have* learned that during the early hours of that fateful day, he was jerked out of sleep by

240

inexplicable terror and felt compelled, even against his will, to go to the summit of the Tor. He was there when the dark mass materialised, and tried hiding himself in the tower of St Michael's Church; but when the darkness surrounded it he ran out again and saw that Glastonbury had vanished. Like you, he found himself in what seemed to be a prehistoric world, filled with animals that have long been extinct. He also saw marshlands and lagoons — and a volcanic mountain.'

Obviously shaken, Frances stepped back, away from Miles Ashcombe. Michael put his hand on hers and felt its febrile burning; he then turned to the man on the bed and spoke quietly to him.

'Tell us what you remember of your past, Miles. Please tell us everything.'

The man seemed perplexed, his eyes as empty as the moon, then he offered a shivering, demented smile and raised both his hands.

'Water and fire,' he said. 'A great light in the darkness. I saw a creature beating wings of skin, but it wasn't a bird. It looked prehistoric — at first I thought it was a pteranodon — but then I saw that it was actually the Archangel, descending from heaven.'

He closed his eyes and took a deep breath, held it in for some time, gasped and eventually stared at Frances, offering his awful smile.

'Wings of skin,' he said. 'Floating between heaven and earth. And he descended out of the blazing heart of God to weigh the souls of the dead. He touched me and I died. He weighed my soul and set me free. My former self cried out and disappeared as I awakened to glory ... St Michael! The Archangel! The Last Day! *I remember it all!*'

He closed his eyes again, held his breath, put his head back, slid down the wall until he was stretched out on the bed, his hollow-cheeked, deathly white face turned towards the ceiling. Only then did he let his breath out, but kept his eyes shut, his hands opening and closing

241

repeatedly by his sides, his shivering lips holding their crazy smile as he drifted away.

Frances shivered also, then moved towards the door, letting her hand fall off Michael's arm as she turned away from him. A choked sobbing escaped her as she grabbed at the door-handle, but Michael quickly grabbed her and jerked her back, making her spin in towards him. She fell into his embrace, breasts and belly crushed against him, hands digging frantically into his shoulder-blades as she sobbed and shook in his arms. He rocked her very gently, offering comfort as he surrendered, feeling something coming out of her that he had known in other women, but never with such palpable presence or fierce, overwhelming intensity. It was heat. Sexual heat.

CHAPTER EIGHTEEN

Though the wind was beating around her, Frances felt hot and drowsy, her thoughts scattering each time she closed her eyes, letting her fall close to sleep. When that happened, she was disturbed, remembering Ravello and Eden, one merging imperceptibly into the other and making her more confused. *Sex*, she thought. *Flesh*. And felt her clothes sticking to her, thus making her open her eyes again to stare out of the car.

No, it was not Ravello. Nor the lush greenery of Eden. Instead it was the low-rolling hills of Salisbury Plain, the grass rippling in the wind like the waves of a green-coloured sea. They had just left Devizes and were driving along the A360, Michael guiding the steering-wheel with his fingertips as if playing with it.

'God,' Frances said, 'I hate the English countryside. Even when the sun shines it's empty, and it makes me feel lonesome.'

'I love it,' Michael replied. 'After the city, with all its filth and noise, this seems so clean and peaceful.'

He glanced at her, grinning, revealing wrinkles under his grey eyes, and she felt the languorous warmth of her blood even in her despair. Laurence was in the rear seat, his troubled gaze downcast, the white-walled village through which they had just passed receding behind him.

'Are you all right?' she asked him.

'Yes,' he said, 'I'm fine. I can think of better days in my life, but otherwise I'm okay.'

He smiled and shrugged, obviously trying to conceal his fear, and she felt a real gratitude for the gesture, knowing how he was feeling. He was suffering guilt over Schul's death, and shame because of his affair with her; and even though their sexual relationship had ended some time ago, she knew that he was still torn between his love for her and his loathing for what she had made him do.

During the past few weeks at home, he had lived like a recluse, only leaving his room when necessary and even then hardly speaking, except to trade polite words with her mother, who always managed to charm him. Thank God for Michael, who had insisted upon seeing him, and, receiving too many refusals, had simply knocked on his bedroom door. Michael must have told Laurence what he had already explained to Frances, because since then, though obviously still not without problems, Laurence had reverted to a semblance of his former pleasant self and gradually conveyed some of that old warmth to her.

Now, returning his smile, Frances felt a little better, less ashamed of how she had used him, but still not without guilt.

Sighing, she turned back to the front, breathing the fresh air. They were crossing West Down, where the British Army held manoeuvres, the fields suitably desolate and windblown, as if the end of the world had come.

'God,' she said, 'have you ever seen anything more dreary? Just send me back to Iraq!'

Michael made no reply but threw her a grin, and Frances, in the warmth of her need, felt herself flowing towards him.

Sex, she thought. *Oblivion*. She would have him sooner or later. So far he had managed to resist her, but she knew what he felt. He wanted her very badly — she knew that as sure as breathing — but the fact that he was her doctor, plus his concern at her sexual hunger, was encouraging him to keep a certain distance and remain in control.

Thinking about that, she blushed, ashamed of her speculations. She shivered in her seat, saw the dark clouds drifting slowly, glanced across the rolling, tree-filled fields and talked to keep herself calm.

'That poor man in the hospital,' she said. 'Miles Ashcombe. What do you think he was trying to tell us? What did he *really* see?'

'I don't claim any *personal* connection,' Michael replied, 'but surely you know about the St Michael churches.'

'A little,' Frances said. 'I know that there are hundreds of them all over the country, and that most of them are situated on top of hills.'

'Exactly,' Michael said. 'And who was St Michael?'

'Some long dead priest, I would imagine.'

'No, Frances, you're wrong. St Michael is the Archangel, the captain of the heavenly host, first mentioned in *Revelations* and *Thessalonians*. According to the Bible, it was Michael and his angels who fought against Satan and his angels and eventually cast them out of heaven. It is also written that he will come down from heaven on the Last Day — '

'Ashcombe mentioned that.'

' — in order to weigh the souls of the dead, as also mentioned by Ashcombe. St Michael is usually depicted as a feathered, winged, sometimes flaming, always sword-bearing creature who floats between heaven and earth in his constant vigilance against the devil — and, indeed, on the tower of the St Michael's church on Glastonbury Tor, there was a carving showing him weighing the souls.'

'So why are the churches usually on top of hills?'

'At first it was assumed that it was merely a symbolic

gesture: St Michael, floating between heaven and earth until the arrival of the Last Day, occasionally settled upon mountain summits or hilltops to intervene in the affairs of men — so the hilltop churches pay tribute to his many supposed appearances down through the ages. However, it has since become clear that the great majority of those same churches were also built over prehistoric mounds covering the convergence of ley lines, and so must have been built there to act as conduits between the earth's magnetic energy and the ionosphere.'

'Oh, Christ,' Frances said, 'we're back to that again.'

'Right,' Michael replied. 'And it gets us back to your question: What did Miles Ashcombe actually *see*?'

'And the answer?'

'Miles Ashcombe is a religious person, a mystic with psychic gifts, and I think that in his terror at what was happening, he grabbed what he could. *Something* descended over him — as it descended over *you* — and then Miles must have seen some kind of being, or beings, and retreating into madness, seeking protection in trauma, interpreted the loss of his sanity as death, and thus viewed that being — or at least the last one he can recall — as St Michael, the Archangel, descended from heaven to inaugurate the Last Day.'

'That sounds reasonable,' Laurence said. 'During *our* particular experience, Frances and I clung to the God we had been told about since childhood: a God quick to anger — and to save. For both of us, though possibly in different ways, he was our hope of salvation.'

Michael nodded his agreement, then picked up on his train of thought. 'The facts fit,' he said. 'Ashcombe was standing, after all, on the ruins of St Michael's church, and that fact, plus his obvious knowledge of the mystical aspects of the Tor itself, would have encouraged such a connection in his mind. Glastonbury disappeared, the landscape changed before his eyes, then he saw a winged creature, a prehistoric pteranodon, and finally was surrounded by brilliant, pulsating light, as some being approached him. It must indeed have seemed like the biblical Last Day — and that pteranodon, observed just before his last moment of sanity, would have become mixed up in his mind with whatever being approached him, convincing him that he had seen the Archangel on Judgement Day.'

'The Millennium,' Laurence added in a surprisingly calm tone of voice. 'I think that's what the disappearing Earth means — we're on the verge of a new age.'

Disconcerted, Frances glanced out of the speeding car, expecting to see more green fields and autumnal trees, but seeing instead the thatched cottages and red-bricked houses of yet another typically empty small town.

'The Last Day,' she said to Michael. 'That certainly seems to be coming. But who will inhabit it? Will it be this child I'm carrying? And is this child one of the links between the past and the future? *I* saw other beings, too. They surrounded me and touched me. I saw them at the dawn of mankind, then saw them in Eden. I existed in both periods — just as much as I do now — and those beings, whatever their nature, filled me with love and fear. Now I burn just to think of it.'

And she was indeed burning: feeling scorched by the events she had already been through and the thought of what might yet be coming. She stared defiantly at Michael, anticipating his scorn, but saw only his roughly handsome profile with the bright sky beyond. He looked serious, almost anxious, very far removed from mockery, and she wanted to reach out to hold him and take comfort from him.

'You may be wrong,' he said. 'That possibility remains. I want a rational explanation — I can't help it: that's what I'm like — and I'm hoping that if things work out as planned, we might find one today.'

As he was speaking, the car moved up over the brow of a small incline and Frances, expecting the familiar prehistoric stones to rise out of a desolate landscape, was surprised to see, instead, an enormous horseshoe of tall directional antennas and dish-shaped parabolic radar antennae towering over a mass of aluminium huts, mobile power units, tents, army transport trucks, and what appeared to be close to a hundred men and women, some in uniform, others in white, knee-length coats, many gathered around what appeared to be a variety of cameras and lamps mounted on tripods, all of them wearing heavy, fur-collared jackets over their normal clothing.

Frances could hardly believe what she was seeing, but Michael stopped the car on the brow of the modest hill, and now, studying the scene thoroughly, she saw that the great stones of Stonehenge were indeed still there, but that the wire fence normally surrounding them had been removed to make way for that mass of men and equipment.

'My God!' Frances exclaimed. 'What on earth's going on there?'

'Do you notice something odd about them?' Michael asked her, by way of reply.

'Yes,' Frances said, taking note of the fur-lined jackets. 'It's a warm summer afternoon, yet most of those people are dressed for the winter.'

'Right,' Michael said. 'Here, just three or four hundred yards from that road, the temperature's about seventy degrees Fahrenheit, but just across the road — in the area starting just before the Neolithic ditch surrounding Stonehenge and ending about twenty yards beyond the far side of that same ditch; stretching out, also, about fifteen yards past the Heel Stone at the most northern tip of the monument and a similar distance beyond its southern perimeter — the temperature has been dropping steadily over the past few days and will, if it continues, eventually fall below freezing-point. So, we think something's going to happen, which is why you see this circus around the monument

— and why I've brought you and Laurence.'

Along the road, nearly half a mile before Stonehenge, armed soldiers were milling about a barbed-wired wooden barrier.

'The whole area around Stonehenge has been cordoned off,' Michael explained, 'and will stay that way at least until tomorrow. So, you are privileged.'

Grinning, he started the car and drove along to the heavily-guarded barrier. Stopping again, he showed his identity-card and official letter of admission to the sergeant in charge and, when the barrier was raised, drove on to Stonehenge, then turned into the car-park. After parking and making them all get out, he opened the boot and withdrew three fur-lined jackets.

'Here,' he said. 'I came prepared. And you really *will* need them.'

As they were putting on the jackets, Laurence smiled nervously at Frances, rolling his eyes in mock despair; then Michael gave them some thick gloves and said: 'Okay. Let's go.'

He led them out of the car park to the monument's entrance area. The ticket-booth and souvenir shop were closed, but the concrete enclosure had been filled with two long trestle-tables at which some of the soldiers and scientists were having the lunch that was being served from a mobile canteen by warmly wrapped women. Smelling vegetable soup, grilling sausages and French-fries, Frances instantly felt hungry; but instead of being invited to eat, she was told to follow Michael into the tunnel that ran under the main road and led back up into the grounds of the monument.

Entering the tunnel, Frances still felt quite warm, but halfway along, obviously under the main road, the cold suddenly bit her. She shivered uncontrollably, saw Laurence and Michael doing likewise, then emerged from the gloomy tunnel to the daylight and a more intense coldness.

Once in the grounds of the monument, Frances was

almost disorientated by the sheer size and scope of what she found there. With Laurence beside her, she followed Michael across the ditch and stopped beside one of the 2,000-year old stones, shivering as she stared past the heads and shoulders of men grouped around a mounted cine-camera at the great Sarsen Circle crowned with lintels and its inner horseshoe of Bluestone trilithons which, even surrounded by the steel and plastic of modern technology, retained their infinitely haunting, mysterious appearance. Nonetheless, the ancient standing stones were, in a sense, dwarfed and aesthetically diminished by the tall steel antennae and gleaming radar bowls which formed a wall around the circular ditch, and by the thick black electric cables that covered the grassy ground between the stones and terminated in the four mobile power-units which were standing at roughly equal distances apart around the inner bank. Beneath the radar bowls were the arc-lamps, also forming a great horseshoe around the monument, while beneath the arc-lamps were milling soldiers and scientists, the latter attending to the quite remarkable variety of scientific instruments that had been placed around the monument, including different kinds of telescopes and cameras, most of which were mounted on tripods.

Frances did not recognise any of the other instruments, so Michael, obviously aware of that, explained what was happening.

'We think the dark mass is going to materialise as soon as the temperature drops below, or near, zero. Since some of us also happen to believe that a human element may be involved in the magnetic and electron disturbances required to create the phenomenon, we've brought you and Laurence along for that very purpose. As you can see, most of the people involved have already moved out of the cold zone to that field beyond the ditch' — at this point, Michael indicated the nearby field, filled with aluminium huts, tents, parked army

250

transport vehicles and humans — 'and in a few more minutes, when the people around you have made their final adjustments, we'll *all* retreat to there and wait for something to happen. Should the dark mass materialise, we are going to try to ascertain, in scientific terms, just what it is. What you are surrounded with, then, are radiation detectors, ionisation measuring devices, ozone-measuring spectrometers, particle telescopes and cameras, infrasonic frequency detectors, geoditic and seismic measuring instruments, and theodolites.'

'I thought theodolites were used for tracking UFOs.'

'That's right. They are.'

More puzzled than ever, Frances was just about to ask Michael what UFOs had to do with the dark mass when a well-fed, rosy-cheeked man wearing civilian clothes, shivering visibly, and blowing into his cold clenched fists, walked up to him and, with a cheery grin, said hello. Michael replied in kind, shook the man's shoulder in a friendly fashion, then introduced him to Frances and Laurence as Lionel Sampson, the London-based Projects Officer for the Ministry of Defence's Department of Atmospheric and Meteorological Phenomena.

After shaking their hands, Sampson said: 'You got here just in time. We think something's happening. The temperature's started dropping more rapidly, and our instruments are showing dramatic fluctuations in the magnetic field. We have five or ten minutes.'

'What about us?' Laurence asked.

With the same cheerful, deliberately reassuring grin, Sampson pointed south to the far side of the area inside the encircling ditch.

'All we want you to do,' he said, 'is sit down on the mound between those two Aubrey Holes, which are marked with white circular chalk patches. Since certain evidence suggests that the human element — at least in the case of certain individuals — could be vital to the

251

materialisation of the phenomenon, we're hoping that your presence within the field of the dark mass will encourage its eventual appearance.'

Frances could hardly believe her ears and, after glancing at a straight-faced Michael, returned her attention to Mr Sampson.

'You want us to just *sit* there,' she said, feeling the rise of her anger, 'while the dark mass emerges? Is *that* what you're saying?'

Sampson nodded, his grin wavering. 'Don't worry,' he said. 'We don't want it to capture you again, and we're not going to let it. All these instruments around you,' he continued, waving one hand in the air, 'will be recording and measuring every conceivable aspect of the phenomenon — magnetism, radiation, temperature, light-intensity, infrasonic frequency, electron and radio-wave density, general particle and ozone content — you name it, we're measuring it — and the minute the phenomenon starts forming, we'll pull you right out of there. We'll be back in the field, near the aluminium huts, but we'll have you wired for sound and as soon as we know it's coming, we'll give you the word to get the hell out of its range and come back to us. Okay?'

'No, thanks,' Frances said.

She was stunned by their impertinence, by their willingness to exploit her, and she let her anger show in her face when she turned to face Michael. She took a step back, moving slightly away from him, filling up with the urge to slap his face and remove the smile from his lips; but he obviously read her thoughts and very neatly took control, reaching out to place his hands on her shoulders and shake her affectionately.

'Please,' he said. 'Do it. It's important that we try this. I know you think we're exploiting you, but we're not — we've got it under control. Believe me, if it starts materialising we're going to know about it before it gathers strength, so you'll have plenty of time to get out of here and join us back at the huts.'

'You bastard,' she said.

'No,' he replied, 'I'm not that. I'm just a man trying to do his job, and I want you to help me — '

'Rubbish!'

' — and, in helping me, perhaps help yourself. It's in your interests, as well as in ours, to find out what that thing is.'

'I won't do it,' Frances said, speaking as angrily as she could, yet irresistibly attracted to his air of authority.

'You must,' he said. '*Please*.'

He was still holding her shoulders, shaking her gently, insistently, and Frances felt the heat of his large hands filtering through her cold clothing. Already his touch was making her helpless, destroying her will-power and pride, doing to her what she had formerly done to Laurence in the guest-room's dark silence.

'No!' she said firmly.

'*I'll* do it,' Laurence offered, surprising them both. 'It's all right. *I'll* do it.'

Frances studied him thoughtfully, wondering what had motivated him; she recognised the panic in his eyes as exactly what she was feeling. So, that was it — he would fight his fear by facing its source — and understanding that, as well as knowing what she owed him, she had to give in to Michael.

'All right,' she said, not sounding friendly. 'I'll stay here with Laurence.'

Michael gave her a small bow, his grin affectionate and knowing, then let his hands drop from her shoulders as he turned towards Lionel Sampson who, managing to get back his grin, was already moving away from them, waving his right hand to indicate that they should follow him.

'This way, children,' he said.

He led them southward across the grounds of the monument, past the open end of the Sarsen Circle and the Bluestone trilithons, then on to the mound located between two chalk-marked Aubrey Holes at the far side of the ancient, encircling ditch. Once there, he asked Frances and Laurence to sit together on the grassy mound; then, when they had done so, a technician, looking bulky in his coveralls and heavy jacket, gave each of them walkie-talkies, put his thumb up encouragingly, but then too hastily headed off across the field beyond the curved ditch.

'They're set to receive,' Sampson told them, 'so you'll hear us if we want you to; but if you want to speak to us, press the switch — that's all there is to it. Okay?'

'Okay,' Laurence said.

He grinned uneasily at Frances, trying to show his appreciation; then Frances glared at Michael, determined to make her resentment obvious, but was defeated when she saw that his gentle smile was hiding concern.

'All right?' he said.

'Why bother asking?' she replied. 'You haven't left me much choice.'

He was visibly hurt, but simply nodded and turned away, walking across the ditch, side by side with Mr Sampson, and continuing across the field beyond it. They both followed the other men who had also left the area inside the ditch and were heading towards the aluminium huts in the middle of the field where, behind a solid wall of heat and impact shields, a great number of soldiers and civilians were nervously gathering.

Frances watched Michael until he had disappeared into that distant throng, behind the wall of large, rectangular heat-shields, then she sighed and turned back to the front.

Deserted, she sat beside Laurence on the grassy mound, staring at the prehistoric standing stones which, with the lintels lying across them, did not look too safe. She glanced sideways at Laurence and saw him gazing skyward, his lips moving as if offering a silent prayer, his eyes sleepless and haunted.

She had liked him in Iraq and now she did so again, understanding that what she had made him do had briefly robbed him of pride. And remembering that, she burned — not with shame, but with helpless lust — then glanced over her shoulder at the wide field behind her, searching for Michael in that ugly collection of aluminium huts, wind-whipped tents, army trucks and milling men and women. Failing to see him, she felt an even stronger desire for him, beyond shame or conscience.

She distracted herself by looking at Stonehenge, at the Altar Stone by the great trilithon. The stones represented history, imprinting its mysteries upon the present, but the electric cables, dish-bowl antennas, arc-lamps, cameras, theodolites and other scientific instruments had made a travesty of the normally haunting beauty of the ancient site, joining the past to the future in a grotesque and ominous technical union. Frances, no longer trusting in logic or science, was disgusted and fearful.

'I'd like to apologise,' Laurence said, speaking quietly, his eyes lowered. 'I've behaved very badly towards you, blaming you for my own sins. So I want to apologise.'

Taken by surprise again, Frances blushed like a schoolgirl. '*Your* sins?' she managed to say after the silence became to much. 'I seduced you. That's all there is to it. Perhaps *I* should apologise.'

'This is ridiculous,' Laurence said. 'How many men receive an apology after being seduced?'

Frances chuckled. 'Not many, I suppose. But in this case it's more than a simple case of seduction. I was fully aware of your beliefs, of your religious sincerity and celibacy, and instead of respecting that, I used it for my own selfish purposes.'

'Why *me?*'

'I can't answer that,' Frances replied, 'because I simply don't know. At first, I thought I was doing it because I needed you to protect me — but now I think I did it simply to keep you here until this situation resolved itself. It was an irresistible impulse, Laurence, instilled in me in Eden.'

Laurence stared directly at her, as if trying to read her thoughts, then nodded, gave a rueful smile and looked back at Stonehenge.

'I love you,' he said simply. 'I want you to know that. I was angry because you made me betray my faith, but throughout it, I loved you. I know you don't love me, but that doesn't matter. I just want you to understand clearly how deeply I feel for you.'

Frances was very moved, but she didn't know what to say. In truth, there was nothing she *could* say, and that made her feel worse. Eventually, still unable to put her feelings into words, she took hold of his hand and pressed it to her lips, then let it fall again.

'God,' she said, 'what a life!'

Laurence smiled at that, and Frances, sighing gratefully, looked back over her shoulder, first taking note of the men and women milling about behind the heat-shields, then surveying the giant radar-bowls and tall, thin antennae encircling the monument right in front of her.

The temperature was dropping and she quietly cursed the cold. Then Sampson spoke through his walkie-talkie, his voice badly distorted, telling her the atmosphere was disturbed and he thought it was starting.

Shivering again, Frances looked up at the sky, saw nothing but the swiftly moving dark clouds and returned her gaze to the monument. The great circle of stones seemed ominous, isolated from field and sky, the horizon, far beyond it, a green, tree-laden expanse that merged with natural tranquillity into a grey haze. It was a typical English summer's day — the sky cloudy, threatening rain — and even as she studied it, feeling more depressed each second, she turned colder and started feeling distinctly heavier, just as she had done in Eden.

'Look!' Laurence exclaimed.

And even as he was rising to his feet, pointing at the sky, Frances noticed that the crackling of her walkie-talkie had suddenly ceased, signifying that the instrument had gone dead. She pressed the switch and spoke into it, vainly hoping for a response, but knowing that contact had been cut off by some mysterious force.

Nothing. Deathly silence. Even the birds had ceased their singing. She followed Laurence's pointing finger, straining to see through deepening gloom ... and eventually saw an odd light flashing out around the Heel Stone, at the northern tip of the three-thousand year old Avenue.

From where Frances stood, the Heel Stone looked like a giant fish-head, bowing slightly towards the monument, its top nearly level with the distant horizon over which, in an impossible manner, the sun was now rising.

It was a huge sun, a tropical sun, rising golden and majestic, and its striations were fanning out along the horizon, first yellow, then red and appearing to flicker rapidly, giving the impression that they were flames licking out of the bowing Heel Stone as it plunged into jet-black silhouette.

'It's two o'clock in the afternoon,' Laurence said. '*The sky must be changing!*'

Frances jerked her head around and stared obliquely above her to see the normal sun, pale as the moon, hovering beyond the dense clouds. She glanced back over her shoulder at the mass of people across the field, observed that the normal sun was reflecting only dimly off the huts and army trucks behind the heat-shields. Disorientated, she turned back to the front, saw that other strange sun rising behind the Heel Stone, then, tugging furiously at Laurence's arm, started to run.

'No!' Laurence snapped. 'I'm staying here! *I have*

257

to know what it's all about!'

Frances stopped and gawped at him, not believing what she had heard, frantically worked on the switch of the walkie-talkie and received nothing but silence. She felt frozen, too heavy, divorced from reality, and knew that the dark mass was forming around her to take her away again. She remembered the child in her womb, was convinced she could feel it kicking, then sobbed, threw the walkie-talkie aside and suddenly found herself fleeing.

She ran over the ditch and bank, then raced across the sloping field, heading straight towards the long line of black shields and the people behind them. She was frightened, almost hysterical, conscious only of survival, and her very loud gasping was the only sound filling the silence. She glanced over her shoulder to see Laurence beside the mound, his head pulled back as he looked directly above him, his hands shading his eyes. She saw no more than that, but looked ahead and just kept running, then mercifully found herself racing between two large heat-shields and falling, almost sobbing with gratitude, into Michael's strong arms.

'It's all right,' he said. 'You're all right. It's still just taking shape.'

She felt his heat at her breasts, at her quivering loins and thighs, and clung to him, pressing herself against him until he turned her away from him. Leaning against him, letting his hands rest on her shoulders, she looked across the field to where Laurence was still standing on the grassy mound, his face turned towards the sky, the Sarsens and trilithons silhouetted behind him in the golden, almost phosphorescent illumination of that slow-rising, alien sun.

'Christ,' Michael murmured, his chin just above her head, his voice floating out of the silence with an eerie tonality. 'I can't believe this is happening.'

Frances glanced left and right, at the people massed around her, saw that most of them were looking at

Stonehenge with fearful, rapt expressions on their faces. Here, also, there were telescopes, various cameras and other instruments, but Frances was only aware of those pale, awe-struck faces illuminated in an oddly pulsating light, which was growing brighter each second.

'I shouldn't have run,' she said. 'I should have remained with Laurence. I should either have persuaded him to come with me or stayed right there beside him.'

'No,' Michael replied. 'You did the right thing. You couldn't have talked Laurence away — and wouldn't have gained a damned thing by staying there with him.'

'Jesus Christ!' Lionel Sampson exclaimed softly.

Frances suddenly noticed the small, plump man standing beside her, his mouth open in amazement . . . then she followed his gaze and saw the great darkness forming around Stonehenge.

It was an immense column of darkness, rectangular, its edges wavering, about half-a-mile wide and reaching up from the earth to the sky, like a pillar supporting the clouds in some mad artist's vision. The alien sun was still rising, beaming its light into the dense mass, and that light diffused to form a brilliance which burned through the darkness. The light exploded, became striations, then turned into countless stars that repeatedly flared up and contracted, giving life to the Nothing.

Laurence was still standing there, dwarfed by that spectacular dawning, then a greater light exploded obliquely down from the clouds to form a great pyramid which, in illuminating Stonehenge, turned Laurence into a silhouette.

'No!' Frances screamed.

She tried to break away from Michael, but he held her close to him, refusing to let her go, while the pyramid of light contracted vertically to become even wider.

Laurence stood there, a silhouette, the brightening

light distorting his shape, then the brilliance of the pyramid, whose base was broadening as its apex sank, eventually, in devouring the ancient stones behind him, erased him completely.

The pyramid's vertical kept shrinking until the light turned into a long, thin blade that stretched horizontally from one end of Stonehenge to the other, erasing the whole monument, while the surrounding darkness, half a mile wide, blocked out the real world.

And then, even as Michael's arms tightened around Frances, she *felt* the darkness advancing upon her and sweeping around her.

'*We're inside it!*' she screamed.

Suddenly it was there — directly above them and all around them — a darkness filled with pulsating light and what might have been shooting stars. Frances looked at Stonehenge, searching for Laurence and failing to find him, instead seeing what appeared to be an immense, glowing disc descending over the ancient stones as they gradually dissolved.

The stars were shining *through* the stones, dazzling her with their radiance, but she managed to observe that the enormous disc was surrounded by smaller discs, and that all of them were adding their light to the greater, pulsating brilliance.

'I can't believe this is happening!' Michael murmured. 'I don't *want* to believe it!'

And even as she heard his voice, Frances stared more intently into that dazzling haze and saw, in its unreal, shimmering splendour, figures moving to and fro, then spreading out to advance towards her, silhouetted, featureless, but obviously standing on two legs, their arms swinging in a normal fashion as they walked out of what resembled the landscape of a very vivid dream, at once frightening and beautiful.

'*It's sucking us in!*' someone bawled.

That single, terrified cry was the signal for panic, and Frances felt Michael's arm around her waist as he dragged her away. She ran with him, sobbing dryly, trying to hold on to her senses, vaguely aware of the mass of other people racing past her on all sides. They were retreating across the field, trying to get away from Stonehenge, and she saw the grey-hued greenery of the normal world again spread out in front of her.

There was shouting and screaming, then a fierce wind beat around her; she felt herself being sucked into a vacuum, but was pulled back by Michael. It was like the eye of a storm — the wind was rushing and howling around them — then there was buckling metal, collapsing antennae and arc-lamps, then the screams of those coming up behind her were sucked back into silence.

'Keep running!' Michael bawled.

She kept running because she had to, being dragged along by him, but eventually they escaped the force that was trying to pull them back, and stopped side by side on the grass at the field's outer limit.

'Christ!' Michael gasped. *'Christ!'*

Together, they turned to look back across the field, noticing that the others were doing the same, most dishevelled and windswept.

The pillar of darkness was still there, rising from earth to sky, but now stretched out on either side for a very long way and covering at least half of the field. That area, now unrecognisable, presented an alien spectacle, its darkness streaked with constantly shifting, shimmering light and what appeared to be exploding or shrinking stars.

Obviously it was another world, extraordinary and confusing, dominated by the great disc that hovered over the vanished Stonehenge and was, in its turn, surrounded by many smaller discs. The latter glowed like lanterns where they floated above the vanished monument, their flat bases emitting light which formed luminous pyramids in the stark, seemingly artificial darkness.

And there, most chillingly, stretched across what had been the field, were the silhouetted, distorted, but apparently human-shaped creatures who were moving to and fro, back and forth, very slowly, reaching out as if to touch the human beings mingling with them.

Then, even as Frances stared at them, they started fading away.

Again, it seemed impossible, an insult to intelligence, turning the senses upside-down even as it was happening.

The great disc flared up and vanished, shrinking back into darkness; then the smaller discs did the same, one after the other, eventually leaving nothing but that alien sky filled with pulsating stars.

The stars illuminated the ground below, and the creatures moving blindly over it, including the soldiers and scientists who had been sucked into the dark mass and, crying out, their voices echoing ethereally, gave the distinct impression that they were not only lost, but oblivious to the alien creatures wandering among them.

Yes, they were lost, and Frances knew it on the instant, as she heard them crying out and saw them fading away into a whirlpool of receding, shrinking stars and swirling streaks of white light. And then they were gone, and only the pillar of darkness remained, and then it also faded away to leave the normal grey afternoon.

Normal except for one thing.

Stonehenge had vanished.

Standing with her spine pressed into Michael's broad body, feeling his heat filtering through to her as his hands slid around her waist, Frances stared, with all the others massed around her, at the chilling emptiness of the field where Stonehenge had recently been.

The ancient stones had disappeared. A fine vapour rose from the green earth. There were no indentations or other marks where the stones had been standing. The great circle was empty. The land beyond was clearly visible. The alien sun had also vanished, and now dense clouds were moving across the sky as if nothing had happened.

Then, making her blood turn cold, Frances heard the voices emerging from that empty area ... disembodied ... despairing.

'Help! Someone help me! Where am I? What's happening? God, help me!'

The voices cried out for a long time — the desperate pleas of the invisible — while Frances and those scattered around her looked on in numb horror. *'Where am I? Please help me! Oh, God, what's happening to me?'* The voices rose and fell, echoing ethereally in an outer silence, until, after ten or fifteen minutes, they started fading away.

They faded slowly but surely, with heartbreaking inevitability, disappearing into the ether, growing fainter as if their owners were moving away over a very great distance. Then they faded away completely, first one, then another, until only one remained, and it eventually faded away also, leaving a vast, eerie silence.

That silence lingered a long time and was infinitely haunting; then a single bird sang, and was shortly followed by another; and soon the birds were gliding across the grey, cloudy sky, above the desolate green earth upon which Stonehenge had stood, and from which arose, for reasons as yet unknown, a fine, marsh-like mist.

'God help us all,' Frances whispered.

CHAPTER NINETEEN

Mrs Devereux examined herself in the mirror and, displeased with what she saw, turned away and went to the French windows overlooking the rear garden. It was late in the evening, the dark garden moonlit, and Mrs Devereux, concerned that Frances had still not returned from Stonehenge, looked down at her very well-kept lawn and found herself shivering. *Damn*, she thought, *will I never forget it? Will it haunt me even into my grave? And now Frances! Dear God ...* And yet she continued looking down, seeing the moonlight on the green lawn, remembering what had happened there many years ago and convinced that it was going to happen again, if in some different way.

Disturbed by such contemplations, she poured herself a sherry and sipped it as she stood by the window. Now, with the seance over and everyone gone, the silence of the four-storey house seemed oppressive, amplifying every creaking of wood and rustling of curtains.

Mrs Devereux closed her eyes, remembering the seance in the dark lounge, herself drifting away into that place where time and space had no meaning. Once there, she became a bridge between one world and the other, allowing the disembodied, who could not speak for themselves, to speak their garbled words through her. She had seen them in the starlight, in the glittering void of the nothing, and had watched them moving to and fro silently, obviously lost.

She had seen nothing else — and certainly not her long-lost husband — and when she had opened her eyes again, feeling exhausted and slightly dizzy, she had been faced with a group of perfectly normal women, all holding hands around the circular table. All old. Her own age.

'Silly cows,' she now murmured over her glass. 'I don't know why I bother.'

But she *did* know why she bothered. It was because she had lost her husband and wanted to contact him, desperate as she was to get answers to the questions that had secretly been tormenting her for years. No-one knew of her torment (they only saw what she chose to show them) but *she* knew that she would never rest in peace until the truth was discovered.

'*That's* why I bother,' she said. 'Those silly old cows aren't silly.'

Nor were they. She, Mrs Devereux, although possessing certain powers, could not get in touch with the other world without aid; so those other old women — frequently grief-stricken but often just intensely curious — had the sort of fierce belief which, when strengthened through their linked hands, could help her, Mrs Devereux, the medium, to break through into the other world.

And what was that world, exactly? Even now, it was hard to tell. Was it actually populated with the dead or with some alien intelligence? Mrs Devereux did not know and was haunted by her own ignorance, sometimes feeling that the more she found out, the less she actually understood.

She knew the other world existed, but didn't know what it really was; she had never seen more than vague figures moving through star-filled darkness. They were strangely insubstantial, wandering silently to and fro, obviously lost, but not necessarily dead or even human by nature. They existed and spoke through her, their language incomprehensible, but she never saw their faces or heard them speaking, so didn't know who or *what* they were.

'Are you still down there?' she asked, staring intently at the moonlit lawn. 'Are you going insane, wondering what's happened to you, or have you simply not realised?'

Talking to herself again. Or to the ghost of her lost husband. She put the glass to her lips and took a sip of sherry, still thoughtfully staring down at the tree-filled, shadowy garden and letting her thoughts turn from her missing husband to her very late daughter.

Why wasn't Frances back yet? Had anything happened to her? Mrs Devereux hadn't wanted them to go — neither Frances nor that poor Laurence — but Dr Phillips, with his charm and gentle firmness, had dragged them both off, insisting that it was all terribly important and could not be avoided.

Stonehenge. Why that monument? What could they do there? It all seemed rather odd, but she knew Dr Phillips well, and doubtless he had very good reasons to do what he was doing, no matter how mysterious they seemed at this particular moment.

Mrs Devereux shivered, still gazing down at the lawn, thinking of her husband and of what had happened to Frances, and wondering how much she was to blame for what was happening now.

I am paying for my secrecy, she thought. *All of this is my penance.*

The front door opened, then closed with a loud bang; Mrs Devereux immediately relaxed in the knowledge that Frances had finally returned.

She finished her sherry, turned away from the window, sat in a deep, faded armchair and tried to look unconcerned. Frances was obviously taking her time hanging her coat up in the hallway, but eventually she appeared, tall and slim in blue jeans, white blouse and high-heeled boots, long brown hair windblown and uncombed, her gaze slightly unfocused.

'God!' she exclaimed. 'I need a drink!' And walked straight to the cabinet where she poured a large brandy, drinking some while Mrs Devereux studied her, before returning her thoughtful gaze to the door.

There was no sign of Laurence.

'You look absolutely *ghastly*,' Mrs Devereux said. 'What on earth have you been doing in Wiltshire? Rolling about in the tall grass?'

'That's not too inaccurate,' Frances replied, looking quite grim.

'And our American guest? I see no sign of him. Has he gone straight to bed as he usually does, hiding his face in the pillow?'

'Laurence hasn't gone to bed,' Frances said, 'but he *has* gone for good.'

'Gone?' Mrs Devereux said.

'Yes, damn it,' Frances replied. 'Laurence has gone, probably for good. He disappeared with the rest of them.'

'The *rest* of them?'

'You're really not that stupid, Mother, so please don't act bewildered.'

'But I *am* bewildered, dear. Absolutely. What do you mean Laurence has gone for good? And who were the others? I don't know what happened down there, dear, so you'll have to *explain*.'

Frances stared angrily at her, sighed and drank more brandy, let the glass rest on her knee while she explained what had happened. She told her story thoroughly, with great attention to detail, and as she continued talking, her voice low and hypnotising, Mrs Devereux saw it vividly in her mind and felt growing fear.

She saw that great pillar of darkness, rising majestically from earth to sky, the alien creatures emerging from that strange, light-filled Nothing,

267

materialising, disappearing, becoming visible again ... as they had also done years ago in this very house ... and as they still did when she went into her medium's trance and became part of that other world.

She watched her daughter's moving lips, heard her words, dissolved into them, and visualised her husband on that lawn all those long years ago. Yes, a very long time ago, though not long enough to forget; and thinking about it, and of how Frances had been born, Mrs Devereux realised that she would finally have to tell her daughter the truth.

' — then they were gone,' Frances was saying. 'They just seemed to dissolve. They vanished as the dark mass was disappearing and didn't come back ... and neither did Stonehenge.'

Mrs Devereux took a deep breath and tried to remain calm; she felt trapped by the silence of the house in which a distant clock ticked. That clock was ticking off her life, remorselessly whittling her time away, and she shuddered to think of what might be coming to those who would follow her.

'All gone?' she said, still stumbling to find an adequate response. 'All those soldiers and scientists just ... *disappeared?*'

'Yes, Mother ... *and* Laurence. We heard their voices calling out and fading away — then there was nothing.'

Mrs Devereux thought of Frances and Laurence upstairs, conducting their affair nightly on the bed in the guest-room, under the delusion that she would not hear a sound. And of course she *had* heard — not much, but enough — and, though shocked a little, had accepted it as a form of catharsis after their terrible experience in Iraq. So, she had ignored them, letting them cling to each other, but also sensing that their meeting had been preordained and that she had to let events take their natural course — which, in view of what had happened at Stonehenge, they appeared to have done.

Now Laurence, like her husband, had served his purpose and been spirited away.

Mrs Devereux studied her daughter and saw lines on her skin, eyes luminous with a terrible beauty, lost in wonder and fear. Trying to ignore that, she leaned a little forward, remembering to keep her voice level.

'And what about those other creatures inside the dark mass?' she asked. 'Was our friend, Dr Phillips, willing to venture an opinion as to whom, or what, they might be?'

'He wasn't,' Frances replied, 'but some of his friends were. It's the opinion of the team of scientists with whom Michael's working that the dark masses are entrances to other space-time frames, and that the disappearing people have been transported into some other world, possibly in some other time-scale — past, present or future. Apparently, scientific examination of the areas involved has shown them to have possessed — at least for a short period after the disappearances — certain similarities to the known properties of black holes, and the scientists are therefore convinced that what is being observed inside the dark mass — the strange lights and wandering creatures — are parts of other space-time continuums that are temporarily rendered visible by certain geomagnetic forces and then, due to fluctuations in those forces, fade back into the space and time they originally came from. In other words, what we might be seeing is a race of totally alien beings, who come from a completely different world . . . and possibly another time.'

'So the people sucked into that dark mass could still be alive?'

'Yes,' Frances replied. 'And could in a sense be still right here on earth, in a kind of parallel world, no longer subject to our own laws of time, and perhaps imagining that they're suffering a bad dream from which they'll eventually wake up.'

Mrs Devereux felt the silence closing around her like a shroud, heard the clock ticking in the hall, sounding distant and unreal. She felt deep relief, as if freed from years of pain, but it sprang out of a deep well of fear and might soon fall back into it.

'And you?' she asked, leaning closer to Frances. 'What do you think?'

'I don't know,' Frances murmured.

'You were *in* another world, in another time, and now you seem to be pregnant. So what do you *think*?'

Frances shrugged, her face pained, her gaze wandering around the room, one of her legs crossed over the other, the almost empty glass of brandy resting on top of it. The lamps cast triangles of pale light on the richly carpeted floor, these separated by small pools of shadow and the carpet's striped patterns.

'I thought I was carrying God's child,' she said, 'and in a sense I still do. I don't know just who or what He is, but I feel that I've been directly touched by Him, and Schul was His instrument. Another world and time. *What* world and *what* time? And if those creatures in the dark mass aren't human, who or *what* are they? I only know that I saw and felt them in Eden, and that everything I did in that place was orchestrated by them. If God truly exists, we're probably *all* His children; and perhaps those creatures, coming out of His light, have been sent here to guide us.'

'Perhaps you *are* God's child,' Mrs Devereux said. 'You are certainly not *normal*.'

'Not *normal*?' Frances replied, looking bewildered. 'Mother, what do you *mean*?'

Mrs Devereux went to the windows, glanced down into the dark, moonlit garden, then returned to her chair, shaking her head.

'I lied to you,' she said, speaking clearly but reluctantly. 'Unfortunately, and to my eternal shame, I've been lying for years.'

She folded her hands in her lap, sat up very straight, fixed her gaze steadily on Frances and spoke as calmly as possible.

'Your father didn't really die when you were a baby,' she said. 'In fact, he disappeared the night you were born — right here, in this house.'

Nervous, and unable to hide behind her usual show of eccentricity, she clenched her left fist, coughed into it, then continued her story.

'A few years after marrying your father, and after trying repeatedly to get pregnant, I underwent a gynaecological examination, after which I was told that I was suffering from a condition that would prevent me from ever having a child. It was a terrible blow. A really *awful* blow. Your father was a good man, a deeply emotional, gentle man, and having come from a loving family, desperately wanted to have children — or, at least *one* child. I was very much in love with him and naturally wanted to please him, so the knowledge that I would never be able to give him a child destroyed all my happiness.'

Mrs Devereux hesitated, barely able to continue, then looked at the rapt face of her daughter and understood that she had to. There was nothing that could stop what was coming, and the truth might be helpful.

'Oh, he was good about it,' she said, 'carefully trying to hide his pain; but I knew how disappointed he had to be feeling secretly, and so the more I thought about my condition, the more depressed I became. In fact, as your father tried to bury his disappointment in work, and as we drifted apart because of that work, I, left alone while he spent long days in the film-studios, gradually came close to a nervous breakdown.'

Mrs Devereux stopped talking, re-living the pain of those distant years, fully aware that the past, present and future all shared the same bed. The pain had not died and could be recalled on the instant; and as she stared steadily at Frances, hardly recognising her child in the mature woman in front of her, she knew that the pain would stay with her even unto the grave.

'I started to dream a lot,' she said, 'and had very bad

271

nightmares. I dreamt of trees stripped of their leaves, and of flat, barren earth. Then the dreams took over my days, making me feel haunted, convincing me that I was being observed by some unseen force. You understand? It wasn't *people* I felt pursuing me: it was some kind of spiritual or ghostly *force*. And so, from that conviction sprang another, more helpful one: that either I was suffering from very odd hallucinations or was seeing what others could not see — that in fact I was psychic.'

She stopped to collect her thoughts, and to control her heavy breathing, feeling a little disconcerted by Frances' large-eyed, unwavering gaze. She sighed, tried to relax, but hearing the silence felt more nervous, her head filled with the ticking of the distant clock and thoughts of mortality.

'I began to see strange things,' she said, 'both at night and in broad daylight. I saw ghosts in this very house, faces floating in the darkness; heard whisperings and indistinguishable murmurings which seemed oddly ethereal. Yes, faces floating in darkness, then softly glowing forms, most of them at night, always indoors — none recognisable. Then all that changed. I started seeing them in daylight. First I saw Kirlian colours around people in the streets, then I saw their astral bodies emerging from them and dissolving above them. And soon I was seeing lights — the kind that people were calling UFOs — hovering in the sky in broad daylight or, much more frightening, glowing like lanterns and descending over Hampstead Heath, usually at night and always in silence, before dissolving to nothing ...'

Dissolving to nothing. Just like her husband. Just like Laurence and the scientists and soldiers and many more worldwide. Mrs Devereux was sick with fear, cheeks flushed, heart racing, and she felt the malignance of the silence which the clock's ticking challenged.

'Finally,' she continued, 'I developed *most* of the signs of pregnancy: the loss of my period, morning

272

sickness and — though even *I* could scarcely believe it — the very *physical* sensation of the child developing inside me ... yet, remarkably, I never gained weight. However, when I went for an examination, my doctor insisted that I was not remotely pregnant — that I was merely suffering from an *hysterical* pregnancy, the product of my desperate wish to have a child. Subsequent visits to other doctors produced the same diagnosis; yet no matter what they said, and throughout the interminable period of the child's gestation — *your* gestation — I retained most of the symptoms of a pregnant woman, and certainly felt you growing inside me. Then, when after eight months another doctor had insisted that I still wasn't pregnant — that my belly hadn't even swollen and there was no sign of a physical foetus — I distinctly felt the non-existent child kicking ... and then I went into labour.'

Mrs Devereux straightened up, turning her face towards the ceiling, closing her eyes and slipping back through the years to that singular moment. She saw the bedroom upstairs, herself lying on rumpled sheets, her elegant beauty distorted by sweat and fresh lines of pain. The room was brightly lit, very warm, the windows closed, and she felt that and saw the curtains whipping as the stars disappeared.

The stars disappearing? She must surely be dreaming! She saw her husband's face filling up with bewilderment; then, with his voice about to break, he asked her to bear down ...

Looking into that bright room of long ago, Mrs Devereux saw the darkness descending over the whole scene — as it had, in fact, done so at the time; then, having seen it, she opened her eyes again, to stare into her daughter's haunted features and take comfort from them.

'It was in this very house,' she said, surprised by her own voice. 'This large house that needed children to fill it with movement and noise. And here I went into labour, impossibly pregnant and bearing down, and your father, that gentle man, that loving husband and composer — knowing what the doctors had said, but taking my word for it that they were wrong — decided to be there when the baby arrived, if indeed it existed. Well, it existed — *you existed*, my dear! I laboured neither long nor hard, but soon felt the baby coming; then, as this was happening, as I was bearing down to push you out, an unnatural darkness slipped down over the house, blotting out the sky, then filling up with a shimmering light, which pulsated with a radiant energy that filled the whole room. And then — oh, dear God, even as I felt you coming! — I saw figures around me, leaning over to examine me, yet transparent and actually passing *through* your father, where he was standing by the side of the bed, looking down at me, clearly shocked speechless. Then I heard their sibilant speech — not talking, something else: an ethereal, melodious kind of *singing* which, though sounding like nothing I had ever heard, filled me with unutterable joy and lifted me out of myself. Then suddenly you cried out — the living child I should *not* have had — and I saw your father holding you in his arms and rocking you gently.'

'But surely, Mother, if there was no *physical* sign of . . .?'

'There was no blood on the bed. No mess at all . . . Yet you seemed perfectly normal.'

She saw Frances staring at her with eyes as big as spoons, their brown depths leading into a universe of infinite mystery. In those eyes she saw awe mixed with dread and disbelief; but she also saw the yearning and hope of all the children to come. Mrs Devereux wanted to look away — to avoid seeing herself twice reflected — but the force of her daughter's gaze mesmerised her and kept her gaze steady.

'And my father? What happened to him? Did he — ?'

'Yes, he just vanished.'

Mrs Devereux heard her own sigh like a breeze far

away, crooning through imaginary bulrushes, over rippling, dark water.

'I must have slept,' she said. 'Or perhaps I even fainted. I remember your father placing you in my arms, then telling me that he had to go outside to see what was happening. First he went to the window. That strange darkness was still there. I couldn't see the sky, but I saw the light inside that darkness, pulsating with a magical, beautiful life of its own while that alien, voiceless singing continued and the shadowy, almost silhouetted figures surrounded my bed. Your father looked into the garden, murmured something like ''Good God!'' and then, as he turned to leave the room, I must have slipped into sleep again.'

'And he never returned?' Frances asked, her voice as quiet as the grave, her eyes glittering with a light that illuminated shocked disbelief. 'You mean he just ... *disappeared?*'

Mrs Devereux sighed, releasing her pain with it, noticing that the darkness between the tall lamps formed an arch behind Frances.

'I awakened soon enough,' she said. 'Hearing your father's voice calling to me — calling up from the garden below the bedroom and sounding quite desperate. He was begging me for help, wanting to know what was happening to him — and terrified by what I was hearing, not knowing what was happening, I placed you in your cot and forced myself across the room to look through the window. The night had returned to normal. There were stars in the sky. I looked down at the moonlit lawn, where your father's voice was coming from, and although I could still hear his voice, the lawn was totally empty. I kept looking, unable to move, horrified and disbelieving, and eventually your father's voice faded away, leaving only the silence.'

Mrs Devereux closed her eyes, opened them again to study Frances, was lost in the pale beauty of that face, wanting to reach out and touch it.

'After that — I don't know why; some animal instinct, I suppose — I simply picked you out of your cot, held you close to me, lay down with you on the bed and fell asleep quickly. When I awakened, the world was normal — daylight beamed through the window — and you were crying healthily in my arms, though your father was missing. I never found out where he had gone ... and he never returned.'

Mrs Devereux shuddered, feeling adrift on a cold, dark sea, wondering if life wasn't but a dream populated with dreamers.

'So, I lied to you,' she said. 'I've been doing so for years. I didn't want you to feel unnatural — to be haunted by the past or frightened of your unknown future — but now, given what has occurred, I think you just have to know ... Your father didn't die when you were two or three years old — he was abducted by whatever came down and surrounded this house — the same kind of dark mass that you experienced in Iraq, and which today spirited Laurence and those other unfortunates out of this world. Now you know why I practise spiritualism — I'm trying to contact your lost father — and why I think that your experience in Iraq was almost certainly preordained. You were not a *normal* child, Frances — nor will your own child be. *God's* child? I don't know if that's true ... but you're certainly not mine.'

She leaned forward in her chair to watch Frances more closely, noting that her dark, tragic eyes were growing larger each second. The room was lit by pedestal-lamps located in the corners, and their yellow light, falling obliquely from wall to carpet, was shadow-filled and too weak. Frances looked like a ghost, a pale ghost, and her gaze wandered blindly.

'I can't ...' she began, hardly able to force the words out. 'I can't accept that — '

'You *must!*' Mrs Devereux insisted, reaching out to take Frances' hand and shake it dramatically. 'Your own

276

birth was not normal — and the child you're having can't be normal — so you must accept the powers you've been given and learn to live with them.'

'*Powers?*' Frances said, sounding dazed. 'I don't have any powers! *I don't believe what you're saying!*'

She tried to snatch her hand away, but Mrs Devereux tightened her grip, staring at her as if wanting to slap her.

'Yes!' she whispered. 'You *have* strange powers — and they'll gradually grow stronger — and soon they'll be so remarkable that you'll find yourself wanting to hide them. *Here!*' she snapped, grabbing Frances' other hand. 'Concentrate! *Look at me!*'

Frances did as she was told, her eyes large and luminous, while Mrs Devereux, tightly clutching both her hands, let the power flow between them.

'Look at the glasses on the cabinet!' she hissed. '*Will* them to *move!*'

Frances stared at the drinks cabinet, too dazed to do otherwise, obeying her mother with the docility of a child, her strained face streaked with shadows. Mrs Devereux held her hands, letting the power flow between them, and eventually Frances started to shake like a leaf in a storm.

Mrs Devereux felt omniscient, her body consumed by flames, and knew that what had possessed her was now entering her daughter. She gripped Frances' hands even tighter, feeling her fear and tension, saw her lips shivering and heard a gasp as her wet eyes grew larger.

Some of the wine glasses were drifting up into the air, hovering about six inches above the cabinet in that weak, yellow lamplight, framed by the panes of the windows and the night sky beyond.

'Yes!' Mrs Devereux cried. '*Yes!* Now make them all *move!*'

Frances shook even more, as if jolted by electricity, and beads of sweat broke out on her forehead as, striped by yellow light and shadow, she concentrated with

277

unleashed ferocity on the glasses floating in mid-air.
The glasses bobbed up and down, wobbled from left to
right, drifted apart, shook violently and then suddenly
exploded, scattering their pieces over the cabinet below
and onto the carpet.

Frances stared at the scattered pieces, at the empty air
where the glasses had floated, then looked straight at
her mother as she sat back, releasing her sweating
hands.

Mrs Devereux said nothing, no longer knowing right
from wrong, wondering what had impelled her to tell
the truth when it could bring no-one happiness. Then
she saw Frances' face, her dark eyes filled with
lamplight, her sensual lips, marked by her own teeth,
searching desperately for words.

'I don't believe this,' Frances said.

CHAPTER TWENTY

'I don't believe it!' Frances snapped into the telephone. 'Of *course* I don't believe it. How can I believe what you're saying when I know how I feel. I *am* pregnant, damn you! *I am!* I don't *care* what your doctors say!'

'You're being hysterical,' Michael replied. 'You've simply got to accept the facts. The examination proved you weren't pregnant, and that's all there is to it.'

'Damn you, I am *not* hysterical!'

'Then why did you rush away this morning?'

'I rushed away from your bloody stupid gynae-cologist and his silly remarks. I can actually *feel* this child inside me — and he says I'm imagining it!'

'You *are* imagining it,' Michael said. 'You're suffering from clinical hysteria. Now I want you to come back here to discuss what we're going to do about it.'

'Damn you!' Frances said, feeling betrayed and humiliated, her cheeks burning in the cool air of the hallway, the light of noon beaming in through the tinted glass of the ornate floor and forming a hazy rainbow at her feet. 'I will not take sedation or your bloody psychiatric treatment. I won't become part of your rotten experiment. I'm pregnant! That's *that!*'

She slammed the receiver down and stared at it for some time, visualising Michael in the hospital, doing exactly the same. That alone could excite her — the very thought of his presence — and *his* anger, which she had felt over the line, excited her even more.

'Damn!' she muttered, shaking her head, trying to clear it and think straight. She stared in bewilderment at the front door's leaded windows, at the kaleidoscopic glass, which let the sunlight fall on her face to make her skin glow.

She didn't hear her mother behind her, but sensed her arrival, and turned around to find her standing in the doorway of the lounge, small and youthfully slim, wearing a loose dress and flat-heeled shoes, her bright eyes magnified by the spectacles, giving her the appearance of an inquisitive bird.

'That was Michael?'

'Yes,' Frances replied. 'He thinks I'm hysterical.'

'Did you tell him about me? About how you were born?'

Frances sighed. 'No, I didn't, Mother. I didn't even think about it. Quite frankly, I didn't believe your story myself — and I assumed that when I had an examination, it would prove that my pregnancy was perfectly normal. Then they told me I wasn't pregnant — God, I couldn't believe it! — and then, still not wanting to believe it, I went a bit crazy.'

'And stormed out of the hospital.'

'Yes. I walked out the minute I heard Michael mention "hysterical pregnancy". I shouted at him — I remember doing that — then I stormed out.'

Remembering it, she blushed, but also felt desire, her embarrassment merging subtly with the lust to make her mind reel. She sometimes hated being a woman, loathed the indignities of her body, but against this was the need to use that body to find sensual transcendence. So, she thought of the hospital, herself stretched out on the examination table, legs parted while the doctor routinely poked and peered inside her, before making his emphatic statement about her not being pregnant. Then she thought of Michael and his disbelieving face, and understood that the fuse to her anger had been lit by her need for him.

Yes, she wanted to possess him, and thus be possessed by him; she needed to transcend her baser self and lose her fear in love's furnace.

'I'm going crazy,' she said, really talking to herself. 'I can't take too much more of this. I can't believe it's really happening to me. It all seems like a bad dream.'

'Alas, it's *not* a dream,' her mother replied, 'and I do believe, my dear, that you should go back and tell Michael about it.'

'I can't tell him. *I can't!*'

As she had stormed from the hospital, so she now fled to the lounge, scarcely aware of what she was doing, impelled by blind panic. She saw the gilt-framed paintings, the fading, antique furniture, the velvet curtains hanging from the ceiling and framing the windows. The room had been like this for as long as she could remember, and as she surveyed it, taking note of its decaying elegance, she felt like a child again.

She turned her back to the ornate white-marble fireplace and faced her mother once more.

'I can't think straight,' she said.

She placed her hand on her stomach, wanting in vain to feel it swelling, then remembered that vivid nightmare in Iraq where she had, on hands and knees, in front of Laurence, behaved like an animal. It had been her, yet not her — it had also been someone else. The real Frances had been lost in Ravello where the church bells still tolled.

She thought of Ravello now, getting it mixed up with Iraq, both places being bathed in the silvery light of a perpetual noon, illuminated in her mind with an intensity borne from sexual release. She was dominated by her flesh, held in thrall by her own desires, driven to seduce and submit until her Self was destroyed. It wasn't natural and never had been (her skin burned with an ethereal heat), and just as she had been used by

281

Schul and had in turn used Laurence, so did she now yearn to use Michael and then be used by him.

She shuddered, feeling fearful, her fingers outspread on her belly, wondering how she could even think of such things, given what was to come.

'It's understandable,' her mother said, 'that you can't think too straight right now; what I've told you must be frightening to hear, as well as totally bewildering. That's why I think you should go back to the hospital: to see Michael and talk to him. You have to talk to someone other than me — someone not so involved — and Michael, with his professional interest in this matter, is the best person for that.'

'You like him, don't you?'

'He has strength, but lacks brutality. I find that an admirable trait in a man — plus intelligence, of course.'

Frances smiled, surprised she could still do so, then looked around the cluttered, Victorian lounge and tried to imagine her father. He would have sat at that same piano, or that Chippendale *secretaire*, composing his music while his pipe lay in its brass bowl, filling the air with its smoke. Her mother had told her he had died, but Frances had never really believed it, and had kept him alive in her mind as someone to cling to. Yet she had felt his loss greatly — much more than she could admit — and had been angry, as well as deeply pained, at being betrayed by his going.

It was a romantic reaction, rising out of his lost presence, and later, when she was caught in the swirling tides of her adolescence, she had been drawn, irresistibly and forlornly, to older men — father-figures. Small wonder, then, that Italy became her personal Waterloo; that the Italian, in his sunlit and white-walled sweltering room, while the church bells tolled noon and Ravello's narrow streets filled with noise, had been able to exact complete submission and hopeless dependence. He had set her on fire and taught her to love the flames; now, when she thought of his singular, debased artistry, and, perhaps more pertinently, failed to separate it from the present, she felt ill and had to turn away from her mother, fixing her gaze on the hallway.

'Yes,' she said. 'Of course. You're quite right. I'll go back and see Michael.'

So saying, she went into the hallway and put her coat back on, then left the house and walked down the street, heading towards East Heath Road. She had to pass the Freemasons Arms, and that temptation was too much for her; she went in and purchased a large gin and tonic, which she then drank too quickly. Instantly feeling illuminated, she left the bar and walked on, turning right at the main road and moving parallel to East Heath, very aware of the lush greenery across the road and the roaring traffic upon it. She soon passed the busy shops and arrived at Pond Street, looked up at the towering hospital, then crossed the road, passed through the main-gate, and entered the building.

Standing in the lift that was carrying her to the top floor, she felt even more removed from her senses, if enslaved by her burning skin. She thought of what had happened to her, and of what she was undergoing, and only managed to deduce from the abnormality of those experiences that her sensuality, extreme at the least, seemed to come from afar. It was more than herself — it was something outside her — and it was making her behave as she did for reasons still unknown.

The lift doors opened, letting her make her escape, and she went along to the main door of the psychiatric wing. There was a person on attendance, but he obviously recognised her, and once he had let her in, she went straight to the room of Miles Ashcombe.

She opened the sliding panel (she was a doctor, after all) and looked through the peephole to see Miles Ashcombe sitting on the bed, his eyes glacial and too bright.

Was he mad? It was possible, though she didn't believe so. More likely he was driven by the mysterious, growing powers which were, at this very moment, at play in that small room.

Ashcombe was sitting in the sunlight pouring in through the window and, with both hands weaving arabesques in the air, orchestrating the dance of the beads he had been given to play with.

The beads were as big as marbles and of many different colours. Having been removed from the strings that had held them together, they were, with the unknotted strings, drifting about in thin-air like the planets of some alien cosmos, rising, falling, forming into Catherine-wheels, coming apart and reforming as kaleidoscopic lines that twisted and turned to his will.

Frances watched, fascinated, remembering her own brand of magic, then glanced at Ashcombe's bright, wandering eyes and turned away in despair. Breathing harshly, she fled from there, taking the lift down one floor, then hurried straight to Michael's office, her heart racing, face flushed.

She opened his door without knocking, walked in and slammed it shut. Michael looked up, surprised, then dropped the pen he had been using. He was wearing a nondescript, open-necked shirt with short sleeves, and she noticed that his muscular arms were tanned, with fine golden hairs.

'I've just visited Miles Ashcombe,' she said, 'and he seems to be developing strange powers.'

'Yes,' Michael replied. 'Very strange . . . and growing more powerful, thus potentially more dangerous, every day.'

'Dangerous?'

Michael shrugged. 'What *else* can they be? The powers you've seen, developing for weeks, have shown no signs of stopping. Ergo, if they continue to develop at the same rate, there's no limit to what Ashcombe might become.'

'Godlike.'

'Yes, Frances, godlike . . . perhaps a new kind of being.'

Michael pushed his chair back and stood up behind his desk. He was wearing fawn-coloured tropical slacks, and his belly was flat.

'I'm pregnant,' Frances said. 'And that's *not* an hysterical statement. I don't know what kind of pregnancy this is, but believe me, it's genuine. Miles Ashcombe is developing some very strange powers, and my pregnancy obviously comes from the same source. Now listen! *Please listen!*'

She told him about her mother, about her own magical birth, and about how her father had disappeared the night she was born. She spoke with controlled urgency, very aware of her racing heart, then noticed the intensity of his gaze as he walked around the desk. He stopped just in front of her, gazing thoughtfully at her, then placed his right hand on her shoulder and leaned closer to her.

'This is true?' he asked.

'Yes,' she said. 'I think it is. I don't think my mother would lie about such a thing — and I know what I'm feeling.'

'What *are* you feeling, Frances?'

'I'm feeling pregnant, Michael. *Very* pregnant ... And my body is burning.'

At that moment she knew she had him. She could see it in his eyes: they widened, then narrowed again as he took a deep breath. Frances smiled and stepped close to him. He moved back against the desk. He couldn't retreat any farther, so she remained where she was.

'What do you mean, Frances?' he asked. 'Just what are you driving at?'

'I need it,' she replied. 'I always need it and want it now. I used to think it was because of the first lover I ever had, but now I know he's only responsible for my predilections — not for my appetite. My body is burning, Michael. It *always* seems to be burning. I always needed it more than most, but since Iraq that need's become abnormal, making me feel that I'm burning. I'm on fire right this moment. I can't help it . . . My body rules me completely.'

She took hold of his right hand and placed it on her breast, breathing deeply to tighten the cloth against her skin and let him feel her warm softness. He tried to slide his hand away, but she held it there, pressing her hand on his.

'It's not me,' she said. 'I'm convinced that I'm being used. Whether God or the devil or some alien beings, I'm being used by a force outside myself, and what it wants is my body. I'm burning up, Michael. Feel me! Spread your fingers and *feel* me.'

He sucked his breath in, held it briefly, let it out. She felt his fingers spreading over her breast, his palm flattening her nipple.

'For God's sake,' he whispered, 'I'm your doctor! I can't . . . *I can't do this!*'

But he didn't remove his hand. In fact, his fingers explored her softness. She breathed deeply to make her breast swell out and give its warmth to his fingertips.

'You want me,' she murmured.

'Frances, *please* . . .'

'You want me badly — I can feel that. Now I want you to feel me, to know my need, and I want that right now.'

'The door's not locked, Frances.'

'Never mind the bloody door. Here,' she murmured, sliding his hand under her blouse. 'Feel the softness of me. Feel my heat. Do it *now*, Michael. *Do it!*'

His hand closed over her breast, fingers squeezing, palm pressing; she was not wearing a brassière and she felt the abrasive warmth of his masculine skin. He breathed deeply and closed his eyes, then started opening them again; but she pressed the fingers of her free hand on his eyelids as her body fell into him. He sighed, almost despairingly, then put his head back, letting the fingers on his eyelids slide down and slip into his open mouth. He sucked her fingers and squeezed her breast, losing his senses, giving in, and she artfully

286

rolled her belly against his groin and heard his soft, throttled groan.

'Yes!' she said. '*Yes!*'

She pulled her fingers from his mouth and slid them wetly under his shirt; his groin quivered against her loins as his hands undid the rest of her buttons and pulled the blouse from her shoulders. She felt the air on her naked bosom, then his lips, his lapping tongue, then his fingers were in her hair, jerking her head back to let his mouth cover hers. She writhed against him, losing herself, letting the flames scorch her skin, then felt herself being gripped, turned around and pressed back down on the desk. There were sounds overlapping — creaking wood, spasmodic gasping, cloth rubbing against cloth — then she felt, as the flames consumed her and she melted, the need to cling to her senses.

She was suffocating, burning, opening her eyes to his sweating forehead, her tongue licking the one deep in her throat as she tried to devour his lips. She jerked her head back, gasping harshly for breath, saw her right leg curved over his spine as he penetrated and filled her.

Her aching throat released a groan as her own knees bent in towards her, then she locked her legs over his straining back and sank her teeth in his shoulder. She tasted sweat, a touch of salt; nipped his skin and tasted blood; heard a grunt and cried out as he pushed deeper and the desk hurt her shoulder-blades. She tightened her thighs, drawing him in, gasped for breath, her lungs on fire, locked her arms and legs around him and quivered, then was dragged down.

A wooden chair fell over, making a nerve-jarring banging. Michael cursed, gasped and groaned loudly as her weight forced her down on him. She was writhing, twisting upon him, being supported as she sank slowly; was stopped, then lowered onto the floor and felt him on top of her. She opened her eyes to the ceiling, gasped for breath, heard him groaning, glanced over the white skin of his shoulder to see the plain of his heaving back.

Edinu: Plain. The plain stretched to a hazed horizon. The light was a whiteness that shimmered with an unearthly glowing. The plain was hot and desolate. Beyond it were the mountains. The peaks of the mountains were distorted in the shimmering heat-haze. She looked away from it, returning her gaze to the immediate vicinity, saw her brothers and sisters huddled fearfully together as the shadowy forms, faceless and silent, moved curiously around them. When she saw them, she cried out. When they touched her, she cried again. That cry was the sound of her terror, but did not last too long. She succumbed to her body's heat, wanting only to please them, then lay down and let herself be opened and entered and filled.

'Yes!' she cried. '*Schul!*'

Frances felt the weight on top of her, the thrusting inside her, opened her eyes as a belly slapped upon her and fleshy hips pounded her. The glistening skin of a sweating shoulder-blade was all she could see.

Where was she? In a room. It was white and filled with sunlight. For a moment she thought she was in Ravello with the Italian on top of her. No, not the Italian. And not Schul or Laurence. That warm hardness withdrew, then entered her again, and she heard the slapping sounds of their union as she melted around him.

Michael! Oh, dear God! They were on the floor in his office! She remembered the unlocked door and the terrible chance they were taking; and this thought, while it filled her with horror, also increased her excitement.

'Don't stop!' she gasped. '*Don't stop!*'

It was a useless command, falling on deaf ears, but she felt the electric jolting of his orgasm as he flooded her insides. The flames consumed her and made her melt, letting her flow into the ether, and she gave herself to him, pouring around him, drowning him, and felt herself becoming one with him as his throttled cry pierced her.

He shuddered and groaned, as if being whiplashed, then shook violently and turned to a block of stone when he subsided on top of her.

She had wanted to find transcendence, to be taken out of her mortal self, to feel the glory of her untrammelled spirit before being recaptured. But that eluded her once more — her churning emotions found no release — and when she opened her eyes and legs, and let her hands fall from his spine, as she lay there on the floor, being crushed by his cooling body, she heard his harsh gasping, his anguished groan, and felt the burning begin again.

'Oh, Christ!' she said. '*Damn it!*'

CHAPTER TWENTY-ONE

Michael groaned again, slowly rolled off her, lay beside
her for a moment, staring blindly at the ceiling, then
adjusted his clothing as she turned away from him,
curling up on the floor like a ball, and slid her hands
between her clenched thighs to hold herself where she
ached. She just lay there, curled up, trying to regulate
her breathing, then heard Michael zipping his trousers,
standing upright and locking the office door.

'Madness!' he exclaimed. 'Pure madness! I can't
believe we did that!'

She remained where she was, holding her aching
centre, letting her racing heart settle and her breathing
return to normal, frustrated even more than before and
burning all over. Was she mad? Not yet. But she could
not stay sane like this. She thought of what she needed
for satisfaction, then shuddered helplessly.

Michael must have seen that, because he suddenly
knelt beside her. He ran his hand lightly down her side
to her raised hip, then very gently rolled her over, onto
her back.

'Are you all right?' he asked her.

The question made her smile. 'Why do men always
ask that after sex? Are their egos that fragile?'

Michael remained grave, his face showing his
concern. 'Maybe,' he said. 'But perhaps I'm just

worried about what really went on here. I'm in love with you — '

'It was sex.'

'No, I'm in love with you — it's not just sex; it's more than that — and I'm worried about what you actually experience when you need sex that badly.'

Frances closed her eyes, trying to look into herself, having to fight back the tears as his words resounded through her, giving life to the love she had sensed in him and washing her clean. She bit her lower lip, choking back her emotions, letting tears fall on her cheeks to cool her warm skin. She loved him — at least she *wanted* to love him — but was frightened of showing it.

'We didn't make *love*,' she said, opening her eyes again. 'We simply had sex.'

He stared down at her, very gravely, then with slowly rising anger. 'Don't speak for me,' he said. 'Speak for yourself — but not for me. It's not just sex — it's love. I know what I feel, damn it! I'm not a child, Frances; neither am I given to self-deception. I love you and want you.'

She remained on the floor, taking deep, even breaths, looking up into his grey, intense eyes and fighting her overbrimming feelings. She had not wanted love — not after Ravello — but she could hardly resist the emotions that were now washing over her, so she nodded to let him know that she had heard him, but made no reply.

'Okay,' he said. 'I just wanted you to know. Now tell me why you called out Schul's name — and I'm *not* being jealous.'

Frances sighed. 'All right,' she said. 'I'll tell you, though I doubt that you'll believe me. For a while there I thought that I was back in Iraq, in Eden, being taken forcibly by Jack Schul while those other creatures stood over us.'

'The *other* creatures?'

'Yes,' Frances said, 'the other creatures. When I went

291

back in time, to what I think was mankind's dawning, I was usually surrounded by other primitives, whom I assumed were just like me — let's say members of the same tribe — but at some point was also surrounded by other creatures like the ones we saw at Stonehenge. I thought of them as God's children because they'd emerged from disc-shaped lights which had, in their turn, emerged from a greater light, which I thought was God. Whether right or wrong about that, I *am* convinced that those creatures, whatever their nature, were controlling our actions, and that even now I'm under their influence and cannot escape it.'

Michael nodded, then stood up and stretched himself, looking very tall and broad above her.

'And your sexual appetite?' he asked levelly. 'Do they control that as well?'

'If you're talking about my need for the kind of things I did with Laurence — '

'I'm not.'

' — then the answer is negative, since all of that — which doubtless disgusts you — I picked up from my first lover at a time when I was emotionally very vulnerable. However, if you don't mean that — '

'I don't.'

' — but are talking about my increasingly abnormal need to simply *have* sex, then, yes, there's no doubt that it began during my experience in Iraq and has been growing stronger ever since. And, if it continues doing so, it will almost certainly drive me out of my mind.'

Michael shook his head, displaying his bewilderment. 'It doesn't make any sense,' he said. 'There's just no logic to it.'

Frances sat up, adjusted her clothing, glanced around her, then seeing the key in the locked door, smiled and climbed to her feet.

'Maybe that's your problem,' she said. 'After all, what *is* logic?'

'You mean, whoever they are, they may not have *our* kind of logic?'

'That's right,' Frances said.

Michael went to the window and looked down upon Pond Street, then turned away and started to place his hands on her shoulders. Frances, feeling the heat of her own desire, stepped back out of his reach.

'Don't touch me,' she said.

Michael sighed, looking hurt, then nodded his understanding; he gave her a slight, knowing smile, but made no move towards her.

'So,' he said, 'who *are* they?'

Frances shrugged, feeling helpless. 'I don't know, Michael. I only know that when I was sucked into the dark mass, I first found myself in a place of lagoons and marshes, then found myself in a completely different time, if possibly the same place. I think it was the same place: it was just thousands of years earlier. I was a primitive creature, living with others at the edge of a great dust-bowl, which I believe became filled with water, probably the sea, over subsequent centuries. So, first I was that primitive creature in a parched, primal landscape; next, I was a recognisable human type, living in lush greenery by the edge of a great lagoon — a lagoon that I believe was originally no more than that very same dust-bowl or, perhaps, meteorite crater. What I'm talking about is reincarnation: the possibility of multiple lives. I now believe that I've lived at least twice before — and that somehow or other that dark mass took me back to my former lives.'

'A parallel world,' Michael said. 'Or alternate universe.'

'Pardon?'

'The theory of parallel worlds is difficult to explain, mainly because of the bewildering nature of time. However, the main point is that if alternate universes *do* exist, they would do so in a completely different timescale from our own, which gives rise to the possibility

293

that there could be a virtually identical *you* living in a different time and place, right now and always. It is also possible that what we dream is as real as *we* are, and exists, side by side with our own existence, in an eternal present containing its own past and future.'

'I'm bewildered already.'

'Once the dream is dreamt, it takes on a separate existence and will therefore create its own world, with past, present and future — and *that* world, in turn, does the same — and so on to infinity.'

'You're driving me crazy,' Frances said.

'It's easy to do,' Michael replied. 'Better minds than ours have gone crazy trying to prove this — but the theory, if hard to grasp, has a high degree of probability, and *has* been used as an explanation for reincarnation, dreams, automatic writing, extrasensory perception, precognition, ghosts and UFOs which, according to many, including Carl Jung, are psychological projections from the common racial memory of mankind.'

'And the dark masses?' Frances asked, sinking into confusion. 'Where do they fit into this elaborate theory?'

'Black holes,' Michael said. 'As I told you before, we've already found out that most of the areas where the disappearances occurred, possessed — at least for a short while after the disappearances — a great many of the characteristics of black holes. Now, we *do* know that matter falling into a black hole disappears from our universe, but the million-dollar question remains ... Where does it *go*?'

'Where, indeed?' Frances murmured, hoping to get a smile out of him, but failing to do so.

'Assuming that the matter doesn't simply *disappear*,' he continued, ' — which, in theoretical terms, it should not — we're left with the choice of it either reappearing in another part of our universe — maybe emerging from a white hole — or reappearing in an *alternate* universe. Accepting this second hypothesis — that the matter sucked into the black hole could reappear in an alternate universe — we have to bear in mind that there'll be no relationship between the time when the matter was sucked into the black hole and the time of its escape into the alternate universe. The black hole, then, could be a doorway through time and space, linking past, present and future together in a simultaneous reality.'

'Which means that the creatures I saw, as well as the people who disappeared, are now existing simultaneously in the past, present and future — right here on earth, in a parallel world that we can't see.'

'Yes,' Michael said, 'put crudely, that's just what I mean.'

'So I could, in fact, have been that primitive creature at the dawn of mankind, as well as the evolving human-being in the Garden of Eden?'

'Correct. Figuratively speaking, an original Eve. And now you're Frances Devereux of Hampstead, England ... giving birth to the future.'

'Oh, no!' Frances groaned.

She covered her lips with her right hand, stopping the scream she felt was coming, then let a shudder of dread ripple through her before controlling herself. She thought of those creatures around her, their wavering, faceless forms, then imagined them watching her this very minute ... silent ... invisible.

Were they actually in this room? Was Laurence still at Stonehenge? Was her father still on the lawn, lost in another time-frame, convinced that he was having a bad dream and would soon wake up? It chilled her to think about it, made her feel that she was suffocating, as if the walls were closing in upon her, threatening oblivion.

'I still can't believe this,' she said.

'It's only a theory,' Michael replied, 'if a rather persuasive one. But you're not physically pregnant — though showing most of the symptoms — and your mother is convinced that you have unusual psychic gifts, which could relate to this. Miles Ashcombe possessed psychic powers of a rather modest nature, but since emerging from that dark mass those powers have been developing remarkably. What about you?'

Frances trembled, stirred to fear by his words, remembering what she had done with the wine glasses at her mother's insistence.

'Yes,' she confessed, 'I'm developing such powers. Already I can do what I just saw Ashcombe do in his room.'

'You can make objects float in the air?'

'Yes.'

'That's just the beginning,' Michael said. 'Ashcombe now *amuses* himself with those games, but he can do a lot more. As I said, we're wondering when, and if, it will end — or if he'll turn into some kind of superman. Come on, let's go see him.'

He took Frances by the elbow and led her out of the office, then straight to the psychiatric wing. As they approached Ashcombe's room, Frances felt her fear rising, a tide of heat that reached up to her face and made her cheeks burn. She stopped just before the room, reluctant to go any further, but Michael, smiling encouragingly at her, tugged gently at her elbow and coaxed her right up to the door.

He slid the peephole open, looked in, his brow furrowing, then stepped aside and indicated with startled eyes that Frances also should look in. She did so — and instantly felt confused and terribly frightened, at first not understanding what she was seeing, then not quite believing it.

There were two Miles Ashcombes in the room. One, perfectly normal, was stretched out on his bed, flat on his back, his face turned towards the ceiling, a gentle smile on his lips. However, the other, not so normal — or at least the same, but surrounded by shimmering light — was hovering above the bed, lying flat on his back in thin-air, his face also turned towards the ceiling, the same smile on his lips.

Frances gasped and turned away, hiding herself in Michael's embrace, shocked and frightened by what she had seen, hardly able to credit it. Michael held her close to him, patted her shoulder-blades reassuringly, then eventually pushed her from him and, holding her lightly by the shoulders, gave her a gentle smile.

'Yes,' he said, 'now you see what he can do ... and now we're going in there.'

'No!'

'Yes,' Michael insisted. 'He's started talking and I want you to listen because it could be of use.'

Again she started to protest, but was given no chance, since he quickly opened the door, pushed her into the room, followed her and closed the door behind him.

Frances stood there, terrified, trying to reject what she was seeing, but that other Miles Ashcombe, that bizarre *doppelganger*, was still hovering in the air above the original Miles Ashcombe, both wearing the same clothing and smiling the same sly smile, both stretched out in exactly the same manner ... the only difference being that the one hovering magically in the air was encased in an egg-shell of shimmering light.

Frances stared at that apparition, then lowered her gaze. When the man on the bed turned his head to stare at her, the head of the man hovering above him did exactly the same.

Frances felt disorientated, rendered dizzy by faulty vision, but then Ashcombe, noticing her, stopped smiling and sighed — and, as he did so, the shimmering creature above him drifted down very slowly. It started fading when it touched him, and soon disappeared altogether, becoming no more than an eggshell-shaped light that shimmered brightly around him, then was sucked into his body until it was all gone.

Ashcombe remained there, lying stretched out on the bed, staring steadily at Frances.

'I know you,' he said, his voice hollow. 'You were there on the other side.'

Hearing those words, Frances felt that she was suffocating, and she stepped back until stopped by Michael's body, by the hands on her shoulders.

'It's all right,' he said. 'Just stay calm. There's nothing to fear.'

His strong hands were a comfort, as was the heat from his body, but Frances still trembled with fear as she gazed down at Ashcombe. Due to his white hair, he looked older than his age, and the smile that was returning to his thin lips seemed slyly triumphant. He examined her face, then her flat stomach, finally nodded judiciously and sat upright, resting his feet on the floor.

'You were there at the beginning,' he said. 'You were blessed, as I am.'

Frances found it hard to speak, but she managed to force the words out. 'What do you mean by the "other side"?' she asked. 'And the beginning of *what?*'

'You know what I mean,' he said. 'You have been there yourself. You were there at the dawn of mankind, and have returned more than once.'

'You mean inside the dark mass?'

'Yes,' he said. 'Naturally. But the dark mass isn't dark — it's filled with light — and that leads to our origins.'

'*What* origins?'

'You were blessed, as I am. You were one of those chosen to link the past to the future, to help plant the seeds of each new age as the old passed away. They came four-hundred million years ago, returned ten million years ago, then came two million years ago to bless those who were chosen. First the reptile, the monkey, the upright ape, *Ramapithecus;* then they returned again, one-hundred thousand years ago, to ensure that Neanderthal Man would evolve into Cro-Magnon Man — the true ancestor of modern Man. You were there even before that, living in caves, eating your own flesh; then the landscape changed, filling with water and becoming verdant, and you — the different you that was passed down through the centuries — learned to worship them and make carvings of them before the next change was ordained. You were there at the start — at every ending and new beginning — as you are here, right now, to take part in the end of the old world ... and the start of the new.'

Frances trembled in Michael's grip, feeling disordered and unreal, her heart racing and making her skin burn with a new kind of fever. She licked her lips, thinking them parched, then forced out more words.

'Who *are* they?' she asked. 'The ones who came ... and are coming back now.'

'The gods,' Ashcombe said, his eyes gleaming with a distant light. 'They come from afar, from the double star, slipping through time and space. They are bodiless, but materialise before us that we might recognise them. They are here to inaugurate the new dawn — and a new breed of Man.'

'A *new* breed of Man ...?' Frances almost lost her courage, but when Michael reassuringly squeezed her shoulders, she found it again. 'What *kind* of new Man? Will the new Man have powers like your own? Like the ...?'

'Yes,' Ashcombe answered proudly. 'Like those of the gods ... the powers that you and I have.'

He raised his right hand to spread his fingers like a web, and the curtains, hanging motionless over the window, started fluttering gently. He kept his hand there, staring steadily at Frances, then the gently fluttering curtains were whipped up dramatically, flapping and snapping as if attracted to his fingers by an invisible force. Then the window exploded, sending shards of glass flying, and a fierce wind rushed into the room and slapped Frances' face.

Startled, she gasped and covered her mouth with her hands. Michael gripped her tighter and pulled her close to him as the wind, suddenly swirling around them, rushed back out, leaving silence. Then the walls of the room cracked and lumps of plaster fell to the floor. The walls spat white powder while their beams split apart, then the cracks became bigger and suddenly criss-crossed the walls like great webs.

'No!' Frances shouted at Ashcombe. *'Don't tamper with this!'*

Yet even as her voice rang out, the walls were spitting more dust and plaster; then the window-frame exploded in a great many pieces from its breaking wall. Frances and Michael both ducked as the pieces shot past their heads, straightened up as the carpet flew off the floor and fell over the bed.

Miles Ashcombe stood up as the floorboards started buckling, rusty nails being shot from the splitting wood like bullets to embed themselves in the ceiling which, now cracking like the walls, was sending down a fine powder.

Ashcombe smiled with sly triumph, eyes gleaming with a distant light, then raised his hands in the air, about three feet apart. Sparkling lines of electric current passed from one to the other, erratically illuminating his face and making him look totally mad.

'Stop it!' Frances screamed. 'Stop it! *For God's sake, don't play with them!'*

But Ashcombe didn't stop. He just stood there, smiling triumphantly. The sparkling lines of electric current jumped between his outstretched hands while the floorboards, still buckling noisily around his feet, started breaking up and flying about the room.

'Let's get out!' Michael bawled.

He started to pull Frances out, moving back towards the door, but large chunks of the walls exploded violently, showering them in plaster, and they both dropped to their knees while more floorboards snapped loose around them.

The noise had reached deafening proportions — a

cacophony of snapping wood, screeching nails and exploding plaster — then the fierce wind rushed back in, sweeping around and beating at them; and as Michael grabbed Frances and pulled her tightly to him, she glanced up and saw that Ashcombe, still standing there by the bed, had turned into a human torch, his fingers blackened and burning from the electricity charging between them, his whole body, from head to toe, surrounded by a phosphorescent light that forced her to close her eyes.

'No!' Ashcombe shrieked. '*No!*'

Frances felt the wind departing, though its roaring still filled the room, and at the sound of Miles Ashcombe's desperate cry, she looked up again.

The wind was still there, forming a whirlwind around Ashcombe, who, frozen in its vortex and surrounded by that dazzling light, was releasing a high-pitched, macabre wailing, which added hideously to the general bedlam. The whirlwind roared and swirled, sucking up plaster and broken floorboards, and Ashcombe, growing fainter in the brilliance inside the storm, remained in that pose of stark, frozen terror while his screaming also started fading away, growing more and more distant. He rapidly became less real, then seemed to be transparent, then dissolved into the dazzling light and faded out with his screaming.

The whirlwind was still roaring and swirling at a furious rate, but now only surrounded the globe of shimmering light — then that, too, started fading away to let the storm settle down. The flying floorboards fell to the floor, as did nails and pieces of plaster, then the wind gave one last, defiant whisper and died out completely, leaving nothing but a devastated room, filled with drifting white powder.

Then Miles Ashcombe called out of nowhere. He was appealing desperately for help. He kept calling out of thin-air, his voice ethereal and haunting, until after a few minutes it faded away completely, being lost at the other side of the universe, leaving a stark, chilling silence.

Frances remained kneeling on the ruined floor, safe in Michael's embrace.

They both stared at the empty room.

CHAPTER TWENTY-TWO

'Yes,' Mrs Devereux said, picking flecks of cotton off her brightly-patterned, Victorian dress and squinting upwards out of the gloom through her spectacles, 'but what did he *mean* exactly? What was he trying to convey before he performed his Houdini act?'

'Please, Mother,' Frances admonished her, 'it's not funny. That remark's out of place.'

'*Nothing* is out of place, dear,' her mother replied. 'Nothing is out of place, anywhere, anytime, and my remark was designed simply to make you feel less gloomy than you look.'

'It seems clear,' Michael said, ignoring the minor altercation, 'that he was talking about the different stages of mankind's development, and about the fact that these creatures have materialised on Earth at each of those stages. The first visit mentioned by Ashcombe was four-hundred million years ago, which would be in the early Devonian, when the first fish crawled out of the sea and onto the land. The next visit, according to Ashcombe, was ten million years ago, which would be about the time of the first upright man, *Ramapithecus*. The next visit mentioned was during the time of Neanderthal Man who, for reasons not yet fully explained, disappeared to make way for Cro-Magnon Man.'

'A disappearance that could be explained by our visitors,' Mrs Devereux intervened.

'Correct,' Michael said. 'He then went on to talk about how the landscape gradually changed, becoming more verdant, and suggesting that the ancestors of Cro-Magnon Man evolved into a race that learned to worship the so-called gods and make carvings about them. Since even *we* know that the aliens materialise out of disc-shaped lights, that would explain why Cro-Magnon Man was known to have carved stones into disc and spherical shapes, and why many of his cave-paintings — the world's first paintings — were basically magical. What Ashcombe was implying, then, is that the so-called gods have visited the earth at each vital stage of Man's development in order to specifically shape, or guide, his progress; and that Frances, and others like her, have been used — and are still being used — as channels through which each new stage of development is ushered in. If the dark mass is a kind of black hole — at least in the sense of being a space-time warp — it *could* contain every event in history, as well as the future; thus Frances, Laurence and Schul — and everyone else sucked into the dark mass — could have re-lived their previous lives, all of which exist simultaneously in the dark mass's space-time continuum.'

'This sounds distressingly complex,' Mrs Devereux said. 'It makes me wish I were dead.'

'It may be complex,' Michael said, 'but it also seems likely — and Miles Ashcombe *did* say that those creatures can slip through time and space.'

'So,' Mrs Devereux said, 'accepting that, where do they *come* from?'

'They come from a double star,' Frances said, 'where-ever that is.'

'I think it's Sirius,' Michael said.

Frances noticed that her mother was leaning forward in her chair, her slim body looking even smaller in the loose Victorian dress. There was only one lamp turned on, beaming its light on two walls, romantically illuminating the paintings on those walls, as well as the area in which they were sitting. Frances' mother, staring up at Michael's broad bulk, seemed spectrally beautiful.

'Sirius?' Mrs Devereux said sweetly. 'I don't believe I recall it.'

Michael smiled at that. 'Sirius is the brightest star in our sky. It is, in fact, a double star whose invisible companion — invisible at least to us — is now known as Sirius B. However, one of the most remarkable things about Sirius is that while its invisible companion, Sirius B, was not discovered until 1862, a so-called primitive African tribe, the Dogon, have always known about it, always described it as the smallest and *heaviest* of all stars, and always knew that it rotates on its own axis, revolves around Sirius A every fifty years, and has an elliptical orbit. Modern astronomical knowledge supports all these facts, but how a primitive tribe like the Dogon could have known them throughout their history is a mystery that has never been solved. However, we *do* know that the Dogon believe all creation originated in Sirius B, that Sirius was the sacred star of the ancient Egyptians, and that an Egyptian dissertation attributed to their legendary founder of magic, Hermes Trismegistos, states that he, Trismegistos, landed on earth to teach men the arts of civilisation, then returned to his home, quote, *in the stars*. It's also interesting that the Dogon are in Africa where the upright ape, the *Ramapithecus*, first appeared during one of the periods mentioned by Miles Ashcombe. Finally, it's worth mentioning that Stonehenge — *and* other renowned megalithic circles built over geomagnetic-line convergence points — had originally sixty stones in its outer circle, which relates to the sixty-year cycle of the astronomy of the Dogon, as well as to that of the Hindus and the Chaldeans, the latter being the founders of astronomy.'

Listening to Michael speaking, Frances had gone into a trance; she now found herself staring past her mother's head at what she could see of the grey sky through the tall window. She was thinking of space, of the boundless realms of the cosmos, and of how, if space were curved, as theoretically seemed likely, it might be possible to travel from one point to another by dropping *through* space, thus circumventing time, instead of travelling around it.

A black hole, she thought. *Where time and space have no meaning* . . . She tried to imagine that place, to visualise that eternal All, to see herself and her father, Laurence and Schul and all the others, repeating their multiple lives over and over, outside all known dimensions. It was like trying to conceive of God — His nature foiled comprehension — so she sighed, sinking back into defeat, that very mortal emotion.

'And can I take it,' her mother asked, undefeated and inexhaustible, 'that we're still talking about bodiless, or incorporeal, creatures who materialise before us only that we might recognise them, or at least relate to them?'

'Yes,' Michael said, 'that appears to be the case.'

'Which gets us to *ghosts* or *spirits*,' Mrs Devereux said. 'And thus back to spiritualism.'

Michael sat back in his chair and stared steadily at Mrs Devereux, then unconsciously reached out for Frances' hand and squeezed it affectionately.

'Yes,' Mrs Devereux said, 'spiritualism. Contact with ghosts or spirits. For years it has been assumed that if we make contact, it's with the dead; but what has baffled a great many, and turned others into cynics, is that the dead, when they talk — either through the speech of mediums, automatic-writing or table-rapping — do not make intelligible conversation or impart worthwhile knowledge. Incoherency, confusion or ambiguity is the standard fare, and since those communicating — the so-called dead — are supposed to be familiar with the

306

living, it has never been explained why that intercourse is on such a low level.'

Mrs Devereux stared steadily at Michael, eyes enlarged behind the spectacles, her head, perched on top of the billowing dress, looking unnaturally small.

'Do you follow my train of thought? It may *not* be the dead. Or, if they *are* dead, they've simply become part of that alternate world, where time and space have no meaning. We may be communicating with *that* world — actually talking across the infinite — and that distance, which may not relate to any dimensions we can comprehend, could well make *all* attempts at communication unintelligible and suspect. No, Michael, we may not be talking of the dead, but of your alternate universe; one — perhaps one of many — which keeps invading our world, in some cases by deliberate design, in others by accident.'

'I'm sorry,' Frances said, feeling the need to hear her own voice, convinced that she would otherwise disappear down the funnel of her own abstract thoughts. 'I'm sorry to interrupt, but all the evidence points to the fact that these creatures have been coming here *deliberately* for a definite purpose.'

'Of course,' her mother replied. 'I've not forgotten that at all. I'm merely suggesting that these creatures, who coexist side by side with us, divorced from considerations of known time and space, may sometimes *accidentally* materialise in our world and be viewed by us as so-called ghosts, or spirits. Similarly, unfortunate souls like your father and Laurence may be sucked into their alternate universe — or, much worse, some ghastly purgatorial void in between, and remain there, convinced that they're having a bad dream, perhaps for eternity. So, we see ghosts — and *they* see ghosts ... and we haunt one another.'

Frances took note of Michael's stupefied expression, then gently jerked the hand she was holding and drew his attention. He smiled and shook his head, obviously weary but fascinated, then squeezed her hand and turned back to her mother.

'Do you understand, dear Michael?'

'I think so, Mrs Devereux. I'm trying to align your theory with mine. What we're saying is that the dark mass is a sort of time-space warp, a gateway through time and space, and that it enables those on Sirius, who are bodiless anyway, to instantaneously materialise in our world at any point in its history, past, present *or* future. We're also suggesting that such space-time warps exist all over the Earth, that they have always waxed and waned in strength and, in so doing, often sucked unfortunate souls in, making them disappear from our own space-time frame. Finally, we're suggesting that those space-time warps, which formerly waxed and waned according to fluctuations in the Earth's geomagnetic field, are now growing progressively stronger, to suck the old earth, piece by piece, into another space-time continuum and, as it were, spit out a new world, which will likely include a new breed of Man — by our standards, a super-race. Finally, we're suggesting that this super-race, which will be incorporeal like those on Sirius, is being given life through women like Frances — all over the Earth.'

Mrs Devereux nodded, no longer smiling, the lamp-light reflecting from her spectacles and distorting her eyes. 'Yes,' she said, 'that sums it up admirably. I think that's what is happening here.'

Frances stared at her, stunned, then shook her head despairingly from side to side and glanced desperately at Michael. He did not turn his head, but instead kept his attention on her mother.

'I am psychic,' her mother said. 'Frances, also, is psychic. I think we should join hands in a seance and try to contact the other world. I believe that with Frances and I doing this together, we should at least obtain some interesting results. It's important to me — I'm convinced my husband is still alive — but it's also of vital importance to Frances, who is involved more deeply than either of us in this singular mystery. Do you agree? Will you do it?'

Michael glanced questioningly at Frances, but with underlying enthusiasm, and she felt the fear descending upon her like a dark, heavy blanket. She closed her eyes, trying to think, wanting the courage to refuse, but knew that no matter her own fears, she would have to consent. She would do it mainly for her mother, and possibly for Michael, but also quite selfishly for herself, out of fear's desperation.

Like her mother, she was obsessed — with her father's loss and her need for him — but unlike her mother, who had tried to assuage her obsession in spiritualism, she had tried to do the same by finding a man who might act as replacement. So, she had looked to older men, to mature men, father-figures, and in so doing had courted the disaster that had subsequently come to her.

Ravello, she thought. *My Waterloo was in Ravello . . .* And recalled that white-walled room above the narrow street off the square, the church bells that tolled for the godly while she writhed on a sweat-soaked bed. She had not found another father, but had found an older man, one with a predator's instincts and a pimp's idle fancies. He had released her sensual self, and enslaved her through that; then, having enslaved her mind and flesh, stripped her down to the naked bone. There was no place for shame, then, no possibility of resistance, no hope for redemption or self-assertion while degradation was paramount. She did all that he asked of her, then more, and more again, and when she was leaving, when he laughed in her face, she saw no future before her.

Yes, she thought, *that was it. I sold my soul for a father-figure. I gave everything I was, heart and soul, mind and body, because I could not admit to myself that my father was gone.*

Now she shuddered, remembering, and felt Michael

squeezing her hand; looked at him, then at her mother, and knew she owed it to both of them.

'I'm agreeable if you are,' she said to Michael.

'I'm agreeable,' he said.

Mrs Devereux nodded, straightened her dress and stood up. 'Fine,' she said. 'Just let me draw the curtains. We can do it right here.'

She went to the tall windows that overlooked the rear garden, drew the curtains to plunge the room into a darkness only broken by the triangular light beaming obliquely from a tall lamp. Next, she removed a potted plant from a small, round table and placed three straight-backed walnut chairs around it. After turning out the light — leaving the room completely dark but for a sliver of greyness beaming through the curtains — she indicated that Frances and Michael should join her. They did so, Frances sitting on one side of her mother, Michael on the other, the three of them linking their hands together in an oddly charged silence.

'You don't have to do anything, Michael,' Mrs Devereux said. 'Just keep holding our hands, irrespective of what you might see or hear. Frances, I want you to close your eyes, as I will be doing, then simply concentrate. Try to block out your thoughts. That's all: simply empty your mind.'

Frances stared across the table, seeing Michael's face in darkness, taking comfort from it before closing her eyes and letting the silence enfold her. At first she felt foolish and even had to resist giggling, then also had to resist the temptation to let go of their hands. Then she felt Michael's grip tightening on her fingers, and the feeling she derived from that contact made her more passive.

She concentrated on her closed eyelids, studying the void behind them, trying to will herself to drift into her mind as if into the sky. It was quiet and very dark, but streaked with white light, and she tried to imagine it as a universe stretching out to eternity. Michael's hand was

310

warm. An electric charge came from her mother. She felt her body glowing with a heat that made her sleepy, that seemed to dissolve her where she sat and let her drift through the ether.

It stayed silent and dark, still streaked with white light, then the lines of light moved in languid loops, coils and circles, until they resembled a great web that stretched out to the infinite. The web was phosphorescent, illuminating the void, then the spaces between the crisscrossing, glowing lines became filled with stars.

The lines of white light moved apart, racing away in all directions, shrinking to nothing beyond immeasurable distances and leaving only the stars. Everything moved towards her, sweeping around her on all sides, surging above and below in great waves that unfurled majestically. Then there was no up nor down, no left nor right; only constant movement around her, an unfurling of space and time.

There were great Magellanic clouds, dark and luminous nebulae, glittering whirlpool galaxies, spiralling solar flares and pulsating star clusters; then a comet streaked across the heavens, leading towards two distant stars which, as space unfurled around her, moved further apart and spread their fierce light through the void. One of the stars disappeared when the other exploded silently around her — then she saw, in the dazzling brilliance of God's fire, the scorched earth in its timeless core. The light flared up stupendously, temporarily blinding her, then shrank back to a bearable intensity, letting time and space perpetually recreate all — the past, present and future.

'It's all right,' a man's voice said in her mind. 'There is nothing to fear.'

She saw Laurence's profile floating in a haze before her, then moved back until she saw him on the grassy mound with Stonehenge beyond him. He was staring at the sky, his hand on his forehead, trying to see the eye of God in the great light descending upon him.

Laurence did not move. He seemed frozen into that position. Frances willed him to move and he dissolved, as did the circle of ancient stones, and there, where Stonehenge had been, but still surrounded by the green grass, a great pool of water, a lagoon, had magically materialised. Beyond the lagoon was more green earth, the glint of other marshes; then, on the grassy mound before the pool, Laurence appeared again.

This time he looked different, his clothing no more than a loincloth, and he stood, gazing over the lake, with a woman beside him. The woman was familiar, body slim, long hair dark, and she stood beside Laurence, perfectly silent and motionless, while a mist rising off the darkly glinting water gradually fell over them like a shroud, until they had disappeared.

The mist became more dense, impenetrable and ominous, then a fierce light, first a pinprick, then a great hole, gradually burned the mist away, revealing a scorched, barren landscape hazed in shimmering heat-waves. A volcanic mountain spewed in the distance. A desolate dust-bowl stretched for miles. There were caves near the dust-bowl, with short, apelike creatures in front of them. One of them was fornicating with another; both were faintly familiar.

She watched them, moved closer, became one of them and looked up, saw unrecognisable creatures gathered around her, silhouetted in a shimmering white light that fell from the burning sky. Then one of them leaned lower to touch her, and she opened her eyes ...

Frances glanced left and right, first at Michael, then her mother, and saw a creature standing behind her mother, placing his hands on her shoulders.

Frances screamed — hardly aware that she was doing do — conscious only of that creature, a luminous figure in the darkness, an oddly glowing silhouette, human-shaped, without features, now placing its hands on

312

her mother's shoulders and making her luminous, also.

Mrs Devereux jerked her head up, staring wide-eyed past Frances — then Frances glanced at Michael as he threw himself away from his chair, behind which another glowing, spectral figure had been silently standing.

Frances heard her own scream. It slashed her free from her paralysis, making her jump to her feet and twist to the side as a glowing hand brushed down her body. Her chair clattered onto the floor, she heard Michael's frightened cursing, then she saw her mother quivering in a ball of light, while the luminous figure standing right behind her kept its grip on her shoulders.

Her mother shuddered and cried out, then shook like an epileptic, fell sideways when the luminous figure released its grip, and just as Frances switched on the nearest lamp.

The light was briefly blinding. Her heart was racing wildly. There was a dull thud as her mother fell to the floor and rolled over to stare up at the ceiling, her face contorting in pain.

'*No!*' Frances cried out.

She rushed to her fallen mother, dropping onto her knees beside her, only realising as she did so that the creatures had disappeared and that Michael was hurrying around the table, cursing under his breath. Then she looked down at her mother and saw her deathly white face, the spectacles askew on her birdlike nose, eyes glassy and lifeless.

A chill slid through Frances, then a fierce, blinding rage; she grabbed her mother and started to shake her and scream into her dead face. She didn't know what she was screaming, hardly knew she was doing so; then someone was holding her shoulders and pulling her back.

She suddenly burst into tears, let herself be turned around, then buried her face in Michael's broad chest as he gently rocked her and stroked her spine. She wept a

313

long time, on her knees, in Michael's arms; then, when she had drained herself of tears, stared down at her dead mother's body and clenched both her fists.

'Damn them!' she said. 'I've taken this for too long. I'm going back to Iraq, I'm going to find the Garden of Eden, and once I get there, no matter what it costs me, I'm going to find out what's happening.'

Michael's lips grazed her tangled hair: a gesture of love and agreement.

PART THREE: THE FUTURE

CHAPTER TWENTY-THREE

Leaving the morning fruit and vegetable market of the Cours Saleya, Michael passed the Opera and turned into Quai des Etats-Unis, letting the breeze from the phosphorescent blue bay erase the sweat from his face. As a young, single man he had often visited Nice, never without the feeling that his future was filled with promise; but now, as he walked along the promenade, past the fishermen's *ponchettes* that had become restaurants and art galleries, he was decidedly less romantic about his future prospects, if such existed at all.

Having flown on an impulse from London that very morning, he hardly felt that he had left and could not stop thinking about what he had committed himself to. Frances' mother had been cremated the previous day at Golders Green, and remembering that sad affair, with Frances pale-faced but tearless, Michael knew that he would have to journey with her to the end of the mystery. So, his future was in doubt, his horizons limited to Iraq, and it amazed him that even the magnitude of the forthcoming adventure could not dim his very human, paternal concern.

He had come to Nice to have words with his daughter, in a two-faced attempt to save her from emotional disaster before embarking upon a journey from which he very likely would not return. Having already deserted her once — eight years ago, when he left his wife — he was now about to do the same thing — and, worse, in a more permanent way. He was therefore not feeling too positive as he walked along the promenade, heading for the restaurants and cafes at the base of Le Chateau.

Cheryl was already seated under a striped umbrella at a table overlooking the port. Michael's heart lurched when he saw her, but he didn't stop walking, merely took in her expensive denims, low-cut blouse and high-heeled shoes, and noting that her blonde hair was much longer, making her look more mature.

Already tired and depressed, what he saw further disconcerted him, but his warm grin was genuine, when, after reaching the table, he had leaned down to kiss her on the cheek.

'*Bonjour, Mademoiselle,*' he said. '*Comment ca va?*'

'Life's fine,' Cheryl replied. 'But please speak English, Daddy. I'm *dying* to have a whole conversation in English. If it's pleasant, that is.'

Michael ignored the warning and took the chair facing her. She was drinking a glass of Chateau Simone from the bottle she had ordered, and he noticed that the bottle itself was already half empty.

'Your hair's longer,' he said.

'Do you like it?' she asked him.

'Yes,' he lied. 'It looks very casual — just like your clothes.'

'Here, Daddy, let me pour you some wine. You look all hot and bothered.'

The defensive edge to Cheryl's voice made Michael realise that this was unlikely to be a pleasant conversation; but he managed to hide that feeling with a smile as she poured him some wine, then held her own glass up in the air.'

'Cheers,' she said.

The wine was white and chilled, with a light herbal

fragrance, and instantly refreshed his dry throat and made him feel marginally better. Putting his glass down, he glanced distractedly over the port, envying those lounging on the many boats, large and small, that sailed colourfully to and fro across the mildly choppy water, under a sky filled with clouds as white and insubstantial as the trembling waves.

'Are you hungry?' Cheryl asked.

'No,' he said. 'Not very.'

'You rarely are at lunchtime, so I've already ordered mussels *and* another bottle of white wine.'

'Isn't that a lot to *drink* at lunchtime?'

'I thought today I might need it.'

She stared at him with veiled defiance, her blue eyes emphasised by her suntan; and again he could not avoid noticing that her long blonde hair, formerly cut in a boyish fringe, made her look considerably older than she was. Dwelling on that, and on her low-cut blouse and high-heels, he wondered how much this new appearance had been designed for her lover — an older man with more mature tastes, which doubtless she wanted to satisfy.

Sighing, trying to stifle a surge of pain, he drank some more wine.

'All right, Daddy,' Cheryl said. 'Here you are. So, why *are* you here?'

'You know why.'

'I told you, I don't want to talk about it.'

'But you told me we could talk on the phone — and then you just disappeared.'

'It's my work, Daddy. I'm here because of *work*. We're shooting a *movie* in Nice.'

'No,' Michael said, 'you're not. The crew all returned to London four days ago. The only ones remaining are you and this producer you fancy. Are you staying together?'

'Yes,' she replied, surprisingly unperturbed to have been caught out in a blatant lie.

'Does his wife know?'

'No. She thinks he's still here working.'

'And this doesn't make you feel bad?'

'That's enough,' Cheryl said abruptly. 'Just stop right there.'

Her visible anger startled Michael, but mercifully, at that moment, the waiter arrived with their large tray of seafood. When he had placed it between them with the second bottle of wine, wishing them *bon appetit* and then departing, Michael filled both their glasses.

'Oh, well,' he said. 'Cheers again.'

They touched glasses and drank, then started on the seafood which, while being as delicious as expected, failed to raise Michael's spirits.

'I'm sorry,' he said, sampling a mussel, 'but we simply can't let this lie fallow. Your affair has caused your mother grave concern; so, if I don't talk you out of it, she might do something drastic.'

'Such as?'

'Well, for a start she wants me to talk to this man of yours — to convince him to end the affair and, if necessary, get you out of his life by kicking you out of your job.'

'You wouldn't dare.'

'I'm afraid I would. I'm a *psychologist*, dear child, and talking to people, no matter how unpleasant the subject, comes naturally to me. I don't want this man playing with my daughter, so believe me, I'll talk to him.'

'He won't listen to you. He loves me.'

'So, when does he leave his wife for you?'

'He wants to, but can't. He's frightened of wounding her and the children. He says he might do it in a year or two, when the children, at least, have finished at university and can stand on their own feet.'

'A likely story.'

'It's *true*,' Cheryl replied, chewing a mussel. 'We've discussed it at some length,' she added, 'and I agree

with him totally. I love him and I want to live with him —
but not with too much damage on my conscience.'

'Oh, I see,' Michael said. 'He also discussed the
damage it would do to *you* if you actually broke up his
family. Obviously a very thoughtful man — omitting no
point of view.'

'Don't be sarcastic, Father. Examine yourself before
you start casting stones at others.'

The transition from 'Daddy' to the more formal
'Father' was enough to signal that the distance between
them was widening; and the pain Michael felt was only
increased by the way Cheryl had thrown his past back at
him.

'Damn you, Cheryl,' he said, 'that was mean. That
was under the belt.'

'You're criticising the man I love for showing more
consideration for *his* family than you showed to yours
eight years ago — so don't expect any fairness from *me*.'

'It's true your mother and I are divorced,' Michael
said angrily, 'but I've looked after both of you ever
since. I'm still your father, I never deserted you, and I
didn't desert your mother, either. We just gradually
drifted apart, that's all.'

'And so you think that David would be a better man if
he walked out on his wife and kids?'

'Dammit, Cheryl, I'm just trying to protect you. My
situation wasn't the same — I didn't leave your mother
for a younger woman. In fact, I didn't leave her for
anyone in particular — I just needed my freedom. I'm not
criticising your David for not wanting to leave his
family; I'm just trying to convince you that this relationship can only bring you suffering; that sooner or later,
you're going to want him on a more permanent basis;
and that in all probability, when that sorry day comes,
your David *still* won't leave his wife and children.'

'So?' Cheryl asked, still trying to sound defiant, but
clearly more nervous.

'You'll then be faced,' Michael explained, firmly

believing his own logic but ashamed of its brutality, 'with the dismal choice of living without him completely or growing old as his increasingly burdensome mistress. Now is that what you want?'

'I want to cross that bridge when I come to it. I don't want to discuss it now.'

Michael just stared at her, hurt and angry at her vehemence, wondering why he should be so concerned about her, now knowing what her future might be. He was naturally thinking of the dark masses, of the places that had disappeared, of Miles Ashcombe, Frances, her dead mother and the mysteries surrounding them.

The world seemed to be disappearing. A new world might be replacing it. He and Frances might be travelling into a future from which there was no return. Did it matter what Cheryl did? Did she have a future at all? Would the earth keep disappearing until there was nothing left but empty marshlands and a desolate, eternal silence.

Asking himself those questions — which he had done ceaselessly for the past four days — Michael suddenly realised exactly why he was going on that singular journey with Frances: if the earth was to disappear, taking those he loved with it, he could not stand by idly and let it happen while there was the slightest chance of finding out its cause and doing something about it. At this point he was willing to risk losing those he most loved because of the faint hope that he might either get them back or find them again in that new world . . . but he could hardly explain that to his daughter, least of all in these circumstances.

'I told you before,' he said instead, 'and I'm going to tell you again: if you don't stop seeing this man, I'm going to have to talk to him — and if *he* refuses to do anything about it then your mother will step into the picture — and she's less liberal than I am.'

'If David says no to you, he'll say the same to Mother.'

'If David says no to me, your mother won't even go

near him. She's told me — and knowing her, I believe her — that she'll go straight to his wife.'

There was a shocked silence from Cheryl as she took in what he had said. She started raising her glass to her lips, but then put it down again, her gaze wandering restlessly around the fashionable, busy port before returning reluctantly to the front.

'She wouldn't!' she finally exclaimed, as if she really could not believe it.

'She would,' Michael replied. 'And you know it — so don't let it go that far.'

Cheryl glanced blindly around her, as if searching for someone who might come and take her away from the real world. She shook her head from side to side, as if denying what she had heard, then sniffed like a little girl, rubbing her face with one hand.

'Oh, Christ!' she whispered.

Suddenly, she jumped up and hurried away from the table, pushing the milling people aside as she made her way across the promenade. Michael called the waiter, quickly paid him and followed Cheryl, likewise having to push rudely through the crowds of tourists until he reached the sea-side of the road. Cheryl was standing with her back to him, looking out at the busy port; and as he approached her and finally stopped by her side, he found himself staring in considerable pain and embarrassment at her suntanned, tear-streaked profile. A light breeze, coming in from the bay, covered her face with her blonde hair.

'Oh, God,' she said, 'you're right. I know you're right, but I can't stop it. I love him and can't stop thinking about him and that's all there is to it. I think he knows that and uses it, but I can't help that either. He just says he can't possibly leave his wife and I have to accept it. I *know* I'm being used. I know it even as I lie beside him. I keep promising myself that each time will be the last, but then, when he tells me that he wants me, I simply go with him. He insists that he *does* love me —

323

but that he owes his wife and children. He often says that we have to live for the moment — and I accept that as well. What can I do? I've tried to stop it, but can't. Each time I see him, it hurts me even more; but it also makes me *want* him even more, and I just can't control that. God, it's made my life a misery, made me mean and contrary, but I can't bear the thought of being without him, so I live on in hope.'

She turned in towards him and let him wrap her in his arms, her body trembling as she silently wept and he patted her shoulders. He was blinded by the light and overrun by emotion, his objectivity melting into the warmth of the love he could not disown.

'You've got to let me work it out myself,' she said, sniffing and stepping back a little to wipe the tears from her eyes. 'Promise me that, Daddy — that at least you 'll give me some time. Don't let Mother go and see his poor wife until I come back to England.'

'When will that be? She'll want to know.'

Cheryl shrugged. 'I can't say. But I promise you, it won't be long — perhaps a week at most.'

'You've got to talk to him,' Michael insisted. 'You've got to make him choose — either you or his family — and this time don't settle for any vague generalities: insist on a straight reply, one way or the other, then make your decision.'

'I'm not sure that I can do that, but I'll try. God, it's all such a mess!'

Michael was shocked at how easily he had lost his daughter — but even more shocked when he suddenly found himself thinking about Frances and the extraordinary journey they would soon be making together. He was not a religious man and had formerly prided himself on his pragmatism, but now found himself floundering in a sea of doubts and self-recriminations, none of which were made any easier by this encounter with Cheryl.

The miraculous events he had witnessed during the

past few weeks had undermined the foundations of his former beliefs, convincing him that his life would be meaningless if he did not pursue the mystery to its source, no matter what that might be. Were this not enough, he also had to face the fact that his affair with Frances, even though based on love, contravened his professional oaths and, even more base, branded him as someone who was placing his own needs above those of his daughter and former wife.

He was, after all, about to leave on a journey from which he might not return, was doing it with a patient with whom he had had sexual relations, and now, even trying to protect his daughter from her own blindness, was going to have to tell her about a decision that might strike her as being considerably more senseless than her own affair.

Michael gazed out over the bay, distracting himself with the sailing boats, seeing girls in bikinis stretched out on the decks while men drank and played around folding tables in the light of a blinding sun. Feeling totally disassociated from that, he sighed and turned back to Cheryl, realising that he was going to have to tell her just what he was planning.

'All right,' he said, 'it's time I made my confession. I have another, more vital reason for being concerned about your future and how that man might affect it ... I'm going away, I don't know how long for, and in fact, I don't know if I'll be coming back. Please,' he added, when he saw her eyes widening, 'just let me explain ...'

He told her about his involvement in the Glastonbury event, about what had happened at Stonehenge, about the dark masses that seemed to be eating the earth piecemeal, about Miles Ashcombe and Laurence, about the voices he had heard crying despairingly from thin-air and the figures that had materialised magically at the seance, about the death of Mrs Devereux — and finally, reluctantly, but with no other option, he told her about

325

Frances, and about why he had to go with her to Iraq to find the Garden of Eden.

When he had finished talking — and saw the shock in Cheryl's face — he knew he had made a mistake.

'What *is* this?' she asked, eyes growing large. 'I can't actually believe what I've just heard. Just what is this . . . *nonsense?*'

'Cheryl, you *know* what happened at Glastonbury. You've read all about it. *And* about all the other places. So please believe me, it's true!'

'I don't give a damn,' she said, her voice rising to incredulity. 'I'm not interested in Glastonbury, nor in your other hocus-pocus; I just can't get over the fact that you came here to chastise *me*, just before running off on some patently crazy basis with a woman who's also one of your patients — '

'*Please*, Cheryl!'

' — a woman obviously sent to you because of her mental problems and who, instead of being cured by you, was actually *seduced* by you. God, the hypocrisy!'

'I did *not* seduce her,' Michael insisted. 'It wasn't like that at all! As I've already explained, Frances was driven by extremely strong needs that were exacerbated by her experience in — '

'Right,' Cheryl intervened, her rage turning to contempt. 'And even knowing that, you — '

'*Please*, Cheryl! I couldn't help myself! It just happened that way!'

He realised what he had said the second the words left his mouth, and watched, in despair, as Cheryl took a step backward, nodding and glancing histrionically around her to express disbelief and outrage. When eventually she turned back to him, her gaze was unforgiving, and her lips, normally ripe with good humour, had formed a thin line.

'Go on your damned journey,' she said, 'and take your demented woman with you. You must be demented yourself to even *contemplate* such a thing! As for me, don't you *dare* talk to me about my future. If you had any concern for that, you wouldn't be running off with that woman for reasons which can only be described as crazy. You left me once, Father, and now you're doing it again — and I doubt that anything my lover will do to me could be worse than you've done. Damn you, Father, *go home!*'

She turned away and rushed off, the wind whipping up her blonde hair, very quickly becoming lost in the dense, lunchtime crowds along the promenade. Feeling naked and torn, Michael wanted to pursue her, but he held the impulse in check, knowing perfectly well that it was useless, and instead just continued to stand there, staring despairingly about him.

The sailboats filled the bay, their brightly-coloured sails flapping, and beyond them the sea was a rippling blue that stretched out to where it merged with the azure sky in a silvery haze.

Michael stood there for a very long time, longing to lose himself in the future, never to return.

CHAPTER TWENTY-FOUR

Frances said little while the removal men did their work. She merely wandered to and fro, from one room to the other, silently observing as her mother's house was stripped bare — furniture, paintings, antiques and musical instruments — each item, as it was carried out, taking another memory with it, as if her history was being eaten away, piece by piece, just like the whole world.

The men, wearing overalls, were fast and efficient, talking constantly as they worked, mostly a stream of ribald banter, oblivious to the fact that their world was disappearing just as surely as the contents of the house.

Watching, Frances wondered why it was happening and what it signified. On the simplest level there was no mystery to it: she was going on a journey from which she would probably not return, so the house had been sold and its contents would later be auctioned off. However, on a more emotional level what was happening was very different: she was getting rid of her past, rendering her personal history obsolete, in order to more readily embrace the future and find her own destiny.

So, as the men stripped the house of its contents, she thought of Iraq, of the Arabs in the marshlands, and, most of all, of that place which she now knew was Eden.

She had to return there — for her lost father and dead mother; for the magical child she was carrying — and as the pieces of her life were carried out to be auctioned off, she felt a curious mixture of dread and quiet exultation.

It was late in the afternoon when the men completed the removal, by which time Frances had almost finished drinking a bottle of Reisling. She could not recall opening it, but that fact seemed unimportant, and when the van had moved off, taking her mother's possessions to a warehouse, she emptied the last of the wine into her glass and stared out the front window.

The light was gradually fading, making the street grey and forbidding, so she turned away and examined the empty room in which she had grown up.

The people buying the house, wanting to renovate and modernise it, had insisted that everything be removed, including carpets and curtains. Now, with the floorboards as bare as the walls, the very silence seemed to be amplified, and the floorboards creaked each time she moved, giving the room, which once had resounded with music and laughter, a hollow, distinctly eerie quality.

Frances sipped some wine and then started wandering about, trying to reconcile what she was seeing with the home she had known and loved. Stripped bare, it was unrecognisable, impersonal, devoid of character, its blank walls, high ceilings and uncovered floorboards making it seem much larger than it actually was.

She stopped in the music-room, imagining her mother at the piano, immediately felt a wave of pain at her loss, so closed her eyes and breathed deeply. She thought of that final seance, felt the power flowing through her, saw the oddly glowing figures in the darkness that surrounded her mother. Those same spectres had been at Stonehenge, emerging out of space and time, as they had done, so many years before, on the night of her own, miraculous birth.

Now, remembering what her mother had told her

329

about her own birth, Frances shook her head in disbelief and walked from the room.

She stopped in the hallway, too aware of the silence, feeling it pressing upon her and forcing her into herself. Buried deeply within her was that other, less known Frances, and she became increasingly aware of her presence as she walked up the creaking stairs.

Michael was in France, having words with his daughter, but she felt his presence permeating the air, as if conjured up by her. He had held her hand during the seance, and she felt that energy now, rising up from her depths like a light burning through veils of mist. Her need for him made her tremble, seeding the wastelands of her grief, and when she thought of her mother's coffin sliding into the flames, she took solace from the knowledge that Michael's love had been gained from that singular loss.

On the landing she stopped again, gazing at each of the bedroom doors. She had intended checking them all, to ensure that nothing had been left behind, but instead, moved by an irresistible impulse, she opened the door of her mother's bedroom, then stepped inside.

Leaning her back against the door, she drank the last of her wine, then stared at the empty space where her mother's antique bed had stood. She kept staring, concentrating, willing the past to return, and eventually saw the room as it had been, with the bed right in front of her. She kept focusing on the bed, sensing the power flowing through her, visualising what had happened at her birth, thirty-five years ago. . . .

The light around her darkened, bringing the bed into relief, and she saw her mother lying there in labour, with an abstracted, kindly man, whom Frances knew was her father, leaning down anxiously. Then the darkness was streaked with silver, a shimmering light filled the room, and in that brilliant haze, tall, translucent figures materialised and surrounded the bed.

330

Frances saw herself being born — as her own child would soon be born — and she gasped, almost weeping at this revelation, then let the present return.

She was shocked and shaken, unable to accept what she had witnessed, but when she studied the room, she saw only the normal bare walls.

Her heart was racing uncomfortably, but she took a deep breath, then walked in a determined manner across the room and set her glass on the window-sill. She gazed at the lawn below, closed her eyes, stared through her eyelids, willed the present to roll back to the past with its numerous mysteries. . . .

The afternoon turned to evening, bathing the trees in moonlight. Another darkness descended and swallowed the moonlight, then filled up with tiny, pulsating lights and an ethereal singing. Her father stepped into that garden and looked up at the sky, then shaded his eyes and started squinting as another light blinded him. He dissolved into that light, his body spreading out like liquid. The light faded away, taking the strands of his body with it — then the moonlight returned and her father's voice came out of thin-air, calling desperately for help. He called out repeatedly, with a naked, haunting fear, but his voice gradually grew weaker, more shaky and distant, then eventually tapered off in some faraway place, leaving nothing but the occasional rustle of autumnal leaves in the night's clinging silence. . . .

Frances took a deep breath, opened her eyes and looked out again, seeing nothing but a normal, overgrown lawn in fading afternoon light. She glanced at her wine glass, saw a vaporous moon reflected, shivered, turned away from the window and walked from the room.

The house was nearly in darkness when she walked back downstairs, but she found that a comfort and therefore did not turn on the lights. She wanted to find herself — that other Frances deep inside — and having just seen herself being born, she understood her own nature. She was frightened and awed by that, scarcely able to grasp its meaning, but she now knew that her destiny lay in the marshlands of Iraq.

She walked back into the almost dark, deserted front room and sat cross-legged on the floor, facing the window. She felt the power flowing through her — the power her mother had said would grow — and closed her eyes to concentrate on the future instead of the past.

She needed something to focus upon, so thought of this very house, watching it taking shape in her mind just a year or two hence. It had been completely renovated and looked modern, if charmless, but the people moving through it were at their ease, clearly not feeling threatened.

Frances was puzzled. The world should have disappeared. How could this house and its new tenants still exist in that future?

She leaned back against the wall, rubbed against it like a cat, stared through the window directly opposite at the lights of the facing house. Above the house the sky was cloudy, its greyness being erased by darkness, and she thought of her first meeting with Michael in the hospital nearby.

Thinking about him, she yearned for him, but managed to cast her mind into the future . . . and *still* saw the hospital. Outside, it seemed normal, the street in front of it filled with traffic; inside, it was business as usual, with no sign of disturbance.

Again, she was puzzled by what she was seeing, having expected to find marshland where the hospital had been and instead seeing an unchanged, normal world.

She kept leaping farther ahead, another five years, another ten, and eventually, in some distant future, saw the building changing — not because of a dark mass or any other unnatural cause, but because of the normal ravages of time and man's redevelopment.

The world, then, had not disappeared: it had simply followed its natural course.

Stunned and bewildered, Frances gazed around the dark room, trying to will herself to get up and leave the house for the last time. In the pocket of her denims was a key to Michael's apartment, and touching it accidentally with her fingers, she was filled with his presence. He would be returning from France this evening and they would meet at his place; in a few days they would leave for Iraq and a problematical future.

What future might that be? And what did her visions signify? Why did her precognition contradict what was happening right now?

Frances sighed and leaned forward, covering her face with her hands. She concentrated on the darkness behind her closed eyelids, trying to gauge the resonance of the silence and lose herself in the Nothing.

The Nothing was seductive, almost lulling her into sleep . . . but suddenly she heard the front door being opened, then clicking shut again.

Her heart gave a leap and made her open her eyes. She looked up to see a tall, deep-shadowed, faceless figure standing still in the doorway of the moonlit room.

'What are you doing, still sitting here?' Michael asked. 'I've already been back to my apartment, expecting to find you there. Is everything all right?'

Frances sighed with relief and let her racing heart settle, then raised her right hand in the air and waved him towards her.

'Come here,' she said. 'Sit here beside me. I want you to hold me.'

He did as he was told, sitting beside her on the floor, kissing her on the forehead, the neck, the lips, then sliding one arm around her and pulling her to him.

'Savouring your last moments here?' he asked her.

'Yes,' she replied. 'Something like that. So, how did it go with your daughter? Did you manage to tell her?'

Michael sighed forlornly. 'Yes,' he said. 'Just about.

Alas, she didn't take it very well, so I'm not feeling too proud of myself.'

'And did you tell her about me?'

'Yes, but it only made things worse. Now, I'm not only deserting her again — I'm also having an affair with one of my patients. In truth, then, our meeting was bloody awful. So, what about you?'

Frances pressed herself into him, trying to lose herself in his warmth, feeling guilt over what she had done to him. That she had seduced him was something which bothered her little; what disturbed her was the fact that he was going to leave with her, probably for ever. She had never met his daughter, but knew how much he loved her; and the sight of the pain in his face was almost too much to bear.

'You know, you don't have to come to Iraq,' she said. 'You're not personally involved like me. Also, I can go because I have no-one left here, whereas you have your daughter and a former wife to look after. I really don't know why you're coming — and I don't think you should.'

He pressed his lips to the top of her head, let them linger their awhile, then tilted her face up towards him. 'You and I were destined to go,' he said, 'and that's all there is to it. Besides, the more I know about this mystery, the more intrigued I become ... and what I learned from the Ministry of Defence today simply heightened my interest.'

Night had since fallen completely, giving the room over to darkness, but the light of the street lamps outside cast a glow on his face. He was smiling, very gently, almost in wonder, then his fingertips brushed lightly across her lips and fell onto her wrist.

'Sampson phoned me just after I got back from France,' he said, his voice sounding oddly ethereal in the dark, empty room. 'The first thing he told me is that monitoring operations conducted by the countries involved have indicated that the time between the appearance of the dark masses has steadily been growing longer, and that there's been *no* new materialisations at all over the past month. Even better, is that all seismic and atmospheric surveys conducted over the past month have indicated that the phenomenon has probably ceased for good — except in a few specific areas where the geomagnetic effects, having produced that marshland, seem to have become permanent features. Those areas include Glastonbury ... and southern Iraq.'

Frances felt as if a great weight was lifting off her shoulders, letting her think and breathe easier. She recalled the visions she had had before Michael's arrival — visions of a world which had not changed as she had expected — then, filled with excitement and hope, pressed herself tighter to him.

'So the world is out of danger,' she said. 'Oh, God, I was right.'

'You *knew* the phenomenon was ending?'

'Let's say I sensed it,' she replied. 'Now what about me?'

Michael sighed again. 'Sampson's surveys have revealed that you're not alone,' he said. 'Other women — all of whom have been involved with the dark masses — have likewise reported their conviction that they're pregnant ... and every one of those women had formerly been told by their physcians that they would never be able to have a child. Also, in every case, it's been confirmed that although those women were displaying *some* of the signs of pregnancy, none of them were in fact pregnant — at least not in any normal, human way. And, finally, it *has* been noted that a lot of those women have recently disappeared without explanation ...'

'You mean they might have gone away on their own accord — exactly as *I'm* going to do.'

'Yes,' Michael replied. 'That's what Sampson suspects: that those women — both here and in the other countries surveyed — have returned to where they first encountered their particular dark mass. They've gone for the same reason you're going — to *complete* this affair.'

Frances closed her eyes and willed the power to her, letting it rise up like a light from her centre to illuminate the geography of the human soul in its flight to perfection. She saw how she had been born, and how her child would be born, then she saw the other women, all of whom were conscious of her, making their secret, solitary journeys back to where the spirit had entered them.

Their old lives had ended and a new life would begin, but the world as they knew it would for the most part remain, coexisting side by side with that equally real world beyond human perceptions. It was the other-world of the spirit, where time and space were one, a world in which consciousness could leap between Sirius and Earth, between the one cosmos and another, illuminating the eternal present with its light and transcending mere matter.

Clearly, she was God's child — and so were all the others — and God was simply the essence of that great, eternal spirit which multiplied throughout time and shrank back simultaneously to the embryonic purity of the universal Oneness. Her child would be God's child — at once embracing the others and being part of them — and the future, which was merely the other side of the past, would be the natural inheritance of the material and spiritual worlds of a thriving Earth.

Frances pressed herself into Michael, taking life from his warmth. Eventually she started laughing, first softly, then hysterically — exactly as she had done when the helicopter descended like God's eye over the river in Iraq — but then her laughter turned into the weeping of someone released.

She was being set free from bondage, from the doubts of her humanity, and she took the warmth from Michael and just as quickly gave it back, pressing herself tighter to him, forcing him down onto the floor, stretching along the trembling heat of his body until he could not resist her. Removing their clothes, they joined together, becoming one in the moonlit darkness, trading souls, then rising as pure energy to the peace of transcendence. And at that moment their flesh turned briefly into spirit, showing them the prismatic glory of their eternal, true selves.

Shortly after, they slept like a pair of new-born babies, then awakened, feeling sleepy and refreshed, but otherwise normal.

After dressing, they left the house, closed and locked the front door, then walked away without looking back, their eyes drawn to the starry sky.

CHAPTER TWENTY-FIVE

Sitting opposite his former wife in what was once his own home, Michael felt a distinctly materialistic yearning for what he had lost. The house was spacious, elegant and furnished with great taste, and on the sofa in front of him, a cup of tea in one hand and her long legs crossed enticingly, Janet looked, in her quietly distinguished way, very much a part of it.

Glancing around him, Michael sighed, hardly knowing what to say. He had dropped in to say goodbye on his way to the airport, but now that he was actually in his old home, he was a bit short on words.

'So you're actually going,' Janet said, saving him any further embarrassment. 'You're embarking upon an obviously mad adventure with an equally mad patient. I couldn't believe my ears when Cheryl told me about it — and can scarcely credit it right now.'

'It's not a mad adventure and my patient is perfectly sane. I simply can't explain the matter in detail, which is probably why it sounds a bit strange.'

Janet raised her fine eyebrows in mock surprise. 'Strange?' she said. 'Of *course* not, my dear. Perfectly normal for *you*. You always needed a little adventure in your life, and this journey, which is odd to say the least, certainly fits into that old, familiar pattern.'

'It fits no pattern, Janet, and has nothing to do with

my personal habits. I simply can't tell you why I'm going, but I *do* have to go.'

Janet sniffed and sipped her tea, then put the cup back on its saucer, while Michael, trying to keep his expression neutral, wondered why he *was* going.

He was in love with Frances Devereux — that much he certainly knew. He wanted her with a passion he had not experienced before — a passion so strong that it would take him to the ends of the earth for her. So, that was one reason, and he could not forget it; but what he also could not forget were the words of Miles Ashcombe who, in a rare moment of sanity, had said to him: '*I know you. You have been there as well. Soon, in the near future, you will go back to where you have come from . . .*' Those words had haunted Michael for a considerable time, but only after an accumulation of knowledge about the dark masses did he understand what Ashcombe had meant.

Ashcombe's 'there' was that other world beyond space and time — the world inside the dark masses — and Ashcombe thought that he had seen Michael in it and would do so again. At first Michael had thought it nonsense — the mere fancies of a deranged mind — but when Ashcombe disappeared just like those at Stonehenge, Michael had started believing in earnest. And now, since the seance with Frances and her dead mother, he believed implicitly in that other world and simply had to experience it.

Thus, he was going to Iraq for two very distinct reasons: the first being an unquenchable thirst for knowledge, the second, his overwhelming love for Frances. Whether or not such reasons compensated for his own betrayals, it was too late to stop.

'I think that *some* sort of reason should be offered,' Janet said, 'when you're telling your only daughter that you might not ever see her again.'

'Did I say that?'

'Yes.'

'I didn't mean to.'

'But it was true?'

'Yes. It's *possible* that I won't be coming back, so at the time I probably thought she should know.'

'Well, damn you, Michael, I want an explanation. When Cheryl phoned me from Nice she was frightened *and* guilty — the former because of what you said about possibly not coming back, the latter because, being so angry about your affair with a patient, she scarcely took in what you were telling her. So, are you coming back or not? And what on earth's going *on*? Being so secretive about it merely makes you seem melodramatic and cruel, which *I* certainly think you are.'

'I'm not being melodramatic and I'd certainly rather not be cruel, but the truth of the matter is that I may not be coming back — and I simply can't explain it any further.'

'But it's to do with that Glastonbury business?'

'Yes.'

'According to the news, the disappearances have ended — hopefully for good.'

'Yes, that's correct — but my personal involvement hasn't ended, and I can't change my plans.'

'And what about Cheryl?'

'I've done all I can. You know exactly what happened between us in Nice, and there the matter still rests. Like you, she disapproves of what I'm doing, so now she won't speak to me. As for this business with the married man, well, there's nothing I can do. I *did* tell her that if necessary you would talk to his wife, but frankly, I don't think you should do so.'

'I won't have to,' Janet replied. 'Cheryl phoned me yesterday to say the affair is over and that she intends coming home as soon as possible. Obviously, once she got over her anger at *you*, she had a good think about it.'

It was a victory, if a small one, and Michael felt good about it, even better because he would not be leaving behind an unresolved situation. His love for Cheryl welled up in him, washing away his lingering fears, and

340

he knew that he could now face what was coming with optimism and courage. Nonetheless, even stepping into the unknown, he had to express very human doubts.

'Are you sure she meant it?' he asked. 'Or might she simply be speaking off-the-cuff and mean nothing by it?'

'I'm *reasonably* sure,' Janet replied in her careful manner. 'She said she'd had a long talk with him, that she'd asked him to choose between her and his wife, and that he had — as you had said he probably would — told her that he couldn't sacrifice his family for her. So, she told him it was over — *and* that she was leaving her job. In fact, *I* weakened at that point, asking her if that's what she really wanted — God, I'm a hypocrite! — and she seemed fairly adamant that it was. I think his response really hurt her — which is why I think she meant what she said about coming back home.'

'Well,' Michael said, '*that's* a relief.'

'Yes, it certainly is. And I have to admit that I think your visit had a lot to do with it.'

'Not *always* a bad father, then.'

'You were *never* a bad father,' Janet conceded, 'when you were actually *here*. It was just that for you the responsibilities of work were always preferable to those relating to more personal matters. You were a good father *in absentia*; you simply weren't a good family man.'

Enormously relieved because Cheryl was returning home, Michael let Janet's reprimand pass without comment, even though he could not avoid the discomfort it gave him by raising a truth he would have preferred to avoid.

He had indeed been a good father, but from a safe distance, and now, when his daughter seemed to need him most, he was once more walking out of her life, this time possibly for ever. Surprisingly, then, overriding such considerations, was the unwavering belief that what he was doing was inevitable and possibly preordained.'

'Anyway,' Janet continued, 'that's in the past now. If you're going, you're going, and that's all there is to it. I just think that you should at least try to give us *some* idea of what's going on.'

'I can't,' Michael said, feeling more remote each minute, his thoughts spiralling off into the ether of that other world beyond comprehension. 'Believe me, I really would if I could, but I simply can't do it.'

Janet sighed, then glanced around the room, as if measuring what she was losing by counting what she had gained. Satisfied, though not exactly happy, she returned her gaze to him.

'Is it dangerous? Can you at least tell me that?'

'No,' Michael said, 'it's not dangerous. If I don't come back, I'll still be okay — you can tell Cheryl that much.'

'Good,' Janet said. 'At least it's something. Although . . .' Her voice trailed off unsurely, then she sighed and shook her head. 'It just seems slightly mad,' she said. 'Even this farewell is crazy. You say you're going away and *might* not be coming back, and we won't have a clue where you are or what's happening to you . . .'

'Do you care?'

'I'm not talking about myself. It's Cheryl I'm — '

'But do *you* care?' Michael insisted, wondering, even as he uttered the words, why he needed such reassurance.

Janet looked at him, frankly amazed, her brow wrinkled in thought. 'Well, *of course* I care,' she said. 'What would make you even *think* otherwise? We were married for a long time, we have a lovely daughter, you're the father of that daughter and she loves *you* — and for all that I'm grateful. *Of course* I care what happens to you, Michael. You represent the major part of my life, and all I value most dearly. So quite naturally I *care*.'

Her patent sincerity made Michael feel cheap.

Ashamed of himself, he realised that he was not the objective thinker he had imagined: that his more emotional, subjective side prevailed over his need for distance — and realising that, and surprised by the warmth it gave him, he found it much easier to accept the unknown's possibilities. In that sense, what he was getting from his former wife, was the courage he needed.

'I didn't know you still cared that much,' he said, actually feeling quite childish. 'I thought that the divorce had killed off completely what we once shared together.'

She smiled, obviously amused that he could think that, then shook her head.

'No,' she said. 'It didn't. You never mistreated me, after all. And you didn't even leave me for another woman, which was a lot in your favour. No, Michael, our separation didn't embitter me; it just made me more careful.'

'And now that I'm leaving?'

'Right now I'm *glad* we've been separated so long; I don't think I could stand this situation otherwise. However, what if you *don't* come back? And when do we actually decide that you're *not* returning?'

'If I'm not back in four weeks, I won't be returning. But whether I do or don't, I've already transferred all my assets to you and Cheryl.'

'That was thoughtful of you, Michael.'

'It was the least I could do. After all, the fact that we're divorced has no bearing on what I feel for you and certainly owe you both, emotionally and otherwise.'

Janet smiled again, aware of what he was doing.

'*Touché*,' she said. 'Anyway, I really *am* grateful — and it takes a real weight off my mind, particularly regarding Cheryl and her as yet — thank God — undecided future.'

'Good,' Michael said. 'That makes it worthwhile. Now I don't feel so bad.' He shrugged, then sighed.

'And that just about wraps it up, I suppose. I have to be going now.'

They both stood at once, both smiling uneasily, then moved closer and embraced one another. Michael kissed her on the cheek, too embarrassed to do otherwise, then hurriedly turned away and walked to the front door, pulling it open, perhaps too enthusiastically, and stepping outside.

The morning light was crystal clear, falling out of a cloudless sky, lending lustre to the lush greenery of this countrified pocket of Esher. Michael took a few deep breaths, savouring the unpolluted air, then turned back and looked again at Janet, appreciating her middle-aged serenity and more mature beauty. She leaned forward and kissed him on the cheek, then gently pushed him away.

'I hate goodbyes,' she said, 'and so do you — so let's make it short and sweet. Goodbye, Michael. And good luck.'

She wasn't crying, but he sensed that the tears were coming, so he smiled, quickly got into his car and drove out of the gravelled drive.

He turned right into a lane lined with trees and headed directly for Heathrow.

Frances was already waiting for him at the Iraqi Airlines check-in desk in Heathrow's Terminal 2, and as soon as he walked through the sliding doors and placed his suitcases on the floor, she rushed forward to kiss him. They clung together for some time, taking comfort from one another, two voyagers on the brink of the unknown, travelling on a wing and a prayer with only their faith to sustain them. Then, as if caught without clothes on, they self-consciously broke apart.

'Oh, God,' Frances said, 'I'm so glad to see you. I was beginning to think you'd changed your mind.'

'No,' Michael replied. 'Never.'

'And how did the visit to your wife go?'

'My *former* wife,' Michael corrected. 'And it was fine. Farewells, like deaths, make us forget the bad times and remember only the good. Also, I learnt that Cheryl's coming home, which made me feel even better. So, all in all, it was worth it.'

Frances hugged him again and he felt her uncommon warmth, the vibration of a magical sensuality that could not be resisted. He wanted to take her there and then, on the floor of this crowded lobby, but instead just stepped back and thoughtfully studied her. She looked drawn, almost haggard, her brown eyes dark-shadowed. But her beauty had an otherworldly radiance that could not be ignored.

'Well,' he said, trying to keep his feet on the ground, 'I'd better check in. Have you done so already?'

'Yes,' Frances replied. 'I arrived half-an-hour ago. Now that Mother's gone, I can't wait to get away — and every minute seems endless. So, let's get moving.'

Michael picked up his suitcases and let her lead him to the check-in desk. There were very few in the queue and the formalities were soon over; then, since Frances wanted to feel that she was actually on the move, they went upstairs and walked along the crowded terminal, towards the departure lounge.

'How do you feel?' Frances asked him.

'Fine,' he replied. 'A bit disorientated, still slightly disbelieving, some pain at the thought that I might not be coming back — most notably regarding Cheryl — but otherwise, I have to confess to a definite excitement.'

Frances pulled him closer to her as they walked. 'Well, that's good,' she said. 'At least you're still clinging to your sanity — and I know that in these particular circumstances that can't be too easy.'

'I'm a psychologist. I'm *supposed* to cling to sanity. It's the *least* I can do.'

'You're not a psychologist anymore. You're one of God's chosen few.'

345

The remark made Michael uncomfortable and he glanced sideways at her, noting her almost beatific smile and the joy in her eyes. She was like a woman transported, vaulting out of her mortal body; and even as he felt the sweeping force of his love for her, he trembled at the thought of what she might be leading him into.

He glanced around the crowded airport, taking in the milling people, trying to accept that he might be seeing it all for the last time. He failed to do so, being trapped in the familiar; but then, as they approached the gates that led into the departure lounge, he saw someone who immediately made real what he was leaving behind.

It was Cheryl.

Michael stopped walking, forcing Frances to do the same, and simply stared, in love and disbelief, at his beautiful daughter.

She was standing near the gate where the boarding-passes were checked, wearing a rumpled sweater, denim jacket and blue jeans, her blonde hair, though still long, now piled up on her head, to once more emphasise her pert features and unblemished youthfulness. She seemed sleepy, but was offering a tentative smile that instantly warmed him.

'Stop staring,' she said. 'It's really me. I came in on a plane this morning and thought I'd wait here for you. I mean, I couldn't let you go without saying goodbye — so, here I am. It's really me and you're not having a bad dream.'

Michael felt Frances' hand falling away from his arm, then he stepped forward, took hold of Cheryl's shoulders, and leaned down to kiss her on the cheek.

'You're not a *bad* dream,' he said. 'More like a dream come true.'

He stared at her for some time, feeling a warm glow of pleasure, temporarily forgetting Frances until Cheryl's blue gaze moved from his face to look past him in an enquiring manner. At that, he glanced over his shoulder at Frances, but she waved her right hand in a

346

negative manner, indicating that he should, at least initially, speak to Cheryl alone.

Nodding, he turned back to his daughter, looking down at her upturned eyes.

'I'm delighted,' he said. 'I can't tell you how much. My heart was breaking at the thought of leaving without seeing you. I thought you'd never forgive me.'

Cheryl glanced at Frances, then back at him. 'I came to say goodbye,' she said softly. 'Not to forgive you.'

'I'll settle for that,' Michael replied. 'And your mother said you'd left that man for good. Dare I ask if that's true?'

'You may. And it is.'

She wasn't smiling now, but simply staring steadily at him, her striking eyes enlarged because she was having to look upward, her body being jolted by the passengers who were pushing past her to show their boarding passes before moving on to Passport Control.

'Well,' Michael said, unable to believe that he was actually leaving her, 'that at least will send me off with a lighter heart. What made you change your mind?'

'I changed my mind because you planted the seed of doubt in me, and when you left, even though I was angry with you, I kept thinking about it. In the end, I knew you were right — that I had to gauge my importance to him — so eventually I decided to do what I'd been avoiding for so long, namely, to put the choice to him: either stay with his wife or definitely give her up and marry me. Try not to look self-satisfied when I say that you were right: when he saw that I was serious, he had no hesitation in dumping me. ''But *mon cheri*,'' he said, ''you cannot *possibly* expect me to sacrifice my family for a mere *poulette*! Please accept two weeks' notice.'' And that, as they say, was that — I walked out and he let me do so, not even coming to the airport to wave goodbye. So, no need to smirk, but you were right — and I've come home for good.'

She was leaning against the railing, still being

brushed by the people passing, and at that moment she seemed very frail, rather than just slim. It was a father's view of her — he understood that immediately — but he still felt a lump in his throat when he studied her pained face.

'You'll recover,' he said. 'Believe me, it's all for the best.'

'Oh, right,' she replied laconically. 'That really helps me a lot.'

'Don't be facetious, Cheryl. Most of the valuable things we learn come at a price — and in this case, you've paid it.'

'I know,' she said. 'Truly.' She smiled and reached down to hold his hand and bring it up to her cheek, letting it rest there for a moment, then gently dropping it. 'So,' she said, 'you're really going off on this magical mystery tour?'

'Yes, I'm afraid so.'

'And you can't tell me a thing about it?'

'Only what I told you in France: that it's related to Glastonbury.'

'I hope you know I want you to return.'

'That's a nice thing to hear.'

She grinned, then glanced over his shoulder. He knew she was looking at Frances, but he didn't say anything.

'That's her?' Cheryl asked. 'Your mad patient? The one you're running away with?'

'Yes,' Michael said, 'that's her. But she's not mad and I'm not running away with her.'

'She's involved in this Glastonbury business, too?'

'That's why she's going.'

Cheryl stared over his shoulder again, standing on tip-toes to do so, then returned to normal and looked at him, a slight smile on her face.

'She's very attractive in a straight-laced way,' she said. 'Are you sure she's worth having?'

'Pretty sure,' Michael said.

'Are you proper lovers yet?'

'Can't you tell?'

'Yes. It's written all over you.' Cheryl's slight smile turned into a wicked grin. 'Well,' she said, 'I suppose you better introduce us. After that, you can go.'

Michael felt the healing joy of a man who has regained his daughter, but he still suffered a slight trepidation as he turned away from her and beckoned to the woman who had come between them. Frances stepped forward immediately, her face grave and self-contained. The women studied one another for a considerable length of time, then Cheryl very formally stretched out her hand to have it shaken by Frances.

'I'm Cheryl.'

'I'm Frances.'

Michael sought for some words with which to fill the brittle silence, but anticipating him, Frances stepped closer to Cheryl, whispered, 'Damn it, this is ridiculous!', then hugged her, kissed her on the forehead and stepped back again.

'So,' she said, 'you're the beauty I've been told about so often. Well, your father obviously wasn't exaggerating. I can see why he's proud of you.'

Cheryl didn't bite, but instead moved in for the kill.

'So you're the crazy patient,' she said, 'who's stealing my father away.'

Frances blushed instantly, as if slapped on the face, but quickly rallied herself and offered a smile that had a hard, cutting edge.

'I'm the woman all right,' she said. 'The one your father's told you about. And I know him enough to be convinced that he hasn't described me as mad. Furthermore, I'm not stealing him away — he's coming with me because he has to — and although you're his only daughter, you're now a woman, not a child, so it's pointless to pretend you're outraged by what's happened between us.'

'All I know is that my father is personally involved

349

with one of his patients — and that morally and ethically it's wrong and should not be encouraged.'

'Oh, my God!' Frances said. 'How pure you are — for a *twenty*-year old! Though, come to think of it, from what I've heard about your *own* life, you're in no position to cast stones at me or anyone else.'

'My lover wasn't a psychologist, and I wasn't his patient.'

'No,' Frances said, stepping closer, her eyes widening, 'but you *were* having an affair with a man who had a wife with two children. Morality? Don't you *mention* the subject in such self-righteous tones!'

'Damn you, I loved him!'

'And what does *that* prove? Only that you're just like me — a woman who was ruled by her feelings and blinded to all else. Sorry, Cheryl, but you've no right to chastise me. You and I are the same.'

Michael felt as though the bottom was falling out of his world, as if everything gained was being lost in this brief, bitter intercourse, He just stood there, helpless, destroyed by feminine reasoning, wanting the world to swallow him and absolve him from choice. He loved both of these women, each in a different way, but that in itself was not enough to help him solve this dilemma.

Then innocence did that for him: Cheryl blushed and took a deep breath. She glanced nervously left and right, at him, then at Frances, let her breath out in a wistful sigh and spoke softly but clearly.

'Fair enough,' she said. 'You're right. I know just what you mean. I was angry at anyone who dared to suggest that I was wrong. So, I was angry with him' — here she pointed at Michael — 'and then I tried to pin the blame on you, which was easy to do. But it was neither him nor you — it was me and what I wanted; it was me, so besotted by my need for that man that I couldn't — or, more likely, *wouldn't* — see how he was using me. So, yes,' she continued, 'you and I are the same. We both loved a man so much, we didn't care about anything

350

else — the only difference being that I was fooling myself, whereas you knew the truth when you saw it and refused to let go of it. So, I'm sorry ... and you really seem very nice ... and I think my father's a lucky man.'

On an emotional impulse, she again stood on tiptoes, this time to kiss Frances on the cheek and give her a hug. She then turned towards Michael, her eyes wet with tears, gripped him very tightly and kissed him, sniffing back her quiet sobbing.

Michael felt her trembling limbs, her warm, cushioning flesh, and his heart seemed to break down the middle to let love and grief rush in. He was leaving her — yes, and now that knowledge seared his soul — and he knew that whatever was to come, he would never forget her. Some things lasted, after all — a parent's love, a child's faith — and in understanding that he was released from the doubts that had burdened him.

Unashamed, Michael wept. Watching his daughter, also weeping. Then he saw her rush away, one hand waving, a pale flower, and he turned into the arms of the woman he would love throughout eternity.

'Oh, my Frances!' he whispered.

CHAPTER TWENTY-SIX

The office of Professor Saddam Khairallah, assistant curator of the Museum of Arab Antiquities in Baghdad, looked more like one of the museum's storage rooms, or perhaps a shop, than an office supposedly used for administration. One rather modest grey filing-cabinet stood forlornly in the corner near the window, but otherwise the office might well have been a part of the Suq al-Shurjah bazaar, with its numerous, often priceless antiques carefully stacked on the wooden shelves or, if they were too large, left leaning against the walls covered with Islamic art.

Saddam himself was a grey-bearded Sunnite Muslim with an amiable, sun-scorched face, but he looked, in his short-sleeved white shirt and grey slacks, like a European just returned from a long vacation. An old friend of Frances' father from before she had even been born, he had obviously been delighted to see her and, having taken her and Michael for lunch in the museum's canteen, was giving them each a glass of *arrack*.

'It is made from dates and grapes,' he explained to Michael, 'and is really quite wonderful. Alas, I cannot drink it myself, but I'm sure you'll appreciate it.'

Frances sipped from her tiny glass and watched Michael doing the same; he let his first sip linger in his

352

mouth, eventually swallowed appreciatively, licked his lips and nodded his approval at the benign Islamic professor.

'You're right,' he said. 'It's delicious.'

Professor Khairallah smiled happily, then sat in the chair behind his desk, clasping his hands under his chin and fixing his attention on Frances. Beyond him, through the window, were the remaining domes and minarets of the old city, glittering in golden defiance between the soaring steel, glass and stone of the high-rise offices now dominating most of Baghdad.

'So, my dear child,' he said, 'I confess, your story intrigues me, particularly your conviction that the Garden of Eden of Christian mythology actually exists and is possibly connected to the bizarre visitations of the past five or six months.'

'We've given you the facts, Saddam,' Frances replied, 'and they seem fairly persuasive.'

Professor Khairallah nodded, fingers lost in his beard, sunlight pouring in through the window behind him to lend a silvery tint to his steel-grey hair.

'Fascinating,' he said. 'Particularly in view of what is happening all over the world, with these extraordinary materialisations and disappearances.'

'Which seem to have ceased,' Frances said.

'Indeed,' the professor replied. 'However, the very fact that the phenomena occurred in the first place — and that certain areas have apparently been permanently changed by them — has encouraged many to think that what we are living through is the beginning of the end — and they don't know what *you* know. And, just as there have been an increasing number of religious conversions, riots, assassinations, suicides and other extreme emotional reactions in every corner of the globe, so we, too, are having similar problems. Some of our great historical sites have disappeared, so the Shi'ites and Sunnites, just to take one example, are already at one another's throats. Therefore, though the disappearances seem to have ceased, we are now suffering the lamentable results of their initial appearance and the fact that some dark masses still remain.'

'That kind of hysteria should die away,' Frances said.

'Perhaps so,' the professor replied.

Frances glanced tentatively at Michael, who was sitting in the chair beside her, and noted that he was giving all his attention to the Arab professor. His expression was thoughtful, but she knew he was tired and fraught, naturally wearied by the sleepless flight from London to Baghdad, then exhausted by the demands she had made in the hotel's luxurious, wide bed.

Thinking about it, she burned, felt the melting of her loins, crossed her legs and tried to keep her expression composed while memories of the last fortnight filled her head.

Since that first time in the hospital they had made love every night, passionately, fiercely, and within normally acceptable boundaries; but last night and this morning, in their expensive hotel-room, overlooking the walls and tower of an ancient, golden-domed mosque, and, more blasphemously, with an *imam's* wailing in their ears, they had ventured into the edge of those waters that had frozen Laurence's tender heart. And Michael had complied, surprising her and perhaps himself, first reacting in a puzzled manner, then with quiet cynicism, eventually acceding to her demands with an expression that veered wildly between repugnance, amusement, bewilderment and — helplessly — love.

Nevertheless, she had been frustrated, unable to find satisfaction, and her frustration, which was great, had only been increased by the knowledge that she simply did not dare ask him to do what she needed. He had orgasmed, groaning softly, until she pushed him off, cursing softly as she rolled onto her side and anticipated his anger. But the anger had not come — he had simply

354

fallen asleep contentedly — and the next morning (this morning) he had awakened with no more than an ambiguous smile.

They had not discussed their night in bed, neither able to summon the nerve, and Frances had found herself floundering like a hooked fish dropped onto a hot rock. Now she thought of the night with shame (she had not felt that before) and wanted to reach out and stroke his neck, though she didn't dare do so.

Instead, she returned her gaze to her father's old friend, who was once more folding his hands beneath his chin and nodding judiciously.

'So,' Professor Khairillah said, 'you wish to know if our knowledge of Mesopotamian antiquity will support your belief that another world, perhaps one parallel to our own, has had a hand in human evolution.'

'That's it,' Frances said.

'Well, certainly Mesopotamia has not been called the Cradle of Civilisation for nothing,' the professor said. 'For a start, the discovery of seven Neanderthal skeletons in the Shanidar Cave in the Zagros mountains confirmed that a good sixty-thousand years ago, when many areas of Europe were still covered by great glaciers, prehistoric man was already well entrenched in Iraq, Turkey and Syria. Then, some time in the fifth millennium B.C., the farmers of northern Mesopotamia emigrated southward to the Tigris-Euphrates plain that stretches from Baghdad to the Gulf — and therefore includes your supposed Garden of Eden — where, shortly after, they were brought into contact with the invading Semitic nomads of the Syrian and Arabian deserts; and the subsequent mingling of those two cultures laid the cornerstone for the world's first true civilisation.'

'Which could account for the Garden of Eden myth,' Frances said. 'The myth of the first truly human man and woman — *and* of the dawning of moral consciousness.'

355

'Quite,' the professor said. 'The time and the place are right. If we treat Adam and Eve as figurative creatures, the myth carries validity. However, if they actually existed as two of the first of an ancient race, they must have done so at the very beginning of a long, tangled saga. Certainly, shortly after the mingling of the Semitic and Arab cultures, in approximately 3,500 B.C., the Sumerians arrived on the stage to become the actual builders of the first real civilisation.'

'That isn't exactly a secret,' Frances said.

'Of course not,' the professor replied, smiling slightly at her impatience. 'But if we know what the Sumerians *did*, that's *all* we know about them. We still don't know *who* they were.'

So saying, he climbed out of his chair, went to the corner of the room, picked up an object and returned with it, resting its base on the desk, balancing the top with his right hand.

'This,' he said, pointing to what appeared to be a roughly rectangular-shaped stone on which numerous hieroglyphics had been cut, 'is a pictograph, an example of Sumerian cuneiform. Perhaps more than any other human invention, *writing* made civilisation possible — and over five-thousand years ago the Sumerians invented writing in the shape of crude symbols etched in with a stylus on clay tablets like this one. And soon — at least by early in the third millenium B.C. — the Sumerian scribes had improved the cuneiform by using symbols *phonetically* and making it possible to spell out any word in the language. At that point, my dear friends, civilisation was truly born — and over the next fifteen-hundred years the Sumerians added to that glory by commercialising agriculture, establishing the first trade routes between Mesopotamia, Asia Minor and Iran, and creating the first politico-religious city-states. As I said, the very cornerstones of civilisation — for good *and* for evil.'

356

He laid the ancient tablet gently on the desk, then sat down again.

'The Sumerians,' he continued, not without a touch of histrionics, 'dominated Mesopotamia for fifteen-thousand years, created the first civilisation, then faded away with the ascendancy of the Babylonians — but to this day, my friends, we do not know the origin of the Sumerians. They remain a complete and tantalising mystery.'

Frances thought of the primitive farmers, the Ubaidians, living in their mud-brick huts and naming their crude settlements Ur, Eridu and Kish. She also thought of the invaders, the Semitic nomads from the deserts, arriving to take over those dusty villages and crude towns, then mingling with the equally simple Ubaidians. No richly creative fruit there. Just the joining of two primitive cultures. And then, out of an unknown past and source, came the mysterious Sumerians to create, from the crude mingling of Ubaidian farmer and Semitic nomad, the most important event in human history: the first civilisation.

It hardly seemed possible.

'The Sumerians disappeared,' the professor said, 'but Mesopotamian civilisation continued, refined and passed down by the Babylonians, surviving the invasions of the Hittites, Kassites, Elamites and Assyrians, rising up to even greater glory through Nebuchadnezzar's dazzling renaissance, then surviving the Persians and Alexander the Great, then the Selucids and the Parthians, until eventually, in 227 A.D., came the equally mysterious Sassanids, better known as the Sasanians.'

The professor distractedly reached across his desk to pick up a grey stone statuette of what appeared to be a bald-headed priest wearing a skirt and with his hands folded over his bare chest. He stared at it as if not really seeing it, placed it back on the desk, glanced first at Michael, then at Frances, and nodded unconsciously.

'We know that the Sasanians were an Iranian dynasty,' he said, 'founded by Ardashir I in A.D., 224 and destroyed by the Arabs during the years 637–651. We also know that they ruled Mesopotamia between A.D., 227 and 636 — in short, until the beginning of their systematic destruction by the Arabs. However, apart from those facts, we know remarkably little about life under their rule. What *is* known is that during the course of their reign, over a period of approximately four-hundred years, many of the ancient cities of Mesopotamia were buried beneath the sands of the desert, and with them perished one of the oldest and most remarkable civilisations of the ancient world.'

Frances had a sip of her *arrack* while the professor, staring keenly at her, scratched his large nose.

'I only tell you this,' he said, 'to give you some examples of the numerous mysteries which abound in Mesopotamian history. The Cradle of Civilisation appears to have emerged from a series of great waves of intense creativity, interspersed with periods so shrouded in mystery that there appears to be no logical connection between them — as if, indeed, that inchoate civilisation was being guided by a god, or gods, who came and went intermittently, perhaps only as they felt was necessary.'

'Necessary for *what*?' Frances asked him.

Professor Khairallah shrugged, looking bemused. 'Evolution,' he said. 'I merely append to what you have already suggested, but the possibility is there.'

Disturbed again, Frances stared through the window beyond the professor's silvery head and saw the black clock on the white wall beneath the domed tower of an ancient mosque. That same mosque had once stood proudly above the mud-brick huts of its Islamic subjects, but now it was almost lost in the surrounding steel and glass of modern, high-rise hotels, offices and apartment-blocks. The wailing of the *imam* no longer fought the braying of camels; instead it had to fight the

358

roaring of buses, taxis and trucks. Down there, on the ground, some bazaars and *suqs* remained, the stalls piled with copper pots, silver bowls, rugs and quilts; but they were rapidly disappearing, giving way to supermarkets, just as the minarets and mosques were giving way to skyscrapers . . .

' — and so it was,' the professor was saying as if speaking at one of his lectures, 'that after the reign of the Sassanids, or Sasanians, when much of the ancient world disappeared under silt and sand, there mysteriously arose out of that desolation and human conflict one of the most magnificent ages in human history — by which I mean, of course, the Abbasid Golden Age, which produced an intellectual awakening that extended in its impact far beyond the borders of the Tigris and Euphrates. This was the age of the founding of the original, legendary Baghdad; of the great storyteller, Scheherazade; and of Caliph Harun-al-Rashid, considered to be the greatest monarch of his time. Also, during this age, Arabic numbers and the decimal system were introduced, as was algebra; the great doctor Avicenna produced what was to be the standard medical text throughout Europe and the Orient, as well as the Arab world; and Maimonides, philosopher and court physician to the mighty Saladin, dealt with religious and metaphysical questions which were to profoundly influence the major Jewish and Christian religious thinkers. So, out of that inexplicable desolation, sprang that even more inexplicable, supremely great age . . . then, alas, it was destroyed by the rapacious Mongols and thereafter endured centuries of a neglect that has yet to be fully rectified. Indeed, a neglect so profoundly irrational that it does lead one to think that it must have been ordained by the gods for their own unknown purposes.'

The glass of *arrack* had made Frances feel pleasantly drowsy and sensual, and she turned her head to glance at Michael's profile, secretly wishing that he would look at her and smile, but aware of why he was avoiding doing that. She thought of her seduction of him and the many times they had made love since, then remembered the ambiguous smile he had offered when her unfulfilled desire turned into frustrated rage.

He had not been able to satisfy her because there was only one way to do that, and so far, for reasons which she had not cared to examine, she had been reluctant to ask of him what she had so bluntly demanded of Laurence. Yet now, when she thought of what that request had done to Laurence, she was forced to admit that she was frightened of turning Michael against her. So, she glanced at him, yearning to kiss his lived-in face, then returned her attention to Professor Khairallah, whose gentle smile gave her comfort.

'What about my Garden of Eden?' she asked him. 'I *know* that when we were sucked into that dark mass, we were somewhere very close to Al Qurna. So do you believe there *is* a connection between that area and my personal experience inside the dark mass?'

'All myths are based on obscured facts,' the professor said, 'and certainly there are reasons for that area being claimed as Eden — and, of course, the place where Abraham once prayed.'

He clapped his hands lightly and gave her a broader smile, obviously delighted to have slyly returned Eden to its Islamic origins.

'I note that when you were sucked into the dark mass, you found yourself in a land of marshes and lagoons, then, in an earlier period, beside the great dust-bowl which you thought might have later become Eden's lake.'

'Yes, that's correct.'

'It is interesting, then, that most of the early Mesopotamian creation myths speak of watery origins — of water from under the earth joining water from the sea — and floods. This almost certainly refers to the marshlands between the lower Euphrates and Tigris

360

rivers — a view supported by the fact that both rivers regularly flood their banks. As to the importance of that area to the history of man's evolution, the confluence of the two great rivers — where your so-called Eden is located — marks the place where the first civilisation *and* recorded history began. Indeed, it was from Basra and its Euphrates' neighbour, Kufah — both of which began as no more than military camps — that there emerged all the literary, philological and historical materials which were to form the basis of Arab-Islamic culture; and from there, also, that those prime foundations of civilisation, grammar and lexicology, came into being. In short, the whole history of Islam — and therefore the basis of Judaism and Christianity — was greatly conditioned by events that occurred in the land around Al Qurna — your so-called Garden of Eden.'

The professor smiled at Frances, obviously enjoying her growing surprise, unaware that the very mention of Eden had churned up her emotions. She saw it all immediately, vividly real in her mind, and felt a wave of fear and desire sweeping hotly across her.

She reached into her handbag, withdrew a cigarette, lit it, inhaled and blew the smoke out to ease her heart's fearful beating. When she glanced at Michael and saw his thoughtful gaze, she looked away quickly.

'I'm still not sure that this relates to the dark masses,' she said.

'Well,' the professor replied, 'there *are*, in those Mesopotamian myths which deal with the time before recorded history, other parallels to your experience.'

'Such as?'

The professor shrugged as if the facts were self-evident. 'Although much of that history is shrouded in mystery, there can be no doubt that during the earliest stages of the evolution of the various Mesopotamian religions, particularly during the 3rd millennium B.C., the gods were firmly characterised as *human* in shape

361

and, just as surprisingly, as having organised themselves into a primitive, prototypal, democratic structure that strongly influenced civilisation thereafter.'

'So these gods,' Michael said, 'laid the guidelines for future social order. They were, in a sense, *teachers*.'

'Quite so,' the professor replied. 'And while the Sumerian myths — our earliest known records of at least the *consciousness* of the time — say little about the Sumerian view of the creation, the epic of Gilgamesh *does* mention an earlier time — I quote: '*after heaven had been moved away from earth, after earth had been separated from heaven.*' The same belief — that earth and heaven had once been close together and were later *separated* — occurs also in a Sumero-Akkadian creation text from Ashur.'

'I'm not sure I've gotten your drift,' Michael said.

'I refer to what happens within the dark mass,' the professor said. 'Given, as it would seem, that the dark mass is a gateway leading from Earth to the other world — a world where time and space are meaningless, and where the living are incorporeal beings who exist simultaneously in past, present and future — given that, there *could* have been a period when the earth and heaven were one — or, at least, when the people of ancient Mesopotamia *thought* they were one, possibly because the incorporeal but human-shaped gods actually materialised before them, having emerged from the other world beyond time and space which, for our hypothesis, we may call *heaven*. Then, when the gods had departed, leaving Man to his own devices, but with certain directions mapped out for him and possibly instilled in his subconscious, earth and heaven — or this world and the other — were indeed separated ... separated by time and space.'

'And now,' Michael said, 'where parts of the Earth have disappeared, heaven and earth may be coming back together again as one.'

'Yes,' the professor said.

He leaned back in his chair, sighing, then moved his gaze from Michael to Frances, a sad smile on his lips.

Frances stared back, thoughtfully studying his old man's eyes, trying to imagine him as a much younger man and friend to her father. She was foiled in that attempt, but still took comfort from him, feeling as if her father was in this room, letting his spirit console her.

She turned towards Michael, letting him see her fear and hope, and he reached out to take hold of her hand and squeeze it gently, encouragingly. He held her hand for some time, staring at her, smiling slightly; then, when the professor coughed for attention, placed her hand back on her thigh and turned his head to the front.

Frances took a deep breath, feeling light-headed and weak, as Professor Khairallah leaned across his desk, eyes bright, his lips straight.

'Finally,' he said, 'and with particular regard to your strange pregnancy, please let me remind you that according to Mesopotamian mythology, however Man may have come into being, he existed solely in order to *serve* the gods. In the scheme of existence, then, Man was never an end ... he was merely a *means*.'

The full import of those words sank into Frances like a heated blade penetrating her flesh. At first she felt a quick, keen pain, which promptly gave way to terror, then she felt that she was losing her senses and sinking into chaos. She stopped sinking soon enough, coming to rest in a sea of grief, then remembered her mother lying dead on the floor at home, her father walking onto the back lawn and never returning. The grief brought tears to her eyes, but then she was raised on high, transported on the wings of a mystery filled with fierce expectation. She thought of the near future, wondering what it might bring, then shook like a leaf in a storm and reached out for Michael.

She heard the cry of an *imam* in the distance, calling the faithful to prayer.

CHAPTER TWENTY-SEVEN

The jeep bounced and rattled painfully along what was, to Frances, a very familiar desert road. Her eyes were protected by sunglasses, but the wind was burning her face, and she brushed her flapping hair off her forehead to glance sideways at Michael. He was obviously fascinated by the desolate flatlands, studying them keenly as he drove, his gaze sweeping across the distant horizon which was, at this moment, obscured in the clouds of sand spiralling under a leaden sky.

'You can look as long as you want,' Frances said, 'but you won't really see much. What you're seeing now is *all* you're going to see until we get to the marshes.'

'I love it,' Michael said.

'There's nothing to love,' Frances replied. 'It's flat, barren and depressing — though it *can* come to haunt one.'

'If you find it *that* depressing why did you return so often? You were, after all, a *voluntary* worker and came of your own accord.'

'At first I came simply because I wanted somewhere foreign, somewhere completely different, and I couldn't imagine anywhere much different than this. I wanted to get away from the familiar — and certainly from my own past. Then, of course, when I got to know the Arabs, the depressing aspects of the desert, which, believe me, are very pervasive, couldn't stop it from haunting my dreams and turning me into an addict. In fact, addiction to the desert is a trait very peculiar to Englishmen.'

'And, of course, English *women*.'

Frances smiled. '*Touché*, Michael.'

She looked straight ahead, following the line of the crude road, and saw that they were now crossing dry, seasonal marsh and racing towards some dust-obscured palm trees that marked the outer edge of the marshes. Observing them, she shivered, remembering her first meeting with Schul, then felt a wave of trepidation sweeping through her to spoil her good humour. The jeep passed the palm-grove, then bounced over a pothole, making the two suitcases, standing together on the rear seats, bounce against one another.

'Are we getting close?' Michael asked.

'Yes,' she replied. 'We'll soon be there.'

'How do you feel?'

'Not too good. The closer we get to Eden, the more nervous I feel. Already, all that happened here is coming back to me with an immediacy that makes me feel I'm re-living it. I'm not only *thinking* of Schul — I can almost *feel* his bloody presence — and I keep waiting to see that dark mass materialising in front of me.'

'We can always turn back.'

'No, I won't do that. I have to see this through. I'm still certain that I'm pregnant and that it happened in Eden; but I'm also convinced that the baby's coming won't be normal, and that whatever is going to occur will do so quite soon. I want it to happen in Eden. I feel *compelled* to go back there. It's almost as if there's a voice in my head, relentlessly nagging me. This was all preordained — I'm sure of it — so what I'm doing, I have to do.'

Even as she was speaking, she saw the glint of distant

water, swaying bulrushes and fig-palms, then more water and reed houses growing larger as the jeep headed straight for them; then suddenly, there, where the desert should have been, was a broad swathe of marshlands, water gleaming between green banks, the tall bulrushes swaying against a cloudy, sludge-grey sky which made the reed houses of the marsh Arabs look impoverished and colourless.

Frances told Michael where to go and, after slowing down, he drove past the reed houses that were nestling under dusty fig-palms, then braked to a halt where the first of the bridges led across the shallow ditches to the centre of the small, oddly deserted village.

No children came out to greet them, as they had when Frances had last been here, and when she climbed down from the jeep, with Michael following her example, she found herself glancing uneasily around her, as if at a ghost-town.

'This is it?' Michael asked.

'Yes,' Frances answered slowly. 'But it seems *different*, somehow ... Where *is* everyone?'

She glanced around her again, looking and listening for some activity, then shrugged and led Michael onto the palm-log bridge that crossed the water-filled ditch and led into the heart of the village. Once across, they did in fact see some villagers, most of them old, wearing the traditional *keffia* and *dish-disha*, their eyes peering lethargically from beneath their headcloths as they squatted, in unusually somnolent poses, at the doors of their reed huts.

'A singularly lifeless bunch,' Michael said.

'Yes,' Frances said. 'Odd.'

Feeling more disconcerted, she led Michael across to the sheikh's large *mudhif* which, soaring high above the more modest reed huts, looked even grander than it was. As usual, there was a servant standing outside the door of the flat end — the end facing Mecca — and once they had kicked off their shoes, he solemnly led them

367

through the arched entrance, into the *mudhif's* dimly-lit interior.

Michael was obviously taken a little aback by the sheer size of the *mudhif*. Frances noticed his eyes scanning along the thirteen high arches before returning to fall on Sheikh Hamaid, who was, as usual, sitting crosslegged on the reed matting on the floor, beside the coffee hearth with its exotic row of brass and copper pots, where another silent servant was kneeling.

Frances greeted the sheikh in the customary manner, let Michael do the same as he had been instructed, then, at the sheikh's invitation, they both sat opposite him on the reed matting.

Sheikh Hamaid smiled at Frances, but the humour hardly reached his eyes; the reed fire crackled beyond him, filling the air with spiralling smoke, casting flickering shadows and light over his thin, ascetic and, now, very weary face.

'It is pleasant to see you again, Miss Devereux,' he said, 'even though these times are unhappy. May I offer you food and drink?'

'The food and drink would be appreciated, Sheikh Hamaid — but I'm sorry to hear of this unhappiness. Do you refer to the village?'

'We are not what we were,' the sheikh replied. 'Which I'm sure you have noticed.'

'Yes, I noticed a certain emptiness. There are only old men and women in the village, none of them smiling.'

The sheikh nodded in agreement, then turned his head towards his servant and lightly clapped his hands, signifying that the food should be brought in. The servant immediately jumped up and hurried out of the *mudhif* while Frances glanced along its high-arched, cathedral-like interior to that dimly-lit far end, her gaze drawn against her will to where Schul had been lying when she first saw him.

She studied that dark spot for some time, thinking of Schul and feeling threatened, but was eventually drawn back to the present by Sheikh Hamaid's soft voice.

'There are very strange things happening here,' he said, 'as I'm sure you have heard.'

'Yes,' Frances said. 'I have heard certain rumours. And most of them relate to what happened to me when your oarsmen were drowned.'

The sheikh nodded again, his face solemn and much older, his eyes no longer studying Frances' body with sensual suggestiveness.

'We have lived here for centuries, but our time has now run out. There are miraculous things happening — miraculous and terrible — and my people, when they are not being devoured with the land itself, are fleeing from this place with their children, leaving only the old behind. I cannot stop them. I have threatened punishment to no avail. They think only of the darkness that comes down to steal the earth and its living.'

Frances heard Michael's sigh, but resisted looking at him; instead she kept her gaze on the sheikh and silently fought her own rising fear.

'Is this darkness like the one I told you about?' she asked.

'Yes,' the sheikh said. 'The same. But not one — more than one — sometimes two or three at once; stretching from the desert floor to the sky and devouring all that they cover. They take the land that we know and replace it with other land, changing the shape of the world we live in — therefore our very lives. Whole lakes have disappeared to be replaced with swamp or marsh; many rivers, which have been here since the beginning of time, have either vanished or taken on a new course far away from our villages. Thus many fishermen are starving and their villages slowly dying — dying when they are not being swallowed completely by the pillars of darkness. There is much fear and despair among the Ma'dan and other tribes, since most of them, when not grieving lost loved ones, are convinced that the end has come.'

'The end of the world?'

'Yes.'

'That is understandable, Sheikh Hamaid. What is happening here, has been happening all over the world, and *many* people think that Judgment Day has come. Religious riots and even wars have broken out in many countries, with Church and State unable to stop it. However, in most parts of the world the disappearances have ceased, so it seems that the world is returning to normal.'

'*Your* world,' the sheikh said. 'Not mine. For us it is too late.'

There was a scuffling of feet behind Frances. She glanced over her shoulder to see the servant holding back the door's woven-reed curtains, while some of the old women, silent and bowing low, entered the gloomy hut, carrying trays of food.

Frances turned back to the front as the servant near the coffee hearth passed around the finger-bowl and, even while she, Michael and the sheikh were rinsing their fingers, the old women were setting bowls of the customary mutton, chicken, gravy and rice on the reed matting between the sheikh and his guests. Frances noticed immediately that the portions were more modest than usual, and that the musician who normally played music on his *al-qanon* was no longer present, both of which observations filled her with sadness and a great deal of sympathy.

'I'm afraid I cannot offer you more,' the sheikh apologised. 'But there are not enough people left to prepare proper food, and the dancers and the musicians have fled with all the other young people. As I said, things are not what they were — and, alas, never will be again.'

'It doesn't matter,' Frances said.

'You are kind,' the sheikh replied. 'Nonetheless,

though perhaps it does not matter, it offends my poor heart.'

The old women shuffled back out of the hut and the eating commenced. Frances noticed, with some amusement, that Michael was having as much trouble scooping the gravy-soaked rice into his mouth as had Laurence during his visit to this same hut; however, that small entertainment was all she had throughout the meal, since the food was eaten in a silence devoid of its usual pleasant nuances, and the sheikh, eating half-heartedly and obviously just to be polite, gave the impression of a man devoid of hope and spirit.

Seeing the sheikh's unhappiness, Frances lost her appetite, but grimly plodded on at her task, letting her thoughts spiral up into the cavernous gloom of the great arched roof and take her back to when she had first met Schul.

Just to think of him made her burn with a mixture of lust and shame, and then she found herself glancing surreptitiously at Sheikh Hamaid who had once had designs on her. She remembered bringing Laurence here, his discomfort during the erotic dancing of the Arab boys, and the pleasure she had taken not only from that embarrassment, but from her own sly sexual parrying with the then sensual, confident sheikh. The man now sitting before her was not the one she had known, but was merely the ghost of his former self, watching his own disappearance. Her heart went out to him, but there was little she could do to help, since anything she might say could only offer a further blow to his pride.

Relieved when at last the meal was over, Frances had just taken her first sip of coffee when the sheikh leaned towards her, his aged, dramatically lined face showing grave concern, the fire from the coffee-hearth casting flickering shadows over his weakening brown eyes.

'Be careful,' he said. 'Where you are going is the worst of all. It is said that that place has become the world's navel, and that those who go there enter the netherworld and never return. That place is the source of all things. The pillars of darkness are gathering there. A few Arabs have seen those pillars gathering from a very great distance. Go home, Frances. Do not go near Al Qurna. If you do, you will not return.'

Frances stared at the sheikh, trying to fully grasp his words, her fear starting to be coloured with an excitement that defied rational thought. *The world's navel*, she thought wonderingly. *The source of all things. I am venturing into the navel of the world and might emerge to the netherworld* ... She glanced automatically at Michael, caught him staring thoughtfully at her; then he shrugged, letting her know the decision was hers, and looked down at the floor.

'It is our belief,' she said to Sheikh Hamaid, 'that Al Qurna, which you consider to be the world's navel, is in fact one of many gateways through time and space, and that just as it can transport human-beings to another world, your "netherworld", so it has also been used by a race of incorporeal beings who, originating near a double-star known as Sirius, have visited earth throughout the ages by means of dark masses like those at Al Qurna, for the purpose of guiding human evolution. It is also our belief that they first materialised near Al Qurna at the dawn of mankind, and that the time has arrived for our world to become part of theirs.'

The sheikh stared at her as if she had gone mad, then a small, sceptical smile curved his lips.

'Oh?' he said. 'And how will this miracle occur?'

'We're not sure,' Frances said.

'And this is why you are returning to Eden? To witness this miracle?'

'Yes,' Frances replied.

The sheikh stopped smiling, but kept his gaze on her face; after a very long silence he shrugged his shoulders and spread his hands as if praying.

'Who knows?' he said. 'Perhaps you are right. Under

372

normal circumstances your story would sound ridiculous, but given what we know about the pillars of darkness at Al Qurna, it is possible that your extraordinary theory is correct. However, I beg you, Frances, do not go back there. I repeat: if you insist on going there, you will almost certainly not return.'

'I thank you for your concern, Sheikh Hamaid,' Frances said, 'but I haven't come this far to turn back. I simply *must* go there.'

The sheikh's face was filled with sorrow and his breathing seemed too loud, but eventually, when the silence became unendurable, he nodded acceptance.

'As you wish,' he said. 'It is not my place to stop you. Clearly you will do as you must. Perhaps it was written.'

'Is your canoe still at my disposal, even knowing that it may not return?'

The sheikh shrugged and smiled forlornly. '*Taradas* are dispensable,' he said. 'Good friends are not.'

The remark touched Frances and made her look away, taking in the darkly-shadowed, high arches that ran all the way to the back of the *mudhif*. She lowered her gaze, seeing that dark corner where Schul had lain, then shivered, remembering her first sight of him and her intimations of dread. Those intimations had come true, turning her life upside-down; yet now, as she returned her attention to Sheikh Hamaid, she felt a hint of excitement rising out of her fear.

'When do you want to leave?' the sheikh asked her.

'Right now,' she replied.

The sheikh nodded in sad agreement, then wearily climbed to his feet. Frances and Michael did the same, their bodies brushing as they did so, then stepped aside to let the sheikh lead them out of the *mudhif*.

Once outside, in the afternoon's unusually dim light, they stood together uneasily for a moment, glancing around the quiet village which, poised precariously between narrow river and wide lagoon, the reed houses on stilts appearing to lean dangerously towards the water, seemed somehow artificial and temporary, like a film-set rather than the genuine article. This feeling of artificiality was, if anything, only increased by the lack of younger people and general activity; and Frances, glancing around her, feeling as if her heart was breaking, thought that even the chickens and wild dogs seemed remarkably lethargic.

She shivered and glanced at the sheikh, who simply shrugged forlornly, then she and Michael fell in at either side of him and were led through the village to the river, where his large, ornamented canoe was tethered.

Once beside the boat, Sheikh Hamaid turned towards them, raising his hands in apology.

'Unfortunately,' he explained, 'I cannot give you any oarsmen. I cannot, in all conscience, force anyone to go with you when we know that they may not come back.'

'I would not expect it,' said Frances.

The sheikh looked at Michael, as if assessing his strength. 'Where you are going is not far from here,' he said, 'so you should be able to manage the boat alone. You just use the pole as you would on a punt at Oxford, while Frances here' — and he smiled sadly in her direction — 'handles the rudder. Do you think you can do that?'

'I *have* punted at Oxford,' Michael replied, 'so I think I can manage.'

The sheikh nodded again, smiling a little. 'One of the benefits of English education,' he said. 'So, it's goodbye.'

He took a step back, turned sideways and waved them on. Michael walked onto the plank that led down into the low-slung boat, but Frances hesitated, stared intensely at Sheikh Hamaid, then, on an emotional impulse, leaned forward and kissed him lightly on both cheeks. She straightened up again while the sheikh shyly touched his cheek, then she smiled, nodded, sniffed a little and boarded the boat.

A few minutes later the boat was moving along the

river, Michael pushing the pole while Frances handled the rudder, looking back over her shoulder as Sheikh Hamaid waved goodbye, his black robes billowing out behind him in the breeze, the reed houses and glittering lagoon receding in a dream-like manner until, as if it had never been, the whole village disappeared, leaving only the streaming water, the starlit sky and the river-bank's whispering.

CHAPTER TWENTY-EIGHT

The canoe drifted along the river between bulrushes and fig-palms, taking them past the smoke of burning reed-beds, more isolated villages huddled untidily on the water, the dripping, hump-backed buffaloes silhouetted in crimson as the sun began sinking behind the horizon and cast its light on the marshes.

The surroundings were superficially the same, yet subtly, more gloomily altered, and Frances realised, as she studied the reed houses perched on stilts, that what was missing was the normally intense activity which had formerly enlivened the river-banks. Now, when the boat passed a village, an eerie silence prevailed, and the Arabs, mostly old, but with the odd, lonesome child, stared at the boat with a marked lack of expression, as if not really seeing it. Even the animals and birds seemed lifeless, and no-one was singing.

Eventually, when the sun had disappeared and been replaced by an enormous moon and brilliant stars, they did hear some comforting sounds: crying geese, croaking frogs, the snorting and splashing of drinking buffaloes; then the yellow flames of camp fires started flickering between the trees, illuminating the moonlit, haunting darkness with a weak, spectral glowing.

Frances was sitting at the stern of the boat, her right hand on the rudder, and when she stared straight ahead she saw Michael near the prow, looking immense and silhouetted against the starry sky, as his body rose and fell over the long pole that was propelling the boat along.

He had hardly said a word since leaving the village of Sheikh Hamaid, but she sensed that his silence was no more than preoccupation with what might be ahead for both of them. He had come here with his eyes open, aware that he might never return, and that he had insisted on coming was a measure of the love he had for her.

Thinking about it moved Frances, making her want to return his love, but there was no way in which she could show him what she felt, since even her desires, broad and seemingly insatiable, overruled sentimental emotions and were apparently divorced from love. He understood that and accepted it, but she knew that it hurt him; so, as she watched him straining over the long pole, his heaving body outlined by the rich, starlit sky, she longed for a release from that unnatural sensuality which, even now, seemed to be quickening her heartbeat and setting fire to her bloodstream.

'Do you know where we are?' he asked her, glancing over his shoulder.

'Judging by how long we've been travelling, we should soon be reaching the lake, but I can't really tell you where we are. I don't recognise anything.'

'Nothing?'

'No. It's like being on a different river. I used to know every bend and village along this river, but now I'm hopelessly lost. Let's face it: we haven't seen a village for some time, which is really quite odd. This landscape has been changed — dramatically changed — and all the people are gone.'

'The dark masses.'

'Yes,' Frances said. 'And I feel strange already . . .'

Michael made no reply, but simply went back to his punting, making the canoe glide more urgently through the water, as if he had decided to get the forthcoming encounter over and done with. Frances shivered nervously, but also realised she was cold, that the temperature had started dropping as the river grew wider, its dark, foliage-laden banks moving further away from the boat, eventually forming the mouth of a broad lagoon.

As the canoe glided out into the lagoon, Frances turned on the portable radio she had brought with her. The sound of static filled the silence while she pressed buttons to find a station, but eventually, after managing to pick up an English-language broadcast from Basra, she heard someone announcing that the world's leading scientists were in agreement regarding the recently reported dark masses, and were convinced — a few exceptions notwithstanding — that the phenomena had ended. In other words, said the newsreader in exultant tones, the threat of a disappearing world had ended.

Frances kept staring at the radio, mesmerised by what she was hearing, wanting desperately to believe it but finding the news too good to be true. She kept punching the buttons, hearing the same news from everywhere, and suddenly, as the canoe drifted out into the centre of the lagoon — and as the cold deepened considerably and made her and Michael shiver — the radio went completely dead and would not come back on.

Frances tried station after station, muttering curses to herself, then set the radio down and smiled tearfully at Michael.

'Well,' she said, 'at least there's something to go back to — if we ever get back.'

'Yes,' Michael said. 'Oh, God, yes! It's all waiting there for us.'

He was looking steadily at her as the tears sprang to her eyes. She smiled and wiped them away with her free hand, then leaned on the rudder.

'So,' she said, 'let's keep going.'

She held the rudder straight, letting the boat stay on

its course, then pressed her free hand to her stomach and plunged into despair. She stifled the urge to scream and sunder the silence with her presence, but could not stop sweat forming on her forehead even as she grew colder. Looking up at the sky, she saw the known constellations, but the vastness of the cosmos pressed upon her and threatened to crush her. She stared longingly at the receding river banks, wishing her feet were on solid earth, then looked straight ahead as the canoe, swaying gently and making silver-threaded waves, glided out into the vitreous, reflecting bowl of the star-covered lagoon.

Michael used the pole more forcefully, hurrying the boat through the water, then glanced back over his shoulder, his features hidden in the darkness. Frances smiled at him, enjoying the breeze on her face, but was actually less happy than she pretended, feeling her unease increasing.

She glanced up at the sky, rubbed her eyes, then looked again.

'Oh, my God,' she murmured.

Michael, having heard her, pulled the pole out of the water, lay it against the hull, then let the canoe drift forward into the lagoon while he, too, looked up at the sky.

The stars were in motion, some fading in and out repeatedly, many winking out completely and being replaced by others, still more drifting up and down, or gliding to and fro, weaving a new tapestry in the sky, gradually make it brighter and much more beautiful. The cosmos was being turned inside-out, revealing its far side: a swimming palette of light and colour beyond the known spectrum, of darkness that blossomed dramatically just to shrink back to nothing, of great suns and moons that took turns at dominating the spectacle while time and space intermingled as in a dream.

'Good God!' Michael whispered. 'You told me about it, but I just can't believe it! I've *got* to be dreaming!'

'No,' Frances said, 'you're not. It's getting cold — *really* cold. Remember how cold it was at Stonehenge? We've arrived. This is it.'

Michael shook his head, looked up again, then sat down like a man in a trance and kept his gaze on the sky. Frances also looked up, saw the birth and death of galaxies, looked down and saw that genesis reflected in the glittering bowl of the rippling lake. Her eyes went up and down, drawn to lake and sky in turn, and soon she started feeling disorientated, her senses flying away and dissolving into the dreamscape.

'Head for the shore,' she managed to say, 'before it's too late. We can't tell what might happen.'

Her words appeared to fall on deaf ears, for Michael made no move; he just sat there, staring up at the changing sky, his face bathed in the moonlight. Then the moonlight shifted, moving across his face and off it, forming a great pool of light in the black water beside the boat, then gradually fading away completely and leaving only the starlight.

Frances saw that the moon had vanished, the stars had stopped moving, and the sky was no longer familiar: its new stars were too large, its brilliance too remarkable, its crystalline, moonless beauty too sublime to be real.

At once enchanted and frightened, she lowered her gaze. Michael was still sitting near the prow of the boat, perfectly still, his hands on his thighs, his face turned towards that strange sky.

'Michael!' she snapped. 'Get moving! Let's get off the lake!'

This time she got through to him, her words jolting him awake, and he stared at her over his shoulder, his normally calm eyes surprised, then took hold of the long pole, stood up, making the canoe rock, plunged the pole into the shallow water and leaned heavily upon it.

The canoe glided forward, cutting through the silky

water, causing silver-capped, black rivulets to ripple out obliquely and disappear, whispering, in their wake.

Frances stared down at the water, into those star-reflecting depths, remembering Schul's body sinking into white-foamed turbulence while Laurence sobbed in anguish on the raft and she looked on in horror. First shivering with cold, then suddenly burning as if with fever, she forced her eyes from the rippling depths and, looking skyward, was again stunned by what was transpiring.

'Oh, my God!' Michael whispered.

He stopped punting on the instant, letting the canoe drift towards the shore, and just stood there, staring at the changing sky as if hypnotised.

The sky was an inverted bowl, filled with large, glittering stars, but those stars were disappearing, one cluster after the other, as if being snatched away in large numbers by an invisible hand. They kept vanishing by the score, leaving patches of darkness where they had been, until the sky had become a quiltwork of shrinking stars and widening darkness. Then the swathes of darkness merged, becoming one great wall, which in its turn widened dramatically, stretching across the wide lagoon, until there was only an immense pillar of darkness reaching from lake to sky, its ragged edges defined by the stars still glittering around it.

'Christ!' Michael said. '*Christ!*'

He pushed harder on the pole, making the canoe leap through the water, while Frances held onto the rudder, balancing herself on the swaying seat, and looked up to see that enormous pillar of darkness moving inexorably towards her.

It grew wider as it approached, spreading out to cover the lake. The canoe suddenly slowed down and was held back by a fierce wind, which, being sucked up from the shore and into the dark mass, eventually threw the boat into a violent spin.

Michael fell back onto his seat, losing his grip on the

punting-pole; it struck the water with a light splashing sound, bobbed back up and then drifted off.

'*Hold on!*' Frances screamed.

The darkness swept around them, filling up with streaming light, then a freezing cold gripped them, as the canoe, vibrating violently and screeching in protest, spun in a whirlpool.

Frances held on as the air was sucked from her lungs; she braced herself in the anticipation of being flung into the rushing water, and heard Michael shouting an obscenity into the roaring wind.

She was not flung from the boat. Instead, the wind died abruptiy, rushing away as if by magic. There was silence and the water calmed down to let the boat drift towards the shore.

The streaming light changed, became a widespread, dazzling white haze. This in turn faded away, was broken up by patches of night . . . and from that jigsaw of light and darkness emerged hundreds, then thousands of tiny, pulsating lights, which moved back and forth rapidly, like sparklers in the hands of invisible children.

The boat drifted towards the shore, illuminated by the sparkling lights. Michael stared at them with wonder, then raised his right hand, spreading his fingers to catch one of the lights and check what it was. The lights passed through his hand, his arms, his whole body, as he studied the glowing darkness, his mouth slightly open but speechless, hand still in the air.

The boat bumped against the shore, rocked a little and then was still. Frances looked left and right, over bulrushes and grassy earth — and there, in the unnatural darkness, slightly obscured by the drifting lights, was a lush forest-clearing with a natural arch of fig-palms at its far end.

'This is Eden!' she whispered.

CHAPTER TWENTY-NINE

Dazzled by the drifting, sparkling lights and foiled by the outer darkness, they spent that first night in the long canoe, wrapped in one another's arms and looking out over the lake at the constantly changing view.

They were inside the pillar of darkness, surrounded by lights, but when they surveyed the lake, trying to see the sky beyond, they saw smaller rectangles forming within the gloom and, within those inky-black shapes, even more distant stars. The rectangles came and went, like windows opening out to the cosmos, and shifted constantly, left and right, up and down, through one another, as if time itself was moving in both directions along curving space.

Frances and Michael watched, fascinated, hardly speaking to one another, both losing themselves in the epic grandeur of what was unfolding. They sat thus for a long time, their arms about each other, and when occasionally they glanced at their watches, the hands were either racing forward or backward, or had stopped completely.

It was uncommonly cold and their weight had increased, but they sat in the boat, which swayed gently and silently, watching those great rectangles filled with stars fading in and out magically. Then sometime during that night they fell asleep, both drugged by the splendour.

Frances woke first, opening her eyes to a dazzling white haze, her skin burning from the fierceness of the heat that was beating down from a sunless sky. She rubbed her eyes and licked her parched lips, squinted straight ahead, saw nothing but the convex bowl of the horizon where the lagoon merged with blinding sky.

Wincing, she shook her head, twisted around, away from Michael, saw him opening his eyes sleepily as she looked across the clearing — that very familiar garden of orange and lemon trees, fig-palms, and tall, untended grass. She saw the natural arch of fig-palms at the eastern end of the garden and, just in front of it, flapping noisily . . . Jack Schul's tattered tent.

She studied that tent for what seemed like an eternity, her fear mingled bizarrely with a steadily rising, glowing sensuality. She felt helpless, enslaved, victimised by her burning body, yet knew that it was no more than the life-force dramatically strengthened.

Michael groaned and sat up beside her, his shoulder rubbing against hers, and that slight touch charged through her like electricity, making her tingle. She placed her hand on her stomach, wanting to feel the child inside it, failed, then stared at Schul's tent and suffered shamed recollection.

She visualised herself naked, legs spread, Schul on top of her, taking her while Laurence wept by the lake, his cries floating in to her. Studying the tent, she remembered vividly, blushing with shame and lust at once; then, placing her hand on her fevered brow, closed her eyes and recalled that earlier time.

Instead of the lake, a great dust-bowl, herself a primitive, grunting creature, on hands and knees, face turned towards the parched earth, someone heaving behind her. There was that *and* God's eye, the great humming light descending, spreading out until it dazzled her vision and silhouetted the others. Either alone, or in the presence of the alien creatures, she had writhed in surrender, beyond self-control, devoid of normal pride but moved by feelings outside herself.

Now, opening her eyes, staring at Michael and the lake beyond him, she again felt removed from herself and controlled from afar. Her very imperfect body, with its pleasures and pains, was no more than a vessel of evolution, a bridge between the past and future, a mere link in time's endless chain.

'It's the life-force,' she said.

'What?' Michael replied sleepily.

'This problem,' she said. 'This sexual fever that enslaves me. It's the life-force — the need to give life — dramatically heightened. The visitants, whoever they are, deliberately made me this way. They made me want to have and give life more than anything else. They ensured my continuance.'

She hardly knew what she meant, but felt compelled to spit it out. Michael stared intensely at her, as if thinking she might be mad, then glanced over the haze-obscured lake and rubbed his inflamed eyes.

'Christ!' he said. 'Everything's so *bright!* What time is it? What's *happening* here?'

He was talking to himself, as if already in a trance, but turned back towards her, his brow furrowing in confusion, sighed and climbed out of the boat to give her his hand.

'We're here for a purpose,' he said, sounding oddly aggressive, 'so we might as well get out of this damned boat and wait for something to happen.'

Frances accepted his hand and let him help her from the boat. Once on the grass, they both glanced uneasily about them . . . then Michael's gaze came to rest on the tent near the arch of fig-palms.

'Schul's tent?'

'Yes.'

'You mean it's managed to stand there all this time?'

385

'It seems so,' Frances said.

Michael stared strangely at her, then returned his gaze to the tent. He quivered as if with rage, waved her forward with one hand, then led her across the attractive clearing and right up to the tent. He pulled the flap back, looked carefully inside, dropped the flap and stared at her again, an unpleasant smile on his face.

'So this is where it all happened?'

'Yes, Michael,' Frances replied.

'And did you get satisfaction?' he asked her. 'Did he do what I can't?'

'Stop it Michael. You sound like a child. It's all beyond you and me.'

His jaw tightened with anger, fists opening and closing; he stared fiercely at her, then eventually, as if realising what was already happening to him, closed his eyes and shook his head from side to side.

'I'm sorry,' he said. 'I don't know what came over me. I just felt this sudden, unreasonable *jealousy*. I've never felt that before.'

'It's all right,' Frances replied. 'It's this place. It brings out very primitive, basic emotions. You'll just have to watch yourself.'

Already on the verge of losing control of himself, Michael stared down at the tent again, quivered visibly with rage, then started walking restlessly around the clearing, as if examining the trees. Frances walked with him, not wanting to leave him alone, noticing as they followed the semi-circular-shaped line of trees that she could still hear the normal chorus of frogs, geese, singing birds and buzzing mosquitoes, and that apart from the shimmering white haze over the lake, the dark line of marshes beyond it looked unaltered.

In fact, everything was the same, except for the sunless sky; it was only the lack of a normal sun and the presence of the mysterious haze which showed that changes had already occurred — and that she and

Michael were still inside the gateway to that other strange world.

'Eerie,' Michael said. 'This place is weird. I wish something would happen . . .'

He glanced back across the clearing, at the tent near the arch of fig-palms, shook his head as if to clear it of unpleasant images, then started walking again. Frances watched him, feeling nervous, sensing his tension and growing confusion; she could see by the very way he walked that he was fighting himself.

'Let's rest,' she said. 'There's not much else to do. Let's just sit and talk.'

'About *what?*' Michael asked abrasively. 'About you and Schul and Laurence in this place? I've heard all that before!' He broke a small branch off a tree, waved it like a whip, snapped it into three or four pieces and threw the pieces away. 'You're never satisfied,' he said. 'You remain frustrated. You just can't get enough of it.'

The remark shocked Frances, but she made no reply, realising that changes were occurring and could not be prevented. She thought of their arrival here, of the gold-streaked, crimson twilight, of the great pillar of darkness materialising and reaching from lake to sky. They had been greeted and then devoured, swallowed into another world, and once inside it, from their vantage point in the canoe, had watched the unfolding of time and space.

She remembered the other dark masses, the smaller, black rectangles, coming and going, materialising and disappearing, bringing with them and taking away again whole glittering, constantly shifting, constellations. Yes, she knew where she was now (or at least where she was *not*) and understood that her normal world — the world she had left behind — was simultaneously very far away and right here, all around her.

Accepting that, she shivered, collapsing into her secret self, touching the burning flame at her core and laying waste to her senses.

She reached out to Michael, placing her hand on his shoulder, but he violently jerked away and then hurried down to the lake's edge. Frances watched him more nervously, wondering what he might do, then joined him where the water met the shore, lapping around the bulrushes. A silvery light covered the lake, making sky and water merge, and she felt a great lassitude falling upon her as the heat started draining her. In that lassitude, which also affected her mind, she felt the rise of desire.

She placed her hand on Michael's shoulder, but he slapped it off and walked away. She followed him until he stopped near the tent, between two groups of fig-palms. He just stood there, glaring at the ground, his fists opening and closing.

'If you want me, you can have me,' Frances said.

'I *don't* want you,' Michael replied. 'I want to hear about Italy.'

'Italy? What *about* Italy?'

'You know damned well,' he said.

There could be no mistaking the harsh imperative in his tone, and Frances, distracting herself by studying the glittering lake, squinting into that dazzling brightness with restless expectation, yearned for God's servants to return and rescue her from this. *Italy*, she thought. *He wants to hear about Italy. We are waiting to be taken into another world, yet he still wants to possess me* ... And she understood, then, that the madness was infecting both of them, that Michael was losing himself just as she had done, and that whatever might now occur between them, it would not belong to them.

'No,' she said. 'I won't tell you about Italy. It's not your concern.'

She walked away from him, feeling drained and unreal, breathing too heavily. She did not walk very far, but stopped beneath the nearest tree, glancing up as a white pollen fell and covered the green grass like snow. Then Michael approached her, face grim, eyes wild, and grabbed her by the shoulder and shook her with unusual violence.

'I can *have* you?' he sneered. 'And what good would that do me? I can come and then watch you roll away and clench your teeth with frustration? No, I don't want that! I want to know about Italy! Your sexual hunger may be tied to what happened in this place, but your tastes relate solely to your past, and I want to know about that. Yes, Frances! I want to know about Italy! I want to know what you learned there. Now tell me!'

'No!'

'*Tell me!*'

His sudden slap closed her eyes and made her head spin; she fell back and covered her stinging cheek with her hand, then opened her eyes again. She saw him through her tears, a distorted figure in the strange light, then the anger gave back her lost will and lent strength to her voice.

'All right, damn you!' she whispered. 'You want to hear about Italy? You want to know how I learned my whore's talents. Well, all *right*, then, I'll *tell* you!'

And in doing so, lost herself, returning to that distant time, re-living every moment with a clarity so lacerating that it flayed her to the bone, leaving her exposed to naked pain and letting her rage take command. It had happened a long time ago, but it seemed like yesterday, and her words, spilling out like pebbles dropped on a pane of glass, broke the silence that covered the clearing, bringing the past to the present . . .

She had been seventeen at the time, far too beautiful to be heartbroken, and the vacation was not soothing her melancholy as her mother had hoped. She had been melancholic for years, ever since she was a child, convinced that her father, who was supposed to have died years ago, was in fact still alive and spoke to her in the night's lonely darkness. Whether dream or halluci-nation, she had refused to deny his visitations; and neither doctor nor psychiatrist had budged her from the belief that her father, if dead, was still in touch with her, materialising magically in the night and imprinting his presence upon her. So, they had thought her mentally ill, deranged by her loss; and her mother, an eccentric (or masquerading as such) had eventually, when Frances was seventeen and no better, taken her to Ravello in southern Italy for fresh air and a long rest.

'It was beautiful,' Frances said, 'but more isolating than home. I painted, read books and gazed out over the sea, obediently followed my mother through the mandatory sights of the area — the Duomo di San Pantaleone, the Grotta dello Smeraldo, the glorious cathedral of Amalfi, the many gardens and ancient palazzos that adorned the cliffs high above the Bay of Salerno — but in truth I saw little and rarely heard what was said, since I was hiding in my own silence, waiting for someone to release me — a man like I imagined my father had been: witty and wise and certainly older than myself; a *mature* man who would take command of me and set free my fearful soul. And eventually, one afternoon, in the silence of the town square, when I was sitting alone, having a glass of *Marsala*, I met my Machiavellian Italian and was swept off my feet.'

The Italian was in his late-thirties, but exceptionally handsome and urbane, charming her with his wit and sophistication, the latter in particular being a rarity in that small mountain town. He had bought her another drink, then ordered another while paying her bill, and she, slightly drunk when they parted, agreed to meet him that evening. After that, she managed to meet him every day for a week, usually in the afternoon when her mother was sleeping, but almost as often in the balmy, star-bright evenings when, while her mother drank with the other guests in their small hotel, she would pretend to be bored with their adult conversation and say she wanted to watch the nightly promenade in the colourful town-square. It was easy, very easy, and soon turned into a game; until, after five days, proving that patience was worth cultivating, the Italian talked her into his hotel-room, thus into his bed.

'He seduced me,' Frances said, 'because I wanted to be seduced, because I wanted someone older and wiser to turn me into an adult. I thought he could do that — that the experience itself would do that — but although I discovered the exquisite pleasures of sex, I also learned that they didn't bring a sense of security, or even herald maturity. Quite the opposite in fact — I simply awakened to my sensual nature — and the Italian, who was diabolically gifted in that field, soon had me confusing sex with love and behaving accordingly. I swore that I loved him and would do anything for him, and once he heard that, he knew that he owned me and could make me his slave — which he did by simply threatening to leave me when I tried to resist him.'

At first she had been in heaven, transcending herself through sexual release, her sweat running in rivulets as her pores opened keenly to receive him; but then he became less loving, more brutal and demanding, eventually making suggestions that simultaneously shocked and intrigued her. When she tried refusing, he threatened to stop seeing her; and, in so doing, gained her often tearful acquiescence. First minor improvisations, then more, and much worse, causing her deep shame and pain, even as she obliged him. She vowed more than once to leave him, often storming out of his room, but at such times she always returned, humiliated, more malleable.

'My sweet angel!' he often crooned, his tongue licking at her ear. 'My little bitch!' he soon started murmuring as she fought back her tears. 'Let's do it this way,' he would say. 'Turn around. Raise yourself. Use the pillow and remember what I told you. Oh, my sweet, my sublime whore!' And she tried to resist, but was defeated by her own flesh; and eventually, when he slapped her face to silence her protests, accepted even that as her due, and soon came to expect it.

'He taught me the hell and glory of complete submission,' Frances said, 'and that there was little that a woman, if in despair, could not turn to her pleasure.'

It all happened within five weeks — the last five out of six. The Italian spent one week charming her, cajoling her into his arms, then another four weeks teaching her the arts of sex and enslaving her by them. Once enslaved, she needed him desperately, unable to imagine life without him — and any hope that she could resist his worst demands was very soon shattered. He promised repeatedly to keep her with him in Italy; kept promising, also, that he would speak to her mother about them ... but as the days ran out and her departure grew more imminent, he refused to make good the latter promise unless she did even more for him. And naturally, she obliged, losing her pride in love's grief — letting him turn her onto her belly, or bend her over the table, or cover her with oil to make her slip through his fingers, or take her on hands and knees as he groaned his obscenities, or make her kneel at his feet to pay him homage with her lips while he turned his hands into a vice that threatened to crush her skull — and although she learned to like it, and certainly became dependent upon it, even she was not prepared for the shock he gave her when he dangled his cords of silk.

'He tied me to the bed,' she said. 'It was the ultimate humiliation. I was tied by my wrists and ankles, spread-eagled and open to him, and for hours he did what he wanted to me while I begged him to stop. And why did I beg his mercy? Not because of my *shame*. Oh, yes, there was certainly shame at first, but that passed soon enough. No, Michael, not that. And not because it was unpleasant. On the contrary, I begged him to stop because I thought I was dying ... of ecstasy. I was that way because he aroused me to a pitch beyond control, and yet, in that condition, I could neither hold him nor give myself fully to him. You understand, Michael? Are you willing to accept this truth? I was writhing in an ecstasy that could neither be shared nor eased — I couldn't stop it or control it or share it with him by touching him — and so, as I lay there, tossing and straining against my bonds, I came, then came again, and again and again, and thought, because my heart was racing so fast, that I would surely expire. And after that — oh, dear God, after that there was nothing else for me: I had to be tied up, to be rendered helpless, in order to get satisfaction . . . So, Michael, you wanted the sordid truth. Well, now you have it!'

For a while he just stared at her, as if not recognising her, but eventually, as what he had heard sank properly into his consciousness, his blank expression was replaced with tight-jawed rage.

'All right!' he said. '*Right!*'

Quivering, he stepped forward and grabbed the flap of the tent's entrance, ripped it back but could not make it move further, so cursed and pulled harder. The canvas would not come off, so he cursed again and kicked one foot out, knocking the nearest upright away and making the front of the tent collapse. He stared at it, breathing harshly, in a veritable trance of rage, then walked to the other end of the tent and did exactly the same: kicking the remaining support away with a demented man's fierceness. The rest of the tent collapsed, a part of the canvas covering his feet, and he viciously kicked the canvas away, muttering under his breath. He bent down and jerked the thin ropes out of the rings on the crumpled canvas, straightened again, glared at Frances, then abruptly walked up to her.

'You like to be helpless?' he asked. 'All *right*, then, let's *do* it!'

She thought of running away, but there was no place to hide; and before she could think of some other response, he grabbed the collars of her shirt and ripped them apart, until the garment was dangling around her waist, leaving her bare breasts exposed.

393

'Now take off the rest of your clothes,' he snapped. '*All* of them! *Now!*'

At once frightened and excited, Frances did as she was told; then, when she had finished, when she was standing naked before him, Michael grabbed hold of her wrist, twisted it up behind her, and brutally forced her down onto her knees, with her back turned towards him.

'Is this what you want?' he almost snarled. 'Let's *see* if it is!'

He twisted her arm again, making her turn around to face him, then threw her onto her back and aggressively leaned over her. She offered no resistance, but simply lay there, letting his rage burn, as he spread her arms and legs on the crumpled canvas and, with the thin ropes, tied her wrists and ankles to the wooden pegs that had kept the tent rigid.

When she was lying there, spreadeagled beneath him, he stood over her, panting.

'You look nice,' he sneered. '*Very* nice!'

Then he took off his own clothes, very slowly and deliberately, looking at her with contempt, and eventually knelt between her outstretched legs to place his hands on her ankles.

'You're mine,' he said. 'All of you. Mine . . . And you can't do a damned thing!'

He pushed her ankles back as far as the ropes would allow, causing her knees to rise slightly and spread farther apart. She watched him bending over, as if about to kiss the earth, then felt his lips down there, between her thighs, on her pubic hair, then pressing over the tender labia and forcing her eyes shut.

She gasped and bit her lower lip, feeling the arching of her spine, the automatic, helpless movement of her thighs as they cushioned his head. He was sucking and licking, greedily drinking her as she melted, then she felt his hands sliding up her legs and under her hips. He spread his fingers to hold her firmly, nails digging into her soft skin, and lifted her higher, giving himself more access, as his tongue coiled inside her.

She heard something — her own groaning — and desperately bit her lower lip, only dimly aware of what she was doing as her body quivered involuntarily, straining vainly against its bonds, forming a bridge over a chasm of infinite space and time.

Yes, she was a bridge, a thread of life joining two worlds, her physical self in thrall to the demands of sensual pleasure, her spirit rising out of that mortal shell to spiral into the ether. She soared like an eagle, returned to earth, soared again, looked down upon herself from afar, but fiercely clung to her feelings. Michael's tongue was like a feather, first stroking, then retreating; it returned to press wetly and lick, preparing the way for his hungry lips. She melted and was sucked up, pouring into his greedy mouth, then felt the air rushing onto thigh and labia, as his lips, which had been draining her of sense, slid wetly over her belly.

At that moment, in a sea of drunken flesh, she simultaneously touched earth and sky.

Her navel expanded to accept his tongue, opening out like a great lake, and she pushed up, straining desperately against the ropes, trying to reach for the sky. He plumbed her depths, scoured her banks, made her belly's fine flesh ripple, let the ripples run up over her ribcage and spread out through her breasts. Her flesh became a desert, grains of sand in constant motion, a terrain of curves and hollows and languid dunes given life by a burning wind.

She was that, but remained herself, drawing her energy from sensual greed. She felt his warm breath — in her ear, on her throat, then caressing her bosom to further excite her yearning nipples — then the lips again, that mouth drinking her flowing flesh; that tongue, its saliva like warm oil, pouring into her open pores. First one breast, then the other; one nipple, then its partner; and she twisted and writhed, straining vainly against her bonds, feeling all of her, every nerve and sinew, aching just to take hold of him.

His hand clamped around her chin, shaking her head, making her open her eyes.

He was kneeling between her legs, but had straightened up a little, his erect penis thrusting out above her, hard and smooth and blue-veined. He stared down at her, not smiling, eyes gleaming with a kind of blindness, than he slid his hands under her, fingers stroking the perineum, then took hold of her buttocks and raised them to thrust his hips forward. His penis lightly touched her, making her groan aloud; she tried to arch her body higher, to spread herself and take him in, but the ropes, not allowing further movement, made all her nerves sing.

She writhed and cried out, trying to will herself around him, her body quivering in its exquisite torment and threatening to turn her insides out. Then she felt his penetration, herself folding around him, and he was quickly inside her, hard and hot, beating rhythmically, swelling more as she tightened, sending waves of heat rippling through her in every direction, soon making her feel that she was glowing with a magical radiance.

'No more!' she cried. '*Stop it!*'

She was about to explode, to burst forth from herself, to become the moon and stars, earth and air, fire and water, and felt that if she failed to find release her racing heart would give out. Fearing that, she also wanted it, her spirit crying for its lost freedom, then understood in a flash of revelation that the gates would soon open. And indeed they did so, letting her spirit have dominion, and she dissolved and flowed away, pouring down to her own centre, becoming no more than the quivering, pulsating heat of her own nether regions.

Her body strained against its bonds, sending pains through her arms and legs, and she cried out again, her voice reverberating in her head, and realised that the self-abasement which for so long had enslaved her was no more than the wall behind which she had hoped to protect her wounded soul. Then Michael's hands were upon her, travelling down her arms and legs. She felt the ropes being untied and falling off her wrists and ankles; then knew, as the opening gates admitted light and air, that her limbs would soon become freedom's wings, letting her fly away.

'We don't need that!' Michael said. 'It's an illusion. We just need each other.'

And she smiled with joy, agreeing, rising out of her imprisoned spirit, and so wrapped herself around him, arms and legs, heart and soul, and devoured him, absorbed him, made him part and parcel of her, let herself find the release which in turn released him, and heard their two voices as one, rising above the earth's bedlam.

'Yes!' they gasped. '*Yes!*'

Then the earth actually moved.

CHAPTER THIRTY

Like the beginning of an earthquake, the ground shook beneath them, then they heard an ethereal bass humming that filled the space all around them. Michael had rolled off Frances and now they both jerked upright, automatically looking over the lake in search of the dark mass.

The ground shook again, growling far down in its depths, then returned to stillness and silence, leaving only the bass humming which, though it seemed to be all around them, was clearly emanating from the direction of the lake. The dark mass had not appeared there, but the white haze had changed: the general brilliance had decreased and now the air was splotched with dark patches that were changing shape constantly.

Michael climbed to his feet, took Frances' hand and pulled her up. They both stood there, naked, still dazed by the act of love, and stared silently at what was happening above the lagoon.

The dark patches were growing larger and more numerous, boiling out of the white haze like irregular holes in a cloud — or like black ink splashed on blotting paper — then filling up with distant stars in a more complete blackness.

No longer frightened, but charged with excitement, Frances squeezed Michael's hand and saw his heartening smile. She wanted to embrace him, but he had already turned away from her, to once more stare out at that great spectacle above the vitreous water.

Frances followed his gaze and saw the multiplying holes, originally in their dozens, now in their hundreds, filling the sky as far back as the horizon where the marshes had formed a dark line on the convex rim of the lagoon.

The holes kept multiplying, changing shape, growing larger, until they looked like dense clouds in a misty luminescence which rapidly diminished in intensity until it seemed like a normal sky. In fact, it *was* a normal sky, but filled with very black clouds — or with explosions of smoke — and within the boiling clouds, those dark smudges in the white, there were stars, very small, yet growing bigger and brighter each minute.

The bass humming grew deeper, then became an infrasound, so low that it formed a vibration which made the ground shake. That phenomenon shook Frances, sent ripples through flesh and bone, making her very aware of her body and the child she was carrying. She touched her stomach with her free hand, no longer fearful, simply curious, then saw that the holes in the sky had stopped multiplying.

'They're getting bigger,' she said.

That was true. The holes had stopped multiplying, though there were a few hundred, and now they were growing dramatically and changing their shape, turning from ragged holes into wavering, perpendicular columns, then widening until their uneven edges became almost straight. They were shaped like rectangles, some close, others far away, and all of them contained glittering stars that grew bigger and brighter.

The rectangles were windows, looking out on time and space, and as they became more distinct, and spread out above the lake, the white haze diminished more rapidly, eventually turning into a mundane, pearly-grey light.

Then the star-filled rectangles began drifting up and down, north and south, east and west, and soon were settling gently upon the marshes and the lake's glittering surface. Once settled, they started glowing, were surrounded by a shimmering aura; and that light, growing brighter, slightly erased the stars within, as well as obliterating the land upon which it was bleeding.

The rectangles were great funnels, descending over earth and water; and as they pulsated and radiated their shimmering light, that earth and water began disappearing in a magical manner.

The earth seemed to melt, dissolving within the star-filled windows, making way for other, very different dark masses, which were forming mysteriously out of that space-time frame. And as that was happening, the lagoon itself was vanishing, but in an equally different, more dramatic manner, the water being sucked up in immense, spiralling arcs that appeared to be pouring backwards into the star-windows — like waterfalls flowing miraculously in reverse. And, as they did so, the remaining water in the lake was sinking, the muddy banks climbing higher as the water sank, thus exposing the circular rim of the giant crater, which the lagoon had been formerly.

It was an extraordinary sight, terrifying and awe-inspiring, and Frances glanced at Michael, wondering how he was reacting, saw that he was sane and in control (if slightly stunned), then returned her own gaze to the front and was again mesmerised.

Where the earth had melted away, the different masses were taking shape, becoming sandy dunes, bleached rocks and jagged cliffs, each viewed like a piece of a jigsaw in the star-filled, drifting windows. And now the stars were fading, receding back into time and space, and the separate pieces of the new landscape, framed within the great rectangles, materialised in ochres and browns, under a new, stronger sun.

So the landscape was changing beyond the sinking

400

lake, while the lake itself, in a spectacle to stun the senses, was sucked up into waterfalls which roared, flowed in reverse, arched back into the hovering rectangles, then disappeared into thin air. The water in the lake kept sinking, turning the banks into high hills, the wet mud littered with tangled weeds, alluvial stones, gasping fish and polished bones, over which, with the rising of a hot wind, a fine dust was swirling.

Frances and Michael just stood there, too stunned to say anything, the small hand of the former held tightly by the latter, the ground continuing to vibrate through them as the surrounding world changed.

The waterfalls poured backwards, vanishing into the landscaped windows, while the water in the lake kept sinking and shrinking in width, causing the crater to grow dramatically and gradually turn into a barren valley. A fierce heat had filled the air and a hot wind was blowing; and as the last of the water was sucked up, disappearing magically into the hovering windows, the muddy slopes of the valley, already drying, were being covered in fine dust.

That settling dust soon covered everything in the valley, including weeds and plants, alluvial stones and dead fish, and the polished bones of creatures, human and otherwise, who had once walked the earth.

The transformation took many hours, mentally and physically draining Frances; but eventually she found herself, in what she assumed must be the late afternoon, sitting near the edge of the enormous, circular dust-bowl — a barren valley, in fact — leaning shoulder-to-shoulder with Michael, staring out, exactly as he was doing, over that vast, chilling emptiness.

The rectangular windows still filled the sky and went as far as the horizon, and there, where the marshes had been, was a completely new landscape of parched rocks, jagged cliffs and, in one instance, a soaring, volcanic peak which, illuminated in a fierce sun, had the colour of burnished gold.

The windows, or gateways, had served their purpose and were fading away, their black edges becoming vaporous, then turning into reams of smoke which, sucked back in upon themselves, shrank rapidly and vanished.

Frances glanced to either side. The same thing had happened around her. The gateways, or windows, had fallen over the verdant land, swallowing the orange and lemon trees, the fig-palms and bulrushes, and gradually turning the Garden of Eden into parched rocks and dry dust, the latter blown constantly by a gentle, though very hot breeze.

Here, too, the great rectangles were gradually fading away until, even as Frances was studying them, they all disappeared, leaving only a sultry sky.

The infrasound faded out and the earth stopped its shaking. Then there was another sound — a jagged, high-pitched squawking — and they both looked up and saw a pteranodon flying above them, its large beak pointing down in their direction, its wings of skin beating awkwardly.

The bizarre creature passed overhead, then they lowered their eyes again.

The dust-bowl was immense, stretching away to the horizon, a great wilderness valley filled with dried plants and bleached stones, and now, to their surprise, containing a few animals, most of which were obviously prehistoric and, mercifully, a considerable distance away.

Frances accepted it, feeling at one with it, realising in some dim manner that she had obviously changed herself, but not really examining that fact closely, putting it out of her mind. She felt heavy, lethargic, devoid of memory and imagination, and let her hand slip from Michael's grasp as she wearily climbed to her feet.

There was a large sun in the sky, a bright, golden orb,

but it was starting to sink behind the distant mountains, its light turning to striations of deep crimson and yellow fire, which were spreading along the horizon like lava poured from a tilting bowl. The cliffs and mountains were changing colour, blackening into silhouette, and the shadow of the soaring volcanic peak stretched across the sloping floor of the cratered dust-bowl like a giant's crooking finger.

'Nightfall,' Michael said. 'Coming fast. Soon darkness will be.'

He pointed across the clearing, his finger jabbing at a group of rocks. Frances dimly remembered the tent — her brain registered a flapping cloth — but now, when she stared across the clearing, she saw the cave she called home. Michael's finger jabbed the air, then he walked towards the cave. Frances glanced around and saw the sinking sun and the forward crawl of the darkness. Shivering, wondering what the night might bring, she hurried after her man.

'Fire,' he said. 'Keep the darkness back ... And no cold to bite us.'

She gathered up the sticks and arranged them into a pile; he made the rubbed stones spit many lights and turn the wood into flame. Then he went into the cave, banging something, saying bad words, emerged with a bloody longtailed creature hanging lifeless from one hand. The other hand held a flat stone honed down to a sharp edge, and he sat by the fire and used the stone to strip the flesh from the animal. He tore the insides out and threw some of them away; the rest he divided between them, and they both ate with relish. The food was bloody, but it filled up their hunger and left quiet contentment.

'Dark,' he said. 'Demon-night.'

An animal snarled from behind the rocks. There was the padding of swift feet. The animal snarled again, something thumped softly against a rock, another animal squealed, then there was silence and a small, settling cloud of dust.

Daybright dying fast. Night creeping over the plain. The demon-darkness edged towards the cave, but was stopped by the fire. He reached out and pulled her to him. She fell against him, feeling better. The dancing flames were dying like the day and letting the cold take its first bites.

'Inside,' he said. 'Warm-safe.'

Dark but warm-safe in the cave where they huddled together. She looked out through the rock-hole, watching as darkness lapped at the flames before covering them up.

Demon-darkness and silence ... Which brought other sounds to life: distant growlings and howlings, an occasional squawk from overhead, the sudden rush of padded feet, beating tails, snapping twigs, whispering windtalk.

She shivered, cold and fearful, knowing not what she was feeling, pressed herself to his warmth and closed her eyes when they felt very heavy.

Frances found herself in dreaming, her thoughts floating away from the past, returning her to the Self with a mind that roamed between past and future. She felt Michael's arms around her and took comfort from his presence, perhaps awakening for a very brief moment before falling asleep again.

In that sleep she returned home, saw her mother dead on the carpet, wept and then went farther back to find her mother alive. She was sitting in the darkness, holding hands with other old ladies; then all of them placed their hands on the table and it started to rock, tapping its legs on the floor. One tap for 'yes', two taps for 'no'. It was a simple, primitive language between the dead and the living, between one world and another; possibly between the past, to which the dead had returned, and the present, from which the living had departed.

Frances watched the rocking table, heard it tapping

against the floor. It stopped moving and the silence rushed in ... then her mother was talking.

'I kill him,' her mother said, her voice ghostly but very masculine. 'Silent, I make him. And still. And then God can return ...' The voice was harsh and guttural, the words as hesitant as an imbecile's, and Frances saw her mother slumping back, her face turned towards the ceiling. 'Me weak,' her mother said. 'He strong. Me need strength in hand ...'

The old ladies joined hands again, two linking up with her mother. Frances watched her mother choking in the darkness, then getting her voice back. It was not her mother's voice: it was a man's voice, sounding sluggish and primitive.

'Kill,' her mother said. 'Need stronger hand. Disappear him forever ...' The voice trailed off into silence, or the hush of heavy breathing, then eventually emanated again from its dim, distant past. 'You, me,' the voice gasped. 'Soon to be. When his silence is always. Kill him with stronger hand ...'

The voice faded away again, as did the image of her unconscious mother; then Frances travelled back, farther back, to emerge in another time. She saw Laurence rising up, his body fine-haired and muscular, his hand holding a thick branch over his head and swinging it down upon Schul.

She witnessed Schul's dying moment.

In that instant she saw herself, linking past, present and future, forming a bridge with her flesh between what had been, what was, and was yet to be. She had lived then, as now, as she would in the future, and she saw it and returned to her beginnings in the dark of her primitive cave.

'Fear is me! I am fear!'

The words dropped from her shivering lips, reverberating in the darkness, perhaps not even spoken but *felt* and then actualised. She rubbed her eyes, still drugged by sleep, felt her mate, looked out the rock-hole, saw a circle of stars, a hint of moonlight, distant rocks silhouetted.

'The fear comes from the demon-night.'

She spoke the language of her man, which made him waken, growling something. She grabbed his hand and placed it on the ground to let him hear the earth grumbling.

'Coming back. *Come for me!*'

Then he felt it and yelped, jerking his hand off the ground. He held the hand up and studied it closely, turning it to and fro, opening and closing his fingers, glancing at the floor of the cave, and finally, spreading his fingers in the air, pressing his hand down again.

She did the same, trying to help; at least wanting to give him comfort. Like him, she felt the bowels of the earth in the convulsion of rage. The ground shook and made much noise, giving life to clouds of dust, then the noise, which they had thought came from the earth, seemed to come from outside the cave.

'We be good and obey them!'

Had he spoken with his tongue or put himself inside her head? She only knew that she understood what he wished to convey, and that whatever it was she would listen and do as he told her.

'Me good, too! *Me obey!*'

They clung to one another, sharing fear and warmth at once, both looking out through the rock-hole at the demon-night stirring. They saw stars, a hint of moonlight, distant rocks silhouetted. Then another light, stronger than the moonlight, made the rocks stand out from the darkness, illuminating their rounded, sun-scorched edges and lengthening their shadows.

Even as that light grew brighter and widened, there was a noise in the sky, first faint, then growing louder, and soon it was a terrible, deep roaring — the breath of a giant that whipped up the dust, and then, not satisfied with this show of anger, reverberated awfully through the cave and made their ears ring.

'Mercy, Masters!'

'We worship you!'

Their voices rang out as one, rising above the earth's bedlam, then they fell on hands and knees and bowed low to rub their noses in dirt.

'Edinu!'

'Plain!'

One word meant the other and both filled their thoughts as they felt the earth shaking beneath them and worshipped the gods of the great plain. The great plain was the dust-bowl, the vast, desolate crater — *Edinu*, the world's navel, winding down to the netherworld — *Edinu: Plain* — the land of Eden, where it all started and ended.

They bowed low, eating dust, feeling the ground vibrating through them, hearing the terrible roaring, the gods' breath, reverberating around them.

Suddenly, there was silence. They looked up and saw bright light. It was neither the moonlight nor the stars nor the campfire, but a fierce and very alien light which pulsated and blinded them. They both groaned and lowered their heads, stifled their groans, *felt* the silence; eventually heard other sounds, short and sharp, penetrating, then a much softer, oddly soothing sibilance that merged into . . . singing.

Singing? What is *singing*? Who shared this word with them? They only knew of noise that rose and fell to make other sound-patterns. It was speaking, yet not so. It was not one: it was many. It was vibration, feeling, a *sensation* that gave life to the silence.

It was something outside the cave.

They raised their faces from the dirt, stared through the rock-hole, saw the distant rocks — now appearing to be much closer — illuminated in brilliant light.

Not the moon. Nor the stars. Not the campfire that had died. What they saw was a dazzling, unknown light, which appeared to be filled with smaller lights that were drifting and bobbing. And those lights, long and thin, like cutting-stones turned on edge, were bobbing up and down, almost dancing, to what they now felt was *singing*.

Singing-talk. *Talk that sings!*

Feeling soothed, they stood upright, holding hands, fingers touching, then shuffled towards the rock-hole that soon became the mouth of their cave. They stopped just before it, weighing fear against curiosity, wishing to go outside and pay homage, but fearful of doing so.

Too late to decide. A blinding light exploded over them. They squealed, staggered back into the cave and covered their eyes with their fingers. The dazzling light multiplied, quickly becoming more than one, then the many lights moved into the cave, illuminating the darkness.

Thin lines of light converging. Moving up and down. Beaming sideways and then along the floor to form a dazzling web.

At that moment they both screamed, two voices as one, rising above the bedlam of the cave with its stabbing noises and singing.

They stopped screaming soon enough, then both looked up in terror. There were silhouetted figures shoulder-to-shoulder before them, all very tall and thin, but not unlike themselves, all with lights beaming from their bellies or upraised hands, all communicating with singing-talk . . . or with talk that sang alien words.

She dived into her terror then, plunging down to hide herself, refusing to raise her head or return to thought until the gods had departed. Then she heard it — dying singing, fading words, inrushing silence — and the light outside changed, the smaller lights winking out, and then the humming began, became a roaring that did not hurt, and the greater light grew weak and shrank as it rose on high, until the rocks shifted back into silhouette and let the stars shine in glory, radiating through silence.

Exhausted by fear, they both slept, possibly sharing the same dream.

CHAPTER THIRTY-ONE

Awakening the next morning, Frances felt almost normal, though her eyes were smarting and out-of-focus, her head light and disordered. Nonetheless, she knew who she was and what had happened the day before, and so, as she glanced around her, letting her gaze linger on Michael, she was able to give him a smile of recognition and love.

He was kneeling on the ground, one knee raised, one on the earth, and she noticed that he had torn his pants off above the thighs, so that now, wearing those rough shorts and nothing else at all, with his chin in need of a shave and beads of sweat on his skin, he did indeed look like he might actually belong in this primitive cave.

It amused her, but only briefly, for then the strangeness crept back over her, making her sit upright and look down at her own dirt-smeared nakedness. She felt embarrassed to see herself, so swallowed dryly and shuddered, then observed that someone, obviously Michael, had placed her begrimed clothing on the earth where her head had been resting.

'I brought them in earlier this morning,' Michael said, his voice reverberating ethereally around the cave. 'I thought you might want them.'

'I do,' Frances replied. 'Thanks.'

She dressed herself without hesitation, though felt

slightly ridiculous, then managed to meet Michael's gaze, which seemed no more than curious.

'Are you all right?' she asked him.

'Yes,' he said, 'I suppose so. I'm back to normal, if that's what you mean, but I feel a bit unreal.'

'You remember what happened yesterday?'

'Yes.'

'We were different people then.'

'I keep thinking I was dreaming,' Michael said, 'but obviously I wasn't.'

'You've been out there. What's out there now?'

'Just that dust-bowl,' he said.

Frances felt the child inside her, but her stomach was flat. She had been here only three earth-months before, but knew the child would come soon, since, in the matter of its gestation, time was irrelevant. She should have felt frightened, but instead was uplifted, raised on high by the radiant unreality of her wondrous experience.

'Were we visited last night?' Michael asked her. 'Or did I simply imagine it?'

'They came in here,' Frances replied, as if talking about old friends. 'We saw the lights of their descent, heard them talking — if that's what it is — then they entered the cave, carrying some kind of torch-lights. They examined us, but then, when we panicked, very quickly departed.'

'If you knew it was them,' Michael asked her, 'why did *you* panic?'

'Because I wasn't myself. At least I wasn't the person I am now. I was my original self, that primitive creature, and thought they were gods.'

'Maybe they are,' Michael said. 'Either gods ... or God's children.'

Frances glanced at him, wondering if he was mocking her, but he was staring thoughtfully out of the cave, his face weary and grave.

'Yes,' she said, after a considerable hesitation. 'Gods

— or simply God's children. Like you and me . . . and my child.'

Michael's expression was still sombre, but he sighed and stood up, reaching out with one hand to pull her to him and warmly embrace her.

'If I seem strange,' he said, 'it's just the weather. Put it down to the weather.'

Frances chuckled at that, then sank her teeth into his shoulder, wanting to draw blood, to suck him into her and make him a part of her.

'Come on,' he said. 'Let's go outside and face the new day.'

Holding hands like two children, they stepped out of the cave — to be instantly dazzled by the light and burned by fierce heat. They shielded their eyes, letting them adjust to the uncommon brightness, then looked around the clearing, at the parched plants, scorched rocks and slowly drifting dust, then across the immense, cratered plain at the irregular sand dunes and cliffs.

The volcanic peak was still there, soaring high and wavering in heat-waves, its long shadow like the black, crooking finger of a giant, stretching down the sloping side of the crater. There were prehistoric animals where the base of the crater levelled out and formed, to all intents and purposes, a vast wilderness valley. The animals, far away, were distorted in the heat-waves that shimmered up from the barren, sun-scorched earth.

The heat was ferocious, clamping around them like a fist, making them both sweat profusely and feel drained of strength. Frances hurried towards some rocks, dragging Michael by the hand, the soles of her feet burning until she reached a shadowed area, where she gratefully breathed cooler air. She rubbed her stinging eyes, glancing around her, having to squint, saw nothing but streams of fine dust winding across empty wilderness. Occasionally an animal growled in the distance, or a strange bird squawked in flight, but

411

otherwise time seemed to be standing still in a great bowl of silence.

'So,' Michael said. 'Here we are. *Now* what do we do?'

'There's nothing we *can* do,' Frances replied, 'except sit here and wait.'

'And what if they don't come back, Frances? What if they never come?'

'Then we'll die,' Frances said.

She hardly knew what she meant, but sensed his intensity, so squeezed his hand and made him sit beside her. They sat on a low, smooth stone, sheltering under the taller rocks, and from that vantage point were able to look out of the shadows, at the panorama of burning desolation that stretched away on all sides. The prehistoric animals still roamed aimlessly in the valley, the volcanic peak beyond wavered in the shimmering heat-waves, and, above all, the sky was a silvery-white sheet, in which the only visible object was a huge sun that blazed gold and orange.

Frances let her eyes roam from that glorious sun to her own feet which, having been bare for so long, were filthy and torn. Then, with a sigh, she straightened up and looked sideways at Michael.

'I'm going to have this child,' she said. 'I know it. I feel it.'

Michael stared sombrely at her, then gazed all around him. Seeing nothing, he coughed into his fist and said, 'Maybe. Who knows?'

'You don't believe it?' Frances asked.

'What I believe is irrelevant. I only know that since meeting you, the impossible has become commonplace; and that right now, as I sit on this very rock, I can't believe that I'm here. And where, for that matter, is *here*? We're both living a miracle.'

'Are you frightened?'

'No. Strangely enough, I'm not. I feel disorientated, a bit removed from myself, and I also feel tremendous anticipation and constant excitement ... And you? What do *you* feel?'

'The same,' Frances replied, without hesitation. 'Like you, I feel disorientated, or at least a bit strange, but otherwise very emotional. I'm moved by a deep sense of joy and gratification, as if I'm in a cathedral and the organ is playing.'

'You were frightened last night.'

'That was the *other* me. The dawn-child: that primitive creature. I'm not her today.'

'Perhaps you will be, before the day is out.'

'I've no doubts about that.'

And indeed, even as she finished talking, there was a distant rumbling sound, a fierce subterranean explosion, and the volcanic peak shook visibly, then spewed molten lava. The lava poured down the mountain in streams of gold and crimson, which soon broke apart and spread over the slopes like burning fingers. And observing that spectacle, the earth shaking beneath her feet, Frances was able to accept that this was indeed a long-lost dawning: that time and space had been rearranged to take her back, not only to her own origins, but to the beginning of the whole human race.

The earth grumbled again, its bowels erupting in flame and smoke. The streams of lava soon formed a glittering necklace around the mountain-peak, and Frances understood, as she lowered her eyes, that she, also, was changing again.

'I love you,' she said to Michael. 'I want you to understand that. Before the day's over, we might be separated — either physically or spiritually — and whatever happens, no matter what becomes of us, I want you to know that I love you. I've never felt this way before — I've wanted to, but never have — yet I now know that what I feel for you is more than just sex. I wasted my life searching for the father I could never have, but when I found you , I also found release from the vanity of that pursuit. Now I don't need other men — nor the self-abasement learned in Italy. I only need your commitment and my own faith to help me face what is coming. So, I love you. *Remember* that.'

Michael gave his reply without saying a word. He simply nodded and reached out to seal her lips with his fingers, held them there for some time, then removed them and smiled gently at her.

'We're all right,' he said finally, lowering his hand and patting her knee. 'You and I, we'll survive. Meant to be, we *will* be. It hasn't ended for either of us yet — and I don't think it will. Relax, Frances Devereux, I'm still here . . . and the day is still young.'

His last words were almost drowned out by the fresh rumbling of the volcano. Frances looked across the sunken plain, beyond the animals in shimmering heatwaves, saw more lava spewing out of the mountain-peak to add its gold to the crimson flow.

'I feel strange,' she heard Michael murmuring. 'I feel very tired . . .'

She wanted to smile and offer words of encouragement, but was distracted by movement and sound where there should not have been any.

Turning her head, she saw a strange group near the cave, gathered around a smouldering camp-fire in front of the rock-face. At first she thought they were normal people, but then realised they were not. They were hairy, ape-like creatures, very small, their shoulders stooped, though those not squatting were standing on two legs, even if awkwardly.

Frances glanced at Michael. She recognised him, but he seemed different. He kept fading in and out, like an optical illusion, and each time he came back into focus seemed that little bit different. He caught her glance and returned it, brow furrowing in confusion, then scratched the back of one ear and turned away from her, leaning forward as if he could not hold his back straight, his head lolling weakly.

Frances studied the cave-men, wondering where they had come from. They were chattering amongst themselves, using a guttural, alien language, and a few of them were poking at the smouldering fire with branches stripped of their leaves. They did not appear to notice her; nor did they seem too real. Like Michael, they were magically fading in and out, as if merely images being projected by a faulty machine.

Then she heard beating wings. Her dazed eyes turned towards the sky. A prehistoric pteranodon flew overhead, its large beak pointing down in her direction, its wings of skin beating awkwardly.

Filled with fear, she cried out. She sensed that someone was coming towards her. She clung to the hope that that someone would disappear with the rest of it.

At that moment, Michael grunted, grabbed her shoulder and led her towards the squatting cave-men. As he dragged her through the dust, she felt more natural, but kept looking around her. There was no-one coming towards her, but strange clouds were gathering, boiling impossibly out of a clear sky and growing bigger each second.

Her man dragged her to the campfire where they crouched low with the others, all of whom were staring at the sky where the clouds were still gathering. The golden sun darkened, a curtain of clouds falling across it, then long shadows crept into the crater and moved across the flat plain. The sky growled and barked, but surprisingly did not weep; then, though the heat was still fierce, a rising wind whipped the dust up.

'Angry wind come,' Michael said.

'Sky no cry,' Frances added.

Michael? *Frances?* What words were these she heard? She scratched herself in rising agitation and glanced nervously around her. The ground was littered with bones and the debris of dead fires, but otherwise there

415

was nothing to be seen that she had not seen before. She felt a little better, less fearful of the unknown; but the sky roared again, like an animal in a trap, and she then saw a mass of black clouds where pure light had just been.

'Sky wearing cover.'

'Warmed by clouds.'

'Making cold where we are.'

She felt a slight chill when the wind blew across her, letting the dust settle on her arms and legs, making whispering noises. She glanced up and saw that he was staring possessively at her, turned away and saw the other one, Schul, reaching out to take hold of her.

Schul? What sound was this? Was it the sound that made him known? She scratched herself again, feeling very confused; and then, looking across the great plain of the gods, saw that the shadows were creeping forward to swallow the animals.

'Dark cold is nearing.'

'Wind talks louder.'

'Sky no the same.'

They huddled closer together, all looking up at the sky. There was an immense circle of dark clouds right over the circular plain, blotting out the light from the plain and making it look bleak and frightening. She felt the fear in herself and it made her lower her eyes. Schul and Laurence were squatting side by side, still studying the brooding sky.

Schul? Laurence? What sounds were these? She felt confused because her thoughts contained these sounds that she had not heard before. *Schul. Laurence* ... She thought of the sounds and studied the man-apes. They both often looked at her with hunger in their eyes, but now were staring at the sky, which was not as it had been.

'Sky breaking!'

'And makes noise!'

The mass of dark cloud was broken up by the many

lights exploding through it, the lights beaming out obliquely to form great ant-hill shapes, which brightly illuminated the desert floor of the plain of the gods. Those lights startled the animals and made them flee in all directions, their hooves kicking up more clouds of dust and making the air dense.

She could hear the animals crying and shared the terror that caused it, then the other sound, coming down from the sky, seemed to vibrate right through her.

Shaking, she looked up, saw the lights shredding the clouds, growing bigger and melting the darkness around them as they started descending.

The clouds had been broken up and now were over the cave-camp, widening as they silently dropped around her to form a dense mist. Those clouds also held light, trying to break through and beam down; it brightened and dimmed, over and over again, as if to the rhythm of the beating inside her heaving breast.

She shook, gibbered and pointed as the clouds pressed down upon her, as the light, finally starting to beam through, gradually forced the clouds apart until they were swirling all around her, darkening the landscape.

The lights dimmed and brightened and repeated that rapidly, as if they were reflecting what was beating inside her breast. They were beating to a distant music, a sound fading in and out, and it gave them a life of their own, a spirit glowing and visible.

Were they lights? Or were they great birds? She could not tell for certain. They were shaped like flat stones (like the ones used to scrape the meat off bone and crack enemy skulls) but they glowed with a magical incandescence that seemed to pulsate to her heartbeat. They hovered there above the mountains, and above the great plain, and they drifted above the rocks all around the cave-camp, their magic light pulsating and fading in and out as their combined noise, which sounded like breathless growling, made the ground shake.

The floating things were dark shapes within dazzling silver-white mist; they growled in an unbroken manner and made the earth shake, bobbed up and down like the dust when the wind did but whisper. The floating things, those flattened balls of glowing fire, cast their shadows beneath them.

Fear congealed her every instinct. She shook, gibbered and pointed. All her brothers and sisters, including her two man-apes, were behaving in a similar manner as they looked up in terror.

The floating fireballs dropped lower, their shadows widening to touch the man-apes, then the wind, which had been increasing in strength, turned into a storm.

She sobbed fearfully and covered her eyes, fingers outspread to give her sight, saw the others doing the same while they yelped and snorted in terror. The wind hissed and swept around them, made them blind and almost deaf, while the fire-balls, still floating above them, beamed their light through the murk.

'Oh, powerful ones!'

'Mercy!'

They all retreated towards the rock-hole, shuffling backwards through the storm, peering up through outspread fingers, through swirling dust and blinding light, to see some of the things that looked like fireballs dropping down even lower. They squealed in terror and attacked each other, taking defence in a frenzy of violence, but soon the cooler darkness of the cave started falling about them.

'Fear is me! I am fear!'

'The gods outside!'

'I *kill* fear! I *want* . . .'

The last one to speak stared at her, his eyes as bright as the things outside, and she felt the fear breaking her in two and confusing her thoughts.

He was staring at her. That one! The one she thought of as *Schul*. Yet why did she think of that word and what did it mean? *Schul*: a hissing sound. Like a serpent creating dust. She sensed it was a sound from some other time or place, but failed, no matter how hard she tried, to attach it to anything.

For that matter, who was *she*? Where *was* she at this moment? What was beating so hard inside her that she felt she would burst?

It was him, the possessive one. He lived in memory and imagination. She saw him, identified as *Schul*, staring at her with burning eyes.

A cloud of dust swirled through the cave, making everyone cough and shout. Their terror aroused other fierce feelings and made them hide behind violence. His nostrils flared as he grabbed her, pulled her to him, pushed her down. She yelped and the other one, the better one who also wanted her, leaped with a hoarse yelp to her rescue. There was growling and pounding, a grunt, flesh on bone; she glanced up and saw Schul's clenched fist, still blurred in swift motion, as it finished its vicious, downward arc.

The other one was still falling, sliding blood-smeared down the rock-wall; he rolled over as a stone held by Schul crashed onto his head. He grunted again, then seemed to sigh and sleep, his body collapsing in a heap as Schul grabbed her again.

He threw her forward on hands and knees, held her slightly, pulled her into him; she squealed when she felt him inside her, pounding against her.

It was over very quickly. She knew it when she heard him howling. He pulled out of her and let her roll away while he waved his large fists, displaying triumph and pleasure.

That, too, was over quickly. The wind howled and filled the cave. She squealed in fear with all the others as the dust swirled about her and the other noise, the vibrating bass-song of the gods, rushed into the rock-hole.

She crawled across to the one in deep-sleep, fighting against the swirling dust, reached him, heard his

419

muffled groaning, then curled up beside him.

The vibrating bass-song ceased and the swirling dust settled down. She put her knuckles in her mouth to stop her cries and watched the others do likewise. In silence, they were silent, ears curling, eyes widening, then started squealing and leaping about when the dazzling lights filled the cave.

'Help-mercy!'

'Me nothing!'

'Me the god's! Me belong to them! Me worship them!'

The lines of light were long and sharp, cutting the darkness, criss-crossing, illuminating wide eyes, pleading lips and hands turned up for mercy. She watched, shaking violently, fear congealing her every instinct, trying to hide behind the body of the one who was blood-smeared and moaning.

Light and darkness, noise and movement. Motes of swirling dust glinting. The thin lights beamed back and forth, up and down, in constant motion, stretching from the middle of the rock-hole as if out of the air itself.

Then a greater light filled the rock-hole, as if the sky had exploded, and it silhouetted the creatures who seemed to be holding lights near their bellies.

Like the others, she howled and covered her eyes with her hands, too frightened to look at the unrecognisable, only aware that the beating within her breast was making her body shake. She heard other noise, a lesser sound, a wordless communication, a rising and falling of tones which were impossibly alien.

It was talk. A *singing*-talk. It was music. But what *was* music? Her thoughts splintered and flew apart, then raced back and forth, and she saw steaming marshlands, the grey glint of water, green grass and flowers of all colours, an arch of fig-palms. She saw herself, very different; and Laurence and Schul, also different; then raced on until she found her mother in a cluttered room in the family home. She was perched on a stool, a cigarette smouldering beside her. Her fingers were dancing lightly along ebony and ivory; and miraculously, out of the large box above her, came the talk that was singing.

Her mother said it was *music*.

Mother? What was *mother*? She lurched between the past and future, sometimes alighting like a bird on the present before taking off again. Her splintered thoughts regrouped themselves, returning order to chaos, shrinking back into their original, narrow focus on what was happening around her.

She heard the wordless communication, the ricocheting speech singing, and looked up, over the body of the one who was just awakening, to see the silhouettes advancing into the cave, the lights beaming from what now appeared to be their upraised hands and, in their silvery motion, illuminating the fear and awe of those crouched in the dirt, all of whom were gnashing teeth and gibbering dementedly, as the lights, forming a bright web in the darkness, finally dazzled her own eyes.

'Me hurting! *Him* hurt me!'

Her squeal of fear drowned his words as she crouched farther back, looking up over his body at the creature looming above to turn his searching light upon her. She grabbed a stone and threw it wildly, saw the light swinging away, heard the singing-talk ricocheting from wall to wall in that confined, light-slashed darkness.

The tall black figures moved away, retreating towards the rock-hole, their lights waving back and forth, forming brilliant webs in the darkness, then suddenly winking off to leave only the greater light outside the rock-hole. The tall figures stood in that light, rendered black and featureless by it. There was a sudden rush and surge of their singing-talk, then they suddenly disappeared.

The blood-smeared one sat up and stared at her, confused. Still confused, he looked at the others where they huddled together. In silence, they were silent, ears curling, eyes widening, then started squealing and leaping about when a monster roared outside.

At that moment the light in the rock-hole blinked out, plunging the cave back into darkness. The roaring outside grew louder, like a monster enraged, then a fierce wind rushed into the cave and filled it with howling dust. The noise outside increased, but then faded quickly; it abruptly stopped altogether and the howling dust settled, then thin strands of grey, natural afternoon light beamed obliquely into the cave's darkness to give warmth to her face.

She looked at the blood-smeared one and wondered what had happened to him, then saw that the other one, the possessive one, was getting his courage back. The others were not so brave, and in fact seemed almost crushed; they moved back and forth in the gloom, avoiding the rock-hole. They kept staring at the rock-hole, then at one another, but their feet, nervously kicking up clouds of dust, remained deep in the cave.

'Me no fear. Me *kill* fear.'

It was the possessive one who had spoken, staring around him with hard eyes, his nostrils flaring to sniff out any challenge, large fists opening and closing.

'Me no fear. Outside go me. Me kill fear and *take* all.'

He stared at each of them in turn, his eyes hard, nostrils flaring, and receiving no hint of an argument took possession of everyone. His eyes focused upon her, tongue licking his lips in hunger, then he clenched his fists, raised them above his head and walked out of the cave.

With beating heart she watched him go. She held her breath and listened intently. For all the days of her life multiplied there was no sound at all.

She looked at the blood-smeared one, sensing his hope without recognising it, but when he took a step towards her, she turned away and studied the others. They were staring at the rock-hole, trying to see what was happening outside. There was nothing to see but the grey light; no sound but a whispering wind.

Then the one outside howled. He was commanding them to come out. They all glanced at one another, not understanding what shame was, then nervously kicked up the dust and shuffled slowly outside.

She left the rock-hole last, fighting fear with every step. Outside, the light temporarily blinded her, but soon sank back to greyness. The possessive one was staring at her, eyes gleaming with triumph, tongue licking his lips to show the hunger which was now his entitlement.

She avoided his stare but glanced around her, seeing nothing but desolation. The grazing animals had returned to the great plain of the gods, and the mountains beyond had lost their colour and were dull in the grey light.

She looked at the sky. Most of the others were doing the same. A few birds with large beaks and wings of skin were flying sluggishly through thin clouds. Otherwise, as it was on the desolate earth, there was nothing to see.

She stood there, trying to define her experience, but was too stunned to do so.

She was silent . . . in silence.

CHAPTER THIRTY-TWO

'I all. *Am* all. *Take* all.'

The aggressive one raised the challenge and again received no response, so he opened and shut his large fists, then slapped one demonstratively against his open palm. The smack was hard and loud, resounding brutally in the silence, making some of the others twitch nervously and hang low their heads.

She moved away, trying to avoid him. The sound 'Schul' rang in her head. She had not thought of the sound before this day, but now it seemed to belong to him. He stared at her, watching her movement, nostrils flaring to catch her scent, then licked his lips, took a deep breath and stared down the others.

All except one — the *good* one, who also wanted her. She heard the sound 'Laurence' in her head, but didn't know what it meant. The good one was growing angry, touching the blood still on his head; he gave a hoarse growl and stared at the other, then kicked up the dust. He glanced sideways at her, his gaze forlorn, but made no move towards her.

'I all. All you *mine*.'

The other was glaring at everyone, letting them know his entitlement. He had been the first one out of the cave and that made him their leader, the one who could take what he wanted and do as he pleased. Now he concentrated on her, licking his lips, nostrils flaring, and she stepped back, feeling a dull, instinctive fear, remembering pain and not wanting it.

With the gods no longer present, the aggressive one was master of his domain. Now he fondled himself, exciting himself as he stared at her, then took a deep breath and raised his clenched fists to display his great strength.

She stared fearfully at him, then beyond him to the wilderness; the sun was breaking through the clouds, pouring golden light on the mountains, making the boiling lava on the volcanic peak glitter brightly, forming phosphorescent streams of many colours.

'I want! I *take*!'

The aggressive one came towards her, nostrils flaring, eyes alight, swinging his fist at those in his way, then reaching out for her. She felt the vice of his fingers, a pain darting along her arm, as he threw her face-down on the earth and moved in behind her.

She turned her head, spitting dust, looking sideways and up, saw the other one, the good one, exploding into violent action. He hurled himself at the bad one — whose sound she knew was 'Schul' — and swept him to the side with his weight as she rolled away from them.

She jumped up to rejoin the others, dodged their waving hands, heard their chattering, then looked down at the two males as they howled and fought each other on the ground, making dust billow densely.

They rolled over the loose stones, arms and legs about each other, fists rising and falling ferociously in that spiralling dust. They grunted and yelped, sometimes howled in rage or pain, then suddenly were back on their feet, both smeared with blood.

The good one shook his head, looking weak and confused, while the bad one took a deep breath and hurled himself forward. His left fist was a blur, sweeping down through streaming dust, then it hit the other's head like a stone and made his body jerk sideways. The good one fell back, hitting the earth with a dull thud, then the bad one leaned over and took hold of his head, hammered it more than once against the ground, then stood up again.

Lying on the ground, the good one quivered and groaned, so the other one, the one whose sound was 'Schul', turned towards her again. Erect, he came at her, breath hissing in his throat, and was grabbing her when the one on the ground suddenly jumped up behind him.

'*No!*' he cried. '*No touch!*'

At that moment the earth shook and a bass humming filled the air — and Frances, abruptly shocked and frightened, went winging out of herself. Her thoughts splintered and flew apart, then raced back and forth, and she saw steaming marshlands, the grey glint of water, green grass and flowers of all colours, an arch of fig-palms. She then returned to the wilderness, drawn back by howls and screaming — and suddenly realised who she was; and that what was happening here had all happened before ... between Schul and Laurence in Eden, in that time that was yet to be.

Now, as the snarling Schul turned away from Frances, she saw Laurence take hold of the thick, gnarled branch that had been lying on the ground beside him and, with his body arched, silhouetted by the dust-bowl's light, raise the weapon high above his head. Schul was already halfway through the air, his greedy hands outstretched, when Laurence, with a quavering, high-pitched, almost feminine wailing, brought the branch down on his skull, making Schul careen sideways and roll over on the earth with blood already splashing from his first wound.

It was the first but not the last, since as Schul attempted to rise again, Laurence repeatedly struck him over the head and face with a fury which, accompanied by his peculiar demented wailing, merely emphasised the extent of his long-buried resentment and anguish.

426

Frances screamed at Laurence to stop, hardly believing what she was seeing, but Laurence kept striking Schul with that fierce, releasing rage, growing more exultant as he did so, not aware of what guilt was. Schul's hands dropped to his sides, revealing a head like a pomegranate, then as Frances managed to pull Laurence away, Schul fell onto his side, tried in vain to get up again, shuddered in a long, drawn-out spasm, fell back and was still.

Along with the others, Frances stared at that fallen body; but as an exhausted Laurence sank to his knees and fell over, lying flat on his back and focusing blindly on the sky, the shaking ground and pervasive bass humming combined to distract her.

Squinting, she looked up, at first puzzled, then terrified, to see a circular, solid blackness growing steadily wider as it broke through the clouds just above and came down upon her.

The descending blackness was bizarre, playing tricks on the eyes, now concave, now convex; now like a flat, solid, featureless object, now like a hole cut in the sky and showing the cosmos beyond. It grew bigger as it descended, spreading out a great distance, then she realised that it was actually sinking into the immense crater, which, as the object roared louder, was being swept by large, swirling dust-clouds.

'Oh, my God!' Michael exclaimed.

They both witnessed the interaction of time and space: the past meeting the future.

Now, where Laurence had been lying, Frances saw *Michael* sitting up, shielding his eyes with one hand and staring directly above him as that blackness descended, grew even wider, then developed a wavering silvery rim. Michael stared at it, transfixed, his body smeared with dirt, then the normal light changed to a dazzling white haze that erased his lined features.

Frances felt her body's weight, the child growing in

427

her stomach, and the energy seemed to be draining out of her as she looked up again. The perfect blackness was still descending, growing enormous as it dropped lower, and she realised that it was going to slot into the wind-swept crater as perfectly as a cork into a bottle.

The navel of the world, she thought. *The world's navel is that great dust-bowl. And that dust-bowl will in time become the deep lake into which, with a dubious finality, Schul's body will sink.*

She kept looking up, unafraid, now simply fascinated, observing the widening blackness as its rim became an immense, flaring circle, dimming the light of the sky above. The earth shook beneath her feet, the bass humming vibrated through her, then she felt her skin beginning to glow with a sublime sensual heat.

'Frances!' Michael called. '*Frances!*'

He was climbing laboriously to his feet, looking absolutely exhausted, and Frances started towards him, glancing around her as she did so, and saw the other people standing there, shaking their heads, clearly dazed. Then, as she froze, trying to recollect who they were, light and sound exploded about her, at once dazzling and deafening, and she looked up to see that the descending mass had become a great flaring globe.

Not a globe, but an immense dome of pulsating light. She found herself stepping backwards, farther away from the crater's edge, while the object in the sky, that mountainous arch of luminous energy, turned the wilderness of that crater into an incandescent, mesmerising haze.

The great cork filled the crater but cast its light on the ground around it, swallowing the distant mountains and volcanic peak, then pouring out around Frances.

She screamed as she was blinded, fell down as Michael cried out, shuddered and saw only the white light that had burned through her skull. She was in the light and *was* the light, and looked into herself, aware of other lights growing out of that spectacle and separating like molecules.

The molecules grew into silvery discs, dark-centred and dome-shaped, and these multiplied until there were hundreds spread out all around her. They hovered silently in mid-air, above and all around her, then spread out across the great crater as far as the mountains.

Draining out of herself, Frances sank to the earth. Kneeling there, she saw Michael, sleeping, curled-up in the pulsating haze. She was blinded but could see, looking through herself to the infinite, and witnessed the future living within the past and arched over the present.

The silvery discs covered the earth, hovering magically in the air, taking energy from the water beneath the soil and rendering it visible. The energy danced electrically, shooting up from the shimmering crater, silvery lines that quivered and swayed, coiled sinuously and crackled, forming phosphorescent bonds between the ground and hovering discs.

Then the discs starting changing, spreading out to touch each other, becoming long, linear lines that formed an immense, glowing web which contained, beneath its countless strands, glittering stars in black space.

Frances looked and was captured, enslaved by time and space. The glittering stars and black depths curved around her while she floated on shimmering light. Then the stars started moving, up and down, to and fro, floating above, below, around and finally through her, pulsating like the discs she had seen previously, then making her melt.

The lights were living energy, the beating heart of the eternal present, and as they circled her, entered her and passed on to somewhere else, they spoke to her of God and His angels and the portals of heaven. And as she looked at them, transported, crossing the heavenly vaults to join them, she saw time and space overlapping around her to give shape to a new world.

That world formed out of the ether as the darkness filled with light, the light melting the stars and letting a golden dawn have dominion. Time shifted back and forth, curved back upon itself, and drew out of itself the other worlds which existed within it. Jewelled domes and gilded spires, glittering bridges and gleaming highways, great cities built in mountains and by rivers that flowed out to the stars. Whether real or imagined, they made the infinite comprehensible, giving Frances something recognisable as an aid to acceptance. The light beneath her turned to sand, then the sand became grass, then trees and bushes sprouted from the grass and in turn produced plants and flowers.

A wind whispered and made the trees shiver, then a white pollen rained down.

Frances looked across the valley, the plain known as *Edinu*, to see, within the towering dome of light, the white molecules dancing. The light reached out to embrace her, surrounding her with its warmth, then the molecules filled up her senses with the speech that was singing.

She watched the molecules, entranced, their music tugging at her heart, their speech, which was singing, releasing her soul to the heavenly hosts. Then the dome of light darkened — or rather, faded away — and then the light returned to normal above the dust-filled crater, though the mountains, which had been there before, could no longer be seen.

Frances thought of her child, but could feel herself no longer; she was adrift on the sea of her own memories and constructing from that. Here, lemon and orange trees in a grove with an arch of fig-palms; there, from the nearest edge of the crater, an immense, dust-filled plain. That plain was the world's navel; it was *Edinu*, the land of Eden. That plain was the gateway through time and space, leading into the netherworld. That world

430

was 'here' and 'now'; it was also 'there' and 'then'. It was a bridge between the past and future — and would become the lagoon.

The great plain was desolate, rendered more drab in normal light, but soon the dancing molecules, the pulsating white lights, had spread out from the garden around Frances to cover the crater. Once there, they grew larger, then turned into glowing discs, and the discs, hovering magically, bobbing gently up and down, suddenly flared up and drew from the barren earth rich fountains of water.

The water bubbled through the soil, pushed the dust up, then the earth, finally geysered into fountains that poured into one another and exploded into more spectacular fountains of silvery spray. The water became a pool, then a lake, then a lagoon, and soon filled the whole crater, reaching the edge of the garden, its surface, lightly rippling and pure, reflecting the discs still above it.

Time moved back and forth, slipping through holes in space, emerging from the funnel of the infinite to create its own future. The calm lagoon rumbled, giving utterance to the earth beneath, then that earth, caught in telescoping centuries, was pushed up in great blisters. Mounds of muddy soil surfaced, making the water boil around them, then grew higher and wider, letting water and mud slide off them, until they had become fecund islets in a vast, steaming marshland.

Frances knew that marshland, having seen it before. She knew it as the world had come to know it when it settled on Glastonbury. Frances watched it being born, saw it settle, then studied its busy sky.

The lights were in their hundreds and pulsated above the marshland, then they moved, changed positions, drifted sideways, up and down, finally settled again but stretched out to one another, joining up to form that same glowing web in which glittering stars formed. The stars flared up and faded, returned and vanished again,

431

moving in and out of space, controlled by time, before being pushed elsewhere. Eventually they disappeared, leaving the great web behind, then this reformed as molecules which, glowing warmly and dancing, spread out over the garden.

Frances stared at the lagoon, trying to drink in its reality, then turned towards the arch of fig-palms and saw Michael sleeping there.

She sighed and was content. She could not feel herself. The glowing molecules came towards her, pulsating with life, surrounded her and bobbed up and down to fill her soul with their singing-speech. She was soothed and reassured, then seduced into acceptance, melting inside her own sensual heat and wanting only to give life.

The molecules danced around her, bobbing gently and glowing, their speech singing in her mind and plucking her heart-strings, raising her spirit on high as she joined with the ether. They merged and flared up, then became a single light, which, though as soft as a fine mist, still pulsated rhythmically.

At first the mist was impenetrable, then dark holes made it patchy. The dark holes grew bigger, as if being torn from fine gauze, and eventually materialised as the human shapes that Frances had seen in the cave.

The ghostly figures were like the cities whose highways reached the stars: they existed to aid her acceptance of what she thought was impossible.

Frances wanted to know who God was, what He was, where He was, but she finally understood, when she gazed at the creatures around her, that she would only find Him within herself, where the mind becomes soul.

Having taught her that, they then willed it, making her one of them.

She sighed and sank back, stretching out on the cushioning grass, listening to the music of the spheres and observing the figures above her. They were human-shaped, but too tall, and they lacked distinct features. Existing as mere molecules, as pulsating energy and thought, they had come from the double-star, from the invisible companion of Sirius, adopting the vague form of human-beings in order to help her.

They were shadows onto which she superimposed what it was she required.

She saw Schul and Miles Ashcombe, then Laurence and her mother, each emerging out of the other where space and time met.

Laurence was standing on a grassy mound with Stonehenge behind him, shading his eyes with his right hand as he stared at the sky. A magical radiance fell upon him. He turned his head to smile at her. She willed him to go and he dissolved — as did the circle of ancient stones — and there, where Stonehenge had been, a great pool of water, a lagoon, miraculously materialised.

Jack Schul was on the bank, staring forlornly across the water. Frances followed his gaze to see Laurence and herself on a wooden raft, pushing someone's body over the side, then watching it sink. When it had disappeared, they both glanced back at the land, but Schul — the real him, or his *doppelganger* — had disappeared, also.

Frances felt no guilt or fear, but was touched by a new compassion; she shed tears for all the sins of the world and man's pained moral growth. Her tears fell like rain on glass, obscuring her view, distorting the real, and when her eyes had dried she saw her mother standing in the bedroom at home. She was holding the curtains open, gazing down on the back lawn, and the radiance that had illuminated Laurence now shone on her loving face.

She just stood there, silent and motionless ... eternally present.

Frances wept again, her tears washing away her mother, then erasing the walls of the house to leave only the back lawn. Miles Ashcombe was there, no longer

433

mad, his face serene; he was walking hopefully to and
fro, the Tor of Glastonbury beyond him, then a pyramid
of shimmering light dissolved him and left only starry
night.

Frances slept in that starry night, a mere infant,
dreaming happily; a door opened and sunlight fell
across her and made her awaken. She cried out and
glanced around her, still attempting to define the world,
then a man with a gentle, caring smile leaned down to
examine her. He was grey-haired, slightly bald, his eyes
brown and abstracted — obviously not a practical man,
though clearly intelligent. He smiled, creating cobwebs
around his eyes, letting his face fill with warmth.

'Frances,' he said. 'You sweet child. Let me play you
some music.'

She heard his singing-talk, then a piano, a violin; and
music being the language of the spheres, she understood every word.

She gurgled with delight, kicked her legs, grabbed his
nose, positively writhing with the pleasure of the
innocent looking up at the face of God. He was her
father, her creator, the only man in the world — a world
divided simply between him and the woman, her
mother.

Frances wept, remembering that. She cried tears,
recognising him. Love and pain coursed through her,
almost managing to divide her, but then merged into
the single emotion that made her whole for the first
time.

Just as those ghostly figures had surrounded her
mother years ago, just as they had looked on during that
singular, bloodless birth, so did they now surround
Frances to observe her child's dawning.

Frances lay on God's green earth, a bridge between
past and future, and watched her father opening his
mouth to blow a thin stream of smoke.

Not smoke: ectoplasm: an emanation of bodily

434

appearance. It took the shape of a foetus, then a baby, then a child, then herself. She saw herself floating above, reflected in Eden's pure air, and she smiled, letting the tears dry on her cheeks, and lay back to give birth.

God's child, she thought. *Give me God's child. For we are all His lost children.*

A sensual heat limned her being, making her spirit writhe with pleasure, and she became a bridge between the sun and moon, to give her breath to the cosmos.

She gasped as her child emerged, breaking through her shivering lips, an ectoplasm that spread like smoke above her and then formed loops and coils. The loops became eyebrows, the coils outlined the eyes; a spiralling strand took the shape of lips and then encouraged a smile.

She gasped again — dying — leaving the old world for the new, passing from one present to another and releasing more of her secret self. It came out of her casually, parting her lips as her spirit glowed, curling into toes and fingers on invisible feet and hands, beneath the blind eyes and smiling mouth of the face not yet fully formed.

She died, entering the new world, not hearing her own final breath, but letting her eyes, which were open, stay that way to see what she had lived for.

Her final breath was her signature, completing her work of art, the ectoplasm spiralling above her face to fill in what was missing. It flowed around the toes and fingers, outlining the hands and feet, then coiled up and curved back in an arc that eventually surrounded the eyes and mouth. The eyes moved and then glowed, radiating an inner life, and that life, which was a pulsating energy, spread down to reach fingers and toes, to fill out chest and belly, to lend shape and definition and character to the child of the future.

Frances briefly lost herself, her heart stopping where

435

time met space, then her heart started beating again and she awakened to glory — soaked in the morning dew, warmed by a new sun, holding her child to her breast in God's mysterious future.

CHAPTER THIRTY-THREE

Michael emerged to dazzling light, to a vast, silvery sky, saw the flying saucers (or what resembled such) hovering in their hundreds above the earth as far back as the eye could see. Fear made him feel weak, but he tried to climb to his feet. He saw Frances at the far side of the clearing and desperately called to her. She stared at him as he fell back, too exhausted to stand upright, and the last thing he remembered before he slept was the hope in her shining face.

He slept and knew the darkness and emerged to a different light, perhaps dreamed that the saucers were hovering nearby, then opened his eyes again.

There was a brilliant sky above him, very blue, smudged with thin clouds, strands of gold and magenta spreading through it from a perfectly normal sun. He blinked uncomfortably, then rubbed his stinging eyes, saw the same scene, so sighed with relief and tentatively sat upright.

There were no flying saucers, but there were steaming marshlands, starting at the very edge of the forest clearing and stretching as far as the eye could see. They were marshlands, not swamps, and possessed a remarkable fecundity. The humidity, a product of plentiful rain and heat, had made everything outsized.

There were lush orange and lemon trees, thick clusters of giant figs, bananas and papayas hanging heavily from very large, bright-green palm leaves. Indeed, the foliage was exceptionally vivid, overwhelming the senses; and slightly stunned, trying to accept it, his gaze roaming over it, Michael took in the clearing and the placid lake beyond it, then followed rippling waves of tall grass to where it was slapping at Frances.

She was sitting up in the grass, still wearing the same clothes, but holding a crying baby in her arms, her long hair falling over it. She looked radiant in the sunlight, at peace with herself; and as she gently rocked the baby and quietly talked to it, her conversation, like that of most new mothers, was more like music than speech.

Michael stared at her, bemused. He wasn't too sure about where he was. He remembered his dream (the wonderful light and flying saucers) and, feeling even more confused, looked around him again.

There they were: the steaming marshlands. They reminded him of Glastonbury. Recalling that place, he also remembered Miles Ashcombe, Mrs Devereux and Laurence, and, finally, his own journey here with the woman he loved. He and Frances had come a long way, travelling through time and space, to emerge in a very different world, outside past and future.

Where were they? *What* were they? Michael actually *heard* his own thoughts, his mute voice vibrating across the clearing to make Frances glance at him. Rocking her baby, she smiled contentedly, then lowered her head again, while Michael stared around him — at Paradise — wondering if it was real.

He nervously touched himself, running his fingers along one arm, felt the fine hairs on his skin and realised he was normal. Returning his gaze to Frances, he studied her gurgling child, aware that that ectoplasmic creation was now a physical being.

The child, which had been born just like its mother,

was the seed of this new world.

Michael pondered his changed future, then impulsively cast his mind beyond it, flying out of himself to traverse time and space, going instinctively where his curiosity led him.

He soared up from where he was, glanced back down at the Earth, passed *through* space and emerged to the double-star, which was the source of his being. Disc-shaped lights bobbed and weaved, forming a bridge between the two stars, a vast arch of pulsating energy, in which all became one. Michael felt it and was renewed, mind and soul fusing together, then curiosity took him back to the Earth he had known before Eden.

Wanting to see his daughter, he caught her in sleep, tossing and turning restlessly in bed because he had left her. In her grief, she dreamed about him. He was sitting near Frances. They were in a forest-clearing filled with flower-brightened foliage, both gazing out over tropical marshlands of unusual beauty. The place looked like Paradise, at once verdant and serene; and Frances, who was crooning over a baby, was limned with a golden light.

Soothed by what she had seen, Cheryl stopped tossing and turning. Still sleeping, she offered a smile to the dark, silent bedroom. Young and healthy, she would endure, find a man, bear his children, then pass on to find her father waiting for her, as he was waiting right now.

Michael knew this as he watched her, casting mind and soul over her, letting her take strength from his presence as she saw him in dreaming.

In her dream she saw her father in the Garden of Eden, turning his loving attention to Frances and the child she was holding.

A light breeze blew off the marshes, rippling the water in the lake, cooling Michael before crossing the clearing to blow around Frances. She shook her head and looked up, saw him watching her and smiled; then her head moved again, bowing towards him, acknowledging him, and in so doing stopped eclipsing the sun and let it burst around her.

He was dazzled by the light, but managed to keep his eyes open, then sat back as Frances straightened up, her smile touching his heart.

Michael wept. The tears felt cool on his warm cheeks. They flowed as they had done with his daughter, Cheryl, so he let them fall freely. He had ventured here in ignorance, borne on wings of faith and hope; and, in traversing time and space, had made them part of him. Now, he could make the past as real as the present, even as he ventured into the future to return to his source. So, in coming to Eden, he had lost nothing, but gained all — and thus, in letting his tears fall to the grass, he was displaying his joy.

Still weeping, he stood up, glanced around him, saw a new world, wondered where his neighbours might be and then touched his own cheeks. He wiped his tears with his fingers, took a deep breath, drank the clean air, then walked very shyly across the clearing and knelt beside Frances.

'Don't ask me,' she said, obviously anticipating his questions, holding her gurgling baby to her breast and rocking it gently. 'I don't know, but it's all right. *We're* all right. You and I, we'll survive. We were meant to continue.'

He saw his daughter, Cheryl, in the depths of her eyes, and understood that what she had said was true. He was here . . . and there, also.

'Amen,' he whispered.

THE END

GENESIS BY W. A. HARBINSON

There is a global conspiracy of such enormity that those who encounter even its outermost fringes are inevitably contaminated. A conspiracy based on incredibly advanced technology of *Earthly origin*. A conspiracy dedicated to the eventual enslavement and subversion of humanity as we know it. A conspiracy with one man – old beyond nature, powerful beyond measure – at its core. A conspiracy stretching through time – across icy polar wastes and jungle hideouts . . . into the cold vacuum of space itself. A conspiracy poised to turn life on Earth into a chilling nightmare of living death.

0 552 11533 9   £2.50

REVELATION by W. A. Harbinson

Without warning, after a night of terrifying disturbance, an event of unparalleled significance occured to shake the foundations of civilisation. It was an event so magnificent, so extraordinary, that it would alter forever the political structure and the spiritual beliefs of western society – be the cause of World War III, as well as, ultimately, a permanent peace . . .

'It has the lot – love, horror, science fiction, political and religious intrigue involving the major religions and world powers, and an extraordinary story of the resurrection of a man hailed by those religions as the saviour of the world.'

– *The Bookseller*

'An extraordinary combination of love story, occult, horror and science fiction based on the second coming of Christ. An electrifying read that deserves the widest exposure.'

– *Publishing News*

0 552 11901 6   £2.50

OTHERWORLD BY W. A. HARBINSON

Deep in the heart of the Amazon rain-forest live the Yano Indians. Dedicated to the powers of darkness . . . a fierce, elusive tribe, whose presence is revealed only by the hypnotic beating of drums and by mysterious lights in the sky.

Laura, a photo-journalist, believes herself to be possessed by evil spirits and offers herself to the Yano in a last effort to release her soul from torment. Alex, whose youthful passion Laura has rejected, follows her into the jungle, where he sees a mystical unveiling of the events that have gone before – and experiences the Otherworld, where good meets evil in a tumultuous confrontation . . .

0 552 12380 3   £2.50

THE DEVIL'S ALTERNATIVE BY FREDERICK FORSYTH

'Whichever option I choose, men are going to die.' This is the Devil's Alternative, the appalling choice facing the President of the USA and other statesmen throughout the world.

As the gripping story gathers momentum, the reader is transported from Moscow to London, from Rotterdam to Washington, from a country house in Ireland to the world's biggest oil tanker which threatens to pollute the whole of the North Sea. The climax is the most exciting that even this master story-teller has contrived, and the last-minute surprises in the concluding chapters take the breath away.

0 552 11500 2   £2.95

THE SALAMANDRA GLASS

A. W. MYKEL

The heart-stopping novel of international suspense and intrigue by the author of *The Windchime Legacy*.

Michael Gladieux thought he'd finished with The Group, a highly specialised unit he'd served with in Vietnam . . . until his father is murdered, his body found with a note accusing him of Nazi collaboration during the war and a glass pendant anchored to his heart with a shiny steel spike.

Who was Michael's father? Why are Washington and The Group so interested? Michael's search for answers leads him on a terrifying quest – to find his father's killer. What he uncovers is far more deadly, as he becomes the one man capable of stopping the twisted legacy of THE SALAMANDRA GLASS

Rivals Ludlum at his best!

0 552 12417 6   £2.50

CORGI BOOKS

A SELECTED LIST OF FINE TITLES
AVAILABLE FROM CORGI BOOKS

THE PRICES SHOWN BELOW WERE CORRECT AT THE TIME OF GOING TO PRESS. HOWEVER TRANSWORLD PUBLISHERS RESERVE THE RIGHT TO SHOW NEW RETAIL PRICES ON COVERS WHICH MAY DIFFER FROM THOSE PREVIOUSLY ADVERTISED IN THE TEXT OR ELSEWHERE.

☐	12639 X	**One Police Plaza**	*William J. Caunitz*	£2.50
☐	12610 1	**On Wings of Eagles**	*Ken Follett*	£2.95
☐	12180 0	**The Man from St. Petersburg**	*Ken Follett*	£2.95
☐	11810 9	**The Key to Rebecca**	*Ken Follett*	£1.95
☐	12569 5	**The Fourth Protocol**	*Frederick Forsyth*	£2.95
☐	12140 1	**No Comebacks**	*Frederick Forsyth*	£2.50
☐	11500 2	**The Devil's Alternative**	*Frederick Forsyth*	£2.95
☐	10244 X	**The Shepherd**	*Frederick Forsyth*	£1.95
☐	10050 1	**The Dogs of War**	*Frederick Forsyth*	£2.95
☐	09436 6	**The Odessa File**	*Frederick Forsyth*	£2.50
☐	09121 9	**The Day of the Jackal**	*Frederick Forsyth*	£2.50
☐	12380 3	**Otherworld**	*W. A. Harbinson*	£2.50
☐	11533 9	**Genesis**	*W. A. Harbinson*	£2.50
☐	11901 6	**Revelation**	*W. A. Harbinson*	£2.50
☐	12541 5	**Dai-Sho**	*Marc Olden*	£2.50
☐	12357 9	**Giri**	*Marc Olden*	£2.95
☐	12662 4	**Gaijin**	*Marc Olden*	£2.95
☐	12584 9	**Deadly Games**	*Fridrikh Neznansky & Edward Topol*	£1.95
☐	12307 2	**Red Square**	*Fridrikh Neznansky & Edward Topol*	£2.50
☐	12583 0	**Submarine U-137**	*Edward Topol*	£2.50

All these books are available at your bookshop or newsagent, or can be ordered direct from the publisher. Just tick the titles you want and fill in the form below.

TRANSWORLD READER'S SERVICE, 61–63 Uxbridge Road, Ealing, London, W5 5SA

Please send a cheque or postal order, not cash. All cheques and postal orders must be in £ sterling and made payable to Transworld Publishers Ltd.
Please allow cost of book(s) plus the following for postage and packing:

U.K./Republic of Ireland Customers:
Orders in excess of £5; no charge
Orders under £5; add 50p

Overseas Customers:
All orders; add £1.50

NAME (Block Letters) ....

ADDRESS ....

....